I0646430

Zinfandel's Grimoire

By Gwen Alyce Clayton

Rivervine Publishing LLC
Ashland, Kentucky, USA

First published in the United States of America by
Rivervine Publishing LLC.

Copyright ©2020 Gwen Alyce Clayton

The publisher greatly appreciates your purchase of an authorized edition of this book. Thank you for complying with copyright laws by not reproducing, scanning, or distributing any part of this book in any form without permission. You are supporting the rightful author and allowing Rivervine to continue publishing books for readers curious about the twain of the worlds of the seen and the unseen.

ISBN: 978-0-578-67038-6

First edition. Fort Wayne, Indiana.

Photography by Kristine Logan. Location: Country Heritage Winery, LaOtto, Indiana.

Fonts used: Interior—Garamond, Copperplate Gothic Bold. Cover—Bookman Old Style, Rage Italic

"Zinfandel's Grimoire" is a work of fiction. Names, characters, places and incidents are either the product of the author's imagination or used fictitiously. Any resemblance to actual persons (living or dead), businesses, companies, events or locales is completely coincidental. However, please check out my Acknowledgements for all the credits.

Dedication:
To Jimmie Chow, my favorite ghost of Amador County

Warning

This book deals with occult concepts, challenges currently held beliefs from various world religions, and presents an alternate view of world history that some may find upsetting. Reader discretion is advised.

Also, this is Book 2 in the Rivervine Trilogy. The author has tried to make 'Grimoire' easy to follow for readers who missed Book 1, "Fermata Cellars," but for a completely congruous experience, we recommend reading the books in order.

TABLE OF CONTENTS

Prologue

WHEEL OF FORTUNE, REVERSED

June 29, 2004

To Glenda Fern
c/o Allied Journalist Network
Sacramento Bureau

Dear Ms. Fern,

I am so sorry to have to write to you at this time. Even though you're in Iraq covering the war, I assume you've heard the news about the June twentieth fire back in Rivervine that reduced the entire city to ashes. I cannot express deep enough condolences to you and Staff Sergeant Humphries in the loss of … well … everything.

I don't know how you can write with such a clear head at a time like this. You *must* be devasted after losing so much. I have to say, though, that you are an amazing writer. My wife, Anna, and I read your coverage of yesterday's transition ceremony transferring power from the Coalition Provisional Authority to the newly formed Iraqi government. I'm shocked there isn't more news about it in the media. Your article was the only mention we saw of the event.

But that is not why I am writing to you today.

I'm not sure if you remember me from the meeting last November when the Rivervine City Council condemned Fermata Cellars Winery. I'm the anthropologist whose testimony you quoted in your article for the *Rivervine Tribune*. As you correctly stated in your story, I am also the one who, back in 1969, encouraged Sage and Xavia Divinorum to purchase the eighty-nine-acre property and start a viticulture business in the agricultural section of Old Town Rivervine.

The only reason I'm bothering you now is because another of our mutual acquaintances, Ms. Xin Vondella—the ghost who was the subject of November's inquisition—asked me to give you the enclosed diary when you safely arrived *home* from what she calls Sumer (but the rest of the world calls Iraq; she often struggles with language among her various incarnations—you will find many such discrepancies in her journal).

Since I did not know how to reach you but knew you were freelancing for the Allied Journalist Network, I am delivering this package in person to the Sacramento bureau in the hope that it reaches you and that you are still interested in migrating from journalist to novelist.

As I'm sure you know, Xin Vondella goes by the name Zinfandel to most people. That is the name by which I will address her in this letter.

She told me about her request to have you author her biography. She said the project was based mostly on your interviews with her in addition to the writings from the enclosed grimoire. She apologized profusely for not writing what perhaps should have been the most important entry of all, but she insisted there was not enough time. She had to grab the book and leave without updating it. She promised to go into further detail with you about that subject another time.

For now, though, I can at least tell you what I know about the fire, although it isn't much.

The entire campus here at UC Davis is going batshit crazy trying to rationalize what happened in Rivervine last week. No one is able to explain a sight that thousands of people claim to have witnessed: a giant, flying, lizard-like creature swooping down from the sky, torching everything within the city boundaries with flames spewing from its mouth (some witnesses say it was the nose).

Of course, the doomsdayers are claiming the dragon (no one knows what else to call it) was Satan exacting vengeance against the city of Rivervine for selling the Fermata Cellars property to Rev. Paul Adamson so he could build his Spiritual Emporium. As a practicing Satanist, I assure you Satan was not involved in the catastrophe. As an anthropologist, I would have to say, based on descriptions of this dragon, the beast most likely originated in the Far East. Witnesses describe it as a long, winged, serpentine creature with a scaled body, claws like a crocodile, and a boxy face with long teeth. Given that the only lifeforms to survive the fire were three trees—an oak, an orange, and a weeping willow, the latter being indigenous to China—my guess is that the event is somehow related to Xin Hsüan, Zinfandel's father, who migrated to the United States from Guangzhou, China in 1800. But that is just a hunch on my part. I have no evidence to support my claim.

What's also suspicious is the residents of Old Town Rivervine—the Comatis as they call themselves—had all evacuated their properties before the fire erupted. Sage and Xavia closed the winery that afternoon and headed west for San Francisco to join their daughter, Brigid, who recently left Rivervine to study at the Conservatory of Music. On their way to the City, they stopped at our house in Davis but did not stay long—just said their goodbyes and left shortly before nightfall. None of us saw any dragon in the eastern sky.

It is just so unexplainably odd that all of the people, structures, pets, livestock, and vegetation in Rivervine have turned to ash, except for the trees I mentioned earlier: an oak at the far west end of town, an orange tree where the farmworkers' quarters were, and a weeping willow standing along the banks of the Vitus River. Two of those trees—the orange and the willow—are located on the Fermata Cellars property. The oak stands in the center of what was a traffic island separating two strip malls.

That night, my wife, Anna, woke me, pointing hysterically to the sight of a female ghost standing at the foot of our bed. The apparition's clothing, skin, and hair were soaked in blood, and she was holding a book.

When I awoke, I recognized the specter. It was Zinfandel.

In her hands was this grimoire. She gave it to me, asking that I save it for you so you can finish your novel. I accepted the book and nodded, swearing that I would ensure the mission succeeded.

Then she vanished. I have neither seen nor heard from her since.

I am sending this to you now in the hope that you will be leaving Iraq soon. We also hope the end of Saddam Hussein's regime will start the healing of the marsh and give the Ma'dān people back their livelihoods. As relieved as we are that the tyrant is no longer in power, we cannot begin to imagine how devasting it is for you or the overwhelming loss you must be experiencing as you go from the warzone of the Middle East to the devastation of Rivervine.

Although you and I do not know each other personally yet, I do want to extend an offer to you and Staff Sergeant Humphries. You two are welcome to stay in Davis with Anna and me until you get settled into a new domicile and heal a little from the grief—however long you may need.

Perhaps then I can tell you how I came to know Zinfandel. It is quite an amazing story and one I am eager to tell, but first, of course, you need to heal. When you are ready to finish your book, please reach out to me.

In frith,
Rev. Todd Caprasen, Ph.D.
Professor of Anthropology
University of California at Davis

The

Grimoire

Ace of Swords

31 October in the Year of Their Lord 2002

It all started with the mice.

There are not usually this many scurrying around here. Between the cats and the rattlesnakes, vermin have always been kept to a minimum. When one of these tiny rodents entered my cellar today, I knew something was amiss.

As the Lady of the Vineyard, I have haunted this place since 1848. For one hundred and fifty-four years, I have known every creature in the Black Land, not by sight or smell but by aura.

My intuition informed me the grounds had one fewer cat. This missing child was not a victim of one of nature's hunts—no fox, coyote, or raccoon had chosen the feline for its feast.

Tonight is October thirty-first—the American holiday Halloween, a time famous for its tradition of children going to each door in the neighborhood dressed as mythical characters, begging for sweets. It is also a time when pranksters perform unconscionable acts of cruelty and mischief in the name of a god they call Sam Hain. Members of his cult have deemed this evening the unholiest night of the year.

The legend of Sam Hain was brought to Rivervine thirty-three years ago when the town experienced a renaissance. Xavia and Sage Divinorum purchased the Black Land in 1969 and built this winery. Other farms, ranches, and businesses followed, as did families looking to build their own homes and schools.

Although the Divinorums were not the ones to invoke the name, Sam Hain, the mystery of the Black Land has always attracted thrill seekers during Halloween. It was only a matter of time before someone weaved his myth into the local folklore.

I assure you, though, that Sam Hain is *not* one of the souls of the vineyard. But after three decades of hearing his name evoked on this night, I have deduced that this imaginary creature is yet another bastardized version of the Abrahamic devil.

When I saw a portly boy dressed all in black and moving about in a dubious manner in the vineyard today, I had no doubt the youngster intended to make the cat an unwilling participant in a ritual for the mighty Mr. Hain.

My first clue was the boy's aura. It radiated with the same energy that maggots raise when they feast on dead flesh.

I do not say that as an insult but rather a fact of nature. Maggots are not evil; they are integral to the death process. The insects ingest rotting tissue, receiving sustenance from the dying animal's vital life essence and becoming strengthened by the energy emitted as the host decays. Without this nourishment, the scavenger would be unable to metamorphose from a larva into an adult fly. And the dead matter would not decompose. Such sacred custodians save carrion from eternal damnation as pollution upon the Earth.

After reading this boy's aura, I could tell he had a fascination with the disincarnation process, as if he himself craved the chi—vital life essence—of carrion. That is how I knew he had taken the cat … and what he intended to do with it.

As a vampire myself, I can empathize with his lust for chi, but I was nonetheless unwilling to share my abode with pests.

There may be other cats that could fill the role of my beloved mouser, but the one this youth had chosen was experienced, cunning, and agile enough to ensure the goddamn mice stayed out of my cellar!

Therefore, I decided to retrieve my dedicated huntress.

I homed in on the boy's psyche, which led me across the road from my winery to the backyard of the property once owned by dear Dr. Castillo.

The estate has fallen into disrepair in recent years. The new owners have improved the house greatly but have done little with the grounds. The weeds are still overgrown, dry, and brittle. It made perfect cover for a group of troublemakers to shear a circle large enough to host a secret ritual on the west side of the property.

I arrived at the site as night was falling. There I found three adolescent boys and two adolescent girls dressed in black hooded robes. My huntress was in a cage—her feet covered in her own feces—in the center of the circle, beneath an altar adorned with myrrh incense, black and red candles, a goat skull, a gong, and a knife.

While the cat was mewing in desperation to be released from its squalor, the youths did nothing to comfort the poor beast.

They instead commenced their ritual by chanting in some language I did not recognize. One of the boys stepped forward and banged the gong three times. When the resonance of the gong dissipated, the portly boy began to speak in English:

"Oh, mighty Sam Hain, we summon you forth this All Soul's Eve. We bring you the requisite offering of live flesh and blood from your sacred feline animal. We shall disrobe our innocent, virgin bodies and smother ourselves with carrion as we engage in intercourse, fellatio, cunnilingus, and masturbation. If our performance pleases you tonight, we request that you empower us with your unholy spirit so that we may utilize this energy to make us stronger disciples of your unhallowed superiority and annihilate our adversaries."

One of the girls—with long, stringy, sandy brown hair, spectacles, and a rather gaunt figure—stepped forward, grabbing the knife from the altar and taking the cat out of the cage, nearly strangling the animal as she clutched its neck and raised its body high above her head.

The young woman paused for a moment and then held the blade against the feline's belly. As the cat scratched in the air trying to escape, mewing frantically, the girl recited more words from that bizarre language. None of the other youths intervened to save the animal.

This little exploit was an act of war. As I quickly assessed the five-piece military corps standing before me, I developed a strategy that would leave them all stupefied. This girl and her allies were about to learn the difference between occult fantasy and the ever-surprising dark side of spirituality.

I decided it was time to introduce them to the source of their fantasies.

After all, if there is anyone who knows the real story of the original sin, it is I, for I am the reincarnation of the initial pit viper that lived among the fruit trees of Sumer all those centuries ago. I am the serpent who frightened a young woman's husband to the point of fleeing the couple's paradise. Without me, the Abrahamic world's terror associated with this or any other night would not exist.

With that said, I must add that my strategy was not merely to scare these youths. I wanted to analyze them—to see if perhaps they were just misled and if by chance, I could steer them along a course directed toward more fruitful goals.

But first, I had to determine their level of intelligence and willingness to join my army. The constellations in the sky show a greater enemy invading my homeland soon, and I need to recruit more soldiers—strong-minded fighters, not just bodies willing to come home in pine boxes. A treaty between me and these five youths could very well be arranged under the right conditions.

The cat's welfare, of course, being the first condition. If I could save my huntress and enlighten five young minds, I would be in a highly favorable position.

Be aware, dear reader, that knowledge does not always come in the form of books or speeches. Sometimes wisdom befalls you like a surge of venom running through your veins. It can be frightening and painful. It might even paralyze you.

With that in mind, I appeared in the center of their circle, taking my original form as a venomous serpent. I lifted myself, balancing on the end of my tail, exhibiting my fangs, and hissing loudly with my forked tongue flickering.

All of them gasped and their eyes grew wide, fixed solidly on me. The lanky girl dropped the cat, which fell to the ground, unable to run away due to its broken leg. Instead, it continued to mew, adding to the terrifying milieu.

I reveled in the flood of adrenalin rushing through the veins of these young hooligans. Everyone's fear fed my chi—not Sam Hain's.

As I weaved and wavered, I produced five apples from my womb—one for each youth standing in the circle. I locked eyes with the portly boy and nodded my head in a circular motion, silently directing him to distribute the fruit evenly among the coven members.

I spoke in a deep, droning voice: "I am the one you seek." As I slowly and purposefully gyrated around and around, I locked eyes with each youngster, hypnotizing them and commanding their full attention. "This is my body, which is given for you. Eat this in remembrance of me."

Panic energy emanated from all five youths. The girl with the cat dropped the knife and released the animal, which tried to hobble away but its broken leg kept it from getting very far. The young woman returned to her place in the circle, trembling.

None of them were brave enough to bite into their apples. They all stood in their places, not knowing the correct protocol for eating fruit produced by the deity they had summoned.

"I am not pleased with your offering!" I scolded the youths. "Only a coward sacrifices an animal's blood!"

The portly boy whimpered in a shaky and confused voice: "But I thought you fed on the fear energy of the cat!"

"Nonsense!" I retorted. "That cat is needed in the fields to kill the pests that spread disease and compete for food with my disciples. Its fear energy is of no use to me. If you wish to appease my lust, you must perform a feat that demonstrates to me that you are raising such energy from deep within your own spirit. You must then form that energy into something that pleases me—do my bidding, pursue my agenda, and manifest my goals."

I glanced around the circle again and asked, "Tell me, each of you, what is it that you fear most, and how can you use it to affect change that benefits me?"

The portly boy spoke first: "I fear my stepfather. Do you want me to kill him?"

I harrumphed at such a question.

"If I feel this man needs to be erased from the earth, I will orchestrate his destruction. I do not want my students to waste time locked behind the bars of man's prison, as would be your fate if you yourself were to terminate this man's life. I need you in the outside world. Tell me what he has done to make you so afraid."

"He teases me constantly," the boy answered. "Nothing I do is right in his eyes."

"Your stepfather is feeding on your sense of inferiority and lack of self-esteem. The next time you see this man, I want you to take a deep breath, stand erect, and hold your head high. Gaze deep past his eyes and if you must speak to him, summon a voice from the pit of your belly. That is the only way to make him understand that you are the dominant one. Do not let him steal your dignity again. My disciples must not be weak. Self-imposed weakness is how others control you. You are the one who must always be in control."

"But my stepfather is right about so many things," the boy whined. "I'm not good at sports. I don't get good grades. My room is messy. He doesn't like the music I listen to. Really, I am a loser!"

"Every day you are faced with choices that determine whether you win or lose," I replied. "My commandment to you is to make your choices wisely. Physical stamina and mental acuity are paramount to one's survival. I want you to focus on those issues immediately. My disciples must be strong both physically and intellectually. You need not be an athlete or scholar, but I insist that your body and mind be in working order, to the extent that you are able. I have no tolerance for people who make excuses for their weakness. And if I visit you somewhere, I want to be comfortable. Do not call on me if the room is not presentable. As for your music, you may listen to whatever appeals to your inner muse, for it is the energy the music inspires in you that is important, not the sound itself. Use what I have taught you tonight to be a stronger disciple. Once you are resilient enough, I will need you to join my army, for I have enemies far greater than this man who shares his bed with your mother. Overcome him, and you can move on to more formidable adversaries."

Tears swelled in the boy's eyes as his pride fought with his sense of humility. The advice I gave this young man was the first step in his self-realization process. His path had just changed from a narrow, unfocused trail to a wide, scenic corridor. It may be steeper and more challenging, for it is not easy to be strong, but he realized that strength is far more rewarding than weakness.

I then turned to the girl with the spectacles, asking her, "What is *your* greatest fear?"

"You!" she screamed. "I didn't think you really existed. But here you are. What are you going to do to us?"

Before I could answer, the other two boys ran off and the second girl interposed. She removed her robe, exposing her naked body. Black paint covered her hair, eye lids, lips, and fingernails, yet her skin was porcelain white. The chilly night air hardened her nipples and covered every inch of her skin with goose flesh. She fell to her knees a few inches from me and in a serpentine dance of ecstasy began wavering back and forth, stroking her thighs with each motion. Her left hand reached up to fondle her left breast. Although the breeze had dried out her womanly lubrication, she nevertheless inserted the index and middle fingers of her right hand into her vagina and began masturbating.

"Make love to me, Master!" she pleaded. "I want to feel the snake inside me. After I reach orgasm, I want to feel your bite on my neck and your venom running through me. When it is all over, lead me to the afterworld. Let tonight be my last upon this earth. Let me be your mistress in hell!"

I reprimanded her by shouting, "I do not take lovers unless they prove their worth to me. What evidence have you demonstrated that you are trustworthy and deserve my affection?"

She gazed at me with a blank stare and open mouth but answered not.

I then turned my attention to the first girl—the skinny one with the spectacles.

"The feline you were holding is suffering from a fractured leg and skin afflictions caused by the filth in which you had it kept," I informed her. "Find the cat and bring it to Doctors Frank and Tony for healing. Present them with a monetary offering—however much you can raise in the course of the evening—as penance for your mistreatment of the poor soul."

She nodded respectfully. The apology expressed in her aura spoke louder than the words "I am sorry" that she managed to choke past her lips. She was still shaking as she looked around for the cat, finding it a few yards away, mewing desperately in the tall grass.

As their excited nerves calmed, I shape-shifted from a serpent to my most recent incarnation as a Comati woman, dressed in my favorite crimson and black dress.

"Forgive me for not introducing myself sooner," I said in my normal tone of voice. "My name is Xin Vondella. The townsfolk call me Zinfandel—the Lady of the Vineyard of Fermata Cellars."

The portly boy addressed me, stuttering.

"M-m-my name is Thomas, Lady Vondella," he said before pointing to the cat girl. "This here is my girlfriend, Tanya."

"And I am Erin Tuft, m'lady," interrupted the snake enthusiast who had put her robe back on. "My parents own this property. We're the newest residents in town, and we welcome you to our home."

I appreciated the hospitable gesture.

"Thank you, dear ones," I calmly responded, thinking carefully how to handle the situation before me.

"If your interest in the occult is genuine," I advised. "Get yourselves an almanac to share and a journal for each of you. Meet me here at sunset on the new moon of each month. And dress appropriately. My soldiers' uniforms shall be warm, comfortable clothing free of distractions but appropriately designed to complement the mood of the ritual. You will also need to use oil lamps instead of candles on your altar; the flame needs a chimney to protect it from the draft caused by my spirit."

The three of them—all huddled around the cat—nodded in agreement.

"We should probably get going, ya know, get this cat to Dr. Frank or something," Thomas said.

I bowed before my subjects, then disappeared, shifting my spirit to where the two runaways had gone. I found them in the sleeping space of one of the boys, smoking sage-scented fags and perusing publications with sexually explicit images. Before appearing to them, I listened to their conversation for a while.

"Look at the tits on this one!" the first boy exclaimed.

"Oh, yeah, she could make a wet noodle hard," the other replied.

"Man, I wish we could have banged Tanya and Erin tonight."

"Well, there's not much of Tanya, but Erin, whoo! We could have shared her and let Tommy Boy have his little popsicle stick."

"Oh, I know. That damn snake kept our dicks dry."

This conversation proved they had no respect for women as powerful individuals—and certainly no reverence for ritual sex as any kind of sacred offering. Instead, they wished only to satiate their own basal carnal desires. They cared not about the energy raised and had no fear that they actually summoned a frightening, venomous, serpentine phantom. The boys showed no reverence for the young women who braved the cold air in hopes of appeasing a higher source of spirituality. Neither Sam Hain nor any other spiritual leader was of any import to these immature lads whatsoever.

So I decided to play a little trick of my own. I appeared through the smoke as a horned, winged demonic character, not uttering a single word. I grabbed the fag from them and put it to my lips, inhaling the magical herb, taking its medicine deep into my lungs. As I exhaled, I blew the smoke into the boys' faces.

The young men dropped their publications and stood dumbfounded, unable to speak or move. Their erections quickly softened. I do not normally consider that a compliment, but under these circumstances, I will.

They were so frightened, their hearts expired right there in the host's room. I dropped the fag, setting the floor tapestry alight. The bed immediately went up in flames; the curtains followed.

The scent of burnt objects caught the attention of the host's mother. Noticing smoke escaping from the bottom of the door, she reached for the handle, felt the heat from its metal and hesitated to turn it any farther. The fortunate woman had enough wisdom to know that had she open the door, the backdraft would have taken her life before she could find her son and his friend … dead, charred from the fire.

That is when I left the scene. The last image imprinted in my mind was of a house engulfed in flames and a mother screaming that her child was dying.

Although I empathized with the woman as she struggled to avoid panic and grief long enough to run to her neighbor's home and fetch help, I felt no regret in what I had done.

Pathetic and weak those two boys were. The world genuinely is better off without them, as they would have grown to become burdens on society, spending their lives in the revolving doors of man's prison, committing one wasteful act after another that would only impede humankind's development instead of progressing it. To think of either boy siring offspring sours my stomach.

I returned to my cellar to find my brother Anton waiting, holding the recovering feline in his arms.

~ Page of Cups ~

Anton was never a handsome man. He was tall, lanky, and sickly from the crazy blood that debilitated him. The blood gave him a frightening look with huge teeth, recessed gums, mottled skin color, and patches of hair growing wild all over his face and hands.

The disease also made him too sick and weak to fight. If he ever became enraged, he would grow confused and start vomiting or fall into a seizure.

So I fought in his stead.

He stayed at home—the gentle monster, caring for the creatures of the vineyard.

Tonight, the fur babe was properly bandaged and purring affectionately. Obviously the three youths had made good on their end of the bargain. But Anton scowled and chastised me.

"You should have obliterated all five of them!" he pontificated. "Look what they have done to this poor cat!"

Anton vehemently despises humans but adores all other animals. For me to have spared the lives of those who caused harm to one of his beloved pets is tantamount to heresy.

If the decision were up to him, none of the five youths would be left breathing. But he himself does not have the courage to take another's life. Therefore, it is up to me to decide who is spared and who is disincarnated.

On this night, I showed mercy upon the three youths who completed the ritual.

I need allies. If I can convert these young minds to my side, it will be to my advantage. Besides, the cat will be fine; Doctors Frank and Tony, two of my Comati friends, have seen to that.

Regardless of whether my decisions were right or wrong, tonight's events have forced me to reflect on my own personal set of ethics.

What is it that I believe to be noble, and what do I find to be shameful? Is there any way to calibrate each moral compass that exists among humanity? Am I to just sit around and watch society decay due to its inability to decide which holds more importance: the needs of the natural world or the journey to a celestial heaven? What role does the human psyche play in all this, and how much is left to the hands of fate? Does such a thing as destiny even exist?

To address questions such as these, I have decided to keep a grimoire, perhaps the only one *written* posthumously.

It shall be a log of my personal revelations, meaningful events, and heartfelt philosophies. I believe that a diary written by a ghost of my competency level shall answer many of the questions laymen have regarding the supernatural realm and correct the myriad misconceptions that have plagued my personal reputation throughout history.

I have spent enough time being the victim of slander, as if I were some poor, wretched waif unable to find her way to the light.

I am here to tell you that the light holds no comfort for me, neither does the counterfeit morality touted by the self-righteous demagogues who think they have all the answers leading to rectitude. They can descend to their imaginary hell slowly and miserably for all I care—and take their spurious virtues with them.

Now, where should I begin? With the Garden, of course.

~ Seven of Wands ~

I have had many lifetimes, but my first and latest have been the two most memorable. As I mentioned earlier, my original manifestation was that of a snake living six thousand years ago in a beautiful fruit tree seven thousand miles from Rivervine in a country called Sumer. The most popular legends claim the fruit was an apple, which is why I gave the youths apples tonight; I figured they would appreciate me more if I perpetuated a myth they recognized. However, the actual fruit from the famous Tree of Knowledge was a pomegranate. Apples are not indigenous to Sumer; pomegranates grow in abundance.

These days, I spend most of my time in a wine cellar in Rivervine—a small city in the Sierra Foothills of Northern California. I have been here since my most recent incarnation, which began on the twenty-fifth of October in the Year of Their Lord 1820.

It is in this cellar where I studied as a young girl, died as a young woman, and will stay as a formidable ghost. It has been my resting place ever since a fire ravaged our home on the sixteenth of August in the Year of Their Lord 1848. The wine cellar in which I am writing this grimoire tonight is a restoration of the original, thanks to my dear friends, Xavia and Sage Divinorum—the first two incarnates worthy of the Comati name in more than one hundred years.

The new Comatis have a whole tribe of their own. Doctors Frank and Tony care for sick and lost animals. Other members peddle various wares. The Divinorums make my wine.

I am also good friends with the Rhoads and Touchkoff families, who farm part of what is left of Rivervine's agricultural lands. The Rhoads family has an herb farm, and the Touchkoffs keep bees to make wax candles and honey. They also supply the honey for the Divinorums to make mead.

I consider myself to be the sentry of the Comatis. I do my best to keep their professions profitable and their land fertile. I also guide them in their spiritual efforts. But I have not yet documented my teachings.

Tonight I realized it was time to record these important testaments because so little remains of any culture that has opposed Abrahamic imperialism.

I do sincerely hope this book is not taken as literally as other discarnates' records have been. My grimoire is not comprised of the words of some almighty being. Neither is it any sort of divine prophecy. Everything written is biased from my point of view and all revelations are truth as I see it. I swear to never intentionally mislead or deceive readers, but I will insist that students seek their own enlightenment, for I am not the only path leading to righteousness.

Spiritual journeys cannot be duplicated, although they often do run parallel and will connect to others at some point. Spirituality grows like an orchard—no two boughs of a particular tree are the same shape or grow in the same direction; therefore, we are all solitary to a point. Yet the roots—our thoughts, words, and actions—connect to the collective mind. I encourage my students to follow if they wish, but once they finish reading, I urge them to forge their own trails, creating sacraments that enhance all realms of their own respective existence. I am happy to be their guide, but I refuse to be their savior. My disciples will need to find their own strength, for I will carry no one's cross but my own.

If you choose to accompany me, be advised of what lies in store for you. My path is full of twists and turns, darkness and dappled light. My companions include creatures with fangs and bushes with thorns. There are times when neither the moon nor sun shine, although the stars go on forever. Modern conveniences are scarce, but nature's perfume is omnipresent. The clarity of the river's water is more precious that the gold in its bed. And the animals offer far greater wisdom than any evangelist. If you are afraid of nature, the Zinfandel lifestyle is not for you.

My students need not be of any particular breeding, for one's character is not a birthright; it is created through an evolutionary process. All my disciples must learn to dance in the fire along with the shadows it creates. This is a place where fear, grief, and rage are embraced and understood as wholeheartedly as confidence, joy, and compassion. Music, literature, and other art forms express those emotions—such are tools not to be lost among society's budgets and inconveniences.

Of course, sexuality is the most sacred of all art forms. Therefore, it must be treated with the reverence it deserves instead of squandered among the scamps who misuse it as a form of basal entertainment or temporary satisfaction.

As for the youths who attempted to summon Sam Hain this evening, my heart is filled with mixed emotions. They are ripe with potential yet waste their energies looking for a messiah to guide them out of their oppressive, isolated, desperate situations. Like most humans, they have been conditioned to believe a divine force will rescue them from their misery. It is with pity in my heart that I advise them of the truth.

Each religion is nothing but some poor wretch's fantasy supported by a cast of mythical figures spawned from the imaginations of those who wish to dominate society. These clerics concoct rules allegedly handed down by an infallible, invisible force that spouts the illusions of an afterlife full of rewards for allegiance and condemnation for misconduct. Even the peace-loving religions wish to control others as they have cursed the darkness and rebuked those who embrace the shadows.

Many in the pious world view me as evil. I care not about those impostors. There is no *one true religion* as espoused by so many sanctimonious crusaders. There is only the strength that comes from the desire, wisdom, and imagination of those adept enough to master their own wills. Keep your wits about you, and you will not fall prey to those predators. Enjoy the pleasures of life as they come to you, keeping ever mindful of the consequences of those delights.

Such are the tenets of Zinfandel.

If anything I have written so far offends you, I advise you to discontinue your studies here and move along your own spiritual path. But if you are intrigued and would like to learn more, I invite you to keep reading.

THE HIGH PRIESTESS

4 November in the Year of Their Lord 2002

Since you have commenced reading the second entry of this grimoire, I assume you must have some interest in the hidden side of spirituality. It pleases me that you have chosen this path because it is one that has been much maligned over the millennia and in need of accurate restoration.

For the average person, the part of the psyche attuned to unseen forces has been locked away in shame and fear. Humanity's rulers have always used storytelling to control the masses. Folklore, religion, and outright lies have plagued the realm in which I exist. Such fallacies are nearly impossible to assuage. It is my sincere hope to reach out to the literate world, so our culture might finally lay to rest the myriad misconceptions creating such cacophony between the living and the dead, the spiritual and the secular.

The more people who are willing to listen, the better.

Tonight is an ideal time to start such a venture. As we enter the Sauin season—the period between the autumn equinox and winter solstice—days become short and nights grow long. With the aid of the new moon—the darkest night of the month—we have no moonshine to distract us. We can focus our thoughts, meditate clearly, and become more introspective.

Darkness is a beautiful thing. It is soothing. It is calming. It is nothing to fear.

This concentration of darkness—the new moon during the Sauin season—thins the veil separating the occult and physical realms, making it easier to penetrate, even for those who are not quite adept. This curtain is not a physical screen but rather a psychomagnetic filter that blocks signals of certain frequencies while allowing others to pass. For average people, the veil blocks the signals throughout the year, but may allow them to pass during the dark time. However, humans attuned to these frequencies can usually pass through the filter throughout the year. For adepts, who are highly sensitive to unseen forces, the signal is intensified during this season.

Anyone starting an occult journey may find it helpful to have spiritual mentors readily accessible at the beginning stages of their course. Although these ethereal advisers are available year round, obtuse learners may have difficulty conjuring them other times of year when the veil is denser and therefore, harder to penetrate. Likewise, stolid spirits may find it easier to graduate from being a residual haunting to having an intelligent conversation with a descendant in the physical realm.

That is why I scheduled a meeting with the youth tonight for their first lesson in *real* mysticism. This was also a good time to meet with them as they are still riding the momentum of their revolting Sam Hain ritual. Had I waited longer, I may have lost their attention, and I could not risk that.

~ Two of Pentacles ~

The success of this army is crucial because these youths are the only hope I have for the left-hand path of the Comati tribe. Xavia and Sage represent the orthodox path of light, peace, and healing. To balance the yin and yang of the occult ocean, I need a crew to navigate the seas of darkness, justice, and liberty. I sense Erin, Thomas, and Tanya are perfect candidates because their auras are heavy with murky waves running deep with torment.

Although the Comati tribe is not based on bloodlines, it does require the seeker to have a modicum of experience as a social outcast. I do not recall any Comatis who were born to privilege. If there were any highborn members, they most likely abdicated their entitlement when they joined our community.

Although you will find wealthy collectors who pay good money for objects associated with the occult—and they have their secret societies rife with elaborate rituals and opulent ornamentation—the Comati path of occultism is humble and modest.

The problem with privilege is that it shelters people from the worries of workaday life. The upper class builds fortresses, passes laws, and commissions scribes to mitigate their anxiety. Yet they neglect to address the root cause of their concern: fear of the unknown.

Humans fear what they do not understand. Ignorance sustains a perpetual state of comfort. Affluence combined with comfort makes for filtered life experiences, which keep people in a bubble of security, and weaken their immunity to leaders who use spiritual terrorism to keep the herd in line.

Many people in today's society fear the occult, especially the left-hand path—perhaps for good reason. History is full of stories about depraved pranksters and nefarious actors claiming affiliation with the path of darkness. But it is my responsibility to call out the scribes—and the rulers who commissioned them— for editing *my* image over the past six thousand years. These self-righteous demagogues blindly obey the agenda of light, where darkness is banished as if it were some poor, pathetic urchin. I am here to tell you that darkness is every bit as worthy of reverence as the light; there is nothing evil or unnatural about it. The color black represents introspection, protection, and transformation. Those of us who embrace the shadows may be a minority, but our spiritual and social value equals that of the shade-fearing majority. We have been tormented long enough!

Our oppressors fail to learn from history. They repeatedly believe that if they shun us, they can erase us. Yet we are still here, even though their ancestors threw nooses around the necks of our forebearers, burned them at the stake, drove spikes through their hearts, and implored everyone to rebuke them.

Having said that, I must emphasize that Comatis— regardless of which path—do not reinforce destructive behavior, irresponsibility, or apathy. However, we do embrace the value of overcoming adversity. We strongly believe the quality of a person's character is defined by the endurance achieved through conquering one's personal battles.

Comatis are also expected to be gracious and generous once they overcome their struggles, thereby helping others triumph as well. We are leaders, healers, caregivers, and teachers.

I accept my commission as captain of the Comati ship in the sea of chaos. Xavia and Sage are the officers in charge of the starboard side. My hope is to have Erin, Thomas, and Tanya maintain the port side. Together we shall board our vessel, sailing through life, battling misinformation, prejudice, and imperialism.

~ Knight of Wands ~

I rested until the appointed hour when the youths had agreed to meet me. We gathered at sunset at the former home of Dr. Castillo—where the dreaded Sam Hain ritual was held last week. The property now is owned by the family of the snake enthusiast, Erin Tuft.

I kept my disembodied persona, watching over the youths as they prepared for ritual.

They had done a beautiful job pulling weeds and clearing a path from Erin's house. It was not much, but respectful. A rust-colored cloth made of soft cotton fabric covered the altar. Instead of the skull, gong, and candles that dominated our last get-together, there was a loaf of fresh bread, carafe of hot apple cider, metal chalice, small plate, and an oil lamp. There was no live animal, but among the decorations of small pumpkins and fallen leaves, I noticed some oranges, which made me wonder if the youths had pilfered them from the tree outside the Fermata Cellars farmworkers' quarters. Before I could hold one to home in on the fruit's origin, the youths started walking up the path.

This time, my charges were dressed appropriately for the cold weather with warm, thick, knitted tunics in autumnal colors of deep gold, orange, and maroon. On the bottom half of their bodies, the girls wore festive, loose-fitting skirts while the boy donned twilled cotton trousers—the kind young Brigid, the Divinorums' daughter, wears. I believe she calls them *jeans*.

The youths gathered in the circle, each one standing at one of the four cardinal points—Tanya in the north, Erin in the south, and Thomas in the west. All were carrying books and pens.

There was an opening in the east that I assumed was reserved for me, so I took my place, readying for the invitation before donning an illusory cloak of flesh.

Finally, they set down their books, raised their arms, and chanted, "At the end of the summer and dark of the moon, we rise to the challenge of learning from you. Your soldiers are we; train us well to be keen. Dear Mistress, please join in our group."

The rhyme sufficed as an invocation.

"Hello, darlings," I spoke, shifting into my human apparition, dressed in my favorite black and crimson Victorian gown.

All three youths gasped, their eyes wide with both fear and surprise, amazed their summoning spell worked—and terrified of what that meant.

They continued the ritual, all three of them trembling but trying to hide their fear by keeping their spines stiffened. Thomas quivered as he poured the cider from the carafe into the chalice, while Tanya broke the bread into quarters, hastily putting them on the plate. When they finished, the two of them held up their offerings, and Erin called out, "L-L-Lady of the Vineyard, w-w-we offer you a feast on this ho-o-oly new-moon night."

Smiling and delighting in the pleasant change of mood since our last meeting, I picked up a piece of bread and put it in my mouth, then took a sip from the chalice. The three youths sighed in relief, happy to see I was enjoying their offerings, and then they too ate bread and drank from the cup. The energy of our gathering lightened.

Erin and Thomas emitted high amounts of energy, as if they were eager and intrigued, but Tanya's aura dimmed, flickering with residual apprehension.

I reached across the altar and gently stroked her hair, whispering assuredly, "Tanya, darling, I cannot alleviate your anxieties, but I vow to do my best to protect you throughout your journey."

She inhaled a deep sigh, sucking in tears and viscid mucus, hanging down her head in humility.

Her aura silently told me, "I do not deserve your attention."

On that note, I commenced our first lesson.

~ Ace of Wands ~

"I am so happy we are meeting here tonight," I told them. "Thank you all so much for your interest. You have done a lovely job of setting up the ritual area."

Looking over at Erin, I added, "And Miss Tuft, thank you for being such a gracious hostess."

She nodded and smiled proudly. Looking around the circle, I noticed Tanya was still frantically trying to control her sniffles and Thomas was growing impatient—his eagerness turning to agitation.

With the ritual part of the evening over, we no longer needed to stand. To make us all comfortable, I conjured some cushions for us to sit on.

"Who knows how long tonight's lesson will last?" I said. "We might as well be comfortable."

They all oohed and aahed, taking their seats as they exchanged glances with each other, their mouths open in astonishment. But as they settled in place, I noticed they still shivered, so I fashioned some blankets as well—thick, wool coverings to match the colors of tonight's ritual.

Once we were seated, I noticed the altar in the center blocked our view of each other. Not wanting to blow out the oil lamp or lose any of the beauty of the ritual ambiance, I telekinctically moved the altar to a spot between Erin and me.

More oohs and ahhs ensued, their auras radiating and pulsating like flames of a campfire. Even Tanya was starting to relax her disposition.

"Did you all bring your journals?" I asked, even though I had seen them earlier. "And an almanac for the coven to share?"

They lifted their books and pens to show me. Thomas also had the almanac.

"This is for 2003," he said, handing me the calendar. "I couldn't find one for 2002, since there were only two months left in the year, but I looked up the moon phases for November and December on the internet and wrote them down in the inside front cover."

"Is that all we need the almanac for—moon phases?" Erin asked.

"An almanac," I explained, "has room to write our own material. It allows us to track our successes and failures and how they correspond with the moon phases, rituals, and other phenomena. Every coven should have one."

"Are we really a *coven*?" Erin beamed. "Like, a real, live group of witches?"

I thought on it awhile. Before I could answer, Thomas blurted out. "Don't we have to have an initiation? Are we getting initiated tonight?"

I feared the poor boy's eyes were going to burst out of his skull, he was so excited. As was Erin. Tanya even perked up.

The mystique of the coven has always attracted humans. Something primal in our psyches finds it thrilling to belong to a clandestine group that shares mystical secrets, elaborate ceremonies, and commemorative rituals. This has been especially so ever since certain cultures started demonizing extrasensory abilities. Gifts such as hedge healing, clairvoyance, and cunning—which most people are unable to suppress—were once grounds for the capital crimes of witchcraft and heresy. Those who suffered from these conditions longed to commune with people with similar aberrations.

These youths were no different. I was certain that in time, the three seekers would uncover their true potential—and that potential may not be accepted in common society. They needed me as much as I needed them. Without leadership and direction, they could be left struggling to tread water in the sea of chaos.

As for the need for initiation, I had to think about it. Most covens *do* require some sort of rite of admission. The Comatis in general do not have any such ceremony; everyone is free to come and go as they please. There is no swearing to secrecy or proof of dedication. We do not give up our previous religious beliefs and commit to new ones.

The left-hand path is different, though. It is so easily misunderstood, and there is so much antipathy against it already that perhaps I should require an oath of some kind. I cannot afford for any of them to betray me.

As I ruminated on the thought, I realized how unprepared I was to initiate them tonight. I had nothing to offer them as a memento, and no ceremony designed. An initiation should be a grand spectacle, something deeply moving and wondrous.

Then it occurred to me: It would be far more appropriate to hold the initiation ceremony over Vampire New Year—the new moon closest to the winter solstice. It is the longest, darkest night of the year. Perfect!

"Yes! We shall have an initiation ceremony," I announced. Looking at the boy, I asked, "When are the new moons for December and January?"

He flipped through the almanac and answered, "December fourth and January second."

"Let us initiate each other as well as the new almanac," I proposed. "On the second of January in the Year of Their Lord 2003, we shall become our own hive—a coven within a coven, so to speak."

All three of them cheered. Dear reader, I wish you could have felt the energy. Elation does not begin to describe it. They were so happy to be part of a chosen family—a family that understood them and accepted their darkness. For the first time in their lives, they were validated. An authority figure whom they respected and wanted to emulate was going to adopt them and teach them something special.

This was a huge responsibility on my part. If I failed them in any way … I cannot even think of the repercussions! And if I failed the Comatis? Rivervine in general? Society as a whole? Oh! I cannot imagine what perils I would face.

Fortunately, I had two months to plan the ritual. As for tonight, though, darkness was starting to fall and we were quickly losing sunlight. Today is Monday and I knew the youths had school in the morning. We had not even begun our studies tonight and there were several items I wanted to discuss before we adjourned.

I conjured a small bonfire in the center of our circle so they could all see each other as well as their written materials. The fire's allure piqued the ambiance and they all stared into the flames as if in a trance. I allowed them a few moments to get lost in meditation before I brought them back into the world of the here and now.

I decided to be blunt and confess, "Let me be completely honest about why I called you here tonight, why you three are different from the regular tribe of Comatis."

The three youths turned their gaze toward me and listened attentively.

"Xavia and Sage Divinorum lead the current tribe. Fermata Cellars is their land and that is where all of the rituals take place. They steer the spiritual direction of the Comati community, and they are doing a wonderful job in terms of the prosperity, health, and happiness of its members. But the Divinorums are pacifists.

Since returning home from the Vietnam War thirty-three years ago, they have had no stomach for fighting, as necessary as it may be at times. The problem with pacifism is that it assumes one's enemies comply with the pacifist's code of ethics, laws, and rules of non-engagement. In reality, if we want to defend ourselves against our adversaries, we may need to use force— force that can be in either the physical or occult realms. And sadly, sometimes it is necessary to make unpleasant decisions, and even sacrifices, to defeat those opponents."

Erin was the first to wander out of the fire's hypnotic stupor. "Is this all hypothetical or do you have something particular in mind?"

Answering truthfully, "I sense a terrible adversary approaching—one who is far greater than the business owners and farmers that make up the current Comati membership. What I need is a special group dedicated to fighting this enemy."

"Hell yeah!" Thomas blurted out. "Sounds spooky. Count me in. Like, what do we have to lose?" His eyes moved away from me and passed back and forth between the two girls, checking their reactions.

Tanya was not as confident about the proposal. "What does that mean, *exactly*?" she quivered.

"Yeah," Erin echoed, "What do you want from us?"

"If you are willing to enlist in my army, I promise to teach you occult principles, so you can be the most astute warriors in the magical world."

"*Most astute warriors in the magical world?*" Erin mocked. "*Us?*" When she finished snickering, she continued, "What's the catch? We're not even the most *astute* students at Rivervine High School and we're supposed to graduate this year. In the meantime,

Brigid is so smart, she's graduating with us and she's two years younger. Why don't you ask her?"

I was taken aback by this revelation. I assumed all four youths were the same age. If the Divinorums' daughter, Brigid, was turning sixteen in two months, that would put these three at the same age recruiters from the United States military approached trainees. I found myself overcome with a sense of relief that I was not preying on minds and bodies that were too young to make sound decisions.

Erin stomped off into the darkness. "I gotta pee."

~ Two of Swords ~

While Erin urinated in the tall grass, Thomas and Tanya locked eyes with each other, as if trying to read one another's mind. Both countenances moped like terrified gamblers. It was easy for me to read their attempted poker faces. Thomas' enthusiasm about joining this coven was tempered by Tanya's skittishness. He saw the group as an opportunity to rise above the hopelessness of his future—*their* future. It meant nothing without his lady by his side. She was, perhaps, the only woman who would ever love a portly, lowborn boy with no financial prospects and no obvious talent. Tanya, on the other hand, feared anything that might compromise her ability to escape her current prison of poverty and misery; being a homely girl with glasses rendered her few choices. Thomas was a kind and loving soul, but would this *dance with the devil* risk their opportunity for a brighter future? Or would the bargain end in their favor after all? Does the devil ever pay dividends that benefit the gambler?

When Erin returned, she plopped down on her cushion, grabbing the blanket, throwing it around her shoulders and snuggling in tight. "It's fucking cold!" she huffed.

The two love birds snapped to attention.

All six eyes were on me, each pair holding a different set of expectations.

"You have several choices," I advised.

I went around the circle clockwise—*jeesle*—as the Divinorums say, starting with Erin on my left. Locking eyes with the young woman, I beckoned her, *come here*, and moved over in my cushion to make room. As she took her seat with careful movements, I placed my hands on the sides of her head, closed my eyes and allowed the visions to fill my mind.

"Anger, rebellion, justice, exposing the truth," were the first words to leave my mouth, followed by, "These feelings are compensating for a life of privilege."

She startled herself back and stiffened her spine. Her face grew three more shades of pale beneath the face powder that contrasted so starkly with the black lip and eye polish.

"W-w-what do you mean?"

"Your parents are wealthy, are they not?"

"Yes."

Still looking her in the eye but nodding toward Thomas and Tanya, I asked, "Your friends are *not* wealthy, are they?"

"Correct."

"Do you have other friends besides Thomas and Tanya?"

"N-n-no. Well, not anymore. I did until a week ago when Darren and Matt died. Darren's house caught on fire the night of our ritual. I talked to his mom a couple days later and she said Darren and Matt were smoking pot in his room. The joint fell and they were too stoned to notice the carpet and drapes catching on fire."

I realized these three youths did not know I was the one who started the fire that killed their friends. If I were to be their spiritual mentor, I would need to disclose this upfront. It would be unethical of me to conceal this important detail.

I stood up, motioning for them to do likewise. The casual nature of our discussion was about to change. It was not one to have sitting down.

"There is something I need to tell you before you make any decisions about following me."

I noticed urine streaming down Tanya's leg. Her heart raced even faster than it did when she dropped the cat during last week's Sam Hain ritual. Thomas looked at me as if I were about to announce some sort of delightful secret. But Erin was the only one to speak.

"What the fuck?"

"Your friends, what were their full names?"

Apparently Erin was the only youth with a voice at this moment. "Darren Miller and Matthew Stone," she answered.

"They died of shock, not fire. It was not an accident."

I gave them a moment to process the news. Before another *what the fuck* could be uttered from Erin's mouth, I continued.

"You three showed bravery and nobility by completing the ritual last week. Therefore you were invited here tonight. Mr. Miller and Mr. Stone ran away during ritual. This is cowardice by any definition, but when practicing daemonolatry, it carries particular consequences."

Tanya found her voice and shrieked, "So you *killed* them?"

Thomas' eyes grew wide and a smile grew even wider. "Cool! I actually hated those assholes. I only invited them to the ritual because I thought we needed five people to carry out the summoning spell. I knew they just agreed to it because they wanted to bang Tanya and Erin."

Both girls shot him a look of anger. Tanya started crying.

"You were going to let them do that to me?" she screamed. "*You're* the asshole! Don't ever touch me again!"

She fell to the ground and started bawling.

"I don't care about this fucking coven anymore!" she yelled. "I'm sorry, Zinfandel. Am I already on the hook for this *army* thing or is there still time to back out?"

Erin plopped back down on her cushion. Thomas went to console Tanya but she pushed him back and yelled, "Get the fuck away from me! I never want to see you again! I'm not your whore!"

He returned to his spot and sat on his cushion, holding his knees and rocking back and forth on his pelvis, wrapping the blanket around him and holding on to it tightly with balled fists.

I shifted over to the distraught young woman and sat down, putting my arms around her, letting her cry on my shoulder. As I rocked her back and forth, I explained the situation in further detail.

"You are free to leave at any time," I told her. "But please listen to me before you go."

Still holding her torso with my left arm, I lifted her chin and wiped away some of her tears with my right hand. Looking her in the eye, I said, "One of the many lessons you all can learn from that night is the importance of explicitly telling ritual participants what is expected of them and making sure you receive their consent before you proceed."

At this point, Thomas dropped the blanket and started crying too.

"I fucked up!" he yelled. "I totally fucked up. This is all my fault."

Erin bolted straight up and yelled, "No, it *isn't* your fault, Thomas. I get what Tanya is saying about you pimping her out, but we *all* agreed to the ritual. We all agreed to get naked. We all agreed to have sex with each other. We all agreed to kill the cat and smother ourselves in its blood. At no time did any of us agree to *not* have sex with you or Tanya. All five of us were fair game. This self-righteous act is bullshit!"

She then sat back down. The ambiance of the ritual area was thick with tension. I decided this was a good time for us to wrap things up.

"Let us take our leave for this evening," I suggested. "Think about things over the course of the month, and if you decide you want to continue, summon me on the next new moon. Otherwise, I bid you all well."

With those words I shed my apparition, planning to shift back to the cave. As I was leaving the ritual area, I sensed Anton standing outside the circle.

"Why am I not surprised you were spying on us?" I asked.

"I still do not trust them, sister. I doubt they will summon you again."

"We shall see."

The two of us shifted to the vineyard, conjured our instruments, and relieved our tensions by playing for the woodland creatures. A few tunes into our concert, two bright lights twinkled across the rows of bare zinfandel vines. As the lights came closer, soft brown fur outlined the approaching cougar. Anton tried to call it over to him but it stopped a few feet from where we were performing. Then it pounced onto something—its first meal of the evening.

My brother and I both felt a rip in our hearts. Whatever had died was something that had left its imprint on our spirits.

When we looked over to see the feast, we saw the carcass of the feral cat that was healed last week.

This is how nature works, my friends. The concepts of loving and cruel are human constructs.

Anton and I are now back in the cave. He is grieving and I just realized I never did tell Erin why I believed she was overcompensating for being wealthy. Another time perhaps.

I also wondered if I should have told the youths that their friends, Darren and Matthew, only had their sights on Erin and dismissed Tanya as "a popsicle stick"—whatever that meant. From an ethical perspective, would this information have mattered?

THE EMPRESS

6 November in the Year of Their Lord 2002

There are some spirits who know me too well. I cannot hide from them my true feelings, thoughts, or opinions on any given matter. I want everyone to think I am strong, that I have everything under control. But when Sauin comes, the veil between the occult and physical realms is at its thinnest, giving even the most languid ghosts a peek through my facade. As the sun set tonight, one of my ancestors called my bluff.

"Why are you so sad, darling child?" our matriarch asked in her thick Eastern European accent. "Tonight is for celebration! But you cannot celebrate if you cannot be happy. Tell Doina your problems. Let me help."

"Greatest grandmother," I replied, "thank you for the offer, but I will find my own solutions in due time. I just need to meditate."

"Meditate on what? Your pride or your humility?"

I sighed in defeat, too stumped to answer. I did not know if I was too proud to admit my failure to form a hive, or too humble to trouble her with something so petty. What she faced back in Romania and again in Massachusetts was far worse than three young people wanting to play witch. Hell, even I have endured worse. Why was I letting this bother me so?

"Tell me, Vondella," she insisted. "You are never a burden! I am a good listener."

That, she is. Many of my tears have fallen on her phantom shoulders. And tonight was probably the only opportunity I would have this year to seek her counsel.

I told her everything about the youths, the cat, Anton, and this grimoire.

"You must write!" she counseled. "Right now, yes! Tonight is Sauin—the festival of the dead! The greatest gift you can give your ancestors is to write their story. Then come back and we will drink wine together. The Comatis will still be celebrating when you finish."

Following her advice, I conjured my grimoire, steel point pen, and inkwell. A quiet spot under one of the oaks in the south quadrant looked like the perfect place to scribble some notes while keeping an eye on the celebration.

~ Five of Cups ~

Tonight is the official twain of the autumn equinox and winter solstice, which makes it the festival of Sauin for the Comatis.

A *twain* is a midway point. It is where, in the physical and occult realms, a clear channel of communication runs between the two worlds. For adepts in either realm, authentic interaction with the other side can occur at any time of the year. But for the average seeker, and especially for more obtuse learners, contact is easier during the twains of the conscious and unconscious mind: waking and sleeping, health and sickness, even life and death. It can also be the twains of time and space, such as sunrise and sunset, the shoreline, a mountain top, or the crossquarters of the solstices and equinoxes.

The solar year has four seasons— autumn, winter, spring, and summer. Likewise, there are four crossquarters: Sauin between autumn and winter, Iemmol between winter and spring, Beltane between spring and summer, and Lughnasadh between summer and autumn.

Each crossquarter is a special cause for celebration. Comatis hold large festivals with bonfires, music, games, chanting, rituals, and dancing.

Sauin honors the ancestors and celebrates the last harvest. In Rivervine, the last yield of grapes is usually around this time of year. In the old country, crops of grains, beans, and vegetables had been harvested by Lughnasadh, but the sheep, cattle, swine, and goats were slaughtered at Sauin, their meat preserved in salt. Meat is rich in iron, which has a magnetic effect on the souls of the dead. Leaving out a plate of meat as an offering for the ancestors became a tradition in many pagan cultures throughout the world. Descendants were able to communicate with lost loved ones and seek their advice from the ancestor's realm.

The polar opposite of Sauin is Beltane, which is in early May here in the northern hemisphere; pagans in the southern hemisphere celebrate it in early November. Beltane is when meat supply is at its lowest and flowers bloom the most. Beautiful blossoms, warm weather, long days, and low iron levels attract the fae folk.

The real fae are not the cutesy sprites imagined by artists and poets. They exist in their own realm—neither occult nor physical. Not only are they sentient, but they are also highly intelligent and quick to seize an opportunity to trick an imprudent seeker. That is why one must always keep one's sense when dealing with these beings.

If a contract with them is done properly, both the fae and the human can mutually benefit. Such is the agreement the Comatis have with the good folk, but I will continue that story another time. For now, let us continue our introduction of the Comati holidays.

In between Sauin and Beltane is the festival of Iemmol in early February—August for our friends below the equator. This is when we celebrate the first signs of spring brought on by the returning light. Its polar opposite is Lughnasadh, the harvest of grain and honey. I will explain all of these in further detail in subsequent entries. For now, let me continue with the overview.

The names of our holidays are Gaelic in origin and come from the Celts, who were one of the tribes that frequently traded with the Dacians in what is present-day Romania—the homeland of Doina and Radu Baleur, my greatest grandparents and the original Rivervine Comatis.

Comati is the Dacian word for *peasant*. Before the Roman conquest, Dacian society was split between the Comatis and the noble class, called the *Tarabostes*. The Tarabostes immediately adopted the Roman religion when Emperor Trajan conquered the region in the Year of Their Lord 106. But the Comatis held true to their local beliefs and customs.

Doina and Radu were Comatis living in a small, secluded village high in the Carpathian Mountains. Their only visitors were the Romani peddlers who traded with them. The Comatis made wine and grew herbs that they made into medicine. The Romanis brought wares from the outside world. Together, they played music.

One old, left-handed, Romani woman had an unusual violin that was specially constructed to suit a left-handed musician. The chin rest was located on the right side of the instrument. The bass bar had been placed under the right leg of the bridge, while the sound post was found on the left. The peg holes and bridge were adjusted to have the strings placed in the opposite order of a right-handed violin.

The old Romani woman eventually developed arthritis and could no longer play, despite her abundant use of the Comatis' ointments and herbal remedies. Doina, my left-handed ancestor, was fourteen years old when she inherited the treasure in the Year of Their Lord 1687.

That same summer, an English woman came to the Comati village seeking an herbal fertility tonic—Doina was famous throughout Europe for her ability to heal a barren womb. The remedy worked, and the woman soon conceived a child. Before heading back to England, though, a night of terror struck the tribe.

A group of Catholic priests from the Polish side of the Carpathians swept through the village claiming a destiny to cleanse the land of its heathen demons and protect it from the influences of the Orthodox Church and Turkish Muslims. They declared the territory in the name of the Pope; anyone who would not swear allegiance would suffer death at sword point.

The priests killed everyone in the Comati village except Doina, Radu, the English woman and her husband, thanks to the matron's generous donation to the church: three gold coins, which served as ransom—and their vow to emigrate.

Doina took her violin to England, and Radu brought his cobza—another Romani stringed instrument, similar to a lute. The woman gave birth and Doina became the nanny for the son. Radu studied as an apprentice under the husband's direction. The man had business in the American colonies, so all five of them— the Baleurs and the English family—headed to Salem, Massachusetts.

Although the Massachusetts Bay Colony was a Puritan settlement, the colonists never voiced opposition to my ancestors' pagan practices until the witch panic of 1692.

By this time, the boy was nearly five years old, and the Baleurs had grown close to the English family. But as the number of accused witches increased, the English couple, fearing for the lives of their beloved servants, insisted Doina and Radu flee into the woods.

Once again, my greatest grandparents faced terror, trauma, and pauperism but this time, there was no one to rescue them. When they called upon their Dacian gods for assistance, their prayers were answered by a mysterious robed figure with a wooden cross around his neck. In his hands were three sets of reins leading to three horses. The trio mounted their steeds and rode through the night. I am unsure how to explain this marvel, but as Doina tells it, their surroundings turned blue during the ride, and when the horses stopped, she, Radu and the mystery man were on the other side of the New World.

The first thing they noticed were the wild grapes growing up the trees along the river. Inspired by this phenomenon, they named their new home *Rivervine*.

As the years passed, Doina and Radu had children of their own, and those progenies mated with the native Miwok and Maidu people. Over time, the English, Russian, and Spanish explorers added their seeds. By the nineteenth century, they became a tribe in their own right, giving themselves the name *Comati*.

The Comatis lived like other local peoples residing in cone-shaped huts made of bark, keeping warm around the fireplaces, cooking on earthen ovens, and sitting on carpets made of pine needles. At night, they slept on tule-reed mats and animal skins.

The Comati gathering place was a large assembly house—about forty-four feet in diameter—that was built three to four feet into the ground with center posts holding up roof beams connected by smaller branches and covered with layers of brush, pine needles, and dirt. In the center of the roof was a smoke hole. The building's door faced east to greet the rising sun.

The Miwoks called it a *hun'ge*. The Comatis called it *The Oppidum*—a word harkening back to the Iron Age, describing an enclosed space. That is where the tribe met for religious ceremonies and stored the most sacred of all elements—wine.

In the Year of Their Lord 1800, a ship sailing from India docked at the bay of Yerba Buena, one hundred thirty-four miles from Rivervine. On board was a sixteen-year-old Chinese stowaway named Xin Hsüan.

For many years, the British had done business in India, the country directly west of China. The English had learned to mix Indian tobacco with the sap from opium poppies, a combination that created a most surreal and addictive intoxication. The original Chinese opium was used merely as a medicinal plant—a part of China's pharmacies and economy since scribes first began to write. But it had neither the habit-forming powers nor the mind-altering effect that has made opium so controversial.

Xin Hsüan was a poor Cantonese boy who had taken a job selling Indian opium to Chinese peasants—a career that did not gain him any favor in the eyes of local politicians. When the area's businessmen began importing opium instead of exporting it, the Chinese economy started to crumble, forcing the emperor to ban the imported drug in 1799.

This mandate left the young man in a quandary. He could not sell Chinese opium because his customers demanded India's narcotic. Yet, if he tried to sell the imported drug, he faced imprisonment.

His only option was to trust his luck and sneak onboard an English ship headed for the New World.

Once he landed in Yerba Buena, he stole a horse and set out with roughly five pounds of Indian opium and a pouch of poppy seeds in his satchel. For some reason I do not know, he also brought a sapling of a weeping willow.

Xin Hsüan's luck was not very plentiful during his travels. The local people had their own teonanacatl mushrooms and no need to purchase another vehicle to dreamwork. Neither could he sell to the Spanish missionaries who feared the Satanic imagery created by the pagan substance.

Frustrated and destitute, he reached Comati territory in the spring of 1800. There was one girl—my mother, Crina—who took a liking to the young man. They found a romantic connection and he decided to stay. It was along the bank of the Vitus River that he planted his damn weeping willow. I will go into more detail about that dreadful tree later.

I was born 25 October in the Year of Their Lord 1820, the youngest of their seven children and the only daughter.

As for my name, it is actually *Xin Vondella*. Xin is my family name, and Vondella is my given name. It means "precious girl" in Dacian. In Chinese society, one's family name precedes one's given name, a practice that opposes Western culture. Since my father was the dogmatic patriarch—despite being embraced by the Comati tribe—he insisted our naming convention follow that of his fatherland.

All of the Comati children were educated by a Spanish Catholic priest named Father Kristobal.

Kristobal and my brother Anton were the only people who brought happiness to my childhood. And they were the only two who defended me against a horrible stranger from Bavaria. I do not know what inspired the horticulturist to visit Comati territory, but he discovered our grapes and fell in love with our wine. However, he often drank too much and looked to me—barely old enough for breasts—to satiate his carnal desires.

He called me, *Zeinferdel.* That is also the name he gave our grapes. Perhaps I should be flattered but I am not.

On several nights, the drunk Bavarian took me in the biblical sense. The abuse tore my womb, which is why I was never able to bear children.

My father and five oldest brothers watched in amusement, cheering the old man and teasing me for crying and bleeding. My mother and the rest of the tribe were complicit, too afraid to speak up against the men.

Anton, who was only two years older than I, tired of me crying so damn much. These painful episodes took too much time away from our musical gatherings and he wanted to put a stop to the interruptions. His close bond with animals served a purpose when he convinced a surfeit of skunk friends to chase the man out of camp.

In the Bavarian's haste to leave, the old man took only what belongings he could quickly grab in his arms. He left behind most of his clothing and supplies but managed to pick up half a dozen specimens of the Zeinferdel grape stock, hoping to sell it back in Munich.

His last stop on his way out of camp was Father Kristobal's hut. Anton and I were already there, confessing to our own sins for playing a trick on the Bavarian. When we saw the old man approach, we scampered away.

Entering Kristobal's hut, the Bavarian yelped, "I am leaving town. I need the Eucharist one last time before I travel."

"You must first confess your sins and receive the act of contrition!" Kristobal insisted. "I know you have violated

Vondella. Such defilement requires more than the body and blood of Christ. You must repent!"

The Bavarian dismissed the accusation and ran from Kristobal's hut, never again setting foot on Comati territory.

We later learned a Swiss aristocrat named Captain Yohan Sooter had purchased several vines from the Bavarian—enough to plant an entire vineyard. As the vines matured and the wine aged in oak vats, Sooter believed he had made the most wonderful libation. He called it *Zinfandel*.

Sooter set out for California in 1839 in the hopes of finding more of these grapes. He even conned Mexican Governor Juan Bautista Alvarado into granting him a specious land grant of forty-nine thousand acres, telling the politician he wanted to establish a sawmill community, which he called New Helvetia. Although the Mexican governor did not actually have the right to grant the territory to Sooter, the Miwok and Maidu people living in the area lacked the weapon power to defend themselves against the despot. The land fell to the invaders and Rivervine became an outpost for Sooter's Fort, which was headquartered in New Helvetia, about forty miles from Rivervine.

By the time Sooter's lumberjacks reached Comati territory, the year was 1841 and I was almost twenty-one years old. We thought of these workers as just another group of newcomers. The men stationed here lived in tents with crude arrangements. But they brought with them guitars, mandolins, hand drums and fiddles. Some even used jugs and jaw harps to make music. Since I was left-handed, I had inherited the Romani violin from Doina. My brother had Radu's cobza, which sounded similar to the mandolins of Sooter's men, only tinnier.

What I loved most was an amber wine they called *whiskey*. The flavor bit my tongue like a rattlesnake hypnotizes prey. The libation was so smooth and warm and comforting, yet it had a kick that led my mind along a new path of altered consciousness. The more whiskey I drank, the more I danced, appreciating every note played by the musicians.

Anton never truly enjoyed playing music with Sooter's men. Although they were fascinated by his amazing musical talent, the men taunted him for his ugliness and treated him as less than human.

Anton did have some joy in his life, though. He loved his animal friends, and at night, after dinner when the rest of the family was asleep, he and I would sneak out to the cave with our instruments and play some more. It became our secret hideaway where we could escape the pressures of our dogmatic father and ruthless brothers.

To reach the cave, we would have to pass the weeping willow. By the time I was an adult, it had grown to more than thirty feet high.

I always hated that tree. The bark on the trunk had a bizarre-patterned knot on it. When I was a child, I envisioned that bulge as the face of a dragon. I could see with utmost clarity the slanted eyes of the beast, its gigantic fangs, and nostrils large enough to inhale my entire body. Nightmares continuously haunted me, and fear scrutinized my daily activities.

My brothers knew of my phobia and played into it by taunting me with late-night tales of the dragon peeking through its draping branches to spy on me. My father, as cruel as he was, would join in the game and tell me that if I did not behave myself, the dragon was going to inflict its vengeance on me. Whatever did I do to that tree to deserve such a punishment?

Luck was on our side, though. Anton and I managed to safely sneak past the tree unscathed every time we met at the cave. It was there that we could play all the crescendos and decrescendos we wanted without disturbing anyone, soothing our souls in the healing sound of vibrating strings.

We gathered whenever Anton was not sick. He had a blood disease that was common in our family, but rarely found in other ethnic groups. Because the Romanian Comatis had been such a small tribe, inbreeding was common, and many children were plagued with blood that was not strong enough to fight the myriad diseases that humans encounter every day. Even though our mother and father were not siblings, Xin Crina still carried the curse. Anton was the only one of us seven children whose body expressed the symptoms.

I remember him having bouts of weakness and dizziness. His skin would become morbidly pale and blister whenever he went into the sunlight. Dark circles formed under his eyes, and sometimes when he cried, his tears filled with blood.

The only remedy that seemed to help was if I fed him my menstrual flow or cut myself to allow him to drink my blood. It was as if his own plasma betrayed him and he needed mine to replenish what he had lost.

My father believed that blood was the root source of *chi*— the Chinese term for universal lifeforce energy. As a young boy, Anton endured the treatment of our father's acupuncture needles that pricked my brother's skin along certain points on the boy's body. The needles allegedly helped the chi flow freely.

Perhaps Xin Hsüan was right to an extent. Who knows at what young age Anton would have died had it not been for our father's intervention? I suppose I should appreciate my old man for the pissant amount of mercy and compassion he bestowed upon his sixth child. Stories such as this make me feel like an ingrate for harboring resentment toward such an alleged hero, but it breaks my heart to know the man was capable of compassion yet chose to deny me an equal amount of empathy.

Unfortunately, neither my fluids nor Father's needles could sustain Anton through adulthood. My brother lived to see his twenty-fifth birthday, but not his twenty-sixth.

After my favorite brother died, I would go to the cave to mourn him—hoping that playing a dirge or other requiem on my violin would aid in my grief. It was difficult to play without my brother, though. I would even place his cobza by my side in hopes that he would mysteriously appear.

My violin stayed silent for four years. It did not make merry again until 1846 when a young lad from Ireland named Lugh O'Byrne marched into town.

Lugh had come to Rivervine from County Kildare in 1845 during his homeland's great potato famine. He spent most of his time that year in New York but the following year, war broke out between the United States and Mexico. Soldiers were needed. The pay was good. Lugh enlisted in the U.S. Army and deployed to California.

From 1846 to 1848, Lugh fought in the Mexican-American War. As time went on, the Irish soldiers—nearly all of whom were Catholic—found themselves harassed, humiliated and tortured by the Americans—nearly all of whom were Protestant.

The Mexican army was mostly Catholic, and since the Irish had no particular allegiance to the United States, many defected to the more hospitable nation south of the border. They joined a band of Irish-Mexican outlaws called Saint Patrick's Battalion, better known as the San Patricios.

Lugh was not among them, though. Instead, he led a small group of Irish Catholics that were loyal to the Americans. They called themselves Saint Brigid's Battalion and set up their headquarters here in Rivervine, California.

He built a church in our small foothill town, but the building burned in 1848 as part of the mysterious fire that created the Black Land. I will discuss more about the fire in a bit.

Lugh was the first man to show me honor. He treated me with kindness, bringing me wildflowers and drawing my portrait in his sketchbook. He made me feel invincible. When we were together, I was strong. I was smart. I was brave. He saw the good in me. Lugh often told me—in his thick Irish brogue, "Beauty is spiritual; it rises from the soul to the surface and glows brighter with each inch of your lovely smile."

Our two religions were not all that different. Even though Lugh was Catholic, he attended our community rituals, and introduced us to this saint named Brigid, whom he called the matron of bards. Being bards ourselves, she was easily adopted into the Comati mythos.

Unfortunately, just like my brother, Lugh left the incarnate realm before I did. The U.S. Army hung him on 17 March in the Year of Their Lord 1848—Saint Patrick's Day—even though they had no evidence of him defecting and joining the San Patricios.

I am not convinced the reason for Lugh's hanging was treason, though.

Two months before Lugh's death, Sooter's right-hand man, John Marshall, discovered gold forty miles north of Rivervine, setting off the great California Gold Rush. My lover was competition—not just for gold, but for me.

Miners came from everywhere—single men, married men with wives back east, fathers with daughters just like me—they were all lonely and needed a rare commodity called female companionship. My exotic features, combined with musical talent and physical dexterity, commanded a pretty penny, and my father took advantage of the opportunity.

He knew that if Lugh were removed from the picture, I would become numb to emotional investment.

He was right. After Lugh's death, sex no longer conjured magic; it was just a meaningless way to kill time. Yes, I worked as a saloon girl. But I did not enjoy it.

I am grateful for the two years I had with my Irishman, but he raised the standard so high that no other lover has been able to replace him. The magic we created was too special to be diluted.

I even stopped playing violin. I placed it in the cave next to Anton's cobza. The two instruments stayed silent together.

I had hoped Lugh would come back as a ghost to visit me, but I fear that being a good Catholic, despite the Comati influence, he ascended to his Christian heaven and has been there ever since. I call his name every Sauin but he never answers.

I will never forgive my father for whoring me out and taking away my one true love.

Perhaps I should have been flattered to have had so much attention paid to me by the gold miners, but the shallow devotion wore thin, and I tired of demonstrating affection I could not genuinely reciprocate. I started to feel that sex should be respected and savored, not consumed like the cheap, watered-down whiskey sold in the saloon.

Two months before my twenty-eighth birthday, the men in camp were having another one of their rousing, liquor-filled nights.

Alcohol stimulates a person's appetite. The dance hall where I worked did not serve food.

On 16 August in the Year of Their Lord 1848, a beer-breathed prospector insisted I make him dinner. I said no.

He started to draw his gun but I was quicker with a kick to his ribs and jab to the neck, using some gung-fu moves my father had taught me when I was young. The beast fell to the floor.

Knowing the men would never accept my claim of self-defense, I ran and hid behind the ceremonial wine in the Oppidum. The miner arose from his emasculation and followed me, locking the door behind him, once again reaching for his gun.

Since I was now trapped, with no other means of defense, I sliced his throat with a swift, deep slash of my long, sharp fingernails. The despicable wretch bled to death right in front of me. I savored the sweet flavor of his essence leaving his body and immigrating into mine. The feed was euphoric.

Drowning in darkness, my mind raced through the available options. It was obvious I could not stay. But where would I go? North? East? West? South? It finally dawned on me that I had never left Rivervine before. I knew nothing of the world around me.

As I was starting to relish the opportunity to go exploring and start a new life of my own, the darkness filled with a billowy gray vapor. The smoke stung my eyes, stole my breath and pilfered my consciousness. The temperature grew so hot so quickly and then, in a literal flash, it was over as the fire hit the bottles of wine.

I do not remember when the torture ended, but at some point, the pain, fear, and anxiety were gone.

Something beckoned to me, though: my violin.

But I had no legs to take me to the cave or fingers to play the notes on the fiddle's neck. And yet, just the thought of the instrument was enough to bring me to its location.

I do not know how I arrived there, but I found Anton waiting for me. Our instruments were safe—right where I left them.

I wanted nothing more than to embrace my brother, but neither of us had corporeal matter; we did not know what to do. My need to hold him went unsatiated.

I called for Lugh but my lover did not answer.

I craved a drink of either whiskey or wine, but my tongue stayed dry.

Death had cursed me.

Remembering the vine-covered woods, my mind wandered back to town.

I found the entire area blackened. The grapes were ashes. The oaks had been charred and our huts and roundhouse were ruins.

Insulting me even further was that ominous weeping willow standing along the edge of the river.

The fir and the alder trees were completely destroyed by the fire. There was not even the tiniest trace of the manzanitas that once covered the land. But the weeping willow? Not a single leaf of that evil thing had been singed. I never knew a tree could be so spiteful. I have tried numerous times to destroy it— chopping it down, lighting it on fire—but it is one of the few creations of the incarnate realm that I cannot affect. No doubt my father had protected it well with all of his Taoist spellwork.

The closest thing to satisfaction I can claim is that the tree my father planted now permanently mourns for the man who gave it Rivervine roots.

Unable to cope with the trauma, I vowed to never let this area live again. With all my magical knowhow, I christened the boundaries inside Comati territory as *The Black Land*. I swore the soil would remain dark, and no plant, tree, or creature would live again until a proper set of guardians came forward. That spell was broken in the Year of Their Lord 1969.

~ Nine of Wands ~

Here in modern-day Rivervine, all Comati rituals take place in the Oppidum—an area on the Divinorum property where eight oaks outline a half-acre patch of bare land. The community decorates the trees with ribbons and fancy ornaments, making each event festive with special colors appropriate for the holiday. Tonight they decorated the area in crimson and black for Sauin. Iemmol will have silver, blue, and gold. Beltane bursts in bright, happy pastel colors, and Lughnasadh features shades of the harvest. Their beautiful handiwork always reassures me that I made the right decision thirty-three years ago when I gave this land to Xavia and Sage.

The story of today's Comatis actually starts two years before I met the Divinorums.

The myth of the Black Land has always attracted thrill seekers because it was such an enigma. There was never any scientific explanation for the land to lay fallow and the soil to remain so eerily dark for more than a hundred years. Rumors and folklore spread, as I knew they would, about the area being haunted. Some tales even claimed it was a portal to hell. That is why I was not surprised when a young man, whom I guessed was in his early twenties, came here alone on the afternoon of 30 April in the Year of Their Lord 1967.

This was before I had learned how to create an illusory apparition. I was able to read his aura and sense his spirit, but he could not see or hear me at first.

I watched him park his automatic carriage by the main road and set out on foot up one of the hills. He was a tall, slender man with long, dark, bushy hair and a long, dark, bushy moustache. His features were attractive but he was dressed in such garish, odd-looking clothes—pumpkin-colored trousers with a wide, leather belt and a bright green shirt patterned with gaudy swirls of purple, yellow and black. He wore no shoes but managed to wander around barefoot for an hour or so looking at various spots as if assessing the position of sunshine and shadows. During his visit, he frequently scratched the dirt, collected vials of soil, and jotted down notes in a journal, the cover of which read, "T. Caprasen."

Right away, I felt a strong magnetism toward this T. Caprasen fellow. As I read his aura, I sensed an intense, dark spiritual side and a deep passion for studying the cultural development of human beings. This is a trait I admired as it signaled to me that he cared about the people of the past. Comatis hold deep reverence for the ancestors because we know that if we treat them with honor and dignity, they will repay us by acting as guardians and guides from the occult realm.

As much as this all pleased me, though, the longer I studied him, the more I sensed he was not the right fit to awaken the Black Land from its slumber. He would be a welcome guest, of course, as his heart was authentic and his mind was strong. But his calling was at university and his spiritual path navigated the sea of chaos, not rows of grapevines. This highly evolved soul was not a servant of the land—a non-negotiable quality I needed in order to reprogenate the Comati legacy.

However, I sensed the correct people were within his sphere—a close friend and the friend's true love. If I could get this colleague's semen and the blood of his consort to fertilize my soil, the combination would form the right amalgam of chi to re-energize the land and bring it back to life.

Menstrual flow, of course, would be the ideal means of harvesting the woman's blood, but in case the ritual occurred when it was not her moon time, I needed to find a guaranteed way of procuring it.

Dear Reader, you may be disturbed by what I am about to disclose, but it is an important discussion for us to have if you are pursuing the Zinfandel path. I do not recommend blood ritual very often, and I never condone involuntary bloodletting in spellwork, but there are times when sanguinary magic is the most effective, if not the only option.

Of all substances in the world, blood has the highest concentration of vital lifeforce energy—what my father called *chi*. Women's blood contains higher concentrations of chi than men's blood because extra-sensory gifts descend through the generations via the matrilineal bloodline. Patrilineal energy, the bloodline of our fathers, has a much lighter density.

With all this in mind, I knew that if my vines were to grow again, I needed this woman's blood. But I had to obtain it without coercion. Free will is of paramount importance in a magical working. All participants in the sacrifice must be sovereign in their own minds and bodies, and they must always consent to take part.

As I pondered how I could affect this outcome, I wandered over to where T. Caprasen had parked his automatic carriage. It was there I found Anton speaking with a gopher.

My brother looked up from his conversation and said to me, "Come here, sister. Look."

He then led me around to the back of the carriage where we peeked in the window at something on the backseat.

"A guitar!" I shouted.

"It appears this lookie-loo is a musician."

We also found several pieces of postal mail with strange markings. Some had ink stamps with some sort of Asian characters, but not the Chinese that we knew. There were also several photos of a place with signs that read, "Saigon."

In one picture, there was a tall, red-headed bean pole of an American man standing next to a short, stocky woman with black hair and piercing blue eyes. Both wore the uniform of the United States Army.

"This is my couple!" I shouted, and enthusiastically reached to embrace my brother.

Turning toward him, I accidentally stepped on something I thought was the poor gopher.

"I am so sorry!" I screamed.

But when I looked down, it was not the rodent that was under my foot but rather the handle of a dagger. I recognized it as the ceremonial knife we used in ritual before the Great Fire. It had somehow survived the blaze.

I did not have much time to celebrate this discovery, though. T. Caprasen came walking back from his site inspection. I dropped the blade back down near the gopher hole. As the academic sightseer approached his carriage, he stepped on the sharp end of the knife with his bare foot.

He did not bleed much, but the bite of the scrape startled him. He bent down to see what he had stepped on and then jumped back. Pulling a handkerchief out of his breast pocket, he picked up the artifact and furrowed his eyes in confusion, as if struggling to recognize the distinctive markings.

He muttered under his breath, "What the hell is this?"

All I could muster in response was, "Comati." By some miracle, the word was audible enough for him to hear me. I was amazed at my ability to penetrate the veil to the physical realm, even if it was only sound. He still could not see me.

His aura piqued in startled surprise and his head swiftly twisted left and right, searching for someone who could have made the noise.

"That is who we are," I explained.

"Who are 'we'?" he called, his voice trembling. "What does *Comati* mean?"

"The ones who bring you this gift," I answered. "It is my offering for your ritual—something from my heritage."

"Your heritage? Are you Miwok or Maidu?"

"Both … and many others."

"So, *Comati* is a tribe?" His aura relaxed. "Are you their goddess? Why are you giving me this treasure?"

"Bring me the lovers and I shall make the purpose of this object clear."

I sensed his hesitation.

"But this is a relic," he countered. "I have to save this for my academic research."

Trying to sound empathetic but still assertive, I advised him, "Your foremost obligation is to use a sacred object for its intended purpose—in ritual. I would not have given it to you otherwise."

I then collapsed from exhaustion. This had been my first attempt at affecting the physical realm for any reason other than instilling fear into a trespasser. The interaction drained me of energy and I could no longer continue our conversation or even read his aura.

The young man returned with three friends on the evening of 6 May and started setting up their ritual site. The prominent item in the center of the altar was a statue of what I guessed to be a god of some sort. It featured a man's body but the head had a long, pointed snout and rectangular ears that pointed upwards. A bowl of musk incense burned in the east quadrant and some animal bones were scattered in the north. They placed a chalice on the west side and my ancestral knife in the south. Before the ritual started, they changed out of their mundane clothing and donned hooded black robes. I did not get a good look at their faces.

As the evening wore on, I deduced this was some sort of dedication ritual. Each member approached the altar, stating his or her name and pledging fidelity to the *Setian Understanding*, which I assumed was the name of their coven. A young man calling himself Frater Babael led the ritual. Throughout the evening, he barked orders at a woman whom he called Soror Carissa. Occasionally Babael called upon T. Caprasen, referring to him as Frater Todd. At Todd's side was a lovely woman who announced herself as Soror Inanna.

I knew from Father Kristobal's Latin lessons when I was young that "frater" meant brother and "soror" meant sister. It is a common title given to members of certain religious organizations.

After they stated their names and pledged their allegiance, Soror Carissa approached the altar and disrobed. Her hair was scarlet red and her figure was not short and stocky like the photo. Frater Babael also disrobed. He was far too muscular to have been the bean pole in the photograph. Nonetheless, I allowed the ceremony to proceed.

The ritual continued with Babael gently laying the bare Carissa on the ground next to the altar. He began fondling her breasts. As her sounds of pleasure increased, the cleric nudged the woman's legs open and inserted his stiffened phallus, gyrating in rhythm with the sounds of the maiden's ecstasy. Carissa's breathing hastened, signaling her approach to climax.

Babael grabbed the blade from the altar and made a small incision in her inner thigh. The nymph continued to moan in ecstasy as the dagger grazed her skin.

Droplets of blood trickled to the ground. Shortly afterward, Babael's semen added to Carissa's honey and the magical potion ran down her buttocks.

At first, I was overjoyed at this union. "Finally! My vines can grow again!" I thought to myself. The energy from my excitement made the soil beneath the woman glow in a vibrant shade of indigo.

But something did not feel right. The blood did not contain the right matrilineal chi and the semen was not complementary.

"Caprasen!" I shrieked, loud enough so all could hear. The color of the ground returned to its black color. Shocked and humiliated, Carissa and Babael fumbled to don their robes. Todd was left stupefied and embarrassed.

"These are not the lovers you were to bring me!" I chastised.

Awashed in shame, Frater Todd struggled to respond.

"Who then?" was all he could mumble.

"Bring me the couple who will respect my land in its entirety and not squander it as a heretical whoredom. My home is sacred. You know the partners of which I speak. Seek them out and do not return until they have made love among my vines."

"What vines?" he asked, waving his arm around to show there was no vegetation growing within sight.

I was too upset to answer.

The ritual ended early; they were all too fretful to stay any longer.

Frater Todd Caprasen did return, though. Two years later, he brought his friends Xavia and Sage with him. I learned that Xavia had been an Army nurse in the Vietnam War. It was there she met a soldier named Sage Divinorum and started teaching him the practice of Druidry. They had recently returned to Yerba Buena from their tour of duty and were looking to buy land away from the city and start a new life together, close to nature where they could live off the land. I sensed their yearning for the sensation of fresh soil enveloping their hands and the experience of watching plants cycle through the changing seasons. I saw their visions of washing away their cares in the waves of music played in a theater of trees, and teaching others the joy of spirituality under the stars.

For their role in combat, Xavia and Sage received enough money from the government to purchase all eighty-nine acres of the Black Land in August 1969. The property was cheap since no one had touched it since the Gold Rush. They were able to buy the land, build a house and start a winery.

That month, when Xavia was having her moon time, she and Sage made love atop the soil of the Black Land. They intuitively chose the area where the Oppidum once stood.

When I invited the Druids to make the area their new sacred space, they accepted, but insisted ceremonies be held outdoors, claiming a need to be uninhibited and exposed to all of the elements, regardless of weather.

I acquiesced. Instead of asking them to rebuild the hun'ge, I allowed acorns to sprout in a circular pattern outlining the perimeter. They call it The Oppidum.

This is now where the new Comatis meet four times a year for the Celtic holy days—Sauin, Iemmol, Beltane and Lughnasadh. They also gather here for occasions such as weddings, funerals, and other sacred ceremonies.

One factor that has remained constant throughout all of the Comati tribes is the presence of a fire pit in the center of the ritual area. We always had a fire—any time of year. Fire cleanses, purifies, and inspires. Its smoke lifts our intentions up to the Miwoks' Grandfather, the Celts' Shining Ones, and the Chinese Immortals. The heat warms our bodies, as we find motivation for physical activity and sweat out impurities. The scent attracts spirits to visit us from the occult realm. The whole experience leads our minds to a higher state of consciousness.

On that note, I need to put down the journal and pen and rejoin my fellow celebrants. They are about to start the reading of the names. I will pick this up again after the ritual has ended.

~ Straif ~

By the time I finished writing my last entry, festivities were well underway. I had not missed much, though, as the first part of the Sauin ritual is more about preparing the living than communing with the dead.

Earlier in the day, the Comatis prepared the Oppidum for ritual. Streams of crimson and black silk weaved their loving magic into knots and bows connecting the mighty oaks, and decorated the torches marking the cardinal points of north, east, west, and south. In the center of the Oppidum, they lit the ritual bonfire, and tended to its gentle flame throughout the evening.

At the northernmost point, Brigid and Sage had set their guitars. There was also a tambourine and some percussion instruments.

Immediately north of the blaze stood the altar. It was built atop a large tub of recently harvested grapes that would be used in the second half of the ritual.

As always, Xavia placed the Awen stone—the signature of her Druid faith—in the center of the altar. To the left side of the awen stood a black candle, a symbolic gesture to honor the dead. On the right, smoke billowed from a tiny cauldron burning incense made from rosemary, cinnamon, and cloves. The ceremonial earthen pitcher, along with a bottle of Fermata Cellars 1998 Requiem, readied themselves for the libation to be paired with bite-sized nibblets of apple bread that sat on a plate to be served as the food offering. Pinecones, dried pomegranates, and crow feathers—all symbols of the folkloric underworld—decorated the space on the stand. A pouch of ogham staves nestled itself among the ornamentation.

Ogham is the script of ancient Ireland. Although the Celts did not have a written language per se, when the Roman Army, and later the Roman Church, invaded the British Isles, the Druids (the educated priestly caste of the Celts and military advisors to the chieftains) needed a form of encrypted messaging in order to communicate with each other. Praying to their Mighty Kindreds (ancestors, nature spirits and Shining Ones) and meditating on the issue, they were able to develop a secret language indecipherable by the opposing forces. The result was a set of cryptographic keys in the form of the ogham alphabet (a series of twenty-five characters they carved onto stones or pieces of wood).

Everything in Celtic spirituality related to trees, as it was believed trees were the keepers of memories, truth, and trust. Therefore, each letter of the ogham alphabet had a corresponding tree that was native to Ireland.

During rituals, one member of the *aicme* (tribe or family) would be designated as the official seer. The seer would pull three staves from the pile—one for each of the Kindreds—and interpret the message. The Comatis of California continue this practice in the Year of Their Lord 2002, although they have transliterated the Irish trees for those native to Rivervine.

A typical Comati ritual has guests entering from the east and walking in a clockwise direction called *jeesle*, which is the Gaelic word for *sunwise*. But on Sauin (the holiday marking the Celtic New Year), they approach from the west and walk *widdershins*, which means *against the direction of the sun*. This is done as a means of sweeping out negative spirits so that they do not follow aicme members into the new year.

Such was the case tonight as guests lined up in the west before entering the Oppidum. While they waited for Xavia and Brigid to finish setting up their smudging and sprinkling tools, Sage offered a bottle of beer to the *outdwellers*.

Whenever a magician in the physical realm opens a portal to the occult realm, any entity can cross through. Humans can burn all the sage they want, sprinkle salt, and declare their intentions, but clever tricksters always try to sneak past. They can even disguise themselves as the specific entities called by name, often emulating the character traits and repeating common words or phrases spoken by the impersonated entity. The imposters range from harmlessly mischievous sprites to completely malicious gods of turmoil. Oftentimes, though, these ethereal misanthropes can be bribed with libations and personalized poems. Sage made such an attempt tonight.

As he spilled the beer onto the ground, the red-headed bean pole uttered, "Mischief and mayhem, you're clever, we know. We offer this ale in hopes that you'll go. Leave us to our rite, you smart little sprites. Clear away from our circle tonight. Awen."

The crowd echoed in unison, "Awen."

Awen is a word Xavia and Sage use often. They claim it is a Welsh greeting for *inspiration* and use it in a similar fashion as the Hebrew *shalom* or Hawaiian *aloha*—as either a salutation or bid farewell. Its symbol is drawn as three dots topping three rays fanning downward. The dots symbolize the spiritual triune of the Mighty Kindreds while the rays represent the physical aspects of land, river, and sky. The image is contained in a series of three circles: The inner round represents reason; the middle one stands for eloquence, and the outer circle is for persuasion. As a whole, the symbol denotes the virtues and elements valued by modern Druids. Today's Comatis have adopted it.

It is this symbol that graces a clay disk in the center of their altar. That stone is present at every gathering, and the word is spoken at the end of each segment of their rituals.

Saying the word at the conclusion of the petition to the outdwellers is the first of three steps the Divinorums take to ensure the purity of their rites.

The second step is the smudge of guests.

Tonight's process was no different than usual. Comatis lined up with their musical instruments in one hand and their chalices in the other. When people approached the ritual area, they set down their objects and stood still at the entrance with their arms outstretched while Xavia waved the smoke of a sage wand around the person's body.

The Comatis are not the first to burn *Salvia officinalis* in ritual. The custom has been practiced by many cultures throughout history. Although it smells similar to the *cannabis* the Divinorums smoke when creating music, *salvia* does not have the hypnotic effects that cannabis does. However, its smoke does affect the collective subconscious. Because so many people throughout the years—millennia even—have believed it cleanses unwanted energies, it has become a means of inoculation against unwanted spiritual intrusion.

Because of this generational reinforcement of belief, sage smoke actually does bolster one's psychic immunity, and acts in a similar fashion to the sprinkling of saltwater, which was the final step in the process of purifying the ritual area tonight.

With the person's arms still outstretched, each Comati then turned to Xavia's daughter, Brigid, who dipped the sprig of rosemary into the bowl of saltwater and tapped it over the three power nodes of each person's body—head, heart, and solar plexus. Rosemary has a long history of calming the mind and tempering chaos. And nothing is more primordial than saltwater.

Their souls were now cleansed and ready to enter the ritual area.

The first thing they saw as they stepped to their right was a stand holding a steel pen, ink well, and the Book of the Dead. As they walked in, participants were invited to write the names of loved ones who either died that year or dwelled deep within their hearts.

Unlike some covens or practitioners of witchcraft, Comatis do not make a full circle in ritual. It is more like a horseshoe shape, allowing everyone to face the northern quadrant where the altar is set. No one other than the priests, acolytes, seer, and herald stands behind the dais.

Once everyone was settled, Xavia took her place in the far north of the Oppidum and lead the group in a meditation. I was not paying attention tonight, as I was still writing at that point, so I am unable to describe the meditation, but I did notice the air grow silent and calm.

With everyone's spirit soothed and mind focused on ritual, it was time for the herald (a member of the aicme appointed to call the names of the dead) to step forward.

For this year's ceremony, it was Doctor Frank.

That was when I set down my journal and pen, and shifted my focus to the here and now.

My mind flashed back to Halloween when the youths held their ritual to honor Sam Hain. Thomas, Tanya, and Erin survived that night because they were sincere. Naïve maybe, but sincere, nonetheless. Their friends who died in the fire—Darren Miller and Matthew Stone—lacked sincerity. Besides, they were mediocre. Honestly, those pathetic wastes of carbon had no redeeming value. I doubted their spirits were here tonight among the many ghosts waiting to hear their names called.

I was not proven wrong.

Neither the name Darren Miller nor Matthew Stone was called. No one missed them. And I did not sense their presence inside the circle. My guess is they are still haunting the house that burned, paralyzed in fear and unable to either reincarnate or enter heaven or hell.

Shaking off the memories, my mind wandered back to the evening's ritual. My gaze drifted over toward Anton and Brigid. She seemed to be the only person who could see him as others kept asking to whom she was speaking.

Xavia called out to me telekinetically.

"It is time to let them go," she uttered.

"It is not wise," I replied.

"Love never is."

Right as I was losing patience for this evening, Doctor Frank finished reading the names. I begged Xavia, "Can we please get this ritual over with?"

She chuckled, somehow amused at my tetchiness, and called upon Doctor Tony to serve as seer and read the ogham. He reached into the pouch and pulled out the first stave. "From the ancestors, we have Straif," he announced, then reached for a second. "From the nature spirits, Edadh." As he pulled the third and final piece, he said, "The Shining Ones offered Ur."

Tony then took a moment to analyze the reading while the rest of the group remained silent.

"Straif represents the chokecherry, a small tree that grows through underground suckers," he said. "Its deciduous oval leaves are about the length of a human finger. They turn red, orange, and gold in the autumn, and the stems burst in clusters of white and yellow flowers in late spring. In summer, they give birth to small fruit. Mature berries may be edible, but unripe fruit can be poisonous to humans.

"If Straif appears in a reading, it is a sign that magic is being routed through a network of unseen forces. In this case, the unseen force is the ancestors. If you still your soul, you can absorb their magic and use it to blossom and bear fruit. But be patient and cautious with your goals and desires. If you try to leave the tree before you are ripe, your dreams could be poisoned."

People nodded. Tony continued.

"Edadh is the symbol for action, and is represented by the cottonwood, a tree known for its rustling leaves and downy blanket covering its seeds. Cottonwoods tremble in the wind, a sign of action, reminding us that vital lifeforce energy courses through us, affecting the way we live. Find your natural rhythm and you will be able to balance, moving forward with determination instead of quivering in fear. In tonight's reading, the nature spirits are telling us to move ahead with positivity and determination."

He mulled over the last stave for a moment before speaking. When he was ready, he said, "The Shining Ones have chosen Ur, which corresponds to the heath plant, a dense mat of evergreen needlelike leaves along short stems with beautiful pinkish purple flower clusters exploding at the end like starbursts with their spiky stamens. The gods are telling us to focus on our direction in life. If we are on the correct path, they will carry us across the threshold of whatever is challenging us. But if we are on the wrong path, the heath could be covering a pitfall or trap. We need to return to our central beliefs and not get distracted. Distractions are pitfalls."

Everyone oohed and aahed. Afterward, Xavia looked at me and telepathically announced, "You're on. Are you ready?"

"I am."

~ Oir ~

Despite Doctor Tony's reading, the honorary ogham of Sauin is always Oir, the zinfandel grape. Tonight celebrates the last harvest from the vineyard. Tomorrow the Divinorums and their crew will begin the process of crushing the grapes and preparing them for fermentation.

When we look to Oir for spiritual guidance, we notice how grapevines climb onto trees or fences for support. Their roots run deep and their tendrils reach for the light, following their passion. As they climb, their broad leaves spread out, creating a wide canopy to shelter the precious grape berries. Once ripe, the fruit is made into a most magical concoction that can be shared with the whole community. From this vision, we learn that we too can absorb the magic from our roots and reach for our dreams, accepting support when necessary. Once we mature, it is our responsibility to share our good fortune with others.

Every Sauin, after the reading of the Names of the Dead and drawing of the ogham, the Comatis have a Blessing of the Grapes ritual and invite me to participate.

Brigid and Sage grabbed their guitars. Lily joined them with my violin. The three of them played a lovely tune, softly enough so Xavia could speak over them.

It is rather awkward for me. Since I know I am going to be summoned, I feel silly waiting to materialize, but I do not want to disrupt Xavia's train of thought, so I wait until she calls for me.

"Oh Lady of the Vineyard!" she finally beckoned. "Xin Vondella! Zeinferdel! Zinfandel!"

I always hated the name, Zeinferdel. I wish she would not call me that. It reminds me of that horrible Bavarian man. But I do not protest because I sense it helps her absorb her thoughts to run through the full evolution of my name. Frame of mind is crucial for magicians.

As she was rattling off the list of my various monikers, two Comati members pulled the tub of grapes out from under the altar, scooting them a few feet in front, and then returned to their places in the circle.

"We call upon you this Sauin night to thank you for this bountiful harvest," Xavia continued. "We ask you to bless these grapes and ensure this year's vintage is flavorful. Please join us in our rite."

That was my cue.

I like to create a dramatic effect whenever I manifest in front of a crowd. So I started off as a swirl of smoke from the bonfire and moved my way to the tub of grapes. At first, I covered the bounty with mist, but as the haze cleared, I slowly rose from the bottom of the giant pile, pushing up the clusters as I stood, giving myself a crown of fruit. I stepped out of the tub wearing a green velvet gown.

Everyone oohed and aahed.

I turned toward the altar and grabbed the bottle of wine, pouring it into the earthen pitcher. I lifted up the vessel and shouted, "The harvest swells. Intention dwells. A tale of magic is yours to tell. As I pour for you, appeal to me. Drink this wine and it shall be."

When I finished my blessing, Xavia picked up the plate of apple bread, and followed me around the circle. I poured a small amount of wine into each person's chalice and listened to their wishes. Xavia gave out pieces of cake. This ritual is much like children making a Christmas wish to Santa Claus. The difference is the adult Comatis know they must set their own goals and follow a plan to manifest them. I can only serve as a benevolent advocate.

After the last person was fed, Xavia and I moved back to the front of the circle and bowed to each other. She took the pitcher from me and I found my place behind the altar.

The priestess closed the ritual by leading everyone in a meditation, bringing their attention back to the mundane realm.

At the end, she announced, "This rite has ended. Let us go in peace."

"Awen!" the Comatis cheered, and then walked out of the circle in a clockwise direction.

After every ritual, the Comatis hold a feast where each family brings a dish to share. At Sauin, they do things a little differently for the Feast of the Ancestors. They set out one plate for the beloved decedents and place a bite-size serving of each dish upon it. At the end of the feast, the plate is scraped into the fire pit and the meal is burned to ash, which is then absorbed by the earth and fed to the ancestors.

Doina and I stayed up talking and drinking wine all night—a tradition we do every Sauin. Unfortunately, she is never strong enough to continue our conversation once the morning sun peers over the horizon. This year, her absence felt especially jarring when she disappeared and there was no Anton to keep me company. In the distance, I could hear his cobza playing a faint duet with a guitar, and his voice harmonizing with Brigid's. I was tempted to interrupt them and make it a trio, but decided to give them their privacy instead.

FIVE OF WANDS

4 December in the Year of Their Lord 2002

Anton has barely spoken to me all month. He does not approve of my taking the "bad seeds," as he calls them, under my tutelage.

"Are you even confident they will summon you tonight?" he argued this morning as we sat in the chilly fog under our favorite orange tree, waiting for the sun to rise so we could finally end our night of bickering. "Last month seemed pretty unsettling. I cannot believe you are even giving them the benefit of the doubt."

"They are young," I retorted. "They are going to make mistakes. All humans do—throughout their lifetimes. Besides, the youths had been misled by a couple of boys who truly were hooligans; the spirits of both those two delinquents are now flowing in perpetual loops of torture."

"What if we rid the earth of humanity altogether?" Anton retorted. "No animal, plant, or grain of sand would miss the *Homo sapiens* species."

"*We?*," I questioned. "Were you planning on helping me with the labor or were you, as usual, too timorous to get your own hands dirty? And what of your precious Brigid? Would you want to annihilate her too?"

Anton rolled his eyes and turned his gaze away from me, returning to his cobza. He was plucking out a new tune—something in the key of E-flat minor.

"Besides, how could we eradicate the top of the food chain?" I asked rhetorically. "And would you honestly want to purge the world of a beast that had enough heart to plant this *Citrus sinensis* under which we are sitting?"

The particular specimen of fruited wood was planted more than twenty years ago by a small boy whose mother—one of the Divinorums' migrant farmworkers from Mexico—had taken him to a market where they bought a bag of oranges. The child begged his mother to plant the seeds outside their housing quarters, and with permission from Xavia and Sage, the boy's wish was granted. This lone tree was the only one of the seeds to survive past the sapling stage.

Although the youngster is now grown and has a life and career outside Comati territory, his legacy here at Fermata Cellars will always be as the architect of ghostly musical space, for it is under this tree that Anton has found his favorite place to posthumously play his instrument, especially during the months when most of the workers are in their home countries and we can play at night without upsetting the hired help.

My violin usually stays with Lily Rhoads, the young woman who lives next door and runs the herb farm. However, I frequently borrow it back when I have no other means of solace than my beloved four-stringed companion.

Anton does not yet have a guardian for his cobza, but he is careful to return it to the cave when he is finished with his music therapy.

"So what is your lesson plan tonight, Professor Xin?" Anton mocked. "Assuming they actually do go to school."

It was an honest question and one I should have been able to readily answer. After all, I had all month to prepare, and even though the American holiday season was upon us, with customers flooding the tasting room looking for the perfect wine to pair with their Thanksgiving or Christmas meals, I still could have carved out an hour or so every night to develop a curriculum.

But the truth is, I have been so afraid of the youths *not* summoning me that I tried to push it out of my mind. If I had invested time, energy, and hope in creating a program of study, the level of disappointment I would feel if they ignored me would be unbearable.

The smell of coffee came through the windows of the farmworkers' quarters. The few laborers who stayed year-round had awakened.

Anton and I made our way back to the cave where he and his cobza rested for the day. I went off to meditate and prepare, just in case my students convened their class afterall.

~ Beith ~

Visitors approaching Rivervine from the southwest must pass through a dense, low shrub thicket before they reach the center of town. The first tree to greet them when they enter this chaparral woodland is the mountain mahogany. Since it is also the first tree of the forest to bloom in late winter, Xavia assigned the mountain mahogany to the character Beith when she created the Rivervine ogham.

Beith is the first letter in the ogham alphabet. The character is designed with a single limb on the right of the trunk. Originally assigned to the birch tree of Ireland, Beith represents new beginnings. Birch trees are not native to Rivervine, but the mountain mahogany has birchlike leaves; therefore it was the most obvious choice for this purpose.

The most intriguing quality of the mountain mahogany is the fruit it bears. It has a silvery, feathery tail that swirls like a galaxy up in the heavens. On a new moon night when the sky is completely dark, the display is quite awe-inspiring.

During my meditations this morning, I walked down to the chapparal woodland until I found the first mountain mahogany tree in the thicket. The area was wet and muddy from recent rains, and being early morning still, the chilly fog continued to blanket the ground. I cleared some space and sat under the tree, drawing a Beith symbol in the sludge in front of me. Although the mist quickly covered my design, just knowing it was there provided enough stimulation to arouse my consciousness.

Slowly I breathed, inhaling the scent of the damp wood surrounding me, listening to the stillness of the mahogany grove, and focusing my inner eye on the drawing of Beith.

The vision morphed into the image of a stick from the mahogany tree—about as long as my forearm, with one branchlet pointing to the right.

I watched it from a dissociative perspective, as if I were not in my own body but rather floating a few inches above the stick as it floated in the Vitus River, heading toward Dr. Castillo's estate, which is now the home of Erin Tuft and her parents.

In my vision, I saw Tanya pick up the stick and carry it over to the ritual area where the other two youths were doing yardwork—pulling weeds, dividing perennials, and planting winter-hardy herbs.

As she arrived back to the work area, Thomas called out to her, asking for help with something. So she set the stick on the altar and went over to assist him in hanging up some sort of canopy that covered four tall chairs—they looked like the barstools from a saloon. There was one placed at each of the four cardinal points and accompanied by a high side table topped with an oil lamp and an empty cup. Three of the tables—north, south, and west—had a journal and a pen.

In the center of the circle stood the familiar altar adorned with pine swags, oranges, and walnuts. The scent of hot chocolate steamed from the libation vessel. Sitting on the offering plate was an interesting white chocolate and peppermint confection.

Erin approached the altar, placing on it an abalone shell, some incense cones, and a box of matches. Her hair was braided in what I suspect was intended to resemble a snake coil, but she was not quite adept enough to imitate whatever image had inspired the look—her hair was actually too short to braid into such an elaborate design. Despite the giant mess of knots and stray hair wound around the crown of her head, I smiled at her attempt. I was honored that she would think so much of this night, even if her ambition exceeded her skill.

Tanya ran up next to Erin. Once she stopped, I could see that she too had been attempting to braid hair, although hers was a more modest, simple design framing her face, the back of her hair flowing freely. Albeit still messy, she had far fewer knots.

All three youths were wearing contemporary mundane clothing—denim trousers and long-sleeved tunics made from a cotton-like material that looked as soft as sheep's fleece.

In Tanya's left hand was a wand of sage. The right carried a bowl of water with a rosemary sprig. She set the bowl down on the north side of the path leading from Erin's house to the ritual area. On the south side, she placed the sage wand and one of those mechanical fire starters for when it was time to light it.

Erin put the seashell on the altar with the incense cones atop it.

Once they finished with the ritual setup, they walked over to the east quadrant and stood there a moment, admiring their handiwork.

"This looks awesome!" Thomas shouted, pulling Tanya close to him and planting a long, wet kiss on her lips.

"Fuck yeah!" Erin added. "She's gonna love this … I hope."

Of course, darling, I said to myself, amazed that they would go to this level of detail.

They left the ritual area and headed back toward Erin's house. I ended my meditation and returned to the cave to rest before the ritual started, so happy to know that my acolytes chose to continue their lessons.

~ Ace of Pentacles ~

When the sun lowered on the horizon, I made my way back to the ritual area, remaining invisible, waiting for them to formally summon me before materializing.

As I watched them saunter toward the ritual site, I could see they were now dressed appropriately for a festive occasion, thanks to what appeared to be newly acquired velvet, hooded cloaks. Thomas wore a dark hunter green robe. Tanya's was royal blue with silver lining. Erin had maroon. All three were secured by pewter clips bearing the design of a viper—jaw opened, fangs bared—swallowing a cluster of grapes.

Thomas approached the chair in the east quadrant and set upon it a rather bulky package wrapped in decorative paper and tied with a crimson velvet bow.

He then returned to the opening of the ritual area where Tanya and Erin were already standing, one on the north side of the path and the other on the south.

They took turns waving themselves with the sage wand and sprinkling each other with the water-dipped rosemary sprig.

Just like last month, Tanya took her place in the north, Thomas the west and Erin the south, saving the east, I assume, for me. They did not sit in the chairs, though. Instead, they remained standing.

Once in position, they lifted their arms and chanted in unison, "Vondella the Wise, honored guest of our feast. Please join our circle. Take your place in the east."

I appeared, wearing my signature black and crimson gown, and headed over to my assigned chair.

Picking up the package, I unwrapped the gift. Thomas admitted, "I can sew. I made one for each of us."

The robe was beautiful—black velvet with gold lining. It too had a clip with the snake-and-grape design.

Tears leaked out of my eyes and streamed down my cheeks. I tried so hard to repress the sentimentality. These three young people respected me enough to present such a meaningful gift and go to such lengths to prepare a ritual.

I truly was a goddess in their eyes.

You are not a Shining One, I reminded myself. *You are just a ghost—Xin Hsüan's whore daughter. Do not let your ego grow too big.*

Shaking off my stupor, I noticed my students were ready to start the evening's gathering—part ritual, part lesson, part social function. They looked at me with hopeful expectation.

"We should ground our energy and invite other spirit guides to join us," I advised sluggishly, still coming to terms with the youths' level of contemplation.

I started by having us hold hands.

"Close your eyes and imagine yourself as a grapevine," I muttered. "Your roots grow deep into the earth, covering this circle and connecting with the ancestors. Your leaves absorb the spirits of land, river, and sky. The Shining Ones fill your fruit with wisdom, strength, and prosperity."

I gave them a few moments to lose themselves in the vision before continuing.

"Once your spirit is full of what you need, prune the dead wood, and pluck the weeds of inappropriate energy. Rid yourself of any energy that does not benefit you."

Another moment of stillness.

"With your soul full of benefaction and cleansed of detriment, return your attention to our ritual tonight. Become the wine of the Comatis and generously pour honor and integrity into your every thought, word, and action."

More silence.

"Now, let us raise our hands toward the sky."

Everyone's arms stretched wide above, our hands still clasped together, eyes still closed.

"Repeat after me: 'Heated in passion. Grounded in justice. Cooled in logic.'"

The four of us shouted the words over and over, each refrain growing faster and louder. I lost count of the repetitions, but once I was able to visualize our spell swirling before us in a cone of energy, I bellowed as loudly as possible, "As we will it, so shall it be!"

The three youths echoed, "As we will it, so shall it be!"

We unclasped our hands, opened our eyes and let out a big sigh, taking a moment to allow the energy to dissipate.

Reveling in the knowledge that we had just raised energy as a coven, we smiled at each other and released a few more deep breaths.

We were all numb with magic. It took a while to regain our grounding in the mundane realm.

Once they were able to compose themselves, Thomas grabbed the carafe of hot chocolate and Tanya took the plate off the altar. They stood in my direction but did not look me in the eyes. I reached for my cup, noticing Erin picked up hers as well.

"Spirits of the East," Thomas called out, focusing his gaze someplace above my head. "We offer you communion this night. Please join us in our workings. Accept our offerings, and fill us with your magic."

He poured a smidgen of the liquid on the ground while Tanya tossed a crumb of peppermint. He then poured some hot chocolate into my mug, and Tanya offered me a piece of candy from her plate.

The boy spoke to me, "Vondella, we welcome you to our rite and ask that you guide us with your wisdom."

"Thank you, Thomas and Tanya," I said, accepting their offering.

They then moved on to Erin and repeated the greeting.

Finally, the two lovers took communion from each other and returned to their places in circle, looking at me to guide them in the next steps

Accepting the honor, I let out a deep breath and admitted, "I am so proud of each of you."

Tears swelled in everyone's eyes. Their auras thinned and I realized none of them had ever received praise from an authority figure before now.

So that is what brought them to the occult. Everyone needs to be applauded. If parents will not do it, outdwellers will.

I motioned for us all to take our seats.

"I see you have all brought your journals," I said, gazing at the young man seated across from me. "Thomas, have your written anything this past month that you would like to share with the coven?"

"I don't know," he whined, looking down at his feet and fidgeting with his fingers.

I called his bluff.

"You do know. You just do not want to tell us."

"I guess …"

He paused for a moment.

Reading his aura, I was able to complete his thought.

"You want to escape," I said. "You want to create an environment where you are respected and valued. Your life at home and school are miserable because you have no power, no authority … no beauty."

Thomas bent over his knees. Covering his face with hands, he started to bawl. Tanya ran over and put her arms around him, holding him tightly, rubbing his back. Their embrace lasted long enough to neutralize the distress, but knowing the conversation was not concluded, I waited for him to regain his voice before asking, "Has your relationship with your stepfather improved since Halloween?"

Tanya returned to her place in circle. Thomas sniffed the tear-filled phlegm back into his sinus cavity and answered with his voice still shaking and angry.

"I'm trying to ignore the asshole."

Once he calmed down a bit more, he continued, "I have applied for a job at Fermata Cellars cleaning wine vats after school. I figured this would be a good way for me to become a full-fledged Comati. Plus, it gets me out of the house and away from that … jerk."

"Why do you hate that man so much?" I asked. "Are you jealous of his relationship with your mother? Do you feel loyal to your father? Does he mistreat you?"

"All of the above, I suppose," he answered, wiping more mucus on his sleeve. "My mom got tired of working the same number of hours as my dad, but he never helped with the cooking, cleaning, or taking care of me. He just plopped on the couch after work and put on the TV. So Mom kicked him out, started dating other men, settled on this asswipe."

Thomas paused for a moment before taking a deep breath and continuing his story.

"His name is Jack. I call him Jack Off. He's constantly making sexually explicit comments about other women, but if my mom so much as makes eye contact with another man, he launches into one of his rages. When I defend her, he calls me a fag."

He looked up at me and yelled, "I'm not gay! I just …"

The boy trailed off, collecting his nerve, mucus running down his nose as fast as the tears falling down his cheek.

"My mom is so beautiful—the most beautiful woman in the whole world, inside and out. He shouldn't be going to titty bars or gawking at women walking down the street. We can't even watch the fucking news without him commenting on how hot the women reporters are."

My heart softened. Continuing our conversation, I offered the following advice:

"My darling boy. My heart aches for you. I wish so much that I had better news, but the truth is that your mother and stepfather are on their own paths separate from yours. You must not get distracted by their actions or attached to a vision of Utopian existence. Focus on your own path—the one that has led you here. I will do my best to nurture your spiritual growth and guide you toward health, prosperity, and happiness. But be forewarned that it will not be easy. The universe is chaotic. Lean into the waves and find your own stream."

The young man nodded and smiled for a split second before losing all control of his emotions. At the onset of his fit of tears, Tanya once again rushed over to console him.

I gave them a few moments to allow his bawling to run its course. Once his tears quieted a bit, I figured he and I were done with his lesson. There was no need to embarrass him further, so I moved on to the next student.

Looking over at Tanya, who had returned to her place in the north, I asked, "How about you, young lady? What are you hoping to get out of this coven?"

"I meditated on it long and hard," she responded emphatically. "I want to be the mother goddess—nurturing, healing, and wise. I want to raise the next generation of Comatis. I want to guide them and shape the future."

"Well then," I said. "It is time I explained the facts of life."

Tanya interrupted with a disheartened tone. "I know the facts of life, Vondella. I am well aware that I'm not pretty enough for a man to want to have sex with me."

"That's not true, Tanya!" Thomas cried out. "I think you're the prettiest girl in the whole school!"

His voice trailed off. The two of them locked eyes for an awkward moment before I intervened and got our discussion back on track.

"You two have much to discuss. Do you want to wrap up our evening now or continue?"

Erin did not approve of that option.

"Wait a minute!" she shouted. "I haven't had a turn to talk. What about me? Don't I count? Or is this going to be the Thomas and Tanya Cult—with Erin as the eunuch or something?"

Thomas quickly dried his eyes and stood firm, returning to his seat in the west.

"No, Erin," he said. "I apologize. My emotions got the best of me. Please, go ahead. I would like to hear about your journal entry."

"Thank you, Thomas," she said peacefully, surprised at his diplomacy. The shock tied her tongue.

"I, I, I, um, well, I don't know, actually," was all she could spit out.

I fixed my gaze deep into Erin's eyes and spoke in a calm, consoling tone.

"My darling girl. Talk to us about your journal. What did you write this past month?"

Gradually finding her steel, she inhaled a deep breath and then uttered, "I … wrote … about … sex. I wrote about danger. I wrote about how I want to learn sex magic and summon demons."

She looked to me and then around the circle to Tanya and Thomas, checking our reactions. The other two youths kept silent and gazed at me, unsure of the most appropriate way to respond.

"I think about sex all the time," she continued. "It's like I can't stop. And I want danger. I want excitement. I don't want to be stuck here in Rivervine the rest of my life, living some boring-ass farmer lifestyle. I don't care about being close to the land or close to nature. I want to be close to the action!"

The young woman held her ground, her gaze firmly fixed on me, unapologetic of the words that had just left her mouth.

I answered with equal honesty.

"Human sexuality is a beautiful thing but one that has been exploited and objectified since the first business transaction," I informed them. "If shared between humans who love and respect each other, sex can raise powerful energy.

"But if any of the participants betray a true love's confidence, disaster surely will ensue. Likewise, if an aggressor seeks privileges beyond one's rightful entitlement, much harm can be done. Like any other trespass, the victim's revenge can be crueler than the original offense. Also, those who treat sex as a banal form of entertainment—even if it is consensual among adults— never will understand the act's true power."

Erin rolled her eyes and snickered, "So interpreted for a general audience, are you saying we only can have sex if it's with our *true love*? I don't know if I can do that. I like it too much. I don't care about true love. I just want to get off. I like dressing slutty. I like *being* slutty. I like bondage. I like being both a dominatrix and a submissive slave. It's all fun and games. It's not real."

But for me, it was real—and certainly not fun.

When I was alive, I was forced into prostitution, and I did not enjoy it at all. The only time sex was ever pleasurable for me was when Lugh—the love of my life—touched me. I could not understand why anyone would willingly subject herself to the whims of men who cared nothing for her health, safety, or emotional wellbeing.

Before I could retort with a knee-jerk reaction, I paused to think about what I knew of the history of sexual power play— domination and subjugation—which has long been a popular game among lovers. I had heard about the Marquis de Sade, a French nobleman who died shortly before I was born, and his writings about erotic violence.

I had felt the rise in auric energy when men would strike me. Some would beg me to strike them—raising an equal amount of auric energy.

Depravity is its own form of magic, and as long as it was consensual, there was no ethical violation.

But do I want to encourage such behavior among my disciples?

As usual when I'm faced with a dilemma, I calmed my mind, grounded my energy, and allowed my consciousness to flow toward the appropriate answer.

Erin grew impatient. "I'm not trying to shirk responsibility," she said, her intonation beginning to rise. "But I'm tired of living this plain ol' ordinary, day-to-day life, doing the same thing everyone else does, believing the same thing everyone else believes, and shying away from the same risks everyone else is afraid of. I want a life that's dark and scary!"

Thomas and Tanya remained quiet, both looking at me for how to respond.

I collected my thoughts and meditated on how best to handle the needs of these three individuals and their expectations of coven participation. Tanya yearned to be part of a functional family. Thomas wanted respect. Erin craved adrenaline paired with endorphins.

When I was ready, I broke my silence.

"Each of you are at an age when sex is at the forefront of your mind," I said. "This is normal and natural—nothing to be ashamed of."

"I sense a 'but' on the edge of your tongue," Erin noted.

"True," I chuckled before putting on an air of seriousness. "But you do need to understand that for every action, there is an equal and opposite reaction. There is more to sex than glamor and excitement."

Once again, Erin rolled her eyes. "I use birth control."

"I am sure you do, but what if it fails? Then what will you do?" I asked.

"Have an abortion, of course. It's legal."

"Legal, perhaps. But if you are going to practice the occult arts, you need to know not only where babies come from but where they go when they die—where we all go when we die."

Her voice escalated to a heated tenor. "But it's my body, my choice!"

I remained cool. "I am not debating that. I am advising you of the inherent risks involved with occult practice—and even sex in general. Anytime a man ejaculates inside a woman's vagina, there is a possibility that a new life may be created. A new life means a new soul."

"But if I have an abortion, the baby's soul just goes back to wherever it came from and reincarnates again, right?

I was not prepared to have this complex of a conversation tonight, but events forced the issue.

"Let me start from the beginning."

~ Ace of Cups ~

Dear reader: I do not mean to belittle anyone's grief, but I do hope to provide a sense of understanding about the process of birth, death, and reincarnation. The following narrative is how I explained it to the three youths. You too should know.

The human amalgam is a trinity comprised of 1) a physical shell including bones, flesh, and fluids; 2) a mind comprised of intelligence, memory, and personality; and 3) chi—the current of vital lifeforce energy.

An individual human's physical shell begins to form when the chi of a mother's ovum unites with the chi of a father's sperm to spark a new type of entity called a zygote.

If the chi current of that newly formed zygote is strong enough, it will move the mass along its path of development. However, most zygotes have chi with too weak a current to advance to the next stage of development, which is called an embryo. If a zygote's energy fades, the physical matter and its chi exit the womb.

If the current is strong enough to become an embryo—around the second week of the gestational period—it forms skin, lungs, muscles, and bones. Once an embryo reaches the fourth week of development, a brain begins to grow.

At that moment, a portal opens between the occult and spiritual realms, clearing the path for any uncarnate or discarnate soul to adopt that baby as its new physical shell. And as mentioned earlier, any occult entity—benevolent or malevolent—has the possibility of entering an open portal, including a mother's womb.

Some spirits are so eager to re-enter the physical realm that they take any fertilized egg they can find. Others are first-timers who have never been part of the physical realm before but jump at the chance to have the full human experience.

"How do you control what kind of entity enters your womb?" Tanya shrieked in horror. "Or can you?"

I nodded my head, calming her anxiety.

"Your womb is a channel of metabiological energy. You can control who enters it ritualistically—immediately before or during coitus—by claiming your body as sacred space and inviting a soul with certain characteristics to reincarnate inside you."

"Can you invite a particular person, like an ancestor or something?"

"Yes. In fact, it is actually common to reincarnate within our own bloodlines."

All three of my students looked at me curiously.

I explained how souls follow their kindred from the occult realm. When they start to miss being part of the family, the yearning to reunite with the clan grows fierce, so they imbue a descendant's womb.

If a soul seeking reincarnation senses the mitochondrial DNA of one of its descendants, it will most likely reach the portal ahead of other entities because its chi recognizes the path.

"Hmm," Thomas hummed. "We learned about mtDNA in biology class."

He and the girls affixed their collective gaze firmly on me, indicating their eagerness to learn more. So I told them.

"Mitochondrial DNA is found inside the mother's egg cell and houses several traits that are passed on to the babe, including parapsychological gifts —what people once called 'witchcraft' but now are known as telepathy, clairvoyance, psychokinesis, psychic healing, and extra-sensory perception."

All three of my students gawked at that remark, unsure of the meaning of all of those words. So I defined each of the terms.

Telepathy is a means of communication between minds.

Clairvoyance is the ability to envision events, objects, or people outside of the current time/space continuum. Clairaudience is the ability to hear such things.

Psychokinesis is the ability to move objects with one's mind.

Psychic healing is, as the name suggests, the ability to heal physical or mental ailments with the mind.

Extra-sensory perception is an umbrella term for any of the above gifts.

"Whoa!" Thomas exclaimed. "That is so cool! What about, like, out-of-body experiences?"

"That is another phenomenon in parapsychology that many occultists pursue, although it is not passed on through the mother's genes. OBEs and near-death experiences are events that happen, not traits or skills that one either is born with or learns."

"I've heard that women's psychic abilities increase when they're pregnant," Tanya said. "Is that true?"

"Sometimes, yes," I explained. "In general, women tend to have more psychic 'powers' than men do because those genes are contained in the ovum. Baby girls are born with all the eggs they are ever going to have, so those genes are present from the day of her birth. As she develops, especially during puberty, her hormonal levels increase, often feeding into that genetic structure. That is usually when her parapsychological abilities present themselves. They can kick in earlier if a young girl experiences a traumatic event."

Thomas started to interrupt, but the question he was about to ask was obvious, so I looked at him and said, "Yes, boys have psychic abilities too. They are just usually not as pronounced."

I then returned to our discussion on pregnancy.

"A woman's psychic energy radiates at its highest frequency during the time she is passing on her genes to the infant growing inside her. Hormone levels rise in order to fuel the spiritual energy of that exchange."

Tanya's eyes widened. Erin winced. I continued.

"In most cases, this is a joyous experience with the mother and child forming bonds that never shall be broken. But on occasion, either party may have second thoughts."

"What do you mean?" Tanya asked, worried.

"The embryonic sack serves as a holding tank until both mother and child feel secure in the transition. As the baby's brain grows larger, the fetus starts to recall lessons learned long ago that were stored deep in the annals of the mind—sometimes repressed through numerous lifetimes. If a sensation or memory experienced in a past life is not relevant to the upcoming life journey, the new physical shell filters out the thought and disregards it in the overall collection of items to be recalled. That is why it is so difficult to remember past lives.

"However, there are times when a previous life has had great influence over the current moment. Such is the case with lovers who are so deeply bonded that they are known as soul mates. Arch enemies are bound to an equally dynamic memory. Any experience that significantly influences a being can carry over from one life to the next. A physical shell can sort out minutia, but traumas, passions, and ardent emotions become calloused on the spirit and cannot be eschewed.

"The new individual is unsure how to amalgamate past memories with the divination of its future."

As our discussion ensued, I explained that during the next thirty-six weeks of gestational development, the child realizes there is no need to carry every memory collected or skill learned throughout its incarnations. Yet its soul must decide which filters to install—what attributes to define, limits to have, strengths to pursue, and memories to keep—all while leaving room for the accumulation of even more knowledge in the new lifetime.

This cavalcade of intellectual, emotional, and spiritual stimuli deluges the mind. Some fetuses give up in frustration, leaving the womb, their spirits once again returning to the occult realm.

Between sixteen and twenty weeks, most souls feel sure of their future outlooks. Quickening occurs, causing a jittery movement, signifying the baby's acceptance of the birth contract.

Even still, a soul has until its day of birth to renege on the deal.

I do not know why babies are born stillborn. The mourning—the loss of hope—I just … have no words … The poor, grieving parents. But we must understand that for whatever reason, our current state of scientific knowledge does not have an explanation for why a soul did not take its first breath.

"So like, I get it," Erin asserted. "If I engage in coitus, then x, y, and z happens, but I'm not a psychopath. I don't intentionally go out and fuck guys just so I can get pregnant and kill babies. Nonetheless, I do *not* want to have kids!"

"You might not intentionally plant seeds in your garden for the explicit purpose of pulling weeds," I retorted with an equal amount of ferocity, "but you *have* demonstrated an obvious lack of reverence toward the sanctity of pleasure. Sex is not cheap entertainment. It is not a means of controlling other people. And it is never to be performed—not even for magical purposes, or as I should say, *especially* not for magical purposes—without acknowledging that another human life *could be* created."

"So hold on a sec," she interjected. "Are you saying that abortion and birth control are forbidden in Comati culture? Because if that's the case, then I'm out right now. I don't mean to sound heartless, but I'm kinda slutty and I like being that way.

If y'all are a bunch of prudes, then there's no point in me staying here."

"Pleasure itself hurts no one," I responded, staying calm yet matching the youth's emphaticalness. "The harm comes from infidelity, disease, and oppression. Sex is the only act that has the potential to connect the body, mind, and spirit of two people—and it does so on a deeper level than any other human activity. It is also the only form of magic that can create life. The more lightly you treat the power of pleasure, the more conscientious you need to be toward those who might get hurt from your actions. Knowing someone could possibly fall in love after intimate relations is a misdeed if that emotional commitment is not returned, as is consciously spreading disease. And conceiving a baby without accepting responsibility for its life is an even greater misdeed."

"But abortion is legal. Unless you're going to tell me there's some sort of karmic counterblow or something, what do I care?"

"Because sometimes birth control fails. And in the case of rape, incest, or unplanned desire, one of your ovum could become fertilized without your control. As the host of this potential new life, you do have a right to evict the tenant, and if you do so before a soul enters the new lifeform, then no harm is done. But once the baby's brain starts to develop—at about the fourth week of gestation—the squatter becomes more difficult to expel."

"That sounds so coldhearted," Tanya chimed in. "Tenant, host, squatter, expel—those are horrible words to describe motherhood."

"Yeah, well, they're all accurate," Erin snickered.

I ignored their outbursts and continued, explaining that few discarnates know the proper etiquette. Protocol dictates a soul *should* ask permission from a woman before entering her womb. But most are so eager they neglect to show the requisite courtesy before taking up residency.

Honestly, they usually do not know any better. And to be fair, few women require tenants to apply. Even fewer men believe they should share the responsibility of attracting the right candidates. Most humans think the concept of deciding prenatal incarnation is silly—maybe even sacrilegious. Both sexes just would rather copulate and enjoy the heat of the moment. Consequences be damned.

But those damning consequences strike viciously once the womb becomes occupied. A mother may not be financially or emotionally prepared to carry a child. The father may have turned tail and run. Either the baby or the mother may develop health complications. The tribe may not have enough resources to support another member.

"For whatever reason, the host has every right to terminate the pregnancy," I affirmed, but cautioned in my next breath. "However, it is never an easy choice to make. There are many physical and psychological effects a woman endures when she chooses to abort her offspring. As sad as this situation is, hope returns when the babe receives another opportunity to be reincarnated into a family that can provide the love, shelter, nourishment, and education it deserves—perhaps even with the same parents, at a more appropriate time."

Thomas looked at Tanya longingly, but his ladylove's watery eyes were affixed firmly on me, begging to learn more. Both youths were imagining the same thing: themselves as parents.

Erin, on the other hand, was disgusted at the thought of being pregnant. That much was obvious by her comments and questions this evening. The young woman nearly retched whenever she thought of raising a family.

As unpleasant as the topic was, our conversation about abortion had not concluded. There were some important factors they needed to know.

"The unborn will be given another chance to incarnate, but the wounds incurred by the host have no remedy," I said. "Physically, abortion permanently scars the womb, possibly compromising future pregnancies. Emotionally, the woman may be left with a sense of speculation or guilt, spending the rest of her life wondering what might have been had she chosen to endure the pregnancy, although some women have no remorse at all."

I went on to explain that every culture throughout history has had some method of terminating pregnancy.

"Usually, if abortifacients are used, they are given to women shortly after conception. It has only been in modern times that surgeons have been asked to enter a woman's womb, kill the formed baby in-utero, and extract the dead material. It is a most barbaric procedure."

Thomas and Tanya both grimaced. Erin shrugged her shoulders.

"The most important consideration from a Comati viewpoint is that we aspire to be in tune with our bodies," I told the youths.

In the old days, if women's menstrual cycles were late or if they started to suffer symptoms of pregnancy, women drank an abortifacient tea made from any of the poisonous plants in the area. The infusion was mild—most women survived, but a few died. Today there are factory-made medications they can take with a much lower risk of maternal death.

The modern surgery, though, is what gives me pause. It permanently scars women's bodies and causes their hormones to follow the same post-partum experience as if they had live births.

The longer a woman waits to have the procedure done, the more the baby develops, becoming more and more human-like—and the stronger the bond grows between mother and the little one inside her. The further the pregnancy advances, the deeper the regret can be.

"What about men?" Erin asked antagonistically. "Do they ever regret dropping their seed and then abandoning their babymamas? They don't risk this 'bond' with the child. If they don't have to accept responsibility for their share of the lives they create, why should women?"

"Wait a minute!" Thomas demanded. "Do babydaddies get a say in this whole thing? It really isn't fair if we're supposed to be responsible for providing for the baby if the mom chooses to keep it, but if we want to keep it and the mom aborts it, we have no rights."

I acknowledged his concern. Nonetheless, he would never have to sacrifice his body or forty weeks of his life—his career or his wellbeing— to host another human life. In other words, when it comes to sex, the risks for men are not the same as they are for women. Therefore, the rights of men are not equal to those of women.

To seem unbiased, though, I kept my response neutral toward the two genders.

"Any time a man and a woman have sex, they should assume it will lead to a child they both have to provide for and raise," I said, attempting to sound diplomatic. "Perhaps if every act of copulation assumed life would be created, far fewer children would be living in squalor or other such misery."

The flames in the oil lamps swelled and the wicks crackled raucously as my anger increased.

I continued—my voice raised and my aura growing hotter, "As far as his 'rights,' no one has a right to another person's labor. The man does not have to sacrifice his body during the gestational period."

Thomas fired back indignantly, "Does the woman have the right to the man's paycheck?"

"Whenever you live in someone else's home, you are subject to their rules. If you spill your sperm inside a woman's house, you are responsible if a life is created. The woman's body is her home. If you do not respect her rules, then you should not enter her house."

"But what if I don't know what those rules are?"

"She probably does not know either. But nonetheless, it is her home, not yours."

"But I don't have a 'home' like that!"

"And you do not suffer the same risks. So again, I advise you to be conscientious of where and when you plant your seed."

Erin interjected.

"But I don't want to have kids—ever!" she yelled. "I like sex. I like the feel of a man inside me, on top of me, behind me. Not only do I crave the whole orgasm thing, I, I, I enjoy the game, the excitement of it all. That is the whole reason I got involved in this stupid Sam Hain cult. The whole ritual aspect of sex is awesome—the theater, the showmanship, the creativity. I want to manifest magic in its highest form."

"Morally, I have no objections, my dear," I replied, trying to calm her down. "But you must realize that unless you are barren like I was, if seed enters your field, it could sprout, even if you take measures to prevent it. You then have to decide either to pull the weed or nurture the sapling. It is not an easy choice. And yes, sex magic is indeed awesome, but it is not immune to the laws of nature."

She sighed heavily and I resumed the lesson.

"The histrionic action that you so desire—with all the drama, smoke, and sorcery—is rooted in a very real, mundane origin," I said. "Because our pedestrian culture has vilified the raising of energy, any candle that is burned or chant that is uttered is seen as some sort of forbidden practice. We are not supposed to eat from the tree of knowledge because it allows us to see what is behind the veil. But if you were to take a peek, you would find nothing exciting—just a group of ancestors, nature spirits, and Shining Ones navigating the waves of chaos and answering petitions for help."

I continued the lesson, explaining that there is nothing wrong with raising energy in a flamboyant manner. If black lipstick and clothing make you feel magical, then wear them. Light the whole house with candles. Fill the air with incense and decorate every room with imagery that triggers your altered state of consciousness and leads you across the bridge to the occult realm.

"Enjoy physical pleasure," I said. "Just be mindful of the consequences."

As my students processed the enlightenment that had just been revealed, their chi flowed and their auras emitted heavy doses of clarified energy.

My soul fed on it. I digested the repast, closing my eyes and breathing deeply, absorbing their chi through my aura until the energy was grounded and I could regain my composure.

I realize they are adolescents on the verge of adulthood and their hormones are raging right now. Somehow I need to reach through to their psyches and train them to become soldiers.

Erin is full of sexual energy and needs anodyne outlets for it. Tanya wants to be a wife and mother so she can create a home life that is better than the painful environment in which she current lives. Thomas seems obsessed with besting his stepfather so he can regain his place in his mother's heart.

It was time to take another break.

~ Luis ~

When we reconvened, Erin was the first to speak up. "Did you have birth control back in your day?"

"Yes, but it was not pleasant."

All three of them listened closely to the tale of conception-prevention for the early American Comatis.

As I mentioned last month, I could not bear children, thanks to a Bavarian man severing my womb when he assaulted me as a young child. But for the average, healthy adult woman in my day, a few methods *were* available, although they were not as effective as the options existing for women today.

In the early years, men would make barriers for their genitals by using the intestines of the animals they hunted. Sometimes women coated their vaginas with a mix of wax and honey from the beehive along with any kind of plants or dirt to make a paste that would soak up the man's semen.

"That paste could *not* have been pleasurable," Erin interjected, grimacing with disgust.

"I would not know from personal experience as I never used it," I answered. "But many women did complain that it was gritty and made them feel unclean."

"Since it soaked up the semen, did it also prevent VD?" she added.

I did not understand the term, "VD" but as her words struck my ears, memories of my old chancre caused me to feel a burning sensation in my vagina and a rash growing on my skin. Before the recollection could reach my nerves, I shook it off and answered the question, assuming she was referring to the pox.

"Comatis did not know about such disease until Sooter's men arrived. The paste may have helped in my case, but the fire hit before we knew what was happening."

Erin perked up. "You mean *the* fire? The one that caused the Black Land?"

"Yes, on the sixteenth of August, in the Year of Their Lord 1848."

I could see the enlightenment glimmer in all three pairs of eyes as they realized the truth about my sickness.

"You didn't use the paste or the homemade condom because you didn't need to prevent pregnancy," Erin speculated. "So you got what? Syphilis?"

"It was awful," I admitted, hanging my head, too ashamed to look at any of their faces. "I was ugly and weak. I could no longer play violin. But the miners still wanted me because there were so many men and so few women. The night of the fire, I had one last rush of energy to defend myself. Of course, my assailant was drunk so he was not much of a match, but still, I was sick and barely able to stand on my feet. Yet somehow his blood found its way under my fingernails."

"Oh, dear God!" Tanya yelled. "Zinfandel, I am so sorry!"

There was a moment of awkward silence as the youths processed the sensitive information they had just received.

I too needed some quiet time—to recover from the unearthed memory. For as much as I had divulged my history with these three youths, I still struggled to talk about the night of the fire or the sickness that would have killed me if the fire had not.

"Maybe someday, in good time, I can tell you more, but for now, let us call it a night."

My acolytes nodded in understanding and I looked over at the young man. "Thomas, would you like to lead us in the closing of circle tonight?"

With eyes widened and chest raised, the young man readily accepted the honor, improvising well.

"Let us hold hands," he directed. "Close your eyes and bow your heads."

We followed his instructions.

"Thank you, Vondella and other benevolent spirits, for guiding our circle tonight. May we leave this sacred ground with wisdom in our roots, peace in our leaves, and prosperity in our fruit. Let us, as a coven, forever be a fruitful vine. Awen."

We unclasped hands.

As the youths cleaned up the ritual area, I asked Thomas how he knew to use the word "awen."

"Brigid taught it to me," he answered, collecting items off the altar. "She is a friend of ours from school. In fact, she's the whole reason the three of us got into the occult. We knew about the Comatis but didn't think they'd want us. We're not from here. We don't belong."

He stopped what he was doing and looked straight at me.

"That's the whole problem. Tanya, Erin, and I don't belong anywhere. Neither did Darren and Matt. They told us Brigid was full of shit and they knew about this Sam Hain cult from the internet. So we tried one of their rituals and well, you know how that turned out."

I reached my arms around him, embracing him tightly as he released all of his pent-up energy, my shoulder quickly drowning in tears.

"Oh, my darling boy," I heard the tree behind him murmur. Looking up, I noticed the mountain ash staring at me, unsure if any of the youths could hear the voice. They must not have because they continued cleaning up the ritual area as if nothing were out of the ordinary.

The second letter of the ogham script is Luis. The farmworkers from Mexico pronounce it "loo-ees," after all, that same word is the Spanish name for Louis. But in Irish, it is pronounced, "loush" and is a word meaning "flame" or "bright." The symbol is drawn with one vertical line and two horizontal lines on the right. When it appears in a divinatory reading, it is a sign of protection. This could mean either the seeker needs protecting, or someone needs the seeker to protect them.

In traditional Irish ogham, Luis is represented by the rowan tree, *Sorbus aucuparia*. In Rivervine, the closest cousin is the mountain ash, *Sorbus scopulina*. The two trees are quite similar. Both have feathery leaves and bright red berries with the trademark star shape on the bottom. The changing leaves make a spectacular show in the autumn, and the berries last all winter, providing food for deer, birds and other wildlife.

The color red and the five-pointed star have always been symbols of protection in many cultures throughout the world, but for Comatis, the mountain ash offers medicinal protection as well.

The bark has long been used to make tonics to fight infection. It is especially helpful soothing sore throats. The unripe berries boost immunity and aid digestion. The ripe fruit, on the other hand, is useful in fighting fatigue and achiness.

"I will watch over them," the tree whispered to me.

"Thank you, my friend," I answered. Before I left, I stopped a moment to conjure my violin and play a tune Lugh had taught me—something in the key of D minor. The words went something like, "Oh! rowan tree, oh! rowan tree, you are so dear to me. Entwined you are with many ties of home and infancy."

The tune may have sounded sad, but the tree appreciated the dedication. I sensed happiness emanating from the wood as if the boughs were trying to embrace me.

SEVEN OF SWORDS

5 December in the Year of Their Lord 2002

The sun set tonight—as is does every night, of course—but this evening's shadow had a familiar figure emerging from the twilight. A light snow flurried in the wind, and as the chill blew into the cave, Anton and I noticed the distinct scent of goat hide mixed with peppermint. Then came the chortle of a couple of jolly old elves.

"Krampusnacht!" we yelled in unison, with the same excitement we had when we were children.

We hurried out of the cave to greet our guests, Anton running out first.

But when I emerged, I was no longer at the cave and my brother was nowhere to be found. Instead, I was inside the ritual area at the home of the snake enthusiast. Erin, Thomas and Tanya were standing around the campfire, listening to tales of Christmas past, told by an old, robed Turk with a long, white beard. Next to him was a silent but animated goatboy decked out in furs.

~ Saille ~

"Krampus my friend!" I yelled to the horned figure before me.

"And Bishop Nicholas!" I called again, wrapping my arms around both characters.

Turning to the wild man, I said, "Thank you for visiting Rivervine on Krampusnacht."

The mischievous imp nodded and smiled as he hobbled around the circle, flicking his long tongue at each of the youths, trying to scare them. They laughed with a nervous mix of humor, awe, fear, and curiosity.

"You do not need to dramatize with these three," I advised.

He looked straight at me, stuck his tongue out as far as it would go, and shook his head with a sardonic expression on his face. He then sat in my chair in the east and crossed his legs, mockingly pretending to drink a cup of tea with his pinky lifted as if he were some kind of upper-class gentleman.

I raised a scornful eyebrow at him and returned my focus to the crowd. Nicholas had gone back to telling stories to the youths. It took a moment before one of them noticed me.

"Zinfandel!" Tanya yelled. "Saint Nicholas is visiting us!"

She was so full of wonder, it was childlike. Then she turned toward Krampus and pointed.

"But who is *he*?"

Her voice was loud enough to distract Erin and Thomas from Father Christmas' ramblings. With all three youths focused on Krampus, and no one paying attention to Nicholas, I stepped closer toward the campfire light and told them a winter folktale of my own.

> *On a silvery December night in the Year of Their Lord 343, two men met their demise—one, a lowly, young goat herder in the Alps of Austria; the other, a benevolent cleric from what is now the country of Turkey. Neither man had known the other before the time when their souls crossed the veil from the physical world into the occult realm.*
>
> *The bishop, dressed in a red hooded robe, chuckled when he set eyes on his new companion. "You look just as lost as me, my friend," he said to the goat herder.*

The young man was unable to speak, but wagged his head furiously, a look of terror shooting from his crusty eyes. As the priest moved closer, the peasant recoiled further, raising his arms across his face to hide from the stranger.

"My friend, I come in peace!" begged the priest. He was hoping to gain the poor man's trust, but the skittish soul continued to shiver in a huddle.

"You do not need to fear me, my friend!" Nicholas assured. "Please, let me see your face so we may talk man to man."

Slowly, the goatboy released his arms and stood up straight, allowing the bishop to get a good look at the full figure of the creature sharing the twain with him at that moment.

In all honesty, the peasant did indeed look like a demon. He had horn-like lesions growing out of his temples, an inflamed tongue that protruded out of his mouth, and a body covered in short, course hairs the color and smell of the ibex that roamed the Alps. All ten fingers curved like eagle talons, and his left foot twisted downward and inward.

Letting his guard down a bit, he took a slow and cautious step forward toward the old man. As he lifted himself up on the toes of his left foot, it appeared as if it were a hoof from one of his goats. His right foot, seeming much larger than the left, flopped when it landed.

Nicholas had heard of the satyrs of ancient myths who were half goat and half man, but standing before him at this very moment was a creature who could quite possibly be the source of such legends. Yet, somehow, he knew this was no accident of nature, but rather a beautiful child of God.

Soberly, the priest asked, "Do you have a name, my friend?"

The boy mumbled something that sounded like "My mom named me Klaus, but other children call me Krampus."

"I am Bishop Nicholas," the cleric replied. He took a moment to study the expressions on his new friend's face and then said, "I sense anger in your heart."

"I hate people!" Krampus yelled. "They are so cruel! They call me a devil."

"Are you a devil?" Nicholas asked, certain the answer was no.

"Maybe," Krampus sheepishly replied. "I look like a devil, so I must be a devil."

"If you were a devil, you would surely know it! A devil has no love in its heart."

"Then that is what I am. How can I have love in my heart when all I have known is cruelty? Not one person has ever shown me kindness."

Nicholas looked around and wondered out loud, "Saint Peter was supposed to meet us here. I wonder where he is. Where are the pearly gates? Perhaps we are lost!"

Krampus guffawed and rolled his eyes, skeptical that such a gatekeeper existed.

"Surely," he thought to himself, "There is no God, no Saint Peter, and no heaven. No human has ever been virtuous enough to deserve such an eternal reward. They are all cruel!"

Bishop Nicholas read Krampus' mind.

"Let us form a partnership, you and I," Nicholas proposed. "Let us ride the skies across the world on the anniversary of this night every year. If I find children who have shown mercy and compassion, I shall reward them. If you find children who have been cruel and malicious, you can punish them."

He reached out his right arm to shake the goatherder's hand, making a gentleman's agreement. Krampus lengthened his claw and the two men shook on the deal.

For one thousand, six hundred and fifty-nine years, the battle has been fought on the evening between the fifth and sixth of December—a night they call 'Krampusnacht.' Krampus punishes naughty children by swatting them with willow switches and filling their stockings with coal. Meanwhile Sinterklaas—also known as Santa Claus, Kris Kringle and Saint Nick—rewards nice boys and girls with sweet treats and toys.

"Wow!" Tanya's eyes grew wide. Her two human friends were equally awestruck.

"You tell a good shtory, Zhinfandel," Nicholas claimed.

"It is mostly true," I insisted, planting myself on Krampus' lap and kissing his forehead, making him blush through the fur on his cheeks.

The good bishop rummaged through his robe as if it had pockets.

"What on Earth are you looking for?" I asked.

"My whishel!"

"What whistle? You mean the one on the string around your neck? Since when do you have a whistle?"

"Ah, thank you. How do you think Krampush and I got here?"

"You trained the reindeer by whistle? That is new since we last met."

"I made it from the red willow growing in the Vitush River, the one with the two trunks."

How appropriate, I thought to myself.

In the middle of the Vitus River grows a tree. It stands fifty feet tall by fifty feet wide and has two trunks growing out of the heavy soil of the riverbed. If you listen closely, you can hear the wood hum. One trunk takes the part of the treble clef. The other, the drone of the bass clef. Together, they symbolize the consonance of the spirit world. That is why Xavia assigned this tree to the ogham character, Saille—the symbol for harmony.

This is the tree that Bishop Nicholas used to carve his magical whistle to summon his caribou that lead his sleigh across the night sky. Together, he and Krampus represent the harmony of reward and punishment.

When Nicholas blew his whistle this evening, the sound was such a high-pitched screech that all three youths convulsed their necks and shoulders. The cacophony warbled in rhythm to the clicking of the caribou's knees as they landed from the sky onto the ground behind the ritual area. The beasts seemed content to munch on the shrubs of Erin's backyard.

I conjured two more chairs so we could all sit and talk awhile. Nicholas found some peppermint candies in his robe. It must have had pockets after all.

~ Phagos ~

"So … you two are dead, right?" the curious Erin asked our guests. "You're ghosts—real ghosts? Are the reindeer ghosts too?"

Nicholas nodded, "Oh yesh."

"So then how does this whole thing work? Because you don't really give out presents to kids. That was our parents when we were little."

Pointing to the horned man, she added, "And I've never heard of Krampus before. But I gotta say, he looks pretty cool."

The goatboy grinned at the remark and raised his eyebrows up and down in a flirtatious manner.

The young woman ignored his overtures. "And the sleigh—how does an inanimate object become a ghost?"

"Ah!" Nicholas cried. "It is all an illuzhion. I better let Zhinfandel explain. My English is not too good."

Once again, all eyes glared in my direction, obligating me to discuss a very complex set of supernatural laws.

As I pondered what I was going to tell the youths, I scried into the campfire, hoping for an answer. A moment later, my inner eye saw an image of Phagos, Xavia's ogham character for the madrone tree. The symbol looks like a checkered flag. When it appears in a divination, it represents the concept of crossing over.

Madrone is one of many trees that sheds its bark back as it ages. The first layer has a rich orange-red covering that over time peels away, exposing the smooth, mature, greenish-silvery wood.

The flowers are tiny, white bells that ring only for the most astute prophets. If you hear the call of the madrone, you discard the outer bark of ignorance and metamorphose into a smooth, mature sage. This shedding of the old paradigm and awakening of the new is where the youths were tonight.

Choosing my words wisely, I explained there were two different principles at play here this evening. The appearance of our two human guests returning from their graves had a slightly different explanation than the soulless sleigh and peppermint candies.

For a *Homo sapiens*, the mind accumulates the necessary skills and learns the requisite lessons until the body's bones, organs, and fluids expire. The physical shell then decomposes, leaving the mind homeless and the chi needing a way to change form and direction.

At that point, one's religious views come into play. If one believes in an afterlife, such as heaven or hell, one's chi carries the mind to such a place and remains there for eternity, enjoying or suffering the fantasies developed when it was part of the physical realm. If one believes in reincarnation, the soul rests and meditates until it is ready to migrate to another corporeal shell.

But if one has a mission to accomplish before going to heaven or a reason not to emigrate, that soul lingers as a ghost.

Such is the case with Krampus, Nicholas, and me.

We do not actually work in the ways storytellers have written about. Nicholas does not sneak into children's homes and place their materialistic desires under elaborately decorated trees. But he can give parents epiphanies about their children needing help with something, and guide both juveniles and adults along paths that solve their problems.

Krampus is a little naughtier. He likes to create illusions that frighten those who exert their physical stature or economic privilege in ways that harass or oppress the vulnerable and less fortunate. He targets youngsters in particular—bullies and emerging autocrats—to ensure their spiteful tendencies do not mature.

"He also likes the ladies," I added.

Krampus grinned. Erin blushed. I continued, getting us back on track.

"A normal human lives until old age and then begins the process of disincarnation."

I explained that when we grow old and reach the end of our lifecycles, our chi current weakens and our minds often start to separate from the physical realm. The body and mind have been attached for so long and have forged such a close bond that both factions struggle to let go.

"Is that why old people get Alzheimer's?" Tanya interjected, looking dejected. "The last time I saw my great-grandpa in the old folks' home, he didn't even recognize me."

"Yes, my sweet girl," I said. "This is a slow and difficult transition for both the person and the family members. Survivors will have their patience tested as they watch their loved ones struggle to remember names, places, and regular routines."

Krampus laughed, pointing to Nicholas and making a noise that sounded like, "That is you, Old Man!"

"Oh, hush, or I will shwat you with a willow switch!" the cleric retorted.

Nicholas walked over to Tanya, reaching again into his robe and pulling out a porcelain doll with curly black hair.

"Is that a creepy, haunted, possessed doll?" Erin suspected.

Bishop Nicholas chuckled. "Oh, no. It is jusht a gift for a girl who shtood her ground and defended her beliefs."

Tanya clutched her present and sniveled, barely able to spit out a meek, "Thank you."

Turning back toward Erin, Bishop Nicholas reached into his robe again and pulled out a silver-plated hand mirror.

"I want you to shee yourself as the beautiful soul you have proven yourshelf to be," he said.

Erin gasped.

Thomas looked down at his feet, trying to make himself invisible.

"You think I will overlook you?" Bishop Nicholas accused.

"I don't deserve anything."

"My young man, you have demonshtrated a love for someone other than yourshelf. The way you guard Tanya and demand reshpect for your mother is the mark of a noble leader."

Thomas collapsed his face into his hands and sobbed, unable to see the gift Bishop Nicholas was holding.

Krampus giggled, grumbling something along the lines of, "It's from one of my goats."

Thomas slowly lifted his head to see Bishop Nicholas standing before him holding a drinking horn.

"Now seems like a good time to take a break," I announced.

The three youths were preoccupied with their gifts from Bishop Nicholas, and Krampus' pungent body odor was starting to get offensive. But we still had not yet covered the subject of illusion, which needed to be discussed before we could proceed with Vampire New Year next month.

My soldiers—all three of them—must be ready by then. I do not have time to worry about Anton's skepticism or any other distractions that may destabilize my faith. The reaction the youths were having to Krampus and Bishop Nicholas seemed to be favorable. I knew I had to continue the momentum. That, of course, meant prolonging tonight's lesson as late as possible.

I turned to Erin and asked, "Do you have any more of that peppermint candy from last night?"

"Yeah, it's back at the house."

"Do you mind going to get a few pieces? We should offer some sort of refreshment to our guests."

"Oh, sure. No problem."

"Can you bring some hot chocolate too? And some cups?"

"I'll be right back."

"Bring enough for all of six of us!" I hollered as she walked toward her home.

While she was gone, I apologized to our guests.

"I cannot believe I did not have milk and cookies waiting for you tonight."

"Zhinfandel, you have much on your mind these days. We understand."

Krampus nodded.

"Erin, Tanya, and Thomas made this fabulous confection from white chocolate and peppermint. Wait until you taste it. It is amazing."

Our two guests smiled.

"Thank you for being so kind and generous to them," I added.

"Thank you for teaching them the wayzh of the Comatizh."

~ Uinllean ~

The meeting reconvened once Erin returned with the chocolate. As we sat enjoying the treats—and more of Nicholas' far-fetched storytelling, Erin looked over at the giant sled parked on her property and the reindeer grazing on the honeysuckle.

How appropriate! I thought to myself. Honeysuckle, according to the Rivervine ogham, is associated with the character Uinllean. In a divinatory reading, Uinllean is a sign the seeker is about to learn some specialized hidden knowledge. Of course that was true tonight.

"That thing looks so freakin' real!" the young woman roared.

"*Real* is a state of mind," I said. "I believe the Asian monks explained it best."

Of all the hidden knowledge humans have procured through the ages, the Buddhist theory of illusion, in my opinion, is the most awesome.

I told them about the Buddha teaching us that our experiences are ever-changing composites of illusions made of five aggregates: matter, sensations, perceptions, mental formations, and consciousness. These five features rhythmically form what are called *psycho-physical configurations*.

"The sleigh, the doll, the mirror, the drinking horn—those are all illusions," I said.

"But it's real!" Tanya cried, holding up her precious gift. "I can hold it. You can weigh it if you want to. I'm afraid to drop it because I don't want it to break."

"Yes, darling," I responded. "One does not need all five composites in equal measure for an illusion to be created. Sometimes, when one sense is missing, another compensates for it. In the case of your doll, Bishop Nicholas telepathically perceived a mental formation of your heart's desire. He then created an illusion so real that our collective consciousness believed it."

"Is that like when a person goes blind and suddenly gets ESP?" Thomas asked.

"Exactly. Matter exists even if no one perceives it. And perception exists even if there is no matter—so long as the sender and receiver have the same mental formation and collective consciousness."

That is how magic works.

If I appear to you, dear reader, the materialization you see is not flesh and blood. It is an illusion I have created. I can take any form I want; it need not be human. I can be as vivid or as transparent as I choose. I can even move about without any physical expression at all.

"Can all ghosts do what you three do—with the sleigh and the doll and all?" Thomas asked.

Krampus shook his head wildly, mouthing something that sounded like, "No, no!"

I explained that most discarnates never learn this skill. Some loiter about the occult realm until they decide to reincarnate. Others are what I refer to as perpetual phantoms— the ones you hear about most often. They haunt particular areas and complete the same tasks habitually—the innkeeper who lights the fire every evening or the woman rocking a baby in her arms. These souls are so confused that all they can muster is to repeat the same movement. Most of their time is spent in a daze, completely unaware that time has moved forward.

But the mental energy of that confusion is so strong that it forms an illusion that those in the physical realm can see, hear— and sometimes even feel, smell, or taste.

Confusion is the worst aspect of disincarnation, even for me. I may be one of the most formidable minds in Rivervine, but even I have days when perplexity overtakes coherence. So many changes happen so quickly that I find it impossible to maintain an adequate level of comprehension. I laugh when I listen to Xavia complain about how she cannot understand the youth of today or when I hear the Mexican laborers struggle to learn the English language. They worry about such trivial hindrances, yet here I am grappling with upgrading vernacular between the centuries and understanding the inundation of new lingo used in workaday life. So forgive me, dear reader, if I write a phrase you do not understand. I may use obsolete jargon or attempt to explain a modern issue without fully knowing if what I wrote makes sense by contemporary standards.

Once I finished my monologue, Erin spoke up.

"Can we talk about consciousness for a minute?" she asked. I nodded for her to proceed. "Last month, we talked about how altering your state of consciousness was a tool for casting spells. Is that related to illusion? If so, are spells real or just illusions?"

"Do not be so quick to dismiss illusions as being unreal," I advised. "Everything in life is an illusion. Reaching an altered state of consciousness just allows the magician to focus on mental formations."

"Is it dangerous?" Tanya squeaked. "Ya know, to get high? That's how you reach an altered state of consciousness, right? With drugs?"

"There are many ways to alter one's mental acumen that do not involve hallucinatory substances," I answered. "There are several Comatis who swear that practicing yoga and eating certain foods improves their parapsychological abilities. They do not use mind-altering medicines at all."

"I love yoga!" Tanya cheered. "So I don't have to get high to cast a spell?"

"Of course not, darling. A substance that leads me to a revelation might take you on a fool's errand. If yoga is your pathway to enlightenment, then follow it."

"Oh, thank you!" she exclaimed, grateful to be relieved of any peer pressure.

The lone male disciple abruptly changed the subject.

"Hey Zinfandel," Thomas blurted out, "Can you leave Rivervine, or are you stuck here?"

"That was random!" Erin responded. "Where the hell did *that* come from?"

"Well, Krampus and Nicholas are ghosts, and they're able to move about," he noted. "But I thought ghosts were tethered to their place of death or something."

The question stunned me as I had not thought about it before. Krampus and Nicholas looked at each other inquisitively; neither of them knew the answer, nor had they ever wondered about it.

"I have never tried to leave—always stayed to protect my vines. It was a vow I made long ago, before the fire. I will have to test that theory someday."

"What about other ghosts?" Thomas followed up. "What's the deal with them? If Krampus and Nicholas can travel, why can't others leave the places where they died?"

As I ruminated on the subject, I explained the situation to the best of my abilities.

Most people assume that when they die, a docent from the occult realm escorts them across the twain to help them assimilate to their new state of nonbeing. This guide is usually the spirit of a previously deceased relative or close friend—someone the decedent recognizes and trusts but who has not yet reincarnated.

In reality, not all souls receive such an escort. In fact, there is no actual heaven or hell. There is no invisible old man up in the sky orchestrating a frenzied puppet show. There is no Saint Peter counting your every sin and cross-comparing it to every act of virtue to determine if you are worthy of entering a glorious kingdom or condemned to a shameful inferno.

"So there is no naughty-or-nice list?" Erin asked, glancing at Bishop Nicholas.

The cleric met her gaze and shook his head.

"You have been deceived," I said, and then proceeded to explain.

For some people, the deception is so vivid that when their physical shells lose their breath and heartbeats, their minds stay locked inside the fantasy. They frolic in their illusory kingdom or suffer the stench and heat of brimstone.

However, those who embraced the fantasy but did not believe strongly enough develop a condition known as *lament*.

Lament traps the mind in a particular place along the time/space continuum. It is often found in the ghosts of people who suffered traumatic deaths such as suicide, homicide, or sudden accidental death. These souls become disoriented, struggling to adjust.

Many of my ilk linger at the point of disincarnation— waiting in dire hope that a hero will guide them to some glorious destination or repay them for all the misery they endured throughout their lifetimes. Instead, they wait at the twain, watching the moon and sun complete their cycles through the sky. But no one ever comes. These poor souls spend eternity disappointed and lonely, like orphans waiting for parents to return. They realize the wastefulness of their previous lives, suffering in abject subservience, denying everything nature celebrates just to play a game officiated by a referee who never enforced the rules.

"How do you avoid lament?" Erin asked.

"You live your life knowing that each day could be your last," I said. "Virtue is its own reward—not a bargain made between you and a supernatural being. You behave ethically because it is the right thing to do, regardless of fear or favor. Do your best to anticipate outcomes and avoid regrets. Accept responsibility for your actions. When the time comes for your body and mind to go their separate ways, have confidence that you spent your life doing the best you could do."

The three students and two ghosts applauded. I smiled and thanked them for their appreciation.

"Can ghosts be healed of their lament?" Tanya asked. "Is it like a disease that has a cure? Like, can you burn candles or incense or something?"

"Possibly," I replied. "The problem is, the longer the soul has been dead, the thicker the callous that covers the wound. Lament is the fiery lake of burning sulfur, the blazing furnace, the chains of darkness, the weeping and gnashing of teeth. It is constant and insufferable. Healing such an injury is a steep gradient."

As my eyes scanned the circle, I noticed Thomas seemed eager to speak. I nodded for him to go ahead.

"So the twain is a place?" he asked. "I thought it meant *in between*, like the cross-quarters of the seasons."

"A *twain* is a point of demarcation separating two boundaries," I told him. "There is a twain between the seasons and a twain separating the occult realm from the physical realm."

"I've heard that the veil is thinner at some times more than others," Erin asked. "Is that true?"

"Yes," I said. "You may have heard folk tales of the veil being thin at particular times of the year—Halloween, full moons, or during a woman's menstrual cycle. In truth, there are indeed certain conditions that lower the level of mental energy enough to ease communication between the living and dead."

I continued, saying that despite conditions being ideal for interaction, not all ghosts are able to converse with the living.

Crossing the veil is no easy feat. Some discarnates frantically attempt to communicate with incarnate beings but fail to convey their messages. I watch them banging at the veil, but no one answers.

Some come close. These ghosts can appear in dreams, hauntings or séances. The rest of the time, they are lonely and miserable. That is why ghosts are frequently portrayed as tortured, gloomy souls. The sadness is due to frustration more than anything. They want so badly to realm shift but do not know how. I have tried teaching a few of them but, alas, it is something one can only master through introspection, meditation, and practice.

"What's it like in the occult domain?" Erin asked. "Can you describe it in more detail?"

Mulling over her request, I told her, "Let me see how I can best distill it."

I went on to explain how the occult domain is a place that cannot be seen, heard, smelled, tasted, or felt by those in the physical realm, even though the two worlds coexist.

For example, I cannot see per se, as I have no rods, cones, irises, or pupils. But I know how an item wants me to see it because I home in on the spiritual frequency of that object. I can sense its shape and color and where it is located in proximity to me. Without ears, I cannot hear the notes of my violin, but the spirit of the music comforts me. Wine and whiskey lead me to an altered state of consciousness even though I have no neural pathway.

"Is death scary?" Erin asked.

"Not once you get used to it," I replied. "The occult realm is a safe place. There is no disease, no discomfort. We are free from pecuniary anxiety and schedules that enslave us. Loved ones are nearby whenever a memory is entertained."

But I warned them: As liberating as it may be, the occult realm is not without consequence. There are restrictions that can be grueling and stressful in their own right. For example, if discarnates love people in the physical realm or witness grave injustices, they will agonize over their inability to affect a world that does not even know they are there.

That is why so many choose to reincarnate. Once a ghost adopts a new corporeal home, it breathes, eats, and bleeds. It enjoys the flavor of a truly fine wine. It engages in acts of pleasure. These physical and psychological sensations guide the spirit along its path during the period of time that it occupies an earthly body.

"But Nicholas and Krampus are doing that now and they're ghosts," Erin said. "They're eating candy and drinking hot chocolate."

The goatboy chuckled, uttering what I think was, "I love chocolate. You should give me more!" He then flicked his willow branch, as if he would swat her if she did not refill his cup. Erin, being a good sport, played into the drama, starting to pour from the carafe but holding back before letting any liquid actually fall into his cup.

"Oh no!" she joked. "The jug is empty! Oh, please, Mr. Krampus, don't be mad!"

She kept giggling as he gently tapped her with the switch. The two of them laughed and then she put her arm around him, looked him in the eye and grinned.

He returned the smile and boasted, "You're my friend!"

"It ish good to see Krampush so happy," Nicholas said.

"Yes, it is," I responded.

At that moment, I remembered Anton. I looked at the bishop and asked, "Have you seen my brother? He was with me in the cave before I landed here this evening."

"Sho shorry, Zhinfandel, but I have not."

"I wonder where he could be."

As I listened closely, I heard the faint sound of his cobza. I followed the music, finding him playing for the reindeer. What a sweet gift to give his animal friends.

THE MOON

2 January in the Year of Their Lord 2003

In the cave tonight, I turned to Anton and asked, "How do I look?"

"What message are you trying to convey?" he replied. "If you are trying to appear pretentious, the black hooded robe is effective."

"One of my students made this for me last month. I like it. It is beautiful and evokes a sense of warmth to others in the circle."

"You *really* think these students are going to save Rivervine?"

"Do you propose a better strategy?"

"Not yet, but the night is still young."

"You sound as though you have plans for the evening."

"Brigid is coming over while you are out with your *acolytes*. We are going to work on a new musical arrangement we started at Sauin."

"You two are growing quite close."

"She understands me, sister. Like you once did before you became obsessed with your little *army*."

"Are you implying I do not understand you anymore?"

"No. I am calling you out for abandoning your brother in favor of some misfits you barely know. I am also putting you on notice that I too have had a revelation: Brigid is my new musical partner."

"What about Lily? I thought she was Brigid's musical partner."

"Lily is smitten with some new worker at the saloon."

There really is no sense in pretending either of us does not care what the other is doing. He knows damn well I am enviousness of his new closeness with Brigid, just as I know he is jealous of Tanya, Erin, and Thomas.

My relationship with my brother is evolving. As difficult as this is for us to confront, we both must lean into the Tao and surf the waves of chaos.

"Oh, well, Happy New Year, brother," I kissed his cheek on my way out.

"Yes, dear sister, Happy New Year to you too."

Anton went about tuning his cobza.

For the first time in one hundred eighty-two years, we were not celebrating this sacred evening together. Both our souls filled with sadness, yet we understood our paths were diverging. Accepting this fact made it no less painful.

~ Seven of Cups ~

I arrived at Erin's house this afternoon about an hour before the four of us were scheduled to meet. Since I had volunteered to set up the ritual area, I wanted every detail to be perfect. This was the most spiritually significant night of the year, and with this being my acolytes' first Vampire New Year, I wanted to ensure they remembered it fondly.

In the south quadrant, to the left of Erin's chair, I heated up some coals in a small, grilled fire pit. Waiting on the side were slabs of beef seasoned with an herbal mix that our neighbor Lily Rhoads had made, along with some long-handled tongs. On the table by Tanya's chair in the north, I placed four plates, as well as small rolls to serve with our beef. Since the youths were too young to legally drink wine, I filled a carafe with grape juice from the Divinorums' late zinfandel harvest and placed it on the table in Thomas' west quadrant. I also tasked the west quadrant with holding a bottle of Lily's special barbecue sauce.

The east quadrant—my dedicated space and the direction in which the youth would enter—needed special care. As I pondered over how to make my section special, I spotted a crow landing on the eastern chair.

When I turned to greet my new feathered friend, two more birds joined him, followed by a much larger avis—a raven.

The crows cawed, and the raven croaked. They all made quite a racket.

As I started to walk toward the birds, each of them scattered, leaving behind several black feathers.

I looked up to the sky and called out, "Thank you, my friends," knowing full well they expected something sparkly in return—corvids love to steal shiny objects. So I conjured some iron pyrite, fashioned it into the shape of four eggs, and set them on my table in the east, saving the feathers for future use.

In the center of the ritual area, I covered the altar with a black velvet, golden-fringed scarf. On top of the cloth, I placed an Awen stone, an oil lamp infused with borage and valerian, an empty cup, and four bloodstone rings.

As the time neared to begin our ritual, I lit each of the four oil lamps on the tables in the four quadrants and put the meat on the grill. Watching my three students walk toward me, I noticed they were wearing the hooded cloaks Thomas had made last month. Underneath, I could see they all donned heavy clothing, boots, and gloves to keep them warm in this extremely cold night air.

During their walk along the path, I set the mood by playing something dark and mysterious in the key of G minor on my violin.

As they came closer, the warmth from the grill put smiles on their faces, and they all oohed and aahed from the smell of the cooking meat.

Once the acolytes reached the entrance of the ritual area, I set down my instrument and greeted them.

"Blessings, my students!"

"Blessings, Vondella!" they shouted in unison.

"Well, this is it! Vampire New Year—your first of what I hope will be many. I welcome you to this most sacred feast."

Everyone looked around and smiled at each other.

"Let us start, shall we?" I commenced. "Go ahead and make a line, please. Erin, we'll start with you in the south, followed by Thomas in the west, and Tanya in the north. I need to make sure that when you enter the circle, you walk counterclockwise to your stations and avoid crossing over any covenmates."

"I thought we walked jeesle in circle," Tanya questioned. "That's clockwise."

"For Vampire New Year, we go widdershins," I responded. "Going counterclockwise is a way of symbolically ending the cycle of the old year."

"Oh!" all three youth bellowed as they formed a line in the order I had requested.

I gathered the black corvid feathers, fashioning them into a fan.

Erin entered the sacred space, standing with her arms and legs outstretched. I waved the feathers over her body and in a singsong voice hollered, "Wings of raven, wings of crow, carry the old year's rubbish and go!"

The young woman inhaled deeply and exhaled slowly, releasing all of her penned up energy and clearing her mind.

With her aura now cleansed, she walked widdershins around the altar and took her place on my left.

Thomas was next, guarding his station in the west, followed by Tanya, who then fanned me before taking her place in the north. With all of our auras now properly cleared, I tossed the feathers outside the circle and cupped the four gilded eggs in my hands.

Lifting the offering into the air, I called out: "Outdwellers, tricksters, tommyknockers, trolls: We offer you a gift as a ransom for your toll. We are opening the veil to the realm of the unseen. We ask you to stand down so our message may be clean."

I tossed the eggs outside the circle and waited a moment for the energy to clear.

Our ceremony could now begin.

Walking widdershins, I handed each of my acolytes a piece of paper with invocations for them to read tonight. When I finished with Erin, I moved to the center and lit the lamp on the altar before returning to my place in the east.

"Let us all take a deep breath," I instructed. "And now raise your arms, reaching toward the sky."

The flame of the altar lamp flared, releasing a mild scent from the borage and valerian. A calming, soothing aroma washed over us, helping our minds focus on the ritual but without detracting from the feast awaiting us. It was a perfect way to welcome our honored guests.

"Tanya, will you start, please?"

She nodded and reached for her piece of paper.

"Ancestors, beloved dead," she called out. "Those who have taught us love, defined traditions, and forged our paths, the honor of your presence is requested on this Vampire New Year."

Thomas barely waited for Tanya to finish before he started calling out his spiel.

"Nature spirits of land, river, and sky: You fill us with wonder and show us divinity and beauty through Earth's creations and mysteries. The honor of your presence is requested on this Vampire New Year."

I looked over to call on Erin, but she appeared to be in a trance. This is a common occurrence during ritual, although not usually so early into the ceremony. Trying to avoid shocking her too much, I gently whispered, "Erin, it is your turn, dear."

The young woman jolted out of her reverie and grabbed her slip of paper.

"Shining Ones—deities, angels, and ascended masters," she called out. "We look to you for wisdom, guidance, and protection. The honor of your presence is requested on this Vampire New Year."

From my position in the east quadrant, I led the rest of the ritual.

"The outdwellers have been placated, and the kindred have been welcomed. Our celebration of Vampire New Year can now begin!"

The aroma of grilling meat was the central focus of everyone's minds. Although it provided a pleasant distraction, we needed to affirm our reason for the celebration before we could feast. Vampire New Year was nothing new to the Comatis of old—Anton and I still celebrate—but the tradition has been lost in the new era. My goal tonight was not to overthrow the Divinorums but rather to add a new branch of the tribe.

I started by saying, "Let me show you, dear ones, why Vampire New Year is so important."

The flames to all five oil lamps extinguished.

"Look above you," I said. "Notice how dark the sky is getting. There is no moon out tonight. Once the sun completes its journey this evening, the stars will be the only source of light in the heavens until tomorrow morning. Since the winter solstice was only twelve days ago, the morning sun will take longer to arrive than it did two weeks earlier. That means tonight—the second of January in the Year of Their Lord 2003—is the darkest, longest night of the year. As vampires, we recognize this as an occasion worth celebrating."

I walked to the center of the ritual space and stood at the altar.

"Throughout winter, there is very little energy fluttering about," I said. "Few plants photosynthesize. Animals do not mate. All is quiet and calm—ever so peaceful for those of us with sensitivity to the hustle and bustle of the mundane realm."

All three of the acolytes focused their eyes deeper on me. Their souls resonated with my words.

"Vampire New Year is a time of power," I continued. "We exhibit great strength because there is very little light to weaken us. The night sky is most vivid, heightening our clairvoyant ability. Strategies become clear. Our light-loving enemies are left defenseless."

The youth stared deeper into my gaze.

I proceeded to inform them that even though astronomers claim that the winter solstice is the shortest day of the year (therefore the respective night would be the longest), no such phenomenon truly exists.

Winter solstice in the northern hemisphere is when the sun stops directly above the Tropic of Capricorn—Earth's southernmost latitude. Likewise, the summer solstice is when the sun crosses the Tropic of Cancer—the northernmost latitude. Seasons are reversed in the southern hemisphere.

Each of the solstices lasts longer than twenty-four hours. This fluctuation occurs because the Earth is not a perfect sphere. It wobbles toward the sun on one turn around its axis and wobbles away from it another time, wobbling forward again and so on.

Equinoxes are when the sun crosses the Earth's equator, bringing spring and autumn to the northern and southern hemispheres.

It takes approximately two weeks for a season to complete its change of guard.

In Rivervine, California, according to the wretched Gregorian calendar, in the Year of Their Lord 2002, the days with the longest nights fell between the fifteenth and twenty-ninth of December. During this period, there were fourteen hours and fifty-seven minutes from the time dusk ended on one day until dawn began on the next. There were two days—the twenty-first and twenty-sixth of December—that had fourteen hours and fifty-eight minutes of nighttime. The new moon closest to this time is tonight—the second of January, in the Year of Their Lord 2003. There are only fourteen hours and fifty-three minutes of nighttime. But I will sacrifice five extra minutes in order to have a blank canvas for an entire night.

Closing my eyes and lifting my hands to shoulder height, I took a deep breath and meditated for a moment. With my thoughts intensely focused, I removed the chimney of the oil lamp, grabbed one of the bloodstone rings and waved it through the flame. I then slid it onto the thumb of my left hand.

Lifting my arm and circling it so the others could see, I called out, "This dark green, opaque rock is known to peddlers and scientists as *green chalcedony*. Ancient mystics called it *bloodstone* because it is flecked with bits of red jasper that resemble drops of blood. To the vampire, blood is sacred because it is the root source of vital lifeforce energy. Tonight I will present each of you with a similar ring and induct you into a new branch of the Comati tree—the Order of Green Chalcedony."

The youth oohed and aahed, smiling, their auras beaming with pride. Looking at their happy faces, it reaffirmed my belief that humans of all ages need a means of taking pride in themselves. They also need to wonder. They need mysticism. They need the freedom to live as they genuinely are, not what social norms, government, or religion have told them to be—or not to be.

Shaking off the epiphany, I rejoined the here and now, realizing that if the Order of the Green Chalcedony was going to be successful, my acolytes needed to enlist by their own free will. I want them to experience love and pride and personal power— not power over anyone else but power to control their own destinies. I wanted them to have a sense of community, that they belonged somewhere. And that somewhere was a special place, someplace rare and hidden from the unenlightened masses. It was a place that they earned entry into—not an illusion, not a false promise, but rather …

"*A kingdom not of this world*," an inaudible voice spoke to my mind. The scent of roses mingled with the borage, valerian, and barbecue.

"A kingdom not of this world," I muttered under my breath as my mind returned to the current notch along the time/space continuum.

"What?" all the acolytes inquired.

"Nevermind," I said, awaking from the trance. Coming back to center, I continued.

"The ring is to be worn on the thumb of your left hand. The left hand, of course, demonstrates the left-hand path—the path of the moon, the dark aspect of yin. The ring is to be worn on the thumb because it is opposable to the other four fingers. You always must be free to resist, fight, or oppose the mainstream."

I then called to Tanya in the north quadrant, asking her to join me at the dais.

"Tanya, based on the lessons you have learned so far under my tutelage, do you believe in your heart of hearts that walking a spiritual path with me complements your own Tao? And are you willing to fight with me for the soul of Rivervine?"

Looking her directly in the eye, I emphasized an important point. "You are free to leave the order if ever a time comes when you believe in your heart of hearts that this path no longer complements your own Tao or you decide you no longer wish to fight on my team. I ask you now to answer from your heart in your own true voice."

With tears streaming down her cheeks, the young woman managed to croak out the words, "Vondella, it is with great honor that I accept your ring. I am beyond flattered that your ancestors have adopted me, and I vow to fight for this family so long as I am able."

"Very well then" I said, waving the ring through the flame of the oil lamp. "Tanya Perino, I hereby induct you into the Order of the Green Chalcedony."

I finished sliding the ring onto her thumb. As she returned to her station, I motioned for Thomas to come forward as I reached for the third ring.

"Thomas Haley," I announced. "You have been summoned to defend the soul of Rivervine under the banner of the Order of the Green Chalcedony. Based on what you have learned so far, do you accept this challenge? I ask you now to answer from your heart in your own true voice."

"Yes, Vondella!" the enthusiastic young man proclaimed. "I will follow you no matter what. I would even sign my name in my own blood!"

"There is no need for such drastic measures," I politely informed him, waving the third ring through the flame and sliding it onto his thumb. "Free will is of paramount importance. But your commitment is duly noted, I assure you."

I kissed his cheek, and he nodded as he returned to his station.

Finally, it was the snake enthusiast's turn to approach the altar.

"Erin," I called, waving the fourth ring through the flame.

"Yes, I accept," she noted, before I could ask her for any type of confirmation.

"Very well," I said, sliding the ring onto her thumb.

As she looked at the new trinket on her hand, the young woman's eyes grew wide for several moments, then narrowed to stare even deeper into the stone. At last she cried out in a panic, "The demon returns! I, I, I can see it!"

Looking up at me, she shakenly demanded, "Wh, wh, what do I do?"

The other two youths became excited. Their mouths opened wide and their hearts started racing.

"I wanna see!" They each yelled.

"No!" I shouted back. "Give her space to see her vision."

I then turned to Erin and instructed her, "Tell me exactly what you see."

Her gaze returned to the bloodstone.

"I see a man—clean shaven, fair skin, blue eyes, short, sandy blonde hair … *very* nice suit, like something out of a magazine."

As her vision grew more vivid, her eyes widened.

"He is counting dollar bills. He has a lot of money. He gives this money to another man—one with long, dark hair and even paler skin."

A moment later, still scrying into the ring, she completed her thought.

"The dark-haired man is sitting at some type of table with other people. He is shouting."

Erin stared deeper, struggling to sustain a fading vision. At last she held her right hand over her mouth, gasping in horror at the image shown from the ring on her left hand.

"The dark haired man is lying on top of a pole in front of a building. The point of a stake is coming *out of* his chest."

She paused for a moment and then added, "He wasn't stabbed *in* the chest, but rather…"

As the image grew more vivid, the grimace on her face soured.

"He-he-he has been *impaled!*" she shrieked. "Oh, dear God … through the *anus!*"

Losing her focus, Erin looked to me and asked, "Can that be right?"

I grabbed her face and pulled her head close so I could kiss her brow.

"My darling girl!" I yelled in congratulations. "You are the first oracle to serve the Order of the Green Chalcedony!"

The young woman recoiled away from me, terrorized by the vision she saw. Her heartbeat raced and her aura trembled, succumbing to the fear.

"What the hell do I do?"

"This is not your problem, my dear," I assured her, trying to calm the energy. "It is mine. I will take care of it."

As Erin shakenly stepped back to her place in the south quadrant, I told her, "I am so sorry you had to experience that vision, but your emotional sacrifice tonight is duly noted."

The young woman slouched in her chair, rocking back and forth, clutching her abdomen, paying no attention to what I was saying.

"I saw it! I *saw* it! It was *real*!" she kept yelling. "It was so, so real."

"Yes, darling," I tried to soothe her. "I know. It was just a vision. It was not your problem to tackle. You are only a messenger. I will deal with the men in your vision."

Erin continued shaking. Tanya and Thomas had become upset—partly because of Erin's hysteria and partly out of jealousy that they were not chosen to assume an obvious role in the order.

Coven jealousy is a common problem when working with mystical groups. There is frequently the accusation of favoritism and political pecking order. But Erin's gift is genuine and none of us can deny it. Stifling it will only cause a form of lament. Nonetheless, I must eventually find a way to lift up my other two acolytes.

While Erin recovered from her fright, I returned to the center and scried into the flame of the oil lamp.

"Tanya, darling, come here please," I called out.

The young woman heeded my call and stepped away from her place in the north.

"Place your hand on Erin's cheek and see what happens."

The student followed my instructions.

Erin shivered at first and then breathed a sigh of relief. The hysterics ceased and the oracle's emotional state stabilized.

"Tanya," I called. The acolyte and her patient both looked at me, as did Thomas. "Your role shall be as the healer of the Order."

The two girls smiled and held each other in a long embrace as Erin continued to release emotional energy into Tanya's body.

Once calmness had been restored, Tanya left her patient, stopping by the center altar to give me a hug before returning to her place in the north.

I looked over at Erin and asked if she would mind turning over the beef that had been grilling in her quadrant. The young woman smiled and obliged.

Thomas watched the whole event anxiously, his aura fraught with wonder over what his role would be. Sensing his fretfulness, I called him forward.

"Thomas, look into my eyes and stay still for a moment."

I studied him for a long while, holding his face in my hands and struggling to divine an assignment for the young man. He was far too immature to be a priest and not athletic enough to lead combat training. From what I knew about him, I could see he was a quick thinker, always in a rush to speak, and fiercely defensive of both his lady love and his mother.

"My darling boy, how old are you?" I asked him.

"Nineteen, ma'am," he stammered. "I was held back in school. I graduate this year."

"When do you turn twenty?"

"July fourteenth."

"So you are by all rights a man, not a boy."

The young man hung his head down once again, ashamed.

"My stepfather doesn't think so. He calls me a retard."

He then started to cry.

"I don't deserve to be here!" he yelled through his tears. "I'm a loser. I have let you all down. I have let Tanya down when all I ever wanted to do was love her. Erin and Matt and Darren were my friends; I promised to teach them witchcraft, but I got Matt and Darren killed, and Erin is over there losing her mind."

He then looked up at me and conceded, "I made those promises in good faith. But I don't know how to keep them."

I embraced Thomas fully into my chest, wrapping my arms around him, holding him tightly and rocking him gently, allowing the acolyte to release all his tears onto my shoulder.

"You have done nothing wrong," I assured him, still locked in our embrace. "In fact, you have done something very, very right! If it were not for you, the four of us would not be here tonight celebrating a holiday that had been long forgotten and creating a whole new branch of the Comati tree."

I released his body but held his face in both my hands. Locking eyes once more, I confirmed, "Thanks to you, I am not fighting this enemy alone."

His hazel eyes—pooled with tears and reflected by the lenses of his spectacles—dazzled me into a trance. I stood there, scrying into those glistening gems, watching the spectacles fog and listening to his nose fight dripping mucus. One loud snort shook me out of my haze, and I conjured a handkerchief for him to relieve his nose and dry his eyes.

"Thank you," he sniffled.

"You are welcome, of course," I replied, still somewhat hypnotized and processing the revelation that came to me.

I am not a devout follower of astrology, but I do know that the human body is sixty percent water. If the moon can influence the Earth's tides, it stands to reason that other celestial objects can affect our bodies, especially our minds, which are the clearinghouses for our personalities.

Thomas was born on the fourteenth of July in the Year of Their Lord 1983.

This tells me he was born in the Chinese Year of the Rat and under the Greek sign Cancer, but close to the cusp of Leo. This information allows me to deduce that he is a clever, quick thinker, optimistic, and energetic. He is sensitive to other people's beliefs yet stubborn with his own opinions. He tends to be kind, but his weak communication skills can make him seem impolite or rude. He is loyal and emotional with a tendency to be suspicious based on a deep-seated sense of insecurity.

The modern zodiac used in the United States follows a 12-month cycle that started with the Egyptians, but was adopted by the Babylonians and later the Greeks, who named it the *circle of animals* that we know today. Although there are oftentimes thirteen new moons or thirteen full moons in a given solar cycle, there is never a full thirteenth month, which is why there are only twelve signs in the Greek system.

Chinese astrology follows a 12-year cycle, with each year also named after a specific animal, albeit not the same animals as the Greek zodiac.

The Comatis have no documented astrological system, although we do use Sirius as a starting point when studying the heavens. This celestial body is relevant not only because it is the brightest star in the northern hemisphere's sky during winter, but it also has the heaviest gravitational pull on the Earth compared to all other heavenly objects. Sirius is so important that the magi used it to guide them from the Orient to a manger in Bethlehem in the first Year of Their Lord.

As the revelation unfolded, it dawned on me that this might be a good task for the young man.

"Thomas," I called. "How would you feel about documenting the Comati astrological system? In, say, thirteen years? That would you give you a full cycle to study the heavens and document your findings. You shall complete the task by the thirteenth Vampire New Year from tonight. I realize the magnitude of this request, and I pledge whatever resources you need to accomplish the task. If you fail, no harm will befall you, but if you succeed, you shall be memorialized as the father of Comati astrology. Do you accept this challenge?"

The acolyte was so overwhelmed that he fell to the ground and started hyperventilating. Tanya rushed over to her beau, cupping her hands over his mouth, forcing him to breathe through his nose.

Thomas took one deep inhale and Tanya removed her hand, allowing him to breathe normally again.

"I accept!" was all he managed to cough out before his sensory and motor skills broke down.

This time, I stepped away from the patient and allowed Tanya to work her magic. This time, it was she who caressed him against her chest. This time, it was her shoulder that collected his tears.

I was so proud!

~ Feast ~

We took a short break, at which time Erin asked me, "When do we eat? I don't mean to sound rude, but the meat is barbecuing in my quadrant and making me hungry."

"If Thomas and Tanya are ready to reconvene, we can eat right now."

The two love birds had been talking throughout break, but when they heard their names called, they yelled, "Oh, we're ready!"

"Then let us resume our quarters."

Once we were all in place, I brought our attention back to the sacred space.

"Let us all close our eyes and center our attention," I said. Once we were all ready, I called out, "On this night of Vampire New Year, the most holy of all festivals, we share this meal with the kindreds, asking them to bless the feast so we may be nourished by their magic. Awen."

The three acolytes echoed, "Awen," and then opened their eyes and looked at me for continued guidance.

Since the plates and bread were in the north quadrant, I started there.

"Tanya, can you please hand everyone a plate with a roll of bread? You will notice there are five servings. One is to be placed on the altar as a sacrifice to the kindreds."

She did as instructed, followed by Thomas in the west, who poured grape juice into everyone's cup and finished by pouring a serving into the cup on the altar.

"What do I do with the barbecue sauce?" he asked.

"Just wait there and we will all come to you if we want it."

"Okay."

For the meat, I had us all bring our plates to the south quadrant where I conjured a serving platter for Erin to place the roast on. She then carved the chunk into individual slices, which she put on our plates. I brought both my plate and the one that had been on the center altar. Once the fifth plate had been filled, I set mine down on the eastern table and returned with the second plate to the center altar.

Staying in the center, I reached for the cup of juice with one hand while keeping the plate in the other. Raising them both, I called out, "To the Mighty Kindred: We thank you for the blessings you have bestowed upon us and ask you for guidance as we continue our journey along the Comati path. Awen."

"Awen!" the youth echoed.

I set down the plate and cup on the altar and let the meal sit there the rest of the evening to allow the kindreds time to digest the spirit of the food.

As the humans and I enjoyed our feast, we talked about the significance of the evening's events.

Erin kicked off the conversation by asking, "What makes darkness so magical?"

"Well," I answered. "When there is less activity in the physical realm, there is less competition for energy with the occult realm. The occult realm is where introspection, telepathy, and creativity reside, so longer, hotter, brighter days are filled with a lot of yang energy while shorter, darker, colder days are filled with yin energy."

"Isn't yin energy feminine?" Erin asked.

"Yes, it is!" I answered, proud she knew the answer.

"So can this also be a reason why women tend to be more clairvoyant than men—their energy is more yin than yang?"

I nodded and smiled at the amazing young woman. She continued.

"So if men are more yang than yin, and yang energy is physical, is that related to the physical oppression of women? Like in an *Art of War* sense?"

"Uh, NO!" Thomas interrupted. "If women are yin, and yin is mental, then women have been mindfucking men since time immemorial. Who's the oppressor now, Erin?"

"Touché!" I cried.

I was amazed at their ability to reason on such a deep level. Tanya piped in.

"If darkness is yin and yin is female, then why do we refer to a *prince* of darkness? Shouldn't it be *princess* of darkness? I mean, like, I realize now that there is no such entity, but from a folklore perspective, I'm just curious how the legend evolved."

"Are you talking about Satan or Dracula?" Thomas asked.

"Both, actually," I told them. "The first use of the term *prince of darkness* was in the Bible with the apostle Paul and his letter to the Ephesians. The city of Ephesus—in what is now the country of Turkey—had a temple devoted to Artemis, who was the goddess of the hunt and queen of the moon. She was a virgin goddess, and even though none of the legends attribute any children to her, Paul wanted to ensure that they city's residents converted to Christianity, so he told them Artemis had given birth to the prince of darkness, who was the adversary to Jesus—the prince of light."

"What does that have to do with Dracula?" Thomas inquired.

"In the fifteenth century, Prince Vlad the Third of Wallachia was thought to be not only a descendent of the son of Artemis—thereby continuing the line of princes of darkness—

but also, because Artemis was the goddess of the hunt, he was believed to hunt humans and drink their blood."

The three of them ewwed in disgust. Erin looked down at her meal and wondered, "By the way, what are we eating? We're not gonna see our dinner listed as a missing person on the nightly news, are we?"

I chuckled and answered, "No, my dear. I stopped by the Ceccarelli butcher shop in Old Town Rivervine this afternoon and picked up a tri-tip roast."

"Whew!" she responded. The other two sighed with relief as well. We all giggled.

My soldiers—acolytes, students, friends, whatever you want to call them—continued their meal, soaking up the beauty and stillness of the night.

After a while, Erin broke the silence.

"I just love the darkness. I know Thomas and Tanya do too. Is that why the four of us were called together?"

"For me," Tanya answered, "darkness is a state of mind. I don't have any distractions. It's comfortable. The plants aren't photosynthesizing. I can just be … still."

"I'm sort of the opposite," Thomas chimed in, "I feel closer to nature at night—like, to the nocturnal animals that hunt in the dark. It energizes me. Is that, like, what you were saying about Artemis being the goddess of the moon *and* the hunt?"

"Interesting hypothesis, Thomas," I replied. "Nocturnal animals hunt and mate at night because they have evolved physical traits that give them survival advantages to their diurnal competitors and prey. Vampires usually hunt and mate at night because their psychic energy is frazzled in the daylight."

"How do you know lower animals aren't frazzled by the sunlight?" Thomas asked.

"Excellent point," I admitted. "I do *not* know that for a fact. It was an assumption I made."

These youth are doing exactly what I was hoping they would do—thinking for themselves, questioning established beliefs, and finding their own paths.

I continued.

"I have, however, noticed animals—even nocturnal ones, even humans—are more active under a full moon than they are during the dark moon, and they are definitely less active in the winter. Some animals hibernate—bats and groundhogs for example. Bears go into a type of deep sleep called a *torpor*. Snakes, however, conserve their energy in the summertime by going into *estivation*, which is a state of lowered activity when temperatures are high, water is scarce and days are long. But I have never seen a lower animal meditate, and I do not know if they have a conscience."

Erin spoke up.

"So what is up with bats and wolves—how did they become part of the vampire legend? Was that all just storytelling, or is there more to it?"

I shook my head as I explained the answer.

"When Christian missionaries came to Africa and Latin America, they had to deal with a species of blood-drinking bats in the rainforests. These nocturnal, flying animals lived in dark places such as caves or under bridges. Since most of the missionaries came from Eastern Europe, they named the bats after their legend of the *vampir*, the word for nightwalker in Dacian. The superstitious Europeans believed these winged mammals could shapeshift into human form and prey on innocent people in the night."

"That is so cool!" Thomas shouted.

Erin rolled her eyes.

"They don't really do that!" she scoffed.

"It's still cool, though!" he countered.

"The Dacian legend of the wolf is just as interesting," I said.

All six eyes lit up in anticipation.

"The wolf found its way into Comati lore because of Sirius, the dog star that we mentioned earlier. Back in Romania when Vampire New Year was a prevalent celebration, rumors circulated that Laelaps—the dog of the hunter, Orion—was the patron of the vampires and ruler of the night sky during our big annual festival."

"Was Laelaps a real dog?" Thomas asked.

"This was during a time when dogs were not commonly kept as pets," I answered. "There were a few domesticated species, but they were rare. This was also during the rise of agriculture. Wolves preyed on domesticated livestock, so naturally, these wild dogs were demonized in civilization's folklore."

"It seems to me that all this folklore is just a bunch of propaganda," Erin noted. "Like, poor Krampus. That guy was such a sweet soul, and they literally demonized him just because he had disabilities. And his ibex goats have become the quintessential icon of Satan in contemporary culture. No wonder he's so bitter and angry and vengeful."

She was correct. I congratulate the storytellers for doing such a splendid job of tapping into the fear of the popular imagination! But I curse them as well for deprecating sacred symbols of my culture. There will always be an air of mysticism surrounding vampires—for such is the fate of any true shaman—

but we are hardly worthy of the reputation great scribes have bestowed upon us.

"So what is the truth about vampirism?" Tanya asked. "Is it some sort of blood disease or what?"

"Vampirism is neither a curse nor a disease," I explained. "A vampire is a soul—either incarnate or discarnate—whose chi radiates at the dark end of the spiritual spectrum. We write music in minor keys and sing in the lower range of the scales. We prefer our meat cooked rare and paired with a well-aged red wine. When empaths encounter us, they frequently describe our auras as physically and psychically overpowering—strong, cold, and filled with dim, murky colors. They cannot explain the power we have; many denounce it and pontificate against us."

I went on to explain that vampires inhale darkness into the cores of their beings. Our abdomens, spines, legs, arms, necks, and skulls tune in to the network of dark energies, fortifying our posture, allowing us to connect with the wisdom and power that one cannot see when light blinds us. This power flows through our speech, writing, art, music, and all other forms of communication.

Some souls—like the *arhats* and *swamis* of the East—radiate on the bright end of the spiritual spectrum. Their auras are warm and comforting. They require very little physical stimulation because they are overloaded with lifeforce energy. They are the light ones. We are the dark ones. Together, we are the yin and the yang of spirituality.

You see, darling reader, one of the downfalls of being a vampire is that we are unable to synthesize certain life energies that are present in the lighter regions of the spectrum. Because a soul constantly seeks equilibrium, vampires must find balance by absorbing these life energies from other sources. Balance can be attained through the consumption of blood, intellectual conversation, psychic bonding, physical activity, or sexual arousal.

Blood is the preferred medium because it carries with it a special sort of mysticism. It represents the most primordial forms of both male and female energies. Unfortunately, social conventions have frowned upon the consumption of blood, making voluntary donors scarce. Horrible diseases can also present themselves during an exchange, decreasing the chances for vampires to safely find sanguinary satisfaction.

Therefore, blood exchange must only be conducted under the most trusted circumstances. Once a reliable donor—what vampires call a charge—is found, supply does not usually present a problem. Fortunately, blood is so potent that only a small amount is needed to satiate an appetite. However, the donor must give willingly, or the fluid will be tainted with bitter energy. It is vital for the charge to be well hydrated, fed, and cared for.

Because incarnate donors are in such short supply, I have trained my students to substitute freshly killed cattle, elk, or deer for human blood. Although it is not as potent as fluid from the original species, red meat is socially acceptable and supply is readily available. Be advised, though, the human digestive system cannot process the meat uncooked. Therefore, the meat must be grilled enough to make it digestible yet rare enough for the chi to still present itself. The vampire must be able to be able to see, smell, taste, and sense the blood. If it is overcooked or if the animal has been dead for too long, the chi is lost, and the vampire will remain hungry.

Semen and vaginal lubrication can also be used to satisfy a hunger, but since each represents only one half of human existence (male or female), sexual feedings are not as effective as sanguinary ones unless the vampire has a charge of each sex. Although sexual partners are usually in ample supply, they too may carry physical diseases, and the vampire must still exercise caution. The relationship also has the potential to create an emotional attachment that neither the vampire nor the charge may be able to reciprocate, which can lead to heartache—a factor amounting to destruction because, just like a sanguinary feeding, the donation must be offered with free will. If bitterness, anger, or hatred is present in the donor's chi, the emotion spoils the feeding.

A third type of procurement is psychic—feeding off the mental or spiritual energy of the charge, sometimes without the victim even aware it is happening. I prefer this method when dealing with my enemies, as it leaves the charge feeble and unable to defend oneself. I do it by homing in on the aura of the victim. I can then identify the strengths, fantasies, and talents of the charge and rob the victim of those powers, thereby adding them to my own complement of skills.

Whether the vampire chooses sanguinary, sexual, or psychic feedings, drinking red wine with a feeding is optimal. The crimson color, inebriation, and way it enlivens the tongue contribute to the overall experience.

"But I don't like the taste of wine," Tanya interjected. "I've tried it lots of times. I just cannot force it past my tongue. Can I be a Comati—can I celebrate Vampire New Year—if I don't partake? Is there another way to *enliven the tongue* and get *inebriated*?"

"My darling Tanya, you are following your own path," I told her. "Your spirit surfs a different wave of the Tao. It is neither better nor worse—just different. There is no shame in having an aversion to wine—or alcohol. Yoga, tai chi, and ecstatic dance are common substitutes in other cultures."

The young woman smiled brightly.

"Oh, thank god!" she exclaimed. "I really did not want to be an outcast again."

She hung her head down and let out a sigh. Thomas rushed to her side, holding her in a consolable embrace. Erin tilted her head and smiled in sympathy.

They were all outcasts, bless their hearts. They wanted so much to belong, to be loved, to be respected, to be family. Here I was, leading them. They put their faith in me. They put their hope in a promise I made to them. If I let them down—if I break their hearts—it will crush my own dreams of creating a better world. I cannot disappoint them.

I went back to my station in the east and closed my eyes to meditate for a moment.

"Radu, my greatest grandfather," I called telepathically. "As the family clairvoyant, I ask you to guide Thomas and help him document the Comati zodiac."

In our culture, one never asks a favor of the kindreds without offering a gift in return. Therefore, I dropped a sip of my juice onto the ground as a sacrifice and pulled off a bite of my barbecued meat and roll, likewise tossing it onto the soil. If Radu accepts the offering, the energy of the material will change form and direction into something that pleases my ancestor.

A few moments later, Thomas perked up.

"Have you ever noticed the shadows between the stars?" he wondered. "There's a whole new pattern that nobody ever talks about."

I took it as a yes from Radu!

"Thomas, darling, tell me what you see!" I called.

Before he answered, he looked down and shook his head, shaking off a bout of confusion.

"Tray ker al chair oo lay day no op tay," he sputtered. "What does that mean?"

"It is Romanian for *tracker of the night sky*," I answered. "Radu must have given you your new name—your Comati name."

Once again, Thomas collapsed and Tanya rushed over to console him.

"Say what?" Erin requested. "How do you spell it, like in our alphabet?"

"Let us just call him Traycor," I suggested. "Keep it simple."

"Traycor it is!" Thomas beamed, holding Tanya tighter. She leaned in to kiss him deeper.

Erin raised her glass, "To Traycor, the Comati astrologer!"

I raised my glass and nodded in salute. Thomas beamed so brightly that even his tears glowed.

As Thomas—excuse me, *Traycor*—absorbed the energy from the epiphany, I explained a little about what I knew of Radu's process of studying the night sky.

Even as a ghost, my ancestor continues to track the patterns seen in the sky before the sun rises each morning. He does not study the stars themselves the way traditional astronomers do, but rather he pays attention to the patterns of darkness that fall between the stars. He sees visions not only in the spaces but also the gradients of blue and black that appear in the hollows.

Radu boasts analyses that are far more accurate than looking directly at the starshine. The moon and stars reveal patterns that appear in predictable frequencies based on their annual journeys. While there is no such thing as "destiny" per se, Radu *can* read the shadows cast from all the sources shedding light on a subject and see paths of energy. The combination of auras interacting with each other—be they starshine, meteors, or other lifeforms—is what creates the mystical patterns. The difference between survival and ruin depends on this level of attention to detail. This is how we know when to plant, when to harvest, when to mate, and when to attack.

The more time Radu devotes to studying the night sky, the better he is able to analyze his visions. That is why the winter new moon is the most sacred time of year for us. Of course, we celebrate by eating, drinking, dancing, and making music.

"But none of us play music," Erin interjected. "Are you going to teach us?"

"In time, if you wish to learn, yes. Right now, I do not want to overwhelm you too much. You have already been given a great deal to digest already."

"Oh, but we must have some sort of music!" Tanya opined. "It's not a celebration without music, and we have so much to celebrate. Traycor got a new name, and we all learned our destinies tonight. I can't just go home and leave it at that."

"Very well," I acquiesced, picking up my violin. I then conjured a pennywhistle for Tanya, a hand drum for Thomas, and a tambourine for Erin. "Just play along as the spirit guides you."

I led the group in an upbeat tune in the key of A major. Comatis do not normally play major keys on Vampire New Year, but this was our inaugural celebration, and with all the joyous revelations tonight, I felt a lively, happy melody was appropriate.

None of my students had any sense of rhythm. The sound was cacophonous, but the joyous spirit overpowered the discord.

We celebrated for several moments until the harshness of the racket finally drove the budding musicians to admit defeat.

"That was fun!" Tanya yelled, as she stroked her flageolet. "I want to learn how to play this thing for real. Vondella, can you teach me?"

"The best teacher in town is Candace Renborne at the music store. Tell her Vondella sent you."

"I will. Thank you!"

I let out a big sigh and looked around the circle at my students. Mysticism, wisdom, respect, belonging—these are human needs. If I can give these youths—these outcasts—what they require, they can become an army committed to the soul of Rivervine, not just the soil.

"Does anyone have anything else they'd like to add to this evening's ritual?" I asked. "If not, we can go ahead and end it."

All three heads nodded. Perceiving no further communication from the occult realm, I moved to the center altar. Lifting the plate of food and glass of juice, I called out, "Mighty Kindreds—ancestors, nature spirits, and Shining Ones—we thank you for honoring us with your presence and blessing us with wisdom and revelation on this Vampire New Year. May you find our sacrifice worthy of your blessing."

I then moved to the south quadrant and tossed the plate and glass into the fire. We all watched the flames flicker, transforming our physical offering into smoke, which then ascended across the veil into the occult realm.

As the smoke disappeared, I returned to the east chair and lifted my arms.

"This rite is over. Let us go in peace, wisdom, and honor. Awen"

"Awen," the three acolytes chimed.

The three of them started to head back toward Erin's house while I cleaned up the ritual area.

"Wait a moment!" I called out.

The youths stopped and turned back to face me.

"The second of February is the feast of Iemmol," I told them. "Meet me at the Oppidum at sundown that night. I want to introduce you to the other Comatis."

They cheered and ran back along the path toward Erin's house, leaving a trail of happy energy behind them.

I am now in the cellar of the winery. As I write this, a revelation has come to me: In addition to the Order of the Green Chalcedony, I need two more allies to defeat the impending adversaries mentioned in the first entry of this grimoire. I must have a solicitor to make Fermata Cellars profitable enough to overcome the egregious newcomers who want to take away my land. I also need a scribe to document my history and inform the populace of the problems we Comatis are facing. Both individuals must have the skills to inspire others to take action.

When the revelation ended, I looked at the floor and saw a racer snake crawling across the floor of the winery.

"You must be lost, my friend," I said, picking up the little fellow.

As he ran up my arm, the serpent rebutted, "No. It is you I seek. Take me to the orange tree."

Queen of Wands Crosses the Fool

2 February in the Year of Their Lord 2003

Pride and melancholia cross paths in my heart right now. The young Brigid turned sixteen today, and we had a lovely celebration for her in the Oppidum.

The celebration was also the Comati ritual of Iemmol—the twain of the winter solstice and vernal equinox. It is our custom on this night to showcase our bardic talents, be it painting, drawing, poetry, or song. While I am proud of Brigid and her musical talents, I am sad to learn both she and my brother, Anton, have planned their future without me.

As I have written before in this grimoire, my family's blood line ended the sixteenth of August in the Year of Their Lord 1848 when the Great Fire swept through Rivervine killing the entire tribe of Comatis as well as four hundred of Sooter's men. This catastrophe left no heirs to the property. No long-lost relatives came forth to claim their rightful place. Captain Sooter had no timber to harvest, and the priests had no savages to convert. Gold lay in the riverbed, but no miner proved brave enough to stake a claim; rumors of haunted waters kept the weak from fighting the devil for a metal that could be found further along without fear of eternal damnation.

With no one to care for the property, I remained its guardian despite my non-physical state of being. My plan was to keep the land fallow and frighten off interested parties until a worthy beneficiary could be found. Those beneficiaries, as you now know, were Xavia and Sage Divinorum.

My vision for the young couple was to have them become the new Comatis. It was my hope that their children and grandchildren would continue the tradition of winemaking and earth-based spirituality. But I have just learned that my vision will end with this one generation unless another successor can be found.

Seventeen years ago, before she went by the name Brigid, I asked the spirit of the Divinorums' unborn child if she would be willing to care for the land upon the death of her parents. I appreciated her honesty and straightforwardness yet was saddened by her answer.

"I cannot commit to such a request," she told me. "I have never experienced a farming-based incarnation, so I have no way of determining if this way of life suits me or not."

"Then why did you choose Xavia and Sage as your parents?"

"Their music. In all my previous incarnations, I had been part of a musical family. The songs of the Divinorums fill my soul with happiness, and I want to be part of that. And who knows? Maybe I will discover the farming/winemaking lifestyle suits me. If not, when I come of age, I will abandon it and migrate to another location."

Today was the child's sixteenth birthday. Late this afternoon, Brigid—shrouded in a murky aura—came down to the cellar and summoned me.

"Zinfandel, I have something to tell you."

Apprehension rung from her quivering voice and wary body language.

"I have experienced enough of life as a grape grower," she said, letting out a long breath and straightening her spine. "I am graduating early from high school this year and going to study music in San Francisco—what you call *Yerba Buena*."

Her composure softened as she tilted her head and continued. "Farm life just isn't for me. Please don't be mad."

This was a difficult conversation for us to have. She anticipated my reaction, which of course was filled with crestfallen disappointment, but she also knew that I would not fault her for being truthful. I cannot allow my vines to be tended by anyone who does not feel joy when caring for their defenseless tendrils.

"My darling," I said, grabbing her hands in mine and kissing her cheek. "I understand. You have my blessing."

"Thank you." She paused, signaling something else she wanted to talk about.

When our eyes met, her aura brightened.

"What other news do you want to share with me?" I wondered.

My brother Anton appeared, embracing her from behind.

"We are in love, sister," he said. "I am going to reincarnate so Brigid and I can be together in the physical realm."

What else could I feel but shock? Even though I knew about their love affair, I assumed Brigid would tire of it and break Anton's heart. This reincarnation plan caught me off guard.

Love is a beautiful thing, but this decision comes with several inherent risks—my loneliness being one of them, of course, although certainly not the main concern. Having said that, they both know me well enough to expect my temper to come to the forefront of any reaction I had. I did not disappoint them. Nonetheless, I tried to sound reasonable instead of jealous and selfish.

"You both realize that once reincarnated, there is no guarantee he is going to remember this agreement?" I scolded. "What if you never even find each other? Even if you do, there will be a large age gap, which might negate the compatibility you two now share. Or she may grow restless waiting for you to come of age and another lover will enter her life—one that makes her even happier than she is now. She is only sixteen; how does she know what true love is? Perhaps she will decide she does not want to wait to bear children until you come of age. She will be thirty-four when you turn eighteen."

"Yes, Vondella," Anton interjected, balancing assertion with calmness without being patronizing. Sometimes he can be much more reasonable than I, especially when he knows it will douse my fiery rage.

"We have considered all of those issues before making our decision. I never experienced love as an incarnate. I was always too sick and ugly. I have been discarnate for more than a hundred years, and no one until now has ever shown me the least bit of interest. You have had an abundance of lovers in both the physical and occult realms. Please let me have my chance to physically share affection with another human being."

I turned to Brigid and sneered, "And what benefit do you receive from this deal?"

"I get to develop my music career without the distraction of love. And then, when we're both ready, we can reintroduce ourselves."

Turning to look at Anton, she continued, "I'm confident we'll find each other and fall in love all over again."

"But you are so young, and he is so desperate!" I retorted, glaring at the two lovers. Afterward, I just looked at the floor, shaking my head.

The scent of roses grew strong, and I felt the presence of a ghost I could not identify.

"Worst-case scenario," a woman's voice whispered in my ear, "is they will not find each other. But from this moment on, Brigid will pursue a career in music, and Anton will have a new physical shell that allows him to experience affection, companionship, and all the other pleasures of life."

"Who are you?" I called out, under my breath.

"Oh, just a fan of your Txakoli wine," she answered.

I did not feel her presence, hear her voice, or smell roses again this evening, but she must have been related to the little Basque girl at Kristobal's church—Saint Bernadette's on the northwest side of town. Txakoli is made from the Spanish *Hondarrabi zuri* grape found in the provinces of Cantabria and northern Burgos near the border of France. It is the only wine the Divinorums make that is not a zinfandel or mead. I made a mental note to ask the Catholic ghosts about it if they came to the celebration tonight.

Returning my focus to Brigid and Anton, I was not quite convinced of the mysterious ghost's rationale.

"This is all my fault," I told them. "I was spending too much time with the new recruits and ignored the needs of my own brother."

"Vondella," Anton's reasonable tone returned. "This has nothing to do with your new recruits. I need this. Please be happy for me, for us."

"You are right," I conceded. "My selfish heart does not want to lose my winery or my brother, but the Tao reminds me you both must follow your own paths and I cannot compel you to alter your courses. My grief will end in time." I kissed them both on the cheek and wished them, "Peace be with you."

The three of us headed en masse to the Oppidum. Anton and Brigid, of course, were both elated and relieved, while I tried to suppress my frazzled emotions.

As we walked, my mind wandered, and I realized that I was now left with the exhausting task of finding another heir for the Comati legacy. The obvious first choice, of course, would have been Lily Rhoads, the young woman who runs the herb farm next door to Fermata Cellars. From the moment of Lily's birth, I sensed her desire to play violin, but her family had its own heritage to which she was bound—a legacy of herbs and vegetables, not vats and corks. And she is so reticent around men that I fear she may not produce any offspring. I must somehow find a way to keep the vines tied to their music. The magic of the wine depends on it.

My contemplative mood ended when we arrived at the Oppidum, where my three acolytes were waiting outside the perimeter. Our eyes met, and they quickly noticed I was with Brigid, their friend from school. I was unsure if they could see my brother until Thomas reached out to shake Anton's hand.

"I'm Thomas," the young man tried to sound diplomatic. "My Comati name is Traycor. You must be Anton, Vondella's brother. We have heard much about you."

Anton scowled at the youth but accepted his hand anyway.

"If you hurt another Comati pet again," my brother threatened, gripping the young man's hand in a tight clasp, "I will haunt your nightmares for all eternity!"

Thomas recoiled without further comment.

That whole exchange puzzled me. Anton's illusion skills are not honed as sharply as mine. I was curious to see if any other Comatis could see him—or at least sense his presence—during the ritual tonight.

Tanya and Erin glanced at each other in frightened disbelief. After a moment, Erin changed the subject. Looking in my direction, she asked, "Are we dressed okay?"

I scanned them up and down, noticing their hooded cloaks covering warm, contemporary clothing. Raising my eyebrows, I nodded in approval.

"Whew!" she continued. "It's freezing out here tonight. I really didn't feel like getting my sexy witch on in this weather."

We all chuckled at the comment as we arrived at the Oppidum just in time to go through the motions of getting smudged with sage smoke and sprinkled with salt water. Being the last ones to enter, we found ourselves at the end of the circle.

The ritual went on as usual with the offerings to the kindreds and all the pomp required to raise and direct supernatural energy.

When the time came to celebrate Brigid's birthday, I looked over at Lily and noticed a heavy, sullen, melancholy countenance. She had barely spoken to anyone the whole night and did her best to appear happy for her young friend as the bonfire roared and the mead flowed from tankard to tankard. But when Brigid picked up her guitar and invited Lily to play a duet on her violin, the fiddle's E string betrayed her confidence, going flat at every measure.

The longer she played, the deeper Lily delved into this depression. The erratic improvisation consoled her—the music making love to her anguish. The vibration of the strings shot through her and echoed throughout the young woman's body. From the split ends of her hair to the calluses of her feet, she unified with the melody.

Lily's body swayed violently, holding the violin under her chin on the right side. Her left hand gripped the bow in sadistic fornication with the stings, the fingers of her right hand pouncing on the poor steel victims until they submitted to her domination.

Once the two women finished their duet, some other guests began playing a lively tune in C sharp major. This was the cue for the Comatis to engage in their traditional spiral dance, a ritualistic promenade conducted in a corkscrew direction, emulating the shape and movement of the galaxy. Xavia headed the spiral while Brigid took the tail end.

We ghosts do not normally directly take part in the Comatis' rituals because we do not want to interfere with any workings they may do or deities they wish to invoke. We listen from the outskirts of the Oppidum and engage in our own frivolities. Tonight, though, the birthday girl looked back at Anton with a gaze that begged him to join her. He took her left hand. I took his, wondering if this was going to be my last dance with him. Doina took my hand, and Radu took hers. Father Kristobal and the little Basque girl from his church made the final tail of the spiral. No sign of the mysterious rose woman.

The whole time we were dancing, a newcomer caught my attention—a man in a suit. I did not recognize him at first because I was accustomed to seeing him donning farmworker attire. It turned out to be Lily's good friend Manuel Chavez—the same boy who had been raised at Fermata Cellars but left a few years ago to find fortune elsewhere. It was he who planted the orange seed that grew to become the favorite spot for Anton and me to play our instruments.

When I spotted Manuel this evening, I realized my petition for a solicitor had been granted.

He still lacked a strong sense of fortitude but had grown from a shy, insecure boy to a man of kind heart and pleasant nature.

I noticed, though, that he winced every time someone shook his hand or patted him on the right shoulder. The scent of eucalyptus blew in the air—a sign of Susan Rhoads' muscle ointment. An even stronger smell rushed past my nose—the musky aroma of a vampire.

After the dance, I asked Xavia about the return of Mr. Chavez.

"Yeah, he's our new marketing director," she informed me.

"With whom did he shake hands today?" I inquired.

"Oh, just Glenda Fern, the editor for the local newspaper. Why do you ask?"

"Is that how he injured his shoulder?"

"Yes. She has a mighty good grip. I had Susan give him a massage when we got home."

The editor of the newspaper is a vampire. I have found my scribe!

Vampires are unusually strong, even when they do not intend to be. It is a result of heightened endorphins released whenever they feed. In the case of Mr. Chavez, the editor must have preyed upon his physical energy somehow when they met today. This release of endorphins leaves behind a bold, earthy scent that other vampires can detect—similar to when an animal marks its territory.

"Can you arrange for her to meet me sometime?" I asked Xavia. "I need to speak with her."

"How on Earth do you want me to approach Glenda? 'Hi, our ghost wants to meet you because you're a vampire and she thinks you're cool'?"

"Just invite her for a tour of the winery, especially the cellar. Do not mention me. I will expose myself in due time."

"Okay," she shrugged, glaring at me with a cynical stare. As she walked away, she turned back to tell me, "Hey, Zinfandel … please don't scare Manuel. He's heard stories about the resident ghost. We really need him to help boost business. If he runs off …"

"I will be on my best behavior."

I now have identified my solicitor and my scribe but still no heir.

Walking from the Oppidum to the cellar, I passed by the orange tree where the racer snake caught my attention. We spoke not a word but locked eyes and understood what needed to be done.

And I realized I had forgotten to ask Kristobal and Bernadette about the rose-scented ghost.

THE CHARIOT

6 February in the Year of Their Lord 2003

Ah, whiskey! My vehicle of choice when traveling to an altered state of consciousness. As much as I love wine, it is whiskey that makes me truly happy. The liquor calms my nerves, awakens my libido and opens the door to my creative mind better than Father's opium. This "amber wine"—as I called it back in the days of Sooter's lumbermill—was the only elixir to ease the pain of the torture I endured when the men violated me. It also kept me warm many a night after I lost Lugh.

This evening, I indulged a bit as I rode along with Lily when she delivered herbs and vegetables to her customers. Her last stop is always the dance hall, one of my favorite places in all of Rivervine.

I did not actually need a ride to the saloon, just like I could have conjured my own bottle of whiskey. But I do need to be around people—to absorb their energy, have a barkeep pour the drink for me, witness lovers dancing, inspire lust among the patrons. I need the game, the companionship, the excitement. And I savor the way whiskey tastes when it has rested in a glass of ice for a few moments. The melted water mellows the flavor ever so slightly while the frozen crispness brings out the sweetness of the liquor.

The trip itself gives Lily and me a chance to catch up on one another's goings-on while the spirits of her plants travel to their new homes.

Usually, my tagging along is not a burden. I simply wait until we reach our destination, create the illusion of myself as an attractive woman, and wait for men to ask if they can buy me drinks. When Lily is ready to depart, I abandon the apparition and return with her—as my spirit self—to the farm.

Tonight was different. Manuel Chavez—the winery's new solicitor—accompanied her, which meant I needed to behave myself. Even though he grew up in the vineyard, the young man has not yet met me *in person*, so to speak. Decorum necessitated discretion.

Lily was clearly agitated during the trip. Throughout the ride, she kept flashing glances at me, afraid I would surely say or do something to upset poor Mr. Chavez. But I stayed on my best behavior—inconspicuous to the average observer. I did not make any noises or allow myself to be seen, although I could not avoid altering the temperature inside of the vehicle. As a discarnate vampire, my chi feeds off other forms of energy— ambient heat being one. I have no control over that. Besides, the nature spirits in Lily's herbs like it. The cold air prevents their delicate leaves from wilting.

Our trips to the saloon typically involve *me* offering *Lily* consolation. But tonight, it was I who needed a friendly shoulder to cry on. Unfortunately, with the good Catholic boy obstructing our privacy, my lament fell on distilled kernels of corn poured by Bobbie the barkeep. She always recognizes me and knows to put my drinks on Lily's tab if no one else offers to pick up the charge.

"What are you up to tonight, Zinfandel?" she asked, handing me my *bourbon on the rocks* as she calls it. This *bourbon* is some sort of American whiskey that I love so much. It has a deeper, richer flavor than Irish whiskey with less bitterness than Scotch and less sweetness than Canadian whiskey. The nose is a perfect mix of buttery vanilla and creamy caramel. "Did you come here with Lily and Manuel?"

"Shhh!" I hushed her. "Manuel does not yet know about me."

She leaned across the bar and whispered, "So how did you get here?"

"Oh, in the van," I answered quietly. "He did not see me."

"Can he see you now? Can anyone else? Or does it look like I'm talking to myself?"

"Do not worry. I made myself viewable to the public once I arrived at the dance hall."

"Whew! Good. So how are things going at Ferm …" she stopped in the middle of her thought to keep our confidentiality.

"That, my dear, is the whole reason I am here tonight," I answered, swirling my glass. "Four days ago, I learned that my brother is leaving me and the heir to the Comati vineyard is abdicating her legacy."

She looked at me with a gaping mouth and furrowed brow.

"I didn't know you had a brother."

"He usually keeps to himself. You may have heard him play music with me, though. He plays a cobza."

With her brow still furrowed, she shook her head, not knowing what a cobza was.

"It is an old stringed instrument that looks similar to a lute," I said.

The barkeep shook her head again and shrugged her shoulders.

"It sounds like a tinny guitar," I explained.

She propitiated me by nodding her head and saying, "Oh!" Even though I could tell she still did not understand.

Realizing I needed to move on with my story or risk losing her attention, I told her, "He and I often play duets late at night.

I play violin. Our favorite places are either under the orange tree on the property or in a cave at the base of the foothills."

Bobbie paused for a moment.

"Now that you mention it, I think I have heard you two," she said. "I usually work the late shift, and sometimes when I'm on my way home, I hear strange music coming from that direction. I always assumed it was the farmworkers. But the music didn't sound Mexican."

The barkeep excused herself to go pour a glass of soda water for Manuel and a man named Desmond Taylor—Bobbie's employer, the person who owns the dance hall. Lily had just formally introduced the two men in the business office, and they came to the bar to discuss wine purchases with Bobbie. While the men were talking, Lily went to the kitchen to discuss menu options with Chef Cheryl who is in charge of purchasing items for the restaurant inside the dance hall.

With no friends left talk to, my eyes scanned the room for strangers who might buy me drinks or ask me to dance. No one obliged, so I just sat there, swirling my glass as the ice water tempered the fiery kick of the liquor.

Lily finally wrapped up her business with the cook and headed back to the carriage. I shook off the illusory disguise and followed her out. Manuel arrived right as Lily opened the door and shot a *be quiet* glance to the back where I was sitting.

I made no sound. Neither did the other two humans. The entire trip home was quiet.

~ Fearn, the Ogham of Defense ~
Reading Lily's aura, I sensed that she was preoccupied with pressure from the local land peddler, Edie Clark, to sell the farm.

Miss Clark has been around Rivervine for decades. In fact, she is the one who originally sold the Black Land to the Divinorums in 1969. In recent years, Edie has approached Xavia and Sage numerous times about selling the property back to her so she can develop it for housing, shopping, and industrial purposes. The Divinorums have always refused. So have all the other Comatis with land she wants to seize.

In the meantime, the land peddler buys property surrounding Comati territory, hoping the pressure will inspire our farmers and homesteaders to sell their land.

The battle is all due to the increased demand for homes that offer an escape from city life but sit below the treacherous snowline of the Sierra Nevada mountains. Farmers want to keep the area because the soil is fertile and lies on a gentle slope, providing good drainage for the roots of their crops; the grapevines particularly appreciate the high ash content of the dirt. Ranchers find the expansive grassy fields ideal for livestock to graze. Non-farming families who live in Rivervine need employment, homes, medical care, shopping, recreation, and entertainment opportunities without having to drive their horseless carriages into New Helvetia or Yerba Buena. There is also a large number of people advocating for the nature spirits; these activists do not want the area developed at all. They would rather preserve the land to allow the wild animals to roam freely and the trees to grow majestically.

Adding to the controversy has been the tribadic love affair between Miss Clark and the late Comati bookstore owner, Dorothy Samuel.

In Comati culture, sex is not shameful, although it does carry inherent risks, as I mentioned in my lecture to the new recruits a while back.

But when the Russian and English men started *taming* the West, they brought with them religious views declaring love between couples of the same sex as an abomination. Once Sooter created New Helvetia, his men dismissed Comatis as savages, especially those who *lay with their own kind*.

Since starting the new era of Comatis, Xavia and Sage have embraced people from all walks of life. The business community of the greater New Helvetia area, however, has not been so tolerant.

When Dorothy died a few months ago after a brief battle with a rare blood disease, Edie grieved in secrecy, shame, and loneliness.

Our community convened a *rite of transition* for Dorothy. The ceremony served as our way of acknowledging that her soul may have left its physical shell but her spirit was still welcome to roam among us as one of the ancestors. If and when she decided to reincarnate, we would welcome her back as our kin.

Edie declined our invitation to attend the ceremony. The request itself was controversial. On the one hand, this rite was a celebration of the life of Dorothy Samuel. As Dorothy's lover, Edie deserved to be recognized as a highly honored mourner. On the other hand, she would have been *persona non grata* any other day—she did everything in her power to swindle our land from us. Xavia and Sage extended the invitation, informing the other community members they were free to boycott if their consciences so desired. Nobody boycotted. Everyone put their personal feelings aside—except Edie, who could not muster the gumption to face us.

No one in Edie's family or circle of friends and business acquaintances knew about the relationship, death, or grief.

Putting animosity aside, Xavia organized a grief basket for Edie that included a bottle of Fermata Cellars wine, a jar of Touchkoff honey, some homemade biscuits, and a crock of jam from Rhoads Home Herb Farm. All of Dorothy's friends signed a letter of sympathy, which was tucked inside the basket.

Lily delivered the present in person. I tagged along, without my illusory image but full of rage and intentions to disincarnate the bitch. However, something stopped my homicidal rage—and it had nothing to do with respect for the grieving.

We arrived at Edie's business office—the structure is quite grand in both height and width, with refined furnishings and decorations at every turn. The likelihood of presenting the gift in person seemed slim, so we dropped off the basket with the woman whose desk was in the front.

While we were there, the head bitch herself stepped out from around a corner and made eye contact with Miss Rhoads. I expected the auratic energy to be volatile, but both women held their ground, neither showing emotion of any kind. The difference, though, was that Lily's aura burned with hatred while Dorothy's widow repressed lustful feelings toward the young herbalist.

We left without a word spoken, but the interaction gave me a devious idea—one I would file away for a later date.

~ Ifin, the Ogham of the Ancestors ~

My thoughts returned to the current moment once Lily stopped the carriage in front of Manuel's new home. He no longer lives in the farmworkers' quarters where the orange tree grows. Nowadays, he resides in one of the apartments in the Mercantile District—a building owned by the Polish immigrant

Casimir Fermanski, who also operates a small restaurant a few blocks away.

Mr. Chavez could easily have walked home from the dance hall tonight, but freezing rain was in the forecast so Lily offered him a ride.

After he left the vehicle, the young woman broke her silence to me.

"Thank you," she said calmly as she headed back to her house. "For behaving yourself tonight."

"Have I ever given you reason to doubt my sense of decorum?"

"No. But we've never been in this situation before."

"What situation?"

"Where we've had to reintroduce a previous farmworker into Comati business. None of the Mexicans believe you exist. They all think we're devil worshipers."

"Satanists who make wine for their Eucharist," I noted sarcastically.

"It's a very fragile, delicate situation, and I don't want to scare him off," Lily contended. "He's not only the Fermata Cellars marketing director." She trailed off as tears started choking her voice. She finally spit out, "He's my oldest friend."

When we finally arrived back at Lily's house, I sensed she needed solitude, so I nodded "goodnight" and left the young woman to her thoughts. As I wandered back to the cave, my own mind wandered back to the days when I knew everyone and everything in Rivervine.

~ Eabhadh, the Ogham of Community ~

Miss Rhoads lives in the small guest cottage on her parents' property. She moved in at the age of twenty, in the Year of Their

Lord 1997, shortly after her father died. The young woman had just completed her first two years of college, but after her father's responsibilities fell on her shoulders, she did not enroll in any further courses. She has kept to herself for the most part ever since. Her only social interactions involve either Comati rituals or business calls. She has no consort or friends outside of work, although now that her childhood playmate Manuel has returned to Rivervine, she might open her heart to someone, but I sense something odd about him—something … queer. It is a queerness that she does not share.

The two children grew up across the river from each other.

The Rhoads Home Herb Farm is a five-acre parcel across the river from the winery. The Divinorums own the eighty-three acres to the north and east. A Russian family—the Touchkoffs—have a one-acre site northwest of Lily's cottage where they raise bees to make honey and beeswax. The mercantile district is the three-acre southwest corner of town; it is a charming mix of stores, restaurants, and offices on the first level with apartments upstairs. The old Castillo manor, which is now owned by Scott and Leslie Tuft—the parents of my acolyte, Erin—sits on the final acre of the ninety-three-acre site formerly known as the Black Land.

The Comati territory today is bordered by Kildare Lane in the north, Kepher Road in the east, Vinefera Boulevard in the south, and St. Bernadette Lane in the west. The Vitus River runs northeast to southwest through most of town.

Saint Bernadette's Catholic church sits in the far northwest corner of St. Bernadette Lane and Soubirous Drive. It was built in April of 1979 to commemorate the one-hundredth anniversary of the death of the young namesake from Lourdes, France.

Father Armando Echeveria had been sent to Rivervine a few years earlier to investigate the mysterious regeneration of the Divinorums' grape vines, to determine if the new growth was divine or sinister in nature. I kept my distance, never showing myself to the priest, but Father Kristobal could not help himself. He was so excited to have another man of the cloth to talk to, he immediately befriended Armando, telling him the full history of Rivervine.

The two men talked for days over many, many bottles of wine. Armando developed such a taste for the zinfandel that he convinced the New Helvetia diocese to let him build a church next to the vineyards.

Fermata Cellars has been making the wine for Saint Bernadette's ever since. At first the Divinorums' produced a young wine that was heavily blended with Mission grapes grown at other parishes in the diocese. This combination became Fermata Cellars' *Tango* blend. A few years ago, Father Armando developed a tremor in his right hand, causing him to frequently spill the wine during the Eucharist. The red liquid stained the white altar cloths so badly that he asked Xavia and Sage if they would mind switching to a white wine instead.

The Divinorums agreed and started researching white wines made in the area near Lourdes, France. They settled on the Spanish Basque *Hondarrabi zuri* grape that was fermented into a dry, sparkling varietal called *Txakoli*.

My reverie was interrupted when I heard a telepathic call from my acolytes.

~ Two of Cups ~

Assuming this was an emergency of some sort, I rushed to their defense, finding Tanya, Thomas, and Erin gathered at the Order's ritual site.

A flame burned from the center oil lamp, giving off the scent of sandalwood oil. Thomas and Tanya were waiting for me in their respective quarters, decked out in hooded robes of bright blue—the Comati color of couples announcing their nuptials. My eyes were quick to notice the sparkling diamond hiding in the braided gold band on Tanya's left ring finger. Turning to the south quadrant, I saw Erin staying warm in a red coat with a matching knit cap and mittens.

Taking my place in the east, I looked to the couple in blue and asked, "I take it congratulations are in order?"

For once, Tanya shouted out an answer before Thomas did.

"Yes!" she cried. "I'm so excited! I can hardly contain myself!"

"Are you happy for us, Vondella?" Thomas wondered, his voice shaky. "I bought the ring with my first paycheck from the winery."

Before I could answer, I spotted my brother watching from the high grass.

"I see what is going on," I thought to myself.

Returning to Thomas' question, I responded gleefully. "Of course, darlings! This is wonderful news. Have you set a date yet, or is it too soon?"

"June twenty-ninth," Tanya answered. "We already have it planned. We're having it at the winery. Xavia is going to officiate, and Brigid is going to sing. Oh, my god, I am so excited! I can't wait!"

Thomas had a fearful look on his face. "Are you mad that we didn't tell you first, ask for your blessing? We didn't know the protocol, so we just started making plans. We were just so excited."

"Shhh" I moved toward him, covering his lips with my pointer finger. Smiling, I assured him with complete genuineness, "My darling boy, this truly is wonderful news."

"Great!" Tanya cried. "So what do we do now?"

"You have much to plan," I answered. "You do not need *approval* from me as you are masters of your own will. But if it is my *blessing* you seek, I give it to you."

Tanya shrieked with joy and rushed over to hug me. Thomas gradually joined the embrace.

As the three of us let go, I tried to gather a sense of what Erin was feeling. Was she happy, sad, afraid, indifferent?

Rage. That was the emotion I sensed from her—not about Thomas and Tanya but something else. I did not know what.

As the three acolytes left, I headed over to the place where Anton was hiding. I knew damn well why he was there.

"So you have forgiven them?" I scoffed. "If I remember correctly, you were quite upset with me for sparing their lives. Hmmm. Whatever made you change your mind? Their fertile loins perhaps?"

"The tribe has adopted them, and they have proven their worth over the last three months," he answered in the reserved tone of voice that has become his trademark. "Thomas and Tanya are going to wed one week after the summer solstice. I want to be with Brigid as soon as possible."

I struggled not to fumble with my words or reveal the true level of my anxiety.

"Do Xavia and Sage know your plans?" I huffed. "Does Brigid? Do Thomas and Tanya? Does Erin?" Finally, with my fury boiling over, I yelled, "Am I the last to know about this?"

"Erin does not yet know about my plan to reincarnate inside Tanya's womb," he said diplomatically. "We decided to wait to tell her or anyone else about the birth. There is too much change going on right now. Besides, her permission is not needed in this transaction. Neither is yours, which is why you were not notified earlier. The only reason Xavia and Sage know is because Brigid and I sought their counsel after Iemmol."

Stifling my rage, I had to ask, "Did you compel my impressionable young acolytes into getting married so quickly? And now that I think about it, did you compel Brigid into falling in love with you?"

"Those are all reasonable questions, sister," he answered. "No. I compelled no one in any of this. I want to start my new life with complete honesty and integrity. No secrets, no shame."

Something was off kilter in this whole thing. It may have been bias on my part, but right or wrong, this was not my decision to make. Thomas and Tanya were both of legal age to marry—Tanya turned eighteen on the twenty-third of September; Thomas, as I learned last month, is nineteen. They have, of their own free will, agreed to this plan, which has been approved by Brigid's parents.

I kissed my brother on the cheek and assured him, "I love you, Anton. But I need to be alone to sort through my thoughts. I will spend tonight in the wine cellar."

"As you wish, Vondella."

We nodded goodbye as I left, choosing to walk to the winery instead of spaceshifting there. During the stroll, I let go of my worries, succumbing to the river's icy vapor as the crispness mollified my spirit.

I realized that with this being February, there probably weren't many farmworkers on the property, so I took a detour by way of the orange tree and conjured my violin. The advantage of being a violinist is you can cry on your own shoulder. The soothing sound of a concerto in G minor mended the cobbled patchwork of my buckskin heart. My friend the racer snake danced as I played.

A few moments later, the dreadful, tinny sound of a cord in E major disrupted my musing. The racer snake scurried away.

Putting down my instrument, I acknowledged my brother as the cause of the interruption.

Looking at him nonchalantly, I asked, "Can I help you?"

"I want you to get your wrath out now—before the next ritual, before the wedding, before any other inappropriate occasion where you might lose your temper."

Closing my eyes and inhaling a deep breath, I exhaled with, "Peace be with you."

"You are thinking more than that; I know you," he insisted, dismissing my attempted olive branch. "Repressing your feelings will not help. They will only fester and cause your temper to explode at a later time—most likely when there are people celebrating a happy occasion. Let us get this out now, in private."

"You do not need to know my thoughts. They will dissipate in good time."

"Oh, dear sister. Still waters run far too deep with you. Let me stick my big toe in that emotional lake of yours. How about … you tell me … how you really feel about Thomas and Tanya getting married this year? Or how you feel about me leaving you so I can reincarnate? Or how you feel about Brigid and me being soulmates?"

"I do not know how I feel about any of this!" I shouted back. "How dare you come at me and disrupt my Zen? I admit my anger often gets the best of me, but you do not need to incite it."

He glared at me, sensing the simmering wrath I fought to suppress. I looked away for a moment, then took a deep breath and spit out the words clogging my mind.

"This decision seems like you are only thinking of you and Brigid," I said. "Two other people—and their respective families—are part of this decision. You may have received their permission, but have you honestly thought this whole thing through? How do you know they are the right parents for you? They are all so young and have so much life to experience. You are interfering with their free will. "

His honesty was equally brutal.

"What do I care about parents? Our father left you to die in a fire while he was off smoking opium. Mother cared more about our other five brothers who did not have the crazy blood like I did. Parents mean nothing to me."

"Do you honestly want another miserable family experience? Thomas and Tanya have only been Comatis for three months. We know very little about them. There are other fertile couples who have been part of the tribe much longer. Why not appeal to them?"

"Thomas and Tanya have auras that radiate on the dark end of the spectrum. The other Comati couples are too light for me. I must have parents that understand me."

"Point taken, but if you reincarnate and your plans do not manifest, have you any idea how brokenhearted you might become?"

"More so than I am now? I have nothing to lose. I hate being discarnate. My new life could not possibly be worse than my last one."

I had no rebuttal to his last statement. Hanging my head in defeat, I asked, "How much longer do I have you?"

"Until Sauin."

"And what of your cobza?"

"I will bequeath it to Lily's friend, the one who once was a farmworker."

"The solicitor? Does he even play?"

"All Comatis play music. Manuel will learn. He is Lily's best friend. Our instruments must stay together."

This was true: My violin needed to be with Anton's cobza for now and all eternity. The legacy of the Romani instruments has lasted for centuries. Now was not the time to break tradition.

"I am so accustomed to being the one who runs off to join a lover," I finally confessed. "Being left behind is not a feeling that suits me. I know it is not because you are angry with me or no longer love me. Yet I still feel rejected. I never thought I could be scared, but you have been my anchor all these years. Losing you now brings not only sorrow but fear as I remember how badly I grieved for you after you died and I was still alive. Now you will be alive and I will still be dead. You may not even remember me after you are reborn. Oh, how I do hate playing solos!"

Anton held me in a tight embrace, which we held for quite a long time. When we finally broke away, he kissed me on the check and headed toward the vineyards to play a lively melody in a major key, drawing his usual audience of foxes, skunks, bats, and other creatures of the night. He strummed with a happiness I have never heard from him before. Although my wrath still simmered below the surface, my love for him outweighed any other emotion at the moment.

THE LOVERS

14 February in the Year of Their Lord 2003

Tanya—bless her heart—called out to me this morning. She was not at the standard ritual site at Erin's house but rather in her own sleeping space in her home on the outskirts of town. When I arrived, I found the young woman sitting cross-legged on her bed with eyes closed and wrists resting on her knees—her index fingers making circles with her thumbs. Her breath traveled heavily through her nose and exhaled through her mouth with a droning chant of, "ah-ooh-mm."

On each side of her bed, a small table was adorned with several oil lamps—the oil had been tinted red. Gardenia incense smoked inside a small bowl on top of the stand on her right side. To her left was a short glass of apple juice and a note that read, "Vondella: I call upon you to guide me this Valentine's Day. Please help me make this day special for my beloved, Thomas. Awen, Tanya."

Accepting her invitation, I stood before her, manifesting an apparition and announcing my presence.

"Hello Tanya. How can I help you?"

The young woman was so giddy with excitement, she could barely yelp out a proper greeting.

"This is my first time having a boyfriend—well, fiancé—for Valentine's Day. I don't know what to do. I want to make this day special for both of us. Can you help me?"

"What did you have in mind?"

"Oh, I don't know. Anything, I guess. Did you and Lugh ever celebrate Valentine's Day together?"

The young woman caught herself in a potential faux pas. "Or is that too heartbreaking to talk about? Oh, Vondella, I am so sorry!"

"Do not worry, darling," I assured her, "I am not offended. To answer your question, yes, Lugh and I had a very nice Valentine's Day once."

"Oh, tell me about it … please!"

The smile could not escape my face as I indulged in a little storytelling.

"It was the Year of Their Lord 1848. The Irish Catholics had just built Saint Patrick's Catholic Church a year and a half earlier."

Tanya looked at me puzzled.

"You know it as Saint Bernadette's. I will explain the name change another time."

"Oh, okay." she said and motioned for me to continue.

"Lugh and I went to mass and listened to Father Seamus talk about a scribe named Valentino, and how when he was alive, the pagan Romans imprisoned him for practicing Christianity. As a prisoner, Valentino was ordered to tutor a young girl named Julia who was the blind daughter of his jailer. During the festival of Lupercalia on February fourteenth, the young girl's eyesight was mysteriously restored. Fearing the populace would interpret this as the will of the Christian God, Emperor Claudius the Second had Valentino executed. The scribe's last act was a letter written to his young student signed, 'your Valentine.' The Christian world has been sending *valentines* ever since."

"Oh my God, that is so macabrely beautiful!"

"Yes, it was," I hung my head for a moment but then smiled. "After church, Lugh and I walked back to his tent, passing by a woman selling apple dumplings. He bought us a couple, and we washed them down with a dram of whiskey."

"Oh Vondella!" Tanya called out. "That is so sweet!"

I wiped away the hint of tears that had started to leak from my eyes. Taking a deep sniff and standing up straight, I answered nobly, "Thank you. It was a beautiful day."

The young woman leapt from her bed and hugged me tightly. Looking me in the eyes, she asked, "Do you want to talk about it? You can tell me anything. Really!"

I had forgotten Tanya was a healer. I should have anticipated her empathy. Nonetheless, she had called me to help her, not unload my deep-rooted, complex emotions. I refocused my energy back to the needs of my acolyte. Taking a deep breath, I advised her, "You should write Thomas a love letter. That would be traditional. Tell him exactly how you feel—what it is that lets you know, without a doubt, that he is your soulmate. You could also bake him some cookies or some other treat that he likes to eat."

"Do you have a recipe for apple dumplings?"

I chuckled, "No, but you might be able to ask …"

It dawned on me that Old Town Rivervine did not have a bakery. Several Comatis baked their own breads and sweets, but no one did it commercially. And no one I knew had a recipe for apple dumplings.

"You're the best, Vondella!" she shrieked and jumped into another hug. Pulling me tighter, she added, "Thank you so much!"

"For what?"

"Every Comati owns a business, right? Well, Thomas and I can start a bakery when we graduate from high school."

"That, darling girl, is a most wonderful idea," I cheered, albeit with a reserved, calm voice.

Thomas and Tanya both still lived with their parents just outside of Old Town. Since their families were not already part of the Comati community, the couple would need to start a life within the sacred boundaries of the Black Land. Establishing a bakery in the merchants district was a fabulous idea. The bakery could be on the ground floor and their living quarters on the second.

With the epiphany clear, I smiled wide and excused myself.

"I should go now and let you finish getting ready for school. I hope you and Thomas have a most wonderful Valentine's Day!"

"Thank you!" she shrieked, then yelled, "Wait! This is for you!" and handed me the apple juice.

I accepted the small glass and lifted it up to her, cheering, "Sláinte!" as the amber juice slid down my throat.

Shedding my illusory image, I left her sleeping space. The glass fell to the floor.

~ Nuin, Strength from Deep Roots ~

Relieved to escape that temporal composition, I took refuge in my wine cellar and allowed the memories to run their course. I had three hours to spare before the doors to the tasting room opened.

Every year on Valentine's Day, Fermata Cellars is abuzz with lovers seeking a romantic escapade filled with wine, chocolate, and candlelight. The Divinorums and I are happy to oblige, of course. Xavia and Sage partner with the Touchkoffs' bee farmers for candles and Rhoads Home Herb Farm for sweet treats. All the items are combined into a basket that is sold as a

Romance Package. They even include a pair of wine glasses with an etched image of a fermata—the musical notation to prolong a note or rest—and the words "Sustain My Love."

Although Valentine's Day is by far the most profitable day of the year for Fermata Cellars, I prefer to spend the fourteenth of February hiding in the downstairs cellar playing my violin. Music is my catharsis, and the guests take great delight in the ethereal sound; it adds to the hauntingly romantic ambiance and mysterious charm of the winery.

This morning, though, whatever grief or emotional turmoil I was feeling needed to run its course before I rosined my bow. Otherwise the E string would go flat and nothing I played would evoke romance for the listeners. Their day would be ruined, and sales would be nil.

I had to repress the festering funk leaking from the annals of my mind.

My soul still yearns for that handsome Irish man who abandoned Rivervine for the Catholic heaven. I have not yet recovered from the trauma of not only watching him die but the rejection of him not coming for me in the afterlife. He could have spent eternity with me, but he instead chose to follow Saint Peter.

Nobody loves me. No one has ever truly loved me. The only man I ever gave my heart to forgot about me. That is not love. You do not forget your one true love, not even when the veil separates you.

When Lugh was alive, he was the only man who valued me. He treasured me. None of the other women in New Helvetia or Yerba Buena could tempt him away from me. He was loyal and kind—he embodied every personality trait that actually mattered when it came to affairs of the heart. And, oh God! Was he ever an amazing lover! He and I could harmonize whenever we climaxed together—which was often.

My heart shattered when our fantasy life was cut short and I had to go back to being a ward of my father.

Xin Hsüan was a cruel son of a bitch, even to his only daughter. He allowed men to violate me so long as they paid him a worthy sum. I was in high demand from a young age. Once Sooter's men arrived in Comati territory, they found my Oriental features enticing. My adeptness for music and dancing added to the attraction, but what the men valued most was my barren womb.

When I was alive, a woman who was raped was considered damaged goods and unworthy of marriage. But her rapist suffered no consequences. If a baby was conceived of that rape, the child was shamed and labeled a bastard with no rights to its father's inheritance. If the rape victim tried to end the pregnancy, she was considered a murderer. If the rapist was married, the victim was considered an adulteress.

If a man raped a young girl and tore her womb so much that she could not bear children, no one cared. With the risk of pregnancy negated, the girl was then considered a toy for men's entertainment. If the girl's father was a lucrative whoremonger, he capitalized on this advantage.

If the girl was Chinese, she was in high demand. Not only did her exotic looks attract men, but she was also not part of the Christian culture that saved sex for marriage—at least for women. Men were allowed to freely engage in fornication and adultery, but white women were expected to stay chaste. There were some tavern girls—mostly widows, orphans, and abandoned wives, who followed the men west and filled the role of temporary sexual companion as needed.

Back in those days, sex was entertainment for men. I am not sure if that has changed at all in the modern era, but there came a point in my life—after my breasts grew in and my figure gained some curves—that I realized I actually enjoyed entertaining men. Well, some of them.

Before I met Lugh, I thrived on an appreciative audience. If the men adored me, flattered me and succumbed to my charms, then I felt almost vindicated that my fathered had turned me out. I at least sensed the power I had over *their* emotions and *their* actions. And because I did not have to worry about pregnancy, I was free to tease these lumbermen unabashedly.

Some of the men were brutes, though. They were vicious, rude, and unappreciative. My father still took their money, but I fled each bed as soon as the customer kicked me out of his sleeping chamber. Every time, I would cry all the way home.

And then there were times when I was too sore to handle another invasion so soon after the last go around. Xin Hsüan did not care. He took the men's money and threatened to stuff my vagina with hot ashes if I did not comply. It was the same threat he used when I was ill or having my monthly cycle—which some men found to be erotic.

This is not to say my life was entirely without gratification. I had my fair share of sexual climax—always through the agency of a customer, of course, as no one would consider me anything other than a temporary plaything to be discarded after use. Some of the patrons even taught me a thing or two about sexual hypnosis and Kama Sutra.

When Lugh came into my life, I regretted having so many lovers in my past—whether they were consensual or forced. I had spread my sexual energy too thin and given too much of my personal power to those who were unworthy. I wished I had concentrated all of my energy on him.

My biggest regret, of course, was the possibility of passing on my sickness. If the Army had not hung him in March of 1848, Lugh might possibly have suffered the same ailments as I did.

When Sooter's lumberjacks first came here in 1841, there were not many of them. Seven years later when James Marshall discovered gold in the American River, it was still quite a while before the Vitus River saw the rush of miners looking for the Mother Lode. By the summer solstice that year, Lugh was gone, my heart was cold, and hard, round bumps covered my vagina.

I thought nothing of them at first because I did not know what they were and they did not hurt. I would not have even known they were there if one of my customers had not complained to my father; the gentleman thought they were a form of leprosy and he feared his penis would fall off he penetrated me. A few weeks later, I developed a reddish brown rash all over the palms of my hands and bottoms of my feet.

The worst part was after our summer solstice celebration. I tried to play my violin, but my fingers would not obey me. People called out to me, but I did not recognize their faces. My head throbbed as if some miserable little sprite were banging a hammer inside my skull. I fell to the ground, and the rest of my life became a blur. After that day, I frequently struggled to know where I was or who I was.

For all my memory lapses, the night of the fire replays vividly through my mind. The voice of the prospector demanding I make his dinner, the fury of my refusal, the smell of blood dripping from the cut I gave him with my own fingernails, the flash of the fire as it scorched my flesh—I remember every detail and the effects of that night on all six of my senses.

But today I am here in the cellar, playing my violin. My fingers are obeying me, and there is no trace of syphilis or fire. I think I will spend the day playing traditional Irish ballads for the lovers upstairs.

We shall see if Mr. Chavez reacts at all to the mysterious music coming from downstairs.

~ Coll, the Ogham of Wisdom ~

Judging by the clamor of footfalls I heard above my head today, I would say the new Fermata Cellars solicitor was too busy to question where the music was coming from. I tried to listen every now and then to the voices upstairs, but I never heard anyone talk about anything other than wine.

When the tasting room finally closed for the evening, I put down my violin and detected a strong odor of goat in the wine cellar.

Krampus?

"We make apple strudel!" There was no mistaking that guttural, bleating voice. He was talking to me telepathically.

"Where are you?" I called.

"Tanya's house. Her mom is at work. Today is Valentine's Day. I am helping!"

I shifted over there to find out what was going on. I found Thomas and Tanya rolling out thin layers of pastry on the kitchen table. My Austrian goat-herder friend was peeling apples.

"Hi, Vondella!" the two youths cried.

Krampus started laughing. "See, I told you!"

"Our bakery is going to specialize in apple strudel!" Thomas cheered. "Krampus is teaching us how to make it."

"It is from Austria—my homeland!" the goat herder boasted.

"Krampus told us it's called 'love letter dough,'" Tanya explained. "It's so thin, you can read your love letters through it! You wrap it in layers around the apple mixture and it comes out all nice and crispy. We thought it would be appropriate for us to make it at our shop, so he's teaching us."

"How wonderful!" I applauded. "I love how you are embracing your induction into the Comati family."

Speaking of families, I took a quick glance around the young woman's home and found the place to be so clean and tidy, it seemed as if she lived alone. With the strudel production making a mess in the kitchen, I thought I could straighten it up before her mother and father came home from work.

"Tanya, dear, will your parents be home soon? Perhaps Krampus and I should take our leave."

She hung her head and rolled the dough with added fury.

"My mom works three jobs. She won't be home until late tonight. My dad is …" she choked back tears of shame. "… In Mule Creek."

I knew she was referring to the state prison, and I knew how embarrassed she was to disclose that detail.

"Do not cry, Tanya!" Krampus rushed to her side. Thomas was already holding her in a tight embrace.

"This is why I want a *real* family, not a shit show like I have now!" Her tears gushed. Both Thomas and Krampus caught them. I walked over and kissed the young woman's forehead.

"My darling girl," I said. "You will always be welcome in our tribe."

NINE OF SWORDS

19 March in the Year of Their Lord 2003

The United States now occupies my homeland.

President George W. Bush has sent troops to Sumer. Even though it has been six thousand years since I first bathed in the holy rivers, my spirit is still connected to the land, and every now and then, nightmares resurface.

The problem with repressing emotion is that it festers. When the feelings stem from a previous life, they must travel through the exhaustive layers filtering one's current psyche. In the struggle to free itself, the mind faces a dilemma between seeking resolution and enjoying the bliss of ignorance. When the agitation finally reaches a tipping point, one's demons escape. Such was the case with me today.

~ Ten of Swords ~

My night usually ends with a visit to the vineyard where I practice tai chi among the vines before the sun rises. I then do a similar routine in the wine cellar before the workers arrive.

With my chi cleared this morning, the rush of information set in. The visions were so vivid—past, present, and future. None of it was good. All of it was overwhelming. The timing was horrible.

I needed to build my own army here in Rivervine. This was not the time to lose my focus. And yet I could not redirect my attention back to the task at hand.

Visions of the current invasion hit me right as the new solicitor and two other employees were arriving to work. Although they had no influence on the distressing political climate, I was unable to spare them the experience of an authentic haunting.

Hauntings as most people know them are rarely *intelligent.* That is, apparitions do not usually converse with spectators. If you ask the phantoms questions, they seldom answer. They are merely imprints of memories left behind by the ghosts of people's minds. The hallucinations themselves are rarely sentient.

As I have mentioned before, a human is comprised of three parts: a physical body, a mind, and chi. Chi is spiritual energy. Energy requires fuel. Mental energy is fueled by trauma, orgasm, memories, or some other emotional experience. Once the chi has consumed the fuel, it produces waste. And that is what a typical haunting is: the effluent of a disembodied mind. Sometimes that effluent is perceived—emotionally, psychically, the through the physical senses—by humans or other animals in the earthly realm. Even plants can be affected.

When my visions today ended, all I could do was stand in the corner of the cellar and pout, but my anger manifested in the form of flickering lights upstairs and clanking sounds traveling up the staircase. From what Xavia and Sage told me later, the young women working the tasting room were agitated with one another, and the screen of the money machine blinked with bizarre codes. These events were all beyond my control.

Xavia was quick to rush down to the cellar with a bowl of incense—a mix of jasmine and oud wood. It is my favorite and she knows that will help calm my anxious spirit.

But I was still so upset that her efforts were of little comfort. By afternoon, she had given up hope and went back upstairs, letting my anger finish running its course. She returned a couple hours later, this time with Sage, who had brought his guitar.

The three of us had a long talk. We sang. We played music. We healed … somewhat.

Our meeting dislodged myriad blocked emotions as memories poured forth from all three of our points of view. We discussed how those memories related to the current status of the world stage and what it meant for our local tribe. The three of us agreed on one thing: Whether it was New World or Old World, the iron shroud of Adam is growing and the world is either too distracted or too apathetic to unravel it.

~ Four of Pentacles ~

Memories are like lucky pennies. They're hard to let go of, even when we know the only *luck* they hold is in our imagination. And yet we cling to them, unable to give away these coins because they carry the value of our belief. We become paralyzed in whatever currency they hold, be it grief, pride, happiness, anger, love, or any other strong emotion.

The seeds of today's tantrum sprouted about a decade after Xavia and Sage returned from Vietnam.

A tyrant named Saddam Hussein came into power in Sumer—a country now known as Iraq. As the years went on, Hussein became obsessed with authority and paranoid of losing it. So he invaded neighboring countries—not just as a push for political and religious control but also for the ability to mine rock oil from below the ground.

Throughout his rise to fame, the United States knew Hussein was a madman with the potential to grow out of control. But America had a greater enemy in Sumer's neighbor to the east. In my day, it was called Persia, but today it is called Iran. Then-president Ronald Reagan gave money, weapons, and information to the Hussein regime in an effort to defeat their common opponent.

Once the threat was neutralized, Hussein moved his attention south to a country that, in my day, was part of Sumer but is now the independent nation of Kuwait. His goal, just like in Persia, was to control the rock oil as well as the spiritual and political leadership.

By this time, George W. Bush was president of the United States. He remains in power today.

Bush stood up against Hussein and led a coalition of numerous countries to impose sanctions against the dictator.

As Hussein's power weakened, he blamed everyone but himself, including the Ma'dān people—the indigenous tribe of Sumer that inhabits the marsh between the Tigris and Euphrates rivers.

This area was the place where I experienced my first incarnation as a pit viper living in a pomegranate tree. Today there are no more pit vipers or pomegranates in the marshes. There is nothing but reeds now. The original flora and fauna have all become extinct. If Hussein has his way, the Ma'dān people will become extinct too.

Truth be told, the tribe actually *was* hiding rebel soldiers in the marshes. When Hussein found out, he retaliated by developing a system of canals that drained the water. Some of the *canals* he built were wider than the Euphrates *River*. In ten years' time, the marshes had turned to deserts and Hussein had begun a full-scale assault on rebel forces, using poisonous gas and threatening to use deadly irradiated minerals.

This man—this brutal, evil dictator—is the single biggest threat to peace and democracy in the region. If the United States *does not* intervene, the Ma'dān people *will* die. Hussein will continue terrorizing his own people, neighboring countries, and the United States, which he sees as "the great Satan." He is the Constantine of the Middle East, the great fearmonger, the false prophet.

Yet if the U.S. *does* intervene, thousands of military service members from not only America but other allied countries as well will die. What concerns me almost as much is the knowledge that a small handful of affluent business leaders will grow their wealth exponentially by selling goods and services to the United States military, other countries, and outlaw militias around the world.

I am additionally worried that this conflict will never end and it will be fought on two fronts: a ground war in Sumer and spiritual battle in Rivervine.

~ King of Pentacles ~

The root cause of the deadly friction in the modern Middle East is the battle over a piece of turf. This *holy land* is not the marsh. Instead, it is a place that did not even exist in my first lifetime. Rather, the location is almost seven hundred miles away in a place they call *Jerusalem*.

My original adversary was a man named Adam. He worshiped the Sumerian god of creation named Anu and believed that he was Anu's *chosen one*.

Adam became jealous of my friendship with his wife, Eve, so he devised a story making me the villain.

The storyteller passed on the false narrative to his sons, and they passed it on to their sons. Twenty generations later, his descendent—a man named Abraham—continued the line of noblesse oblige and enjoyed great wealth as a prosperous sheep herder and peddler who roamed between Ur, Canaan, and Memphis grazing his sheep and selling his wares.

But Abraham had a little problem.

He was old. So was his wife, Sarah, who had long since stopped menstruating; biologically, there was no way she could even conceive a child, let alone bear one. They had no children to inherit either the great wealth he had amassed or the hereditary line of spiritual nobility.

Storytellers agree on the abovementioned facts, but here is where I deviate in my scholarship.

I suspect Abraham started suffering from dementia. Add to that the temptations of the flesh at bazaars where he frequently vended, and it is no wonder that he happened upon a pagan dancer named Hājar one day when he was in Egypt.

Funny how no matter how old and ugly a man is, if he is wealthy, beautiful women still flock to him. Abraham was no exception. He may have been suited to old age, but he knew lust when he felt it. Acting on his male impulses, he took the young woman back to his tent and lavished her with fine jewels and even finer wine. Unable to resist his urges, he soon found himself in a position to sire a child.

With Hājar now pregnant and unable to dance for a living, she appealed to Abraham to be a responsible father and take her as a second wife. Attempting to explain this arrangement to his first wife, Abraham told Sarah that Anu had spoken to him, telling him to become the *progenitor of nations*. He was not only commanded to plant his seed as widely as possible, but he was additionally tasked with building a holy kingdom in the mountains on the banks of the Jordan River.

It was a difficult conversation, but Sarah, heartbroken that her husband had been unfaithful and grudgingly jealous of the beautiful young immigrant, agreed to the arrangement, so long as Hājar served as her slave.

"Oh, I can do better than that, my Queen," Hājar told Sarah. "I can help you too to have a child."

In pagan Egypt and Sumer, dancing was done not only to enchant men but also to act as a form of shamanic medicine. Women danced for other women to ease the pains of menstruation, overcome barriers to conception, ensure women's survival of childbirth, and deliver healthy babies into the world.

Sarah was skeptical, but, desperate to feel her own child grow inside her, she agreed.

After twelve years without any luck, Sarah finally conceived a child. Nine months later, a beautiful, healthy boy named Isaac was born.

Hājar's son, Ishmael, was thirteen years old at this point. Until the birth of Isaac, Abraham had doted on Ishmael, promising *him* the inheritance of God's kingdom. But with Sarah now the mother of what their tribe considered the "legitimate" son of Abraham, jealousy and rage started to infiltrate the ranks.

"You are *not* a holy man!" Sarah scolded Ishmael. "You were born out of demented lust to a harlot witch. She is Egyptian. I am Sumerian. My son, Isaac, is the rightful heir!"

Ishmael fired back. "Do not speak to me with such insolence, woman! I *am* a holy man—the twenty first generation of Adam, the *first* son of Abraham, God's chosen progenitor. This is *my* land. *Your* son—who is only here because of *my* mother's witchcraft—shall bow to *me*!"

Both Abraham and Hājar overheard the scuffle. The young woman turned to her husband and pleaded, "Sarah is old. She will die soon. I am young. I can give you many more sons. Send

Sarah and Isaac out into the desert. No one will miss them. Your destiny is with *me*."

Abraham considered Hājar's proposal. The deeper he meditated, the more shame he felt for betraying Sarah all those years ago. She had been a loyal and loving wife, keeping true to her commitment to help her husband build his empire. How could he have broken such a beautiful heart?

The patriarch meditated on the moral dilemma. His knee-jerk reaction was to search for a means of concealing his sin, but the more he thought about it, the more guilt consumed him.

One late autumn night, during a full moon, he built a large bonfire and asked the ancestors for advice.

Of course, Adam answered.

He told Abraham to advise the tribe that Isaac was indeed the rightful heir and they all should immediately begin building the holy city on top of the hill.

Adam then commanded the three of us to leave.

Yes, you read that correctly. There were *three* of us. I was Ishmael's twin sister and this was my *second* incarnation. One I have tried to forget until now.

My tantrum today in the wine cellar was caused by the cavalcade of memories pouring forth. They were all so vivid. And I could feel the soul of my long-lost brother from eight thousand miles away. He is following Adam's instructions, this time in Sumer, still fighting the losing battle for his rightful place in his father's empire.

~ The Gods ~

There is no mention of me in any holy scripture because daughters were not considered important enough to document their births. I was actually born first, which makes *me* the eldest of Abraham's children.

When we were cast out, I begged my mother to take us back to the city of Ur where scribes were writing in cuneiform and studying math and astronomy. I wanted so badly to devour the knowledge and wisdom of the ancients.

Ishmael was not so keen on scholastic pursuits, but he *was* good with his hands. I told him that in Ur, he could learn masonry and agriculture—and he could find a nice Sumerian woman to marry.

My brother would have none of that. A teenage boy filled with ego and hormones, he considered himself the *rightful* heir to Anu's kingdom; it was an insult for him to accept any fate less than that. Ishmael vowed to get his vengeance on the ingrates, Sarah and her usurper son, Isaac.

As we wandered the desert, Ishmael's hatred toward women festered. He blamed our mother for seducing Abraham and using sorcery to help Sarah give birth to Isaac. He then blamed *me* for being headstrong and refusing to join a harem where a wealthy husband would pay for the three of us to live comfortably.

But I did not want to join a harem. I wanted to learn. I wanted to go east to the city of Ur. Ishmael said it was not proper for women to be educated, so he had us press on, taking us south into the barren desert.

Our constant bickering did nothing to preserve the scant amount of water that our father had left for us in an animal skin. The dehydration and anxiety caused our mother to become hysterical. She started running back and forth between two mountains, searching for water, claiming she could force herself to lactate and thereby feed us, but she needed to hydrate herself first.

Ishmael and I were way too old to suckle from our mother's teats, but she was not in her right mind. To be honest, none of us were. We were anxious and desperate, hungry and thirsty.

By some miracle, we happened upon a lone agarwood tree in the desert, where my brother and I stayed and enjoyed some shade while Hājar continued her frantic attempts to fetch water.

A stranger appeared out of nowhere, claiming to be a Shining One named Gabriel. This angel—or whatever he was—led us to a turquoise fountainhead. When Gabriel stomped his foot on the ground, a spring of water sprouted out of the rock, and several smaller pieces of the greenish blue stone fell to the ground.

Hallelujah!

We had water but still no food. It had been days since we'd eaten.

The next morning, a peddling caravan came by on its way from Memphis to Ur. We were able to trade the turquoise stones for food. They agreed, and we feasted gloriously with lamb and bread. To this day, my memory recalls that meal as the most fabulous feast of all my lifetimes.

One of the travelers was a beautiful woman in a white dress and gold jewelry adorned with a gorgeous purple stone. Entranced by the shimmer of her treasures, I was drawn to her like a divining rod. When our eyes met, she did more than just look at me—she gazed deep past my eyes, shooting right into my skull.

I slept so soundly that night. Although the water in my veins and food in my stomach certainly played an important role in that slumber, my dreams gave me peace as visions of the woman in the white dress led me to salvation.

The next morning, the caravan broke camp. The woman in the white dress held out her hand to help me climb aboard her camel.

That was the last I saw of Hājar and Ishmael. The woman in the white dress became my mentor, teaching me how to read, write, and study the stars. She even taught me calculus.

I remember feeling so happy that I had the opportunity to learn and the agency to make my own decisions in life. I was able to choose my own husband, and we lived in our own house. I even had a little garden where I grew vegetables, herbs, and flowers.

I died in peace, surrounded by my children and grandchildren. Waiting for me in the occult realm was my loving husband, who had preceded me in death a few years earlier. As we walked across the veil together, the woman in the white dress and purple jewelry nodded and smiled.

When I met my beloved Lugh in 1846, I recognized the soul of the man I had loved all those years ago.

~ Duir, the Ogham of Mightiness ~

Abraham managed to build his empire, and the city of Jerusalem has become a bone of contention between the followers of Ishmael—known as Muslims—and the followers of Isaac—who are called Jews. Christians follow the line of Isaac because their messiah, Jesus Christ, was a Jew. No other world religion, especially atheists, have an opinion on the subject.

Neither God nor Abraham left a deed or any other certified record specifying which son was the rightful heir to the Kingdom of Heaven.

Three hundred years after the death of Jesus Christ, Emperor Constantine finally converted the Roman empire from pagan to Christian. However, in order to rule the hearts and minds of both the local pagans and the Christians, he would need to merge the peasants' customs and celebrations with the new faith.

The amalgamation did not go well. The emperor instituted martial law against anyone who did not convert, but to propitiate the populace, he bastardized pagan rituals, rewriting astronomical folklore to become Christian holy days. The gods and goddesses were named as saints and given a whole new folklore compatible with the new regime.

Pagans were compelled to convert to the new religion or face deadly terror. Long-held and deeply revered cultural customs and religious beliefs became hidden, only to be resurrected when the heavy hand of the emperor's thugs were out of sight.

As more world leaders adopted Christianity and converted their protectorates, a group of malcontents in Arabia noticed how effective terror was, and chose to use similar methods.

For fourteen hundred years, the world has been brutalized by two versions of a myth that have no empirical evidence to support either claim.

Granted, *I know* that Ishmael and Isaac existed, but I cannot prove it. Even if I could, I do not care which one of them is the *rightful heir* to our father's legacy.

I teach my students that truth is self-evident. If Anu were real, every human being on Earth would instinctively know of his existence and what he commanded of us. There would be no difference of religion. There would be no discrepancies among denominations. We would not need to rely on missionaries, crusaders, or inquisitors to convince us. All of us would be on the same spiritual path.

Religion is a byproduct of something in the human psyche that believes we each have a spirit. That spirit is subject to all the frailties of human limitations. To overcome those limitations, we invent *gods*. In every culture throughout history, humans have created lore based on characters that embody our personal ideals.

Some people are naturally smarter—or should I say, *more clever*—than others. Clever people who lack moral compasses can easily find religion as a means of rising in power. With an uninformed or distracted populace, no one will question the dictates of the despot. Therefore, the first step to gaining supremacy is controlling information and suppressing ideas that do not conform to the narrative.

That is why the fruit from Eden's tree of knowledge was forbidden.

Even though Jerusalem is almost seven hundred miles from the original marsh, the words of Adam—the world's first false prophet—have been responsible for more misery, destruction, and death than any plague or famine in world history. And it continues as Judeo-Christians and Muslims battle over land, power, and heavenly favors.

That leads us to where we are now: fighting a war that cannot be won. The most we can hope for with this current occupation of Sumer is to overthrow the dictator, restore democracy in the area, and repair the marsh. If we are lucky, we may dissuade other potential tyrants from rising to power. We will have to wait and see.

THE MAGICIAN

21 March in the Year of Their Lord 2003

I love when it rains the day of the vernal equinox. Land, water, and sky unite to charge the planet. The sun and moon dance in equilibrium to the rhythm of thunder. Lightening ignites our hidden motivation. Water cleanses away hinderances blocking our success. The fresh scent delights us while the mist refreshes us.

My nature spirit friends can't help but frolic as the electricity in the atmosphere tingles their toes, leaving behind trails of pixie dust to enchant passersby.

I was not alone in this enchantment. My dear friend Carmelita joined me in the frolicking. We have a steady date on the morning of the spring equinox every year, and a little rain is not going to stop us. In fact, the weather made our ritual all the more delightful.

Carmelita Anza immigrated to Rivervine from the Dominican Republic as a young woman. I, however, did not meet her until the twentieth of March in the Year of Their Lord 1998. It was her thirty-ninth birthday, and she finally mustered the courage to petition the Lady of the Vineyard.

At the time, Miss Anza had been working as a clerk for the Rivervine City Council. After ten years as a civil servant, she tired of being subject to the institutional inertia and political pandering at City Hall. She knew of changes that needed to be made in order for the government to run properly—and by "properly," she meant *efficiently capable of serving the whole community, not just the cronies or partisan pets*—yet, as a clerk, she had no power to effectuate those changes.

If she were to achieve her goals, Carmelita knew that she herself had to acquire a seat on the city council where she could make decisions and influence government operations. However, rising in status is challenging, especially when one is a dark-skinned woman who has no affluent husband or father with coattails on which to climb. She was also a solitary witch—a *Bruja*, as they called her back in her homeland. Although she knew about the hospitality of the Comatis in general and the Divinorums in particular, she still felt a need to be alone in her craft.

Being a member of a religious community is not necessary for spiritual growth and expression, but it does offer a sturdy limb of encouragement and support in times of struggle. Those struggles have added weight when one is not part of the inner circle of influence. Success breeds success and like attracts like. When one does not look like the mainstream of success—or know someone who is willing to promote you—the currents can be impassable.

When she could tolerate no more, Carmelita turned to me.

Five years have passed since our first meeting, but I still remember that morning well. It was dawn—several hours before the Fermata Cellars tasting room opened for the day. The sun was starting to rise, bright as fire coming over the mountains.

Miss Anza arrived at the northeast corner of the vineyard—the part that backs the river and begins the slope upward into the mountains. It is a mostly private place, especially before the spring thaw when few farmworkers present the risk of exposure. There is not much space between the rows of grapevines, but if one is creative, one *can* find enough room to conduct a ritual. Carmelita made it work.

She wore a white cotton, mid-length, off-the-shoulders dress that was transparent enough to show the undergarments that lay beneath—a strapless white lace brassiere and a pair of delicate white lace drawers beneath it. Her thick, braided, black hair fell down her shoulders. Not a drop of makeup spoiled her pleasant face. She looked so simply elegant that I had to stop for a moment to appreciate the beauty that was about to summon me.

Once she settled on a site, the *Bruja* set down her satchel and pulled out several items: a jar of Touchkoff honey, an orange, a small paring knife, a shaker of cinnamon, two long-stemmed/small-rimmed wine glasses, a bottle of Fermata Cellars mead, a taper candle, and an automatic wick lighter.

Her first order of business was to prepare the taper. Seekers always bring candles the first time, not knowing the flame will extinguish once I appear. In subsequent rituals, Carmelita knew to bring a glass-encased candle that offered much better protection for its illumination.

She took the knife and cut a hole in the center of the orange that was large enough to fit the taper. She then placed the unlit candle inside the fruit and set the makeshift candleholder on the ground between two rows of vines. But she did not yet light it. Instead, she took the jar of Touchkoff honey and poured some around the orange and then stood up and, with the candleholder in the center, she walked in a circle pouring the honey and calling, "Dama de la Viña. Ella es divina. Escucha mi oración." When she came back to center, she sprinkled cinnamon on the orange and then sprinkled the spice in a second loop around the circle, reciting the same prayer. With her circle now cast, she sat back down, lit the candle and poured the mead.

Taking one glass in each hand, she raised them both toward the sky, closed her eyes, and mumbled the chant several times under her breath, going faster and louder with each round.

At last, she let out a raucous cycle of the spell, finishing with a giant breath, and then, tilting her head back and opening her mouth wide, she poured both glasses of mead over her mouth, letting the honey wine spill down her throat, face, and dress.

At that point, she collapsed and fell to the ground.

Accepting her offering, I entered the circle, taking my usual full-bodied form.

"¡Oh!" Carmelita gasped, staring at me with wide eyes and racing heartbeat, her voice too startled to say anything more. She immediately sat up as I sat down facing her, the orange in the center between us. As always, the unprotected flame on the candle extinguished, leaving a pooling trail of hot wax.

I could not help but notice the spilled mead on her white dress. Her hardened nipples showed through every layer of clothing. The musky scent of her desire hypnotized me.

She grabbed the top of her dress and straps of her brazier, pulling them down to expose her breasts. Arching her back and closing her eyes, her chest throbbed from the excitement.

Her plan to raise energy became obvious.

This is where the ethics differ from the Order of the Green Chalcedony. Miss Anza was not asking me to mentor her. Teachers and students should never comingle sex with education. Amorosity *always* clouds the mind and imposes a level of emotion that overpowers the learning process. Carmelita, however, was petitioning me to help *her* raise energy so she could then direct it toward her goals. In this case, sexual arousal and orgasm *were* appropriate tools to use. I was honored to oblige.

I picked up the dripping candle and poured the delicious mixture of orange juice, honey, cinnamon, and wax across her chest, watching it run in a stream between her breasts. As the hot wax hit her skin, she quivered slightly and let out a heavy sigh.

I then leaned over to kiss her cheek, letting my lips move down her neck, shoulders, and chest. My tongue lapped up all the spilled ingredients along with her sweat.

Carmelita moaned in pleasure as I leaned her onto the ground, stroking my tongue across her right nipple and fondling her left one.

When I sensed she was reaching climax, I continued suckling her right breast while my right hand moved down to her Venus mound, where I began massaging her clitoris. Once her vaginal honey flowed in a stream to the ground, I reached my index and middle fingers deep inside her vagina and found her sweet spot.

My lover gasped in sudden pleasure and released a gushing river of honey.

I grabbed one of the wine glasses and gently scooped up some of the lusciousness that was flowing between her legs.

Carmelita took the glass from me, added some more of the mead and handed it back saying, "Mi cariño, tu cariño, bendita sea."

"¡Bendita sea!" I echoed, taking the glass and sipping from it. I then gave it back to her so she could do likewise. Carmelita poured the remainder on the ground, shouting, "¡Para las uvas!"

Over the next fifteen months, Candidate Anza organized a campaign for city council—raising money, recruiting volunteers, and developing a platform. The only help I gave her was a push start that first day in the vineyard. She accomplished everything else on her own. I merely served as the conduit that bridged her psyche from follower to leader.

In June 2000, Carmelita Anza won the election with fifty-four percent of the vote in a three-way race.

On the spring equinox each year, we repeat this ritual, although she now uses glass-encased candles instead of tapers to ensure the flames do not blow out. Each year, her ecstasy grows stronger and she raises energy more powerful than the year before.

There is wisdom in her ecstasy. I also sense compassion, humility, and integrity. Those are all important—and yet rare— qualities for a government official.

Unlike some cities, the voters of Rivervine do not directly elect a mayor. That position, as well as the vice mayor, is selected by the city council members from among its membership. In January 2003, they chose Carmelita as mayor and local mortician Warner McCain as vice mayor. She is up for re-election in 2004. Today's ritual was an appeal to her gods for guidance on that issue.

I cannot say what answer the gods gave her, but from my personal, selfish viewpoint, it was beautiful seeing her white dress all wet—translucent and clinging to her voluptuous body.

I am sure our little *voyeur* agreed.

Each year, I sense another presence watching us. He's a stealthy one, though, for he escapes before I can home in on him. Because I am so focused on the ritual, I never pay attention to this intruder. Since he has never caused any harm, I do not worry too much. However, this year, his presence weighed heavy over our ritual.

Perhaps I am just being paranoid, but I need to identify this man and find out why he is fascinated by our tribadic sex magic.

I do not believe it is Thomas. He is far too devoted to Tanya.

It cannot be the solicitor. He has not been on Fermata Cellars' property the past three years. Besides, I sense something queer about him.

Sage knows better than to trespass on a private rendezvous.

I am at a loss for who this mystery man could be.

KNIGHT OF CUPS

3 April in the Year of Their Lord 2003

Xavia came down to the cellar this morning to restock the inventory in the tasting room. I was practicing my tai chi among the barrels and bottles but stopped to follow up on the status of the scribe.

"It has been two months since I asked you to invite Miss Fern to visit the winery," I noted. "Why has she not accepted the invitation?"

"I don't know, Zinfandel," the Druid replied. "Glenda's a busy woman. I called her the day after Iemmol, but she hasn't made it out here yet. She's the news editor. She covers government and stuff. Why don't you go after David Lynne instead? He works the business beat."

"Mr. Lynne is not one of us," I informed her. "Miss Fern is."

With an exasperated sigh, she asked, "What do you want me to do?"

Realizing her powerlessness, I said, "Nothing at this point. I will take care of it."

Xavia grabbed the cases she needed and headed back upstairs.

I homed in on the scribe's whereabouts and found her covering the grand opening of a new wildlife sanctuary.

I rambled among the crowd without a physical apparition, remaining in my spirit form. Nonetheless, the rattlesnakes hissed en masse when they sensed my presence, shaking their tails franticly. The hawks screeched and mosquitos hummed.

Zeroing in on my target's aura, I finally got a good look at Glenda for the first time. She appeared to be about thirty years old with shoulder-length dark hair and spectacles so thick her eyes seemed to swim in fishbowls. Judging by her tall, curvy stature, I guessed she was of Slavic descent, which immediately appealed to me. Her modest features were understated, with a lack of face makeup and fine clothing, but then again, we were in a meadow in the middle of spring; her attire was appropriate.

My potential scribe was interviewing Mayor Carmelita Anza while a scantily clad woman sang—well, more like *warbled*—on a makeshift stage.

The young singer may have graced a beautiful outer shell, but her vapid expression and pathetic performance perpetuated the stereotype of the weak *ingénue* who has nothing more to offer the world than a vision of loveliness and attitude of entitled privilege. Few women are able to maintain such a pretense throughout their lifetimes; it is an unhealthy role for any human to play. What was worse was that she could not carry a tune! Her tremulous voice repeatedly went off key, and whenever she tried to convey emotion, it was so contrived that it made a mockery of the lyrics.

As the insects buzzed around my aura, I commanded them, "Feast on the dolt, but spare me the leaders."

The vermin assaulted the young vocalist. Her saccharine sex appeal was not strong enough to ward off the attack, leaving the woman faint and nauseated, ending her performance prematurely.

As the crowd focused on the commotion on stage, I took the opportunity to catch Miss Fern alone. She did not see me. I spoke to her mind instead.

"You would much rather be wine tasting today," I suggested telepathically.

"Um … I'm not much of a wine drinker," her psyche responded.

"Perhaps you should try it. I can show you how to judge a good wine. Fermata Cellars is a good start."

"Yeah, they've been bugging me to come out there. But I have no idea what to do."

"Meet me there and I will guide you."

"Let me get a few more photos and interviews from this event and then I will head over."

"Sounds like a marvelous plan. I will meet you there."

A few hours later, Miss Fern walked in to the tasting room, not entirely sure what to do. To help her overcome her awkwardness, I put her in a semi-catatonic state so that I could control her mind.

Manuel was working the bar today, which is unusual. During the work week, he is typically upstairs in the office or out in the community. One of the regular employees must have been out sick or on vacation. Whatever the reason, he was the one who poured the flight of wine for Miss Fern.

They bantered a bit while he started the samples with the winery's lightest offering: Pianissimo, the white zinfandel. Again, I spoke to her psyche without manifesting any visual apparition.

"Swirl the glass, raise it to the light, and then gave it a good sniff," I telepathically instructed. Miss Fern obeyed, but grimaced at the taste and emptied the rest of the glass into the dump bucket sitting on the bar.

"This is too fruity for my tastes," she told him. "What do you have that's a little drier?"

Manuel refilled her glass with the Requiem, my personal favorite. He also told her about his plans for taking out an advertisement in her newspaper.

Before taking a sip of the wine, Miss Fern pulled out a device from her purse and started speaking into it.

"Hello, Leonard?" she said. "Can you stop by Fermata Cellars? I have a lead for you."

She then stopped speaking, put the device back in her purse, and resumed her flight. After swirling her glass once again, she held it up to the light and commented about how dark and rich the color was. As she took a small sip, she exhaled, closed her eyes, and euphorically uttered, "Oh, now *this* is good."

Manuel and Glenda continued making small talk until this *Leonard* person arrived a few minutes later. Miss Fern then meandered through the gift shop, tasting the samples of comestibles available for guests to enjoy.

"Tell Mr. Chavez that you want a case of the Requiem," I persuaded telepathically.

She followed my instructions, and Mr. Chavez rung up the sale and then carried the heavy box of wine to her horseless carriage.

The solicitor hurried back to the tasting room to talk to Leonard, leaving Miss Fern alone in the open lot as she organized her wagon to fit the big box containing her precious purchase.

I found a shade tree behind her, offering me a safe place to shift into my physical apparition without others seeing me. I chose to appear in a nice skirt and blouse, something modern but not too casual.

"Miss Fern," I called with a softened firmness but startling her nonetheless. She flinched just a bit, then turned around to see the owner of the voice.

"Yes … can I help you?" Her voice was equally firm, speaking from her chest with a deep tone of authority.

"My name is Zinfandel, and I am a friend of the Divinorums. I am also a fan of your writing. I appreciate your coverage of local goings on."

"Oh, thank you." She smiled and started to head toward the tasting room but then stopped and asked, "*Zinfandel?* Your name is Zinfandel? Really? Like the wine?"

"Yes, like the wine." I tried to be as stoic as possible, maintaining my telepathic hold on her.

"Can you meet me at Trails sometime?" I bellowed as she walked away. "I have a news tip I would like to share with you."

She stopped and turned back to face me.

"And what would that be what? Can you tell me real quick?"

She is not afraid of me. I am a stranger. And I approached her from behind, catching her off guard, which should have intimidated her further. Yet no fear energy emanated from her aura.

"It is a matter that is best discussed over cocktails," I said. "Do you drink whiskey?"

Nodding her head and shrugging her shoulders, she answered with a simple, "Sometimes, mostly over ice with plenty of Coke."

"Then I will buy the first round. Can we plan on a day and time?"

"How late in the evening can you meet? I have time tonight after I put the Friday edition to bed. Might not be until nine o'clock or so."

"Oh, I have all night."

"Great! I'll see you then."

"Until then."

She returned to the tasting room. I thought I heard her whisper under her breath, "A woman named Zinfandel drinks whiskey. Hmm. Interesting."

I headed to the cave to meditate and compose my business proposal.

~ Huath, the Ogham of Challenge ~

"I cannot believe I am so nervous!" I told Anton after rehearsing my lecture a dozen times in front of him.

"What makes you anxious, sister?" he asked.

"I am actually doing this—realizing my dreams!"

"A dream you have had for what? Six months?"

He obviously did not comprehend exactly how significant tonight's meeting was.

"Anton … I am going to be *immortalized*," I emphasized. "This scribe, if I can persuade her, is going to write my life's story. If I fail to convince her to do it, I will be lost in the sea of obscurity."

"You can always find another scribe, a bigger sucker perhaps. Writers are a dime a dozen."

"But not all scribes are vampires. This one *is*, although she may not know it yet."

"So your plan is to a) explain what a vampire is; b) tell her that she is one, whether she wants to be or not; and c) coax her into using her writing skills to tell the world that vampires are living in Rivervine and you are the star of the show?"

Scowling at his sarcasm, I explained, "I saw the poor condition of the horseless carriage she was driving, and the clothes she wore were definitely made by a sloppy seamstress. She could make a fortune as a novelist. I am offering her a subject that has never been written about before. And there is no ethical violation in using witchcraft to boost one's success, so long as the proper effort in the mundane realm has been expended, which it will be."

"I see your point, sister, and I wish you well," he acquiesced. "Now go. You do not want to be late."

I kissed his cheek and left the cave. Before shifting to the saloon, I peeked in—without a physical apparition—on the status of the scribe at the newspaper office to see if she was running late. It appeared she was wrapping up her business and telling her fellow journalists goodbye.

I stayed with her as she got into her horseless carriage.

"God, it sure is stuffy in here!" she cried to herself and rolled down the windows. "I can barely breathe."

When we arrived at the dance hall, she parked in the lot and walked into the saloon. Still unapparitioned, I rushed past her and found an empty high table for two where I shifted into my physical illusion, dressed in the same skirt and blouse from earlier today.

Bobbie spotted me right away. Instead of waiting for a waitress to take my order, she came out from behind the bar and walked over to me.

"Hello, Zinfandel. Why are you not at the bar? Are you expecting company?"

"Yes, and here she is," I replied, waving to Glenda, who was scanning the crowd. The scribe looked right at me, smiled, and headed toward the table. As she took her seat, Bobbie asked her, "I know Zinfandel wants bourbon on the rocks, but what can I get you?"

Glenda looked at me as if waiting for approval and then answered, "I'll have a bourbon on the rocks as well."

Bobbie left to get our drinks. I asked Glenda how her day had been.

"Oh, same ol' same ol.' Edie Clark wants to put in *another* subdivision. She took out a permit from the land use agency today. Looks like she's going to block in Fermata Cellars until the Divinorums have no choice but to sell. It's egregious, but there's nothing anybody can do to stop her, unless the planning commission finds a reason to deny the permit. Even then, she will just appeal it to the city council. Carmelita Anza has been the Divinorums' ally on the city council, but now that she's mayor, she can't actually *vote* on projects unless there's a tie between the other four council members, and there's never a tie. Sometimes that creepy Warner McCain votes against Clark, but the other three are totally on Clark's bankroll—she's even listed on their campaign disclosure paperwork. Of course, the neighboring farmers *could* refuse to sell their land, but there's just too much money involved."

Bobbie arrived with our drinks. With the bartender still standing there, Glenda took one sip and grimaced.

"I'm so sorry, but I can't drink this stuff straight after all," the scribe apologized. "I tried. Would it be possible to get this in a pint glass with some Coke?"

"No problem," Bobbie answered.

"Thank you," Glenda said, then looked at me. "I'm so sorry, Zinfandel. I tried to drink it your way."

"No problem," I replied.

A few moments later, Bobbie arrived with a fresh drink for the scribe. As Glenda took a sip, she closed her eyes and exhaled in joy. "Oh, this is so much better!"

With the small talk over and our minds slightly lubricated, Glenda initiated the conversation.

"So what is this *news tip* you have for me?"

"Have you ever wondered *why* Edie Clark—or any other land peddler—wants the Fermata Cellars property? It is, after all, *haunted*. Why would a piece of bewitched land be so contentious?"

"What are you getting at? Those are just ghost stories. They're not true. Are you hinting that the property is sitting on top of an oil reserve or diamond mine or something? It isn't *really* a portal to hell is it?"

"Not exactly, but there is a spiritual significance to the land, particularly the cellar of the winery."

Glenda guffawed—a response I anticipated.

"How do you know all this?" she asked.

"Because I am the vampire that haunts it."

Whiskey and Coke flew out of her nose.

"Excuse me?" she sneered.

I altered my apparition, changing into my crimson and black gown and giving myself some fangs. If Anton were here, he would laugh at the elongated canine teeth, but just like the apples at Sam Hain, I needed to make a dramatic effect in order to capture her attention.

Glenda jumped in horror, spilling her drink. I used my psychokinesis skills to clean the mess and refill the glass.

"Okay then!" she shrieked. "So you want me to do a story on this, I take it?"

"Not just a story—a whole book," I proposed, changing back into my contemporary appearance.

She sat in her seat, quietly bewildered. A few moments later, she asked, "There are other writers in town. Why did you pick me?"

"Because you too are a vampire, and the story needs to be told by someone who understands us."

Glenda laughed. "I am not a *vampire!*" she blurted out, then looked around to see if anyone heard her. Finding the coast to be clear, she added, "You don't even know me. How can you say that?"

As the indignant writer stood up to leave, I conjured a grilled steak on a plate in front of her. The drippings of blood and juicy fat soaked the dish.

"Are you hungry? I will buy you supper if you stay and listen to the rest of my proposal."

Her aura radiated with pride, skepticism, fear … and lust for the large piece of rare, red meat before her.

Gazing deep into her eyes, I commanded her attention and spoke with a firm but gentle tone.

"Imagine being a famous author—award winning, wealthy, revered. You schedule book signings and speaking engagements all over the world. Your work has been translated into thirty languages and adapted for actors to perform. You dress in the finest clothes and live in an elaborate house with fancy trimmings. Your books will be taught in prestigious schools and universities. History will remember you as a master of the craft."

Her chest heaved from anxiety and excitement. Breaking eye contact with me, she glanced down at her steak. I conjured a fork and sharp knife for her, and then created a matching plate of food and silverware for myself.

She returned to her seat and we both ate our suppers.

As we dined, I explained, "I am keeping a diary for you to use as notes. I need you to cobble them together in contemporary parlance and get the book published."

She appeared oblivious to my words as she devoured her steak, reveling in the injection of chi from the red meat into her own blood stream. After a few bites, she gulped her cocktail and with a mouthful of steak said, "I'll need more than just your notes. I need at least three sources and they can't all be favorable to your side of the story. I'm going to need to talk to the opposition."

"As you wish," I replied, continuing to enjoy my meal, eating it gracefully like a properly bred lady should. "Now let me order us a bottle of wine to pair with our meal. Would you also like a potato and a salad?"

"Oh yes please!" she exclaimed. "Thank you."

I looked for Bobbie, but she was away from the bar. Our regular waitress stopped by our table, so I placed an order for a bottle of Requiem.

"Where did those steaks come from?" the server asked. "They're not on tonight's menu. You know you're not allowed to bring in outside food?"

Once again, I had to invoke my hypnosis skills.

"We have a special arrangement with Fermata Cellars. Now, please … bring us our wine and two glasses. Thank you."

The awestruck Glenda watched as the waitress obeyed my command. The scribe then leaned over the table to me and whispered, "How did you do that?"

Leaning back in my seat, I told her, "Oh, my darling, I have so much to tell you."

By the time the bottle was empty, I had summarized the same story I had told the youths at the beginning of the year, and Glenda had a general understanding of why this project was so urgent.

"Two weeks," she said. "Give me two weeks to think about your offer."

"As you wish, darling."

Bobbie stopped by our table to let us know that the bar was closing in an hour. She turned to my guest and, noticing the editor's inability to sit up straight asked, "Glenda, do you have a ride home?"

"Psh! I live within stumbling distance of here. I can walk."

"Okay, then."

Bobbie turned to me and said, "Goodnight, Zinfandel. It was good seeing you."

"You too, darling."

I stayed with Glenda until we reached her apartment. Once she opened the door, she staggered to her sleeping chamber and fell asleep.

When I shifted back to the cave, Anton was gone. So was his cobza. The harder I listened to the silence, the clearer I heard the sound of a duet between cobza and guitar.

KING OF SWORDS

10 April in the Year of Their Lord 2003

"Hello, Sister."

It was not Anton's voice.

"Ishmael?"

Who else could it have been? But the last time I heard his voice he warbled like the vapid singer from the wildlife sanctuary. He is no longer the adolescent boy I knew four millennia ago.

Our souls stood facing each other, unable to advance the conversation. The longer we waited, the queasier my stomach grew. Before I could retch, I spit out the words, "Was that you they killed yesterday or one of your proxies?"

I had heard the Americans assassinated Sadaam Hussein, but I did not know if the Iraqi dictator was the reincarnation of my twin or just another sultan working at his behest.

"It does not matter," he answered. "Jerusalem will be mine soon. Join me and you can have the marsh. You can return it to the glorious jungle you loved so much when we were children."

"I will never leave my vines here."

"You are going to lose the vines. However, if you are a good girl and mind your manners, you can have the marsh when we are done."

"We?"

He disappeared.

QUEEN OF PENTACLES

17 April in the Year of Their Lord 2003

As usual, I accompanied Lily and Manuel on their weekly marketing rounds tonight, continuing to remain disembodied and silent so as not to frighten the solicitor. The last stop of the tour, of course, was the dance hall where all three of us noticed Glenda Fern sitting alone at the bar. I was especially overjoyed to see her as today marks a fortnight since I broached the idea of having the newswoman author my biography; she had agreed to give me an answer by now.

My two companions, who knew nothing about my proposal to the editor, seated themselves on either side of Glenda, striking up a conversation with her while I hid in the background and eavesdropped. It was apparent by her slurred speech and blank stare that she was already inebriated—freely opening her vault of knowledge about city politics, local folklore, and plans to overcome poverty by writing a book about the *vampires* in the cellar of the winery. Lily scoffed at Glenda's publishing aspirations while Manuel gasped in fear.

Since my presence in the room seemed to frazzle the already stressful energy, I shifted back to the horseless carriage and waited for them to wrap up their business. Lily arrived at the *van* (as she calls it) before Manuel; she had some choice words for me outside of the solicitor's earshot. Miss Rhoads shut up once her passenger arrived. During the entire drive home, my fellow riders bickered about Glenda's drunken ramblings. Although I stayed silent, Lily chose to fire foul glances at me the entire ride home.

When we returned to Lily's house, the two of them said goodnight to each other, and I shifted over to Glenda's apartment.

~ Two of Wands ~

I sensed the editor's mind settling into that sweet spot between drunkenness and sobriety. She was now clearheaded enough to discuss our *gentlewoman's* contract yet still riding the wave of whiskey-induced creativity.

I found her sitting at a desk engulfed in a dark, deep, musky ambience. Nary a light shown in the place save for a small lamp next to the machine on which she was punching keys. The contraption looked similar to the one the solicitor uses to inscribe his thoughts.

Remaining disembodied, I walked around her apartment, noticing there was only one sleeping chamber and a conspicuous lack of photographs of children or lovers. Ergo, I figured the scribe lived alone.

Overhead, recorded music played—a beautiful violin sonata in the key of G minor.

I also noticed a scent floating through the air. It was a familiar smell—a smoky, fruity, evergreen essence, like a cross between apple and cedar but not quite either of those specifically. It was something I recognized, but it took me a while to put my finger on it. The longer the fragrance lingered, the more it haunted me until at last I was able to identify it: ghafwood, the tree of the forsaken desert.

Hājar? I muttered silently to myself.

Peeking at her jewelry, I saw turquoise gems dangling from her ears. Around her neck, a silver necklace sparkled with a modest turquoise stone hanging from the center, and her hands were graced with silver bracelets and rings studded with turquoise centers.

To the right of her contraption was a vessel of some sort of odorless, colorless liquid. *Water?*

To test my theory, I hummed a melody from Egypt—one her soul would hear but not her ears. Her reaction shocked me to the point of tears.

Miss Fern jolted, looking up from her project and staring off into the distance, losing herself in thought as she hummed along with me. A moment later, the scribe closed her eyes and shook her head as if clearing away mental cobwebs. Her attention then returned to the writing machine.

Realizing this woman's true identity, I felt heat and sweat radiating from my forehead, even though I had not yet manifested an apparition. I sensed my hands trembling and tingling in a strange mix of hot and cold. My chest tightened as if someone had stolen the air, and my heart raced like a thief avoiding capture.

As I experienced the panic attack, Glenda physically manifested all of the abovementioned symptoms.

Falling to the floor and clenching her chest, the newswoman started to retch. Before the bile could rise to her throat, I shifted into my regular apparition and lifted her limp body over to the couch.

"Zinfandel!" she shrieked.

"Shh!" I hushed. "Do not fear. All is well."

As she lay on the sofa with her head in my lap, I stroked her forehead like a mother caresses a child, trying to calm her nerves.

"How did you get in here?" she inquired, still on edge. "I thought vampires needed to be invited in."

Shaking my head, I answered, "Without a physical shell to encumber me, I can go wherever my imagination takes me."

"Well, how long have you been here? Do you normally spy on people? Have you spied on me before?"

Unsure of how best to answer these questions, and ashamed that I did not follow proper etiquette, I chose to be direct, yet seemingly imperturbable.

"I have only been here a few moments, and no, I have never been here before. The only reason for my visit tonight is to discuss the biography project I proposed a couple weeks ago."

"Fine, but you should have knocked first. I'm kinda freaked out that you were here without my knowledge."

"You are correct, and I apologize."

I admit this moment was awkward. I am unaccustomed to being the instigator of a conversation. Usually, flesh-bound souls seek *me* out. If I *do* pay them an uninvited visit, it is rarely a social call.

With her head still in my lap, I stroked her hair and continued humming the Egyptian melody. Again, she started humming along.

Once her nerves calmed and her head cleared, Miss Fern sat up straight and looked me square in the eye.

"Where do I know that tune? It sounds so familiar!"

"Oh, my dear. That is a long story to tell."

"Well, that's what we're here for, isn't it? Tell me. Is it an ancient vampire song? It doesn't sound Eastern European, though. It sounds more like what they play at the hookah bar."

"The vampires of Rivervine have a complex history that covers not only Transylvania, but the Middle and Far East as well."

Glenda's mouth gaped open as she struggled to respond. A moment later, she sighed and looked around at her austere environs, seemingly dejected and longing for more material comforts.

Returning her focus back to me, she asked, "How gory is this story going to get? Do the Divinorums hold blood rituals or anything like that—animal sacrifices, orgies, acid trips? Is there any criminal activity involved?"

"Oh, no," I chuckled. "I assure you, everything is quite benign. The truth about vampires, witches, Druids—the occult in general—is fascinating on its own without all the fearmongering, misinformation, and slanderous myths that precede our reputations."

That seemed to propitiate her initial fears, although more surfaced.

"If I agree to your proposal, am I making a pact with the devil?" she asked. "Am I going to go to hell?"

"Hell is a state of mind, not a physical place. So is heaven. And no, I am not *the devil*."

"What if I say no to this?"

"I leave your apartment now and never speak of this again. No harm will befall you, I promise."

"If I say yes now and decide later to back out of the project, what happens to me?"

"We part ways, hopefully as friends, but one never knows how relationships will evolve. If it goes sour, we can try to resolve our differences diplomatically, but I will not tolerate betrayal, dishonesty, or malice. Neither should you."

Pausing for a moment, she changed the subject, eyeing me with deep curiosity. "Have we met before? You look *really* familiar."

"I will explain our connection another time. It is a long story, and you are tired, I can tell."

"So you *chose* me? And it's a long story? If I say yes, I get to learn that story. If I say no, I walk away from that story, never knowing what *could be* an important truth that I and the rest of humanity could benefit from."

"You could say that, yes."

"How do I know this project will be successful, though? What if I invest all this time and effort and we only sell a handful of copies?"

"That is a gamble we both take. But at least the truth will be documented. If we do not at least *try* to publish my side of the story, Adam wins … again. *And I am tired of losing to that lying, cheating BASTARD!*"

My anger caused a surge of psychokinetic energy, throwing some books off the shelves; her drink tumbled onto the floor.

"I am so sorry!" I bellowed, getting up to find a rag to mop up the spillage.

"Oh, don't worry about it," she consoled. "It's just water."

~ Six of Swords ~

"So yeah, let's do this!" Glenda decided after I returned to my seat on the sofa. The scribe reached for a small device and pushed a button.

"Okay, we're rolling now," she said. I assume that meant she was recording our conversation.

"First off, tell me who this *Adam* is that you're talking about," she continued. "How has he lied to and cheated you?"

Miss Fern's ignorance granted her a blissful privilege. Meanwhile, my tongue was paralyzed from knowledge.

"Take a deep breath," a disembodied woman's voice whispered in my ear as the fragrance of roses drifted past my nose. "Calm your mind. Come to center. Let the kundalini speak."

"Of course!" I thought to myself. The *kundalini* is the coiled serpent of divine inspiration that lives at the base of each dancer's spine.

I followed the lady's instructions. She did not disappoint me; somehow, I managed to summon the words to dictate to my scribe.

"You know Adam from the Bible?"

"Yes, of course!"

"Do you believe that whole story about apples and gardens and snakes?"

"Not really. I was raised Catholic, but I know the Earth is more than six thousand years old, as the Bible claims. Granted, civilization—agriculture, architecture, academia—is thought to have started in that part of the world around that time, but that whole business about the flood and some old guy building a big boat and traveling the world in search of two of each species of animal, and they all lived for forty days and nights and none of them ate each other or died from the filth—and the termites didn't destroy the wood? Yeah, that doesn't pass my sniff test. But then, neither do vampires, so … what's your point?"

"Humor me for a bit," I instructed. "Close your eyes. Take a deep breath, and when I say a name, tell me what your immediate response is."

"Okay," she said, as her eyelids shut and her chest heaved.

"Ibrahim," was the first name I offered.

She shuddered and yelled through her gritted teeth, "Asshole! Broken promises. You devastated our children and me just so you could hide your shame, appease that *bitch* of a wife, and manifest your empire. FUCK YOU!"

Startled, Glenda opened her eyes and howled, "I am so sorry! I do *not* know where that came from."

"It is all right. I *do* know where it came from. Let us try another word. Go ahead and close your eyes again."

She did as instructed.

"Nisaba," I said.

"Viper, heiress, darling girl," she swiftly answered, surprising herself again. Her blood pressure started to rise as she began to panic over her responses.

"Nisaba was the name my mother gave me three thousand years ago," I told her. "I was the eldest child of Ibrahim and his wife's handmaiden, Hājar. My twin brother was Ishmael; he was born a few minutes after I was. We were the twenty-first generation from Adam, the originator of the bloodline."

Glenda scrunched her eyebrows.

"So how come the Bible doesn't mention a daughter?"

"Girls were not valued back then. Women were chattel—whores, breeders, cooks, and maids. Our births and deaths were not recorded, and we held no value in society."

"Wait a minute!" she insisted, shaking her head in disbelief. "The math doesn't add up. If a generation is *twenty* years, and you were the *twenty-first* generation from Adam, that's only four hundred and twenty. Adam and Abraham were supposedly three thousand years apart, if my catechism teacher was correct. I realize Abraham—or Ibrahim as you call him—was ninety years old …"

Glenda's voice trailed off as her mind remembered details of her past life.

"Oh, dear God, that's gross," she nearly retched again. "I … no, I, I couldn't have done *that*!"

"He was wealthy and you were beautiful. There was nothing odd about it back then."

"Me? Beautiful? I have a hard time believing *that*. I am so plain. And I wear glasses. Was I nearsighted back then? How did people live without glasses?"

"Shh! You are thinking too hard. This is a lot to absorb. I understand. But let us focus on the task at hand."

"Oh-kaaay …" I sensed the wheels in her mind shifting gears. "So what does this have to do with *vampires* and what do you want from *me*?"

"I want you to write my biography and tell the Comati story. Adam has controlled the conversation for more than six thousand years. It is time I received equal representation."

After contemplating the deal, she groaned, "Oh, dear God, I need a drink. Would you like a glass of wine?"

"I never turn *that* down!"

~ Ailm, the Ogham of Overview ~

With our glasses full, we settled onto her couch for a long lesson on how the Comati line managed to go from Sumer to Rivervine.

I started with the same story I mentioned earlier in this grimoire about my original incarnation as a pit viper living in a marsh at the confluence of the Tigris and Euphrates rivers. I told her all about my friendship with Eve and how the young wife chose to forego her own educational and spiritual development to submit to her domineering husband, who only wanted to isolate, control, and manipulate her.

"So you were a snake," she interrupted. "Could you speak? Like, did you two talk, or was it all just mental telepathy? And aren't pit vipers poisonous? Why would a human talk to a venomous creature?"

"My venom was very mild. I would gently bite her neck or wrist or ankle, releasing a small amount of a hallucinogenic substance—toxic in large doses but benign if controlled. She would then slip into a hypnotic trance where her mind met me across the veil of the occult realm. From there, I revealed to her the wisdom of the Tree of Knowledge."

"Interesting," Glenda remarked. "So let me guess what happens next: Her husband, Adam, sees her all doped up, fears she is possessed by the devil, and takes her out of the Garden of Eden. Is that correct?"

"Exactly," I answered. "From that day on, I have carried with me the scourge of being the ultimate antagonist."

"Were there any other reincarnations between the snake and this Nisaba character?"

"Not that I remember."

"Do you remember *anything* about what you did in those three thousand years between incarnations?"

"No."

"So fast-forward to two thousand B.C. …"

"Yes?"

"Did you hate me?" Glenda started to cry. "I failed you as a mother!"

I wrapped my arms around the scribe and let her tears fall on my shoulder.

"Oh, no," I consoled her. "I do *not* hate you and you did *not* fail me. You did everything you could for us!"

Catching her breath, she sat back up, recomposed herself, and asked, "So what does this have to do with modern day Rivervine?"

"I sense Adam is here. I do not know what name he goes by or what he looks like, but I feel his aura."

"What does his aura feel like?"

"Painful, like slander that cuts deeper with each lie. Heavy, like oppression that grows denser with each retelling of the lie. Hopeless, like defense that weakens with each believer of the lie. Those are the sensations and emotions I feel whenever I am near Adam."

"What does he want with Rivervine?"

"I do not yet know."

The scribe paused for a moment, a curious look forming on her face. She topped off our wine glasses and took a large sip from hers. She was once again getting tipsy, but her recording device was running, so I continued talking, even though I was unsure how closely she was paying attention. I talked about ghosts, Comatis, witchcraft, and vampires—everything that I have mentioned earlier in this grimoire.

"Are Xavia and Sage vampires?" she asked.

"No. Just Anton, me … and … "

"And?" she wondered.

I stared directly into her eyes, yet was unable to utter a simple three-letter pronoun: *you*.

"Your recording device," I pointed out. "The light at the top turned from green to red. Is that important?"

"Dammit!" she yelled. "Those were *brand new* batteries!"

"My apologies, darling. Ghosts tend to drain the energy from the room in order to manifest their apparitions. We can continue another time."

"Probably for the best" Glenda exhaled. "This was a lot to digest tonight … so many … wow." She took a moment to collect her thoughts and then asked me, "How is any of this going to help you fight Adam?"

"I need to change the direction of the Comati legacy," I said. "Our history shows an ongoing cycle of persecution, exile, and loss. I am hoping that by analyzing our past, we can chart a course for our future that will unite the strength of the rational mind, the foresight of intuition, and the empathy of a compassionate heart."

She smiled and said, "That sounds beautiful."

THE SUN

6 May in the Year of Their Lord 2003

The three youths in the Order of the Green Chalcedony make me proud. We have been meeting on the new moons at the ritual space in the backyard of Erin's house. Most of our attention has been on planning the wedding for Tanya and Thomas. This month, however, they are spending a great deal of time preparing for their school graduation. Thomas wants to go to university afterward to study business. Tanya dreams of a bakery full of children helping her roll out dough and chop apples. Erin is unsure what she wants to do after graduation, but her distaste for academics precludes her from advancing her education.

Our last meeting was five nights ago when the moon was new. All three of them spent the evening working on their occult arts.

I have been training Erin in gung fu and tai chi; she excels at martial arts, a discipline that will help her learn how to center her focus and hone her clairvoyance skills. After she completes her routines, she likes to eat hallucinogenic mushrooms, which she claims help her reach the deepest levels of her consciousness and produce the most vivid, thorough visions.

Thomas also likes the *shrooms* as the youth call them. He chews a small handful at the beginning of the ritual and spends the rest of the evening charting the night sky.

His betrothed, however, refuses to use anything she deems to be a toxin. Tanya does not smoke sage-scented fags or even drink alcohol. She is taking her motherhood role *very* seriously.

During our monthly get-togethers, she has been studying something called *reiki*. I have never heard of it before, but it appears to be some kind of healing technique that channels her own energy into the patient. She brings books to the circle and reads while the rest of us do our own respective tasks. Every now and then, she will ask me a question about chi—how it flows and how it's used in healing the body. Of course, I am happy to answer those inquires.

Tonight the three of them will be attending the Beltane ritual at the Oppidum with the rest of the Comatis.

The solicitor will also be there. He is another source of pride for me. Right now, he is so naive, yet I sense he is coming into alignment with his true self.

~ Four of Cups ~

This morning, I found Mr. Chavez sitting under the orange tree—the one he himself planted as a young boy.

I remember that day so vividly. Manuel and his mother, Graciela, brought home a bag of mandarin oranges from the market. As he peeled away the rind, the juice squirted down his hands, and when he bit into the fruit, he spit out the seeds, imagining an entire orchard growing where they landed.

Graciela picked up most of the pips, knowing the feral cats and cold weather would prevent them from sprouting. She taught her son how to plant the seeds indoors and give them proper attention so they would be ready to place in the ground come springtime.

Despite her meticulous supervision, only one of the boy's seedlings grew strong enough to plant outdoors. More than twenty years later, that tree has grown taller than the man who planted it. It also has become the favored spot of the local nature spirits—one of whom is a racer snake that has taken the solicitor under its tutelage.

Racer snakes are harmless. Their venom is not dangerous to most humans, and they do not prey on animals larger than lizards or small rodents. Yet because of millennia of character defamation, most humans are afraid of the benign slithering creatures. This particular serpent has a whimsical side to him and likes to play with his new pal.

"Manuel's here every morning, Zinfandel!" my frolicking snake friend advised me. "He's not even afraid of me—pets me and everything."

"Oh really? Tell me more."

"He learns best if you make it a game. Like … he sits on the ground. I wiggle down the tree and tickle his neck. He talks to himself—pretends he's talking to me. Then, when a leaf falls, he pets me on the head and I run back up the tree. He doesn't hear me talking to him. He thinks he thought of it all himself. He types up the words I give him and heads back inside. I'm okay with that, I guess—him taking all the credit. It's better than getting beat over the head with a shovel."

"Interesting. Do you mind if I stand in for you sometime?"

"Go ahead. I could use a vacation. Got a girlfriend in the Fairy realm. I'm gonna ask them tonight at the Beltane ritual if I can visit her. Do you have anything shiny I can give them as an offering?"

I conjured a gold band and slid the ring onto his tail.

"Will this work?" I asked.

He coiled his body to take a peek.

"Wow! Thanks Zinfandel! This is beautiful!"

"You are so welcome. Thank you for clearing a path for me."

The racer snake nodded his head in the direction of the winery.

"You're on," he said. "Here comes Manuel right now."

That was the last I saw of my little friend.

~ Onn, the Ogham of Fertility ~

I shifted into the form of the serpent just in time to see Mr. Chavez open his writing contraption and strike some keys that produced words on a screen. From over his shoulder, I could read what he had inscribed:

"I will probably edit out this part when I write my wrap-up of the Beltane ritual, but right now, I am really hoping Xavia and Sage let me pitch my idea of the Zinfandel Festival to the Comatis tonight. The Divinorums normally have a policy of no business in the Oppidum, but since it's Beltane and the theme is fertility, I'm praying they'll let me penetrate the economic womb by letting me discuss the event as well as my cooperative advertising plan for the Old Town merchants to participate in."

"Oh, yes!" I rejoiced silently to myself, wiggling my tail behind his ear. "This is exactly what I wanted him to do!"

It was humbling to read about his desire to name the festival after me, even though I am sure he was referencing the wine, not the Lady of the Vineyard. But it was an honor nonetheless.

As I looked on, I saw him add, "This better not be bullshit. I'm not sure I buy this whole *fairy magic* thing, but if it's true, and good neighbors want to sprinkle some fairy dust on my marketing plan, I'll take it!"

Bless his heart. His naivety is great, but in time, he will come to appreciate the Beltane traditions with the fae folk in

Rivervine. They are far more complex than a simple sprinkling of sparkly dust.

The local origins date back to 1969, when the Divinorums bought the property. As part of their neo-Druid religion, they brought with them some entities as old as the pre-Christian Celts. They were called The Good Neighbors—beings made of substances other than flesh and blood that lived in a dimension beyond the occult and physical realms, one that differed in time and space. They called it *the Fairy realm*.

It was home to all sorts of fantastic creatures such as unicorns, Sasquatch and the Loch Ness Monster—beings that had been sighted throughout the ages but left no skeletal remains, excrement, or other proof of their existence.

When I was a little girl, the English explorers would tell us children tales of *the fae folk*. They were tiny creatures that flew around on wings like dragon flies and granted wishes or played tricks.

My beloved Lugh told the same tales, except he called the characters *shee*.

In any language, their personality types are the same. Some fae thrived on being helpful, while others could be mischievous. Several just made a fleeting appearance and disappeared. Quite a few, though, were morbidly cruel.

When Xavia came to Rivervine, she explained the relationship between the fae and humans.

The shee were adept at planning, especially when it came to choreographing fate. From their vantage point in the Fairy realm, they were able to see the waves of chaos here on Earth and manipulate the flow. If they favored a particular human, they could raise the tide high enough to overcome hurdles. Likewise, if they wanted to scorn someone, they might throw stones in the person's path.

Their goodwill, Xavia said, could be ensured by forming an alliance with them. The price for their benevolence was usually one shiny or colorful object for each request.

Contrary to what most artists and storytellers have claimed, the land of Fairy is not full of splendor and spectacular hues. Quite the opposite, in fact. On its own, the place is dark and gloomy as there is no sun to create flowers, twilight, or ripening fruit. Anything bright and beautiful must be procured from the earthly realm.

Although the Black Land was barren at the time the Divinorums brought The Good Neighbors to Rivervine, the slated eighty-nine acre vineyard promised to make quite a lovely sanctuary for the fae folk. They could even help with its fertility.

We asked Sage for his opinion, but he was rather ambivalent. Being new to Druidry, he did not fully understand the concept of the Fairy realm or how its magic worked. All he wanted was a life outside of the city. Whatever Xavia wanted to do was fine with him.

Over the next few days, I took some time to ponder the situation. I even sought advice from the Comati ancestors. None of us could find a reason to object to the treaty.

So in 1969, with Xavia acting as a representative for the fae folk, the Comatis established a new tradition.

~ Quert, the Ogham of Support ~

The fae folk's favorite time of year to visit the earthly realm has always been Beltane—the crossquarter between the vernal equinox and summer solstice. This was when the flowers bloomed the most abundantly and fruit began to ripen. The days grew longer, which gave them more time to enjoy the vivid skies of twilight.

This year, the Comatis welcomed their otherworldly guests by decorating the Oppidum with festive ribbons of white, bright green, and cherry red, and they hung sparkling ornaments from the branches of the mighty oaks.

Sage always builds two bonfires for Beltane—one in the west and one in the east. Both pits are three feet in diameter and burn a mix of woods from the Rivervine ogham. Each wood brings with it an aspect of the human psyche. As the woods burn, the smoke sends their magical properties into the air. When Comatis pass through the two bonfires, they are blessed with those gifts.

Sage keeps the flames low all night because unlike other ceremonies, the Beltane fires have a … special purpose.

For this ceremony, guests enter the Oppidum from the north. There is no need to smudge them with sage or sprinkle them with salt water. Instead, they walk between the two fires. The smoke from the east purifies. The one in the west nourishes. Each guest is asked to bring a shiny trinket as an offering for The Good Neighbors. If the person wants to clear their path of something blocking a particular goal, they toss the offering into the bonfire on the left. If the person wants to manifest a particular aspiration, they throw the object into the fire on the right. They then proceed to the south, where they turn to either side and find a place to stand in the circle until the entire tribe has entered.

Tonight Thomas followed Tanya into the circle, walking several paces behind her; most people in the crowd did not see Anton standing between them, although three bits of iron pyrite danced in the western flames. Brigid was next, offering a metal string from her guitar.

Manuel, bless his heart, was so enthusiastic. He threw a gold coin into the fire on the right. The smile on his face matched the gleam he had as a boy spitting out orange seeds.

No one saw me, of course, but I too passed between the bale fires. My gift needed to be something big, something extravagant, something worthy of the request I was about to make. Recalling a memory from many lifetimes ago, I conjured a gold necklace with a purple stone in the center: a lapis lazuli. Throwing the trinket into the fire on the left, I uttered, "I banish my enemies from Riverine!"

As the evening wore on, lovers, friends, and other couples held hands and leapt across the fires, sealing their contract with the fae.

Of course, Thomas and Tanya jumped. Brigid and Anton jumped. So did Lily and Manuel. Erin grabbed my hand and had me join her in bounding across the flames. To the average onlooker, it appeared Brigid and Erin were alone in their leaps, but no one cared.

The whole night was beautiful and magical.

THE DEVIL

30 May in the Year of Their Lord 2003

The merchants were all at a meeting tonight, but I did not attend. My intuition compelled me to stand guard over Lily's cottage instead. It is a good thing I did.

A large, white horseless carriage pulled into the driveway while Miss Rhoads was away. Stepping out of the monstrosity was that rotten, self-centered concrete peddler Edie Clark, who has been flaunting her money and tempting all the property owners in Rivervine to sell their land.

Every farmer and rancher in northern California knows Edie. Some hate her so much that they would rather die in poverty than sell to her. Others are so financially destitute that they sign over their heritage—family farms that are several generations old—because there is no other way to secure a livelihood for their offspring. It breaks my heart to see the Comatis forced to make that choice.

The bitch knocked on the door.

Since Lily was not home, I shifted into an apparition of the young woman's image. Opening the door, I welcomed Miss Clark inside.

"Lily, I know you're not happy to see me, but hear me out," Miss Clark said in a very professional and calculated tone of voice. "I know you're struggling. I know that grocers are buying their food from Chile and Mexico, but that's just the way the ag business is these days. Let me help you. Sell me your five acres. I can pay you eight hundred thousand dollars in cash. You should be able to provide for your family quite comfortably with that. That's a bigger profit than you can make selling basil."

My rage grew inside. Disbelief, shock, fury, and denial struggled for control of my mind, forcing me into a stupor. I was unable to verbally respond to her proposal.

"Lily, please, I'm not your enemy," she continued. "Think of all the good your sacrifice will do for the local economy. Hard-working middle-class families will be able to afford new homes. Construction workers will have jobs. People won't have to drive so far to go shopping. Urban sprawl is a *good* thing."

I still refused to speak or even offer her the customary peppermint tea and biscuits that Lily always put out as her signature act of hospitality. The tea kettle remained dry. The oven never heated. The butter and jam stayed in the icebox.

I calmed my mind, brought my attention into focus, and floated on the waves of chaos where my mind drifted into a strategy.

"I will consider your offer, but not now, not here," I said. "If Mother sees me talking to you, she will get upset. And I do not want to meet at your office either. I cannot face your staff. I do not want anyone to know. I cannot ruin my reputation as well as my land."

Miss Clark nodded in agreement. I continued with my proposition.

"Can we meet, say, in an hour? At the Prospector Inn outside of town? I hear they rent rooms hourly. I do not know anyone who works there. Do you?"

"No." Miss Clark shook her head. "I think that sounds wonderful. Should I meet you in the lobby?"

"Sounds like a plan," I said bluntly, shaking her hand and walking her to the door.

Miss Clark left in her monster carriage, leaving a trail of noxious fumes.

I planned my attack, scrutinizing every detail. I knew Edie was tribadic, even though the town never discussed it. Although Lily herself was not of that persuasion, I could easily play the role in her stead, harnessing the farm woman's hatred for the land peddler, knowing Miss Rhoads would relish the opportunity to inflict as much emotional and physical damage as possible onto Miss Clark.

When the hour came, I shifted to the lobby of the Prospector Inn, dressed in a tight-fitting red silk dress that had a long slit up the back and very low neckline. With matching black stockings, a small sequin purse, high-heeled shoes, and a diamond necklace and earrings, I—or rather Lily—sparkled like the stars in winter. Putting her long, soft brown hair up in a bun, I left a few loose tendrils sneaking down to shape *our* face. I powdered our face and added some rouge and red lipstick, and voilà—Rivervine's latest debutant was ready for business.

Edie was already there, waiting in the lobby, dressed in the same silk navy suit from earlier today.

"Wow!" Miss Clark exclaimed. "You look amazing. Are you going somewhere afterward?"

"No," I answered, trying to make Lily's voice sound sweet—I am not sure I have ever actually heard her use that kind of tone before. I then dropped the tenor to something sultrier. "I wanted tonight to be … *special*, if you understand what I mean."

Edie was stunned, her eyes zeroing in on my hardened nipples. Standing before her was definitely *not* the peasant girl who showed up to city council meetings in overalls and work boots.

"I booked the room for two hours," she said.

"Wonderful," I purred. "What room are we in?"

"Two thirty-three."

One sexy leg led the other as I catwalked in front of Edie, climbing up the stairs to the second floor, my silk dress clinging to the curves of my derrière. Stopping in front of the door to our room, I whipped around and announced, "This is it!"

Edie had the key in hand and opened the door.

I thrusted her onto the bed and started ripping off her clothes, pinning her down and biting her neck.

"Oh my God, I love this," she murmured.

I reached down to feel between her legs. Her wetness soaked through her suit, confirming how much she was enjoying it.

Then she suddenly dried up and pushed me aside. Catching her breath, she told me, "I can't do this. It's too soon … Dorothy."

Unable to feign respect her grief, I stood up, straightened my dress, and told her, "You should wash up. I think we are done here."

She nodded and headed into the wash room. Before closing the door, she turned to me and asked, "Are you actually interested in selling your land or was tonight meant to be a cruel joke?"

"You did not even attend her funeral."

"Is that what you are mad about?"

"No. I think you are rotten scum. The Black Land will never be yours. It is sacred space, and you are not worthy of it."

I sensed the bile churning in her gut. Her arms shook as she closed the door to the wash room.

When I heard her lift the toilet lid, I shifted into the form of a black widow and joined her on the commode. Digging my teeth into her labia, I shot venom into the bitch's bloodstream. The poison flowed through Edie's body, causing excruciating convulsions and stopping her heart. She was dead within a few minutes—long before the real Lily returned home from her meeting.

.

EIGHT OF SWORDS

14 June in the Year of Their Lord 2003

I am unwell tonight. My frailty comes as a result of the beginning of the summer season. Over the next two weeks, the lengthening days and shrinking nights will torture vampires like Anton and myself.

As I suspected, my scribe Glenda will suffer as well.

I mentioned earlier in this grimoire that the Earth is not a perfect sphere. It wobbles back and forth on its axis. Therefore, there is no actual *longest* day of the year. Today commenced a two-week period with only eight hours and *forty-two* minutes between sundown and sunrise. However, there will be two days—the nineteenth and twenty-fourth of June—that have only eight hours and *forty* minutes of nighttime, making them both *the shortest nights of the year.*

My greatest grandfather, Radu, has been working with young Thomas, whom we call Traycor now, to develop a Comati system of astrology—one that uses the shadows of the stars as opposed to the constellations. As part of their work, they are measuring the hours of darkness in each night. Traycor is using information provided by the United States Navy to track the movement of the sun and moon. According to their records, the sun will cross the Tropic of Cancer on the twenty-first of June at ten minutes after two o'clock in the afternoon, signaling the official start of the summer season in the northern hemisphere. It will be winter south of the equator.

But I do not need military intelligence to tell me spring is ending. My energy is weak. My thoughts are cloudy, and my emotions are unstable. Creativity escapes me. When I was incarnate, I would get horrible headaches, nausea, and exhaustion during this time of year. There is so much buzzing and stirring, growing and blooming—creating a commotion that fills the vicinity and competes with the comfortable stillness of the vampire's refuge. The sensory overload is unbearable.

I had planned on sequestering myself in the wine cellar during this period. But my solitude lasted only a moment before I sensed the call of my scribe. The signal weighed heavy with illness and physical torment.

I shifted to Glenda's apartment and found her lying on the floor next to the toilet—her body curled into a half circle with a pillow under her head and a well-worn yellow baby blanket clutched in her arms.

I knelt beside her, lifting her head into my lap and rubbing her forehead. She cried out to me, begging, "Just put my head in a guillotine, please! My head is killing me. And I've been puking all morning."

I looked at her quizzically because I did not understand the term she just used. "What is *puking*?" I asked.

"Vomiting," she whimpered. "I'm sorry. I keep forgetting you're not familiar with contemporary colloquialisms."

"That is quite all right, dear," I responded, continuing to stroke her brow. "Why do you hold a baby's blanket?" I asked.

"Oh, this was mine when I was a little girl," she answered. "I still snuggle with it when I have one of my episodes."

"How long have you had these headaches?"

"Since I was four years old. I call them 'migraines,' but they're not technically *migraines*. I don't see flashing lights or silver halos around objects. But I have these brutal headaches, violent vomiting, and extreme sensitivity to light, noise, and fragrance. Even with thick, dark curtains, there is still too much light coming through my bedroom window. I've been going to doctors for decades, but no one can ever diagnose what's causing my headaches. My blood-sugar levels are all normal. My white and red blood cells are all normal. There's nothing identifiably wrong with me. I have taken every pain killer and migraine medication on the market, but nothing helps."

"Are your headaches worse in the summer?"

"Summer is sheer misery for me! The long, hot, sunny days nearly kill me every year."

A gloomy ambience enveloped the room as she continued her commentary.

"The biggest problem is that I just don't have time to be sick," she sobbed. "Summer is the time of year when the most car accidents occur, the most criminals prowl, and the most special events take place. I have to cover these stories! I'm a journalist for chrissakes! If I don't write them, someone else will, and I'll be out of a job."

As her tears pooled on the floor, I scried into the reflection. The image showed me what I suspected all along—her illness was caused by her chi, not her physical body.

"The doctors are correct, dear; there is nothing physically wrong with you," I told her.

"What the fuck do you mean?" she charged. "Jesus Christ, Zinfandel, I thought you of all people would be on my side."

Understanding how difficult this was for her to hear, I held Glenda tighter against me and rocked her weakened body back and forth with gentle motions.

"This is going to shock you to hear this, but … you are a vampire."

She shot up out of my lap and incredulously demanded, "What the hell are you talking about? There's no such thing as *vampires.* I know there are freaks out there who are into sucking blood and gothing out …"

I interrupted her: "What does *gothing out* mean?"

Falling back down into my lap, she answered, "Oh, *goths* are those punks who dress in all black and wear black lipstick and listen to that really heavy music about death and Satan and all that crap. They're really into vampires too."

Like Erin, I thought to myself.

"I'm not like that at all!" she continued. "I'm normal!"

"No, dear. You are *not* normal," I corrected. "There are many forms of vampirism. You are what we call *sanguinarian.* Sanguinarian vampirism has nothing to do with outward appearances or lifestyle choices."

I explained that blood is the source of chi—vital lifeforce energy. Some people are born with the inability to generate chi on their own. Therefore, they must consume this essence from other sources. Most people survive in polite society by eating red meat—usually cooked rare instead of well done so the blood is still present. Blood is the only complete conductor of spiritual energy.

"*Spiritual energy?* Are you gonna get religious on me, Zinfandel?" she asked, laying her head back down into my lap. "If so, can it wait until I feel better? I'm really not in the mood right now."

I chuckled, then rolled her head and body toward my face so I could look her in the eye. "This is important, darling," I told her emphatically. "This goes far beyond religion. You need to know this because it is the only way you are going to be able to deal with your disposition."

Glenda groaned with a sense of skepticism and turned onto her side facing away from me. "I am so sick," she sobbed. "Can you just kill me and spare me the small talk? I don't care if you take me to heaven or hell. Just put me out of my misery."

"Heaven and hell are states of mind, not actual places, dear," I told her, stroking her scalp and running my fingers through her fine, dark-brown hair. "Vampirism is a condition of one's soul. You see, darling, every animal, vegetable, and mineral has a spirit. Those spirits emit energy that radiates at particular frequencies along the spiritual spectrum. Because of our nature, we vampires are extremely sensitive to higher frequencies such as bright light, crowded rooms, high-pitched noises, and strong scents. If we are exposed to too much energy, we become very sick—just like you are now."

She sighed again, her skepticism obvious.

"Are you gonna make me calculate the coefficient of spiritual friction or something?" she asked sarcastically. "This is starting to sound too much like physics class. I've been out of college for a long time. I've forgotten all that stuff. Besides, my head …"

She moaned horribly. I kept quiet and continued stroking her brow. A moment later, her eyes squinted and she asked, "Do you know why it's worse in the summer?"

"The sun is a giant ball of energy that bombards you with its warm, bright rays," I answered. "During the summer, the days are longer; therefore, you are exposed to more of the sun's power. Light inspires plants to grow and animals to mate. Humans become more active. Even the ground emanates heat waves. There is so much energy vibrating at such high frequencies that vampires cannot handle the overstimulation."

"So what do I do?" she barked. "I don't wanna drink blood. That is so gross! I like sex, but I'm not into BDSM."

I did not know what *BDSM* meant, but this did not seem like a good time to ask, so I just ignored the comment.

The scribe wept for a few moments and then gazed at me with an embarrassed expression on her face.

"I'm sorry, Zinfandel," she said. "Do you mind giving me some privacy? I have to pee before I puke. I've learned that when my bladder gets full during one of these episodes, I need to empty it before I throw up again. Otherwise, I lose control of my bladder and urinate all over the place. So far, I've been lucky to have my stomach hold out long enough for my bladder to relieve itself."

With a feverish daze, she apologized: "That was kind of gross, wasn't it? I'm sorry."

I respected her privacy and left her alone so she could take care of her needs. While she was busy urinating and vomiting, I shifted to the home of Susan Rhoads to get some herbal tea.

This time of year, she always keeps her icebox filled with jugs of tea made with feverfew and lemon balm. She has given aid to so many vampires that the tea has become a staple in her home during the summer. The spiritual frequency of both plants radiate at low, vampire-friendly levels. Drinking cold tea made with these herbs helps counterbalance the high frequency of summer's energy. It also alleviates the headache and settles the stomach.

When I returned to Glenda's home, she had managed to make it to her sleeping chamber to lie down. "The worst is over, I think," she told me. "I usually get so sick the first few hours that I can't leave the bathroom. But once I puke up everything, I usually pass out for the rest of the day."

"*Pass out?*" I asked.

"Fall asleep," she answered. "I'm sorry. I did it again, didn't I?"

I chuckled and handed her the jug. "Drink this," I told her. "It will comfort, rehydrate, and soothe your soul."

"Is it blood?" she grimaced.

"No, no," I chuckled. "It is cold tea. The herbs in it will help balance your yin and yang. When you are this sick, you cannot digest blood. You need something light and refreshing. The blood is needed once you have purged the excess energy."

"I really don't want to drink blood," she said as she accepted the tea and swallowed a large mouthful. Then she set the jug on her nightstand, turned on her side facing the outer edge of the bed, and curled into the same half-circle position I found her in earlier. I crawled into bed behind her and rubbed her forehead.

As she drifted off to sleep, she softly uttered, "Your cold fingers feel good on my face."

I kept watch over her the remainder of the day, although I rested awhile too. She awoke a few times throughout the afternoon, running to the toilet and attempting to vomit without anything actually coming up (she referred to the problem as *dry heaves*), but she quickly fell back asleep upon returning to bed.

By sunset, the headache and nausea were gone, but she was still very weak. I told her to just relax while I conjured some poached eggs and toast—foods that were easy to digest after a summer episode.

~ The Star ~

When nightfall came, Miss Fern seemed to be in pleasant spirits, albeit extremely frail. This seemed like a good time to introduce her to sanguinary feedings. Her apprehension to drinking blood was obvious, but I knew it was the only way for her to get her strength back.

I instructed her to bathe and dress in her sexiest attire.

"I don't have any sexy attire," she whimpered.

"I'll take care of that," I said, conjuring a low-cut black silk dress. I also drew her bathwater, filling the tub with some lavender bath salts I found on her counter.

She soaked for about half an hour, allowing the salt from the bathwater to leach away her migraine and soften her skin. When she emerged and dried off, she smelled fresh and her aura emitted a healthy glow.

I painted her face and curled her hair, then had her slip into the dress. It clung to her curves nicely, although her self-confidence spoke otherwise.

"I feel like such a poser in this thing!" she scoffed. "And this is way too much makeup, Zinfandel."

"But you need that much to bring your eyes out from behind those glasses."

"I look like a drag queen."

I shook my head, not understanding the term.

"A man who dresses like a woman for entertainment. They're extremely talented, but damn, they cake on the makeup."

"Oh posh!" It was my turn to scoff. "Besides, you don't have a masculine figure. You have a very appealing chest, and your legs are long."

"But my feet are *huge*. My ass is wide, and my gut looks like Santa Claus. I'm a freakin' cow! I have no business wearing this dress."

She paused for a moment and stared in the mirror as if wheels were turning in her mind.

A moment later, she called out, "Zinfandel …"

"Yes, Glenda, darling."

"Can you conjure another dress for me? Black, of course, but one that is a little longer, say calf length, and instead of slinky, can you make it billowy like a belly dancer? And for the top, can you make it look like a corset but give me long bell sleeves? Keep the neckline low, of course. That part is okay. I do kinda like my breasts."

"Perfect!" I admitted, adjusting the illusion per her request. "My dear, you look stunning."

She smiled a graceful "thank you," and we headed out— myself dressed in a modest black outfit so as not to detract attention from my protégé.

Glenda was still in a state of quasi-catatonia—deficient in mental acuity, with glassy eyes and sluggish motions. This is actually a good condition for a vampire to be in prior to feeding. The absence of cerebral and physical distractions conserves energy for the chase. One of the setbacks of vampirism is that the incarnate is part wild animal hunting for prey and part human existing in a functioning society. By reducing the human factor of the equation, the vampire is able to focus its efforts on satiating its lust. My job was to act as animal trainer.

The scribe and I walked to the dance hall as it was not a long-enough distance to warrant taking the horseless carriage. When we arrived, a lively band played and a group of people dressed in decorated green jackets filled the room. Their uniforms boasted numerous ribbons and medals, and the air carried conversations centered on an upcoming military operation in my homeland. I could not distinguish their faces, though—a five-pointed star radiating in blue light obscured my view each time I attempted to look them in the eyes.

Glenda's aura homed in on a man with the arc of three chevrons gracing the upper shoulder of his jacket sleeve.

"Is he handsome?" I asked her. "I cannot see his face."

"Yes," she replied, her voice slow and low. "But there is something about him—more than just his looks."

"What do you mean by *more*?"

"He has a story to tell me. A story he *must* ... tell ... *me*!"

"How do you know this?"

"The blue star. Do you see it ... hovering above Father Armando? It is speaking to us."

I looked to the left and noticed Fathers Armando and Kristobal approaching our table.

"Hello, Glenda," the priest greeted. Reaching to shake my hand, the incarnate introduced himself. "I'm Father Armando. I don't believe we've met."

Kristobal shushed me before I could even speak.

"They cannot see me," he telepathically cautioned me. "Glenda sees me as a blue star. Armando does not see me at all. He knows the legends about you, so don't give him your name or our mission will be jeopardized."

Looking in his direction, I blinked, assuring our confidence.

Although I recognized Father Armando from my previous hauntings, I realized I had not yet formally manifested before the priest.

"Nice to meet you," I answered, accepting Armando's hand but eschewing an equal introduction. "What brings you here?"

"Tonight is our gala to celebrate the retirement of Father Donovan. I am going to oversee the chaplaincy once he leaves. The troops and I are deploying in January."

As the barmaid passed our table, Armando stopped her to order three whiskeys on ice. When she returned with our drinks, the padré raised his glass, encouraging us to follow suit.

"Let us all toast to the men and women of the United States military, without whom our freedom would not exist," he asserted.

"Cheers!" Glenda and I concurred as the three of us clinked glasses.

Armando bobbed his head to the music while Glenda's attention returned to the man with the arc of three chevrons. Homing in on the metal tags around his neck, I noticed they read, "Humphries Patrick W" followed by a nine-digit number and references to O Neg and No Rel Pref.

Blood type O? The perfect donor. And No Religious Preference leaves the door open to Comati culture, I thought to myself.

When I looked her way, the blue star now coated Miss Fern's face and skewed toward her mate. She left our table and walked to this Humphries Patrick W person, who took her hand and led the woman to the dance floor. Father Armando continued sitting at my table, drinking his whiskey and bobbing his head to the music.

"What are you doing?" my telepathy questioned Kristobal.

"I am here to oversee these travelers."

"What does this have to do with Glenda?"

"She will follow Staff Sergeant Humphries' deployment to Iraq as both a journalist and a love interest."

The heat of my aura blazed.

I was familiar with the various ranks of the United States Army from my time with Lugh, a.k.a. Sergeant O'Byrne, so I was well aware that it was the lower ranks that were first put in harm's way before the officers joined the fray. They were also paid pittance for salaries and given the cheapest weapons to fight with. Worst of all … they made the most widows. This was *not* the prophecy I saw when I commissioned my scribe.

"No! You cannot take her away from me!" I silently charged to Father Kristobal. "And for an *enlisted* soldier? Can you at least find a higher-ranking officer to complement her?"

"She is going to write about the war from a lower-echelon point of view—a side nary a reporter has covered as most prefer to speak with the officers in command," he replied. "This will boost her career and satisfy the longings of all enlisted men and women who dreamed their memoires would be documented in a national publication."

"But I need her to write my biography!"

"Vondella," Kristobal tried to calm me. "She needs to return to Sumer. And you know why … Join us!"

Father Armando interrupted my stupor.

"I should get back to my soldiers," he said, excusing himself.

"It was very nice meeting you," I nodded politely. "Safe journey."

As he walked away, I saw Glenda and Humphries swaying back and forth to some song about *forever yours, faithfully.*

What on Earth was I thinking? Vampires do not usually marry. No spouse would understand our condition—the sickness, the unpredictable creative impulses, the need for darkened living quarters and lengthy periods of solitude.

Not all lovers can be Lugh, I thought.

People of our ilk seduce consorts, feed off them while they are strong enough to sustain us, then set them free to heal and enjoy the rest of their lives in normal society. How do I make Glenda understand?

The ballad ended and the band played a new song—something upbeat but still seductive. Instead of returning to her seat at my table, she continued dancing with Humphries. Pushing my concerns aside, I chose to act as an erotic guide and coached her telepathically.

"Very good, my darling. Sway back and forth. Now breathe to the rhythm. The song is in a 6/4 time signature, so inhale with the downbeat; exhale with the backbeat—in two, three, out two, three."

She followed my instructions, her gaze holding steadfast on the man with the arc of three chevrons. Whiskey, music, breath, and movement—such fine ingredients contained in an elixir aligning her chi with that of her prey.

I noticed the soldier responding favorably to Glenda's dancing. His heart raced and the star covering his face slanted further toward her—his capture imminent. I continued the choreography:

"Now visualize a serpent coiled at the base of your spine. The snake heeds the call of the music, uncoiling vertebra by vertebra."

Glenda rotated her hips slowly, protruding her pelvis, allowing the imaginary serpent to rise up her abdomen. She arched her back, jutting her chest forward, spreading her bosom wide and isolating it from the rest of her spinal column. As she rotated her ribcage, her wondrous cleavage played peek-a-boo with the audience of one.

The scribe's arms rose above her head to allow the snake to grow even higher—her body moving in sinuous motions that spanned the entire length of her luxurious body.

"At this moment, my dear dancer, you and the snake respire as one. Feel the breath flowing on your forked tongue as you exhale. When you inhale, focus on the oxygen rising up your nasal passage. Once it reaches the junction of your eyes and nose, imagine a special pit there, anchoring your chi, allowing you to sense the fluctuations in your prey's aura, enabling you to detect his movements—physical, mental, spiritual, and sexual."

Glenda obeyed, shedding the mundane world and drawing the fantasy realm closer to the soldier. Her focus homed in on the bronze medals embellishing the warrior's chest—the metal emitted an energy that synchronized their breath, coordinated their brain waves, and complemented their moods. Their groins throbbed with excitement at not only their prospective romantic encounter but also the potential realization of their mutual life dreams. The energy was so great that even I responded.

"He is perfect! Remember, you need very little blood to satiate the hunger. Too much, especially at first, can make you very sick."

"Blood?" she screamed out loud, shaking loose her psychic connection. "I don't want to drink blood. That is so gross!"

The music was so loud that no one heard the words shouted, but Glenda's dance partner noticed her outburst and started to walk away. Unsure how to explain herself, she reached for him and shook her head, "Oh, no, not you, sorry. I was spacing out, thinking about a conversation I had earlier today."

"Oh … okay," he hesitated, unsure if this new dance partner was crazy or not.

Recovering from her faux pas, she said politely, "I am so sorry. This has just been a day. Can we start over? Hello. My name is Glenda Fern, and I'm not normally this weird."

The man with the arc of three chevrons chuckled and said, "I'm Patrick Humphries. Nice to meet you. Hey, aren't you the editor of the newspaper?"

"Yes, I am," she answered with a low, mesmerizing tone.

With their eyes firmly locked, she led him to the table we had been sharing.

"Glenda!" I cheered, acting as if she were rescuing me from my loneliness.

Her new friend and I shook hands as we introduced ourselves. I gave him my name as Vondella, instead of Zinfandel, assuming he was less familiar with my given name than my moniker.

"Do you two ladies drink wine?" Patrick asked. "I'm a huge fan of Fermata Cellars' Tango blend. Can I order us a bottle to share?"

When the barmaid returned, Patrick poured our drinks and gestured for us to lift our goblets.

"To Saint Christopher!" he cheered. "Patron saint of travelers. May he protect us during our tour of Iraq."

"Yes, to Saint Christopher," I echoed. "Slántcha! That's Gaelic."

"Nostrovia!" Glenda responded. "That's Polish, but if you say it when you're really drunk, it sounds like *nice driveway*."

We all laughed, and the two of them continued staring into each other's eyes. The couple made small talk during the remainder of the evening, never breaking their gaze with one another. As I listened to their conversation, her adeptness at the language arts became apparent. She tuned into his mind, asking him questions that spawned conversations about music, childhood influences, and places of interest. The ice broke without the awkwardness of appearing too forward.

I was obviously in the way, so I excused myself.

"If you two will pardon me, I need to get home to my sick brother."

They both nodded and bid me goodnight, although I doubt either of them noticed my absence at all.

After leaving the dance hall, I eschewed my physical apparition and shifted back to the table to eavesdrop on Glenda and her consort.

"I actually want to drink this guy's blood," her thoughts admitted, unaware that I could hear them. "That sounds so gross. I wonder if I'm going insane. Maybe it was just the power of suggestion. Thanks, Zinfandel. Now I'm going batty."

Before I responded, I paralyzed Glenda's face for just a moment in order to avoid what inevitably would have been a panicky reaction. I did not want her to break the hypnotic, seductive eye contact with her prey.

"You are not crazy," I answered. "Stay calm. Keep focused on him. You are doing an excellent job building confidence with the man. Once he trusts you, he will feed you."

"I don't want to feed! Can you make this go away?"

"Darling, it is who you are. And it is who he wants to be."

"What do you mean by 'he wants to be'?"

"In time, you will learn to identify donors by reading their thoughts. You will tap into their innermost fantasies. And you will be able to sense the aura of their blood to know if it is safe to drink."

"Oh, that is so gross! Stop it right now! I'm not ready for this!"

"Very well. I will leave you to your consort. When you are ready for a sanguinary feed, call for me. I will guide you. It must be handled with extreme caution for your wellbeing as well as his."

I unfroze her face and left the dance hall, returning to the cave where I found Anton just as sick as Glenda had been.

Instead of playing music, we spent the night along the riverbank, bathing in the mist and enjoying the company of nocturnal creatures. One of his cougar friends brought him a fresh kill—a domestic cat.

"When I am human again, I am never letting my pets outdoors at night," Anton asserted as he drained the feline of its blood.

Hermit Crosses Three of Swords

21 June in the Year of Their Lord 2003

This summer evening has me weak—very, very weak.

An adversarial feeling has long filled the air and had I not been so frail, I could have dealt with it much more efficiently. I could have divined the approaching opponent and prepared a strategy. Instead, I overlooked several important clues signaling the enemy's growing occupation in Rivervine.

The last customer to leave the tasting room this afternoon was the local mortician, Warner McCain. My guard dropped at the sight of this beautiful creature in my tasting room. He is a handsome man who reminds me of Lugh—tall and lean, about the age of forty, with long black hair, beautiful blue eyes, and high cheekbones.

He sits on the city council with Carmelita Anza, whom you may remember from my entry about the vernal equinox. She is serving as mayor this year; he is the vice mayor.

Although the councilman has *spied on* me since he was a young boy, he has never *summoned* me. His voyeurism has increased in recent years, as he seems to enjoy watching the bruja and I making love in the vineyards.

I allowed his intrusions in the past, assuming he was just another member of my audience. But tonight, his intentions were of a more malefic nature. This lesson cost me dearly. I will never again assume I know a petitioner's objective without proper divination.

Mr. McCain purchased a case of Requiem, the winery's old vine zinfandel, shortly before leaving the tasting room this afternoon. He did not go directly home. Instead, he parked his horseless carriage off the main road a short way from the winery. There he stayed, waiting for the winery workers to leave.

The tasting room closed at six o'clock, but he hid in his spot until the sun set at eight minutes after eight. That is when he left his carriage and headed to the exact spot where Carmelita always sets up her spring rituals.

My eyes could not help but study him. His all-black clothing fit quite snugly, showing off his statuesque physique. He stood with a grand posture and solid countenance, emitting an air of power and prestige. A pentacle pendant graced his delicious neck, and an athame hung from his belt. The trinkets and clothing gave me the impression that he was Pagan and could therefore be trusted.

Comatis do not use either athames or pentacles in our practices, but the items *are* often used by our friends in other mystical groups.

An *athame* is a double-edged dagger, usually ornately decorated, that some modern witches use for creating sacred space or directing magical energy. It does not actually cut anything in the physical realm. Its power comes from the visualizations of the witch.

A *pentacle* is a five-pointed star with intersecting lines. Each point of the star represents a different spiritual element—earth, air, fire, water, and spirit. The intersecting lines represent the connection among the elements.

I am unsure what religious, spiritual, or magical beliefs Warner McCain subscribes to, but his intent and actions tonight were definitely not aligned with any ethical or moral standards set by any Pagans that I have known in modern times.

The son of a bitch tricked me. But not in the way the fae folk play tricks. He was not being whimsical or clever. And he did not want something shiny in return. Instead, the mortician tried to extort my liberty.

He brought the case of wine and a satchel with him to the vineyard, surveying the surroundings to see if anyone had him in sight. When he felt confident that he was alone, he set down the wine and satchel in the center of the circle. From the satchel he pulled a black altar cloth, red candles in glass casings, a censer, cones of cedar incense, and a bouquet of the darkest red roses I have ever seen. He laid everything in a beautiful circular arrangement on the ground and waited for night to fall.

Once there was no trace of sunlight, Mr. McCain lit the candles and incense and began his invocation. He took the athame, pointed it away from his body, and walked in a circle around the Oppidum chanting, "Zinfandel darling, star of delight. Make love to me as the sun dies tonight."

When he finished, I shifted into my usual apparition and announced, "I have heard your plea, Mr. McCain. But what makes you worthy of my attention?"

He pointed to the box of wine and answered, "I bought a case of your winery's 1999 Old Vine Zinfandel."

"Very good! But what gift did you bring for me?"

"Roses, my love!"

"You make me blush with your devotion, darling. What exactly do you seek of me?"

I assumed he wanted me to disrobe while dancing, making the removal of his own garments part of the performance. He most likely wanted to kiss my breasts, run his fingers along my thighs, and mount me, inserting his penis into my vagina.

I was wrong.

"I have wanted you since I was a teenager," he announced. "I have studied you for decades and know you better than anyone. As I prepared corpses for burial, I listened to every rumor spouted from the families of your victims. I should have been frightened, but I found the stories titillating. Their fear made me want you even more. I find your verve just as seductive as your beauty. It makes me want you all to myself. I alone understand you. I will do anything to make you want me."

His breathing hastened as he grabbed my shoulders and shook me before pushing me to the ground. He sat on top of me, pinning me down and ripping the front of my dress, exposing the entire front of my body. He reached for a bottle of wine and poured the entirety of its contents on my chest, voraciously licking it off as his erection stiffened between us.

In a very stern tone of voice, he threatened, "You know, I have been studying folk witchcraft, Zinfandel."

"Oh really? And what have you learned?" I still wondered if this was part of the lover's game. His aura was murky and I was too weak to see through it.

"I am in a position to make eternity very difficult for you if you refuse me."

"How cliché!" I scoffed, pushing him off me, regaining my composure and conjuring a fresh dress. This was obviously no longer a lover's game.

Catching his breath, Vice Mayor McCain continued, "There are five of us on the city council. The mayor is the only one who supports your agricultural and historical preservation."

"Your point?"

"I have learned how to summon your enemies, Zinfandel. There is one in particular from your past who has reincarnated and is living in Rivervine these days. I can banish him … or …

empower him. The choice is yours. Marry me and I will join Mayor Anza's alliance to preserve the winery. I will also persuade the other three city council members to join as well. Deny me, and I will see to it that your vines are covered in concrete and the words of your enemy rewrite history."

How did I not see this coming? HOW DID I NOT SEE THIS COMING!

I had to think quickly, but I could not think clearly. I settled for trying to appeal to his better judgement.

"You proclaim your love for me, yet you're willing to hurt me like this? Take away everything that I hold sacred? How is that love?"

"If you are going to break my heart, then I want you erased from my memory."

"So who is this *enemy*? Napoleon Bonaparte? Vlad Ţepeş? Erzsébet Báthory? Edie Clark returned from the grave?"

I was playing stupid, of course. I knew damn well who he was talking about.

"Someone who has promised significant financial support to my re-election campaign if the Fermata Cellars property was condemned and sold to him."

The sound of Anton's cobza rang from the east. Doina's violin echoed in the west. This was no joke or sexual play about dominance and submission. Warner McCain was seriously trying to coerce me into being his bride. And he knew my greatest fear, my greatest hatred.

I am not the marrying type, but if I were, it would need to be under sacred conditions—because I had found my soul mate. I could not be blackmailed into making a vow. Besides, how would a ghost and a flesh-bound human live together?

The bellowing from the phantom music grew louder. Father Kristobal chanted Hail Marys. The howls of the wolves, the shrill of the bats, the rustling of elk antlers—the sounds of every discarnate creature that ever roamed this place became so insufferably strident that I burst into hysterics.

I fell to my knees, swayed back and forth, covering my ears, begging for the sounds to stop. No one obeyed. The noises continued. Fear had not controlled me so overwhelmingly since the night I died. Once again, I did not know how to escape.

This was the first time I allowed an incarnate to witness my weakness. From my knees, I looked at him and cried, "There. You have received the performance you paid for. Now take your wine and roses and leave me before I disincarnate you here and now."

"Go ahead and kill me," he challenged. "I have been studying how to realm shift. I will gladly fight you either way, Zinfandel. Make me discarnate and I will still take your land away from you, even from the occult realm."

"With your folk witchcraft?" I heckled, finding my composure and wiping the tears from my face. "There is far more to the craft than summoning ghosts and casting spells."

A strategy finally came to me about how I could battle him. I realized that if I broke his concentration, I could tap into his spirit. So I ripped the athame from his belt and sliced the wrist of his right hand. I stared at the wound, making it drip faster.

Ah, success.

He wavered back and forth—his left hand cuffing his right wrist, trying to control the pain and suppress the bleeding. His eyes turned from beautiful blue to neutral gray, and those luscious cheekbones became ghastly white.

I asked the councilman, "So how does it feel to die? It is not so easy leaving your physical shell, is it?"

He answered not.

"Who is the benefactor that controls you?" I demanded. "Remain silent, and your fantasy of fighting me on the discarnate realm will manifest. I have far more experience than you. Go ahead and push your luck."

I glared at his wound once again, making the bleeding stop, leaving no evidence other than psychological torture. At that point, his aura decrypted, and I tapped into it.

He is in league with Adam. THAT SON OF A BITCH!

"Open your circle and leave this place," I demanded. "I have lost my patience for the evening."

"Think about it, Zinfandel. If you kill me, there will be just another puppet to take my place. And it will be highly unlikely that the new city council member will be willing to negotiate with you."

His fear energy dissipated, but since his plan had not worked the way he had hoped, I figured Mr. McCain had no other choice but to temporarily retreat.

I too retreated for the evening. I am too weak to continue fighting tonight. Tomorrow, though, will be another story.

THE EMPEROR

22 June in the Year of Their Lord 2003

I spent the night on the banks of the river, allowing the energy from the flowing waters to rejuvenate my soul. When dawn came, I shifted to the home of Warner McCain. Without apparition, I spied on him throughout the morning.

Today was Sunday. I already knew that he spent this day of the week hopping from one church to another throughout town. Churchgoing provides him an opportunity to chat with the community and secure potential clients for any of their funeral needs. His associates include every member of Rivervine's clergy—except Xavia Divinorum, of course.

Today his final visit was the First Church of Rivervine at eleven A.M. After the patrons had left, the councilman met the minister in the church office for a private conversation. I remained disembodied as I followed them; my aura already simmering with hatred.

The minister took his seat at the finely constructed walnut desk. Mr. McCain sat opposite the pastor. When the pastor turned around, I obtained a good look at his face—deep into his eyes. At that moment, I saw the soul of an enemy I had not encountered in six thousand years.

Reverend Paul Adamson read the name plate. So that is what he is calling himself these days.

Not much has changed about the marsh dweller, although his skin is now pale and his eyes are blue. I may no longer be a snake living in Sumer, but that man is still the vile piece of refuse he was millennia ago. He continues to spread lies, assert his dominance over nature, and deny equal standing to anyone who does not pledge allegiance to his myth.

Once I learned exactly with whom I was dealing, I realized that Mr. McCain was correct last night when he said he was just a puppet for someone else's ploy. Adam always had a knack for manipulating people, getting them to do his bidding, then having them carry on his legacy even further. I believed with no uncertainty the vice mayor would suffer the same psychological fate as all the others in a long line of liars. The lineage had to stop. Mr. McCain could not be allowed to advance the unholy agenda of the false prophet.

Fortunately for Warner, my fury over Adam time took precedence over dealing with the current heir to the counterfeit throne.

I waited for Mr. McCain to leave the church office before I shifted into my most current apparition and appeared before the Reverend Adamson. I was curious to see if he possessed any recollection of his long-ago past life. Very few humans recall memories of previous incarnations. However, when a relationship exists that is as powerful as the one we shared millennia ago, recognition is often a certainty.

Once he saw me, the bastard did not even flinch. The expression on his face assured me that even though I no longer had fangs or scales, the enemy did indeed recognize me.

"Well, Viper, I see you have changed," he said in a most condescending tone of voice. "So *you're* the ghost of Rivervine. Too bad you've gone *down* the evolutionary scale. You are now a lousy slut with a mix of Gypsy, chink and redskin blood in you. You should have stayed a serpent in the fruit tree."

"I thought you did not believe in evolution," I challenged. "Or do you only deny empirical evidence when it conflicts with your arrogant, self-righteous agenda?"

"Viper, please be fair," he retorted. "My *agenda* to which you allude is based on reason, not selfishness."

"Oh?" I inquired. "What *reason* do you have for killing all the snakes in the marsh? My *entire species* was annihilated; there are no more of us in Eden or anywhere else. And your tirade continues millennia later as you repeatedly oppress women, slander people who are different than you, and insist that you have some sort of divine dominance over the Earth … yet you eschew any responsibility for it?"

"Responsibility?" he refuted. "I'll show you responsibility! This country—the United States of America—is great because of the traditional Christian values that *I* developed. Had it not been for *me* and the divine providence of generations of *my* offspring, *you* would not be here today. And you, dear Serpent, would not have enjoyed the fruits of *their* ingenuity as you reincarnated over the years. You are such an ingrate, you pathetic mutt!"

"You call that responsibility?" I mocked. "You enslaved the Indians, the Africans, the Irish, the Chinese, and anyone else you could force your brutality on, just so they would work for free in order to build your civilization. *You* have been responsible for the murder of millions in the name of righteousness—the Crusades, the witch hunts, the Holocaust, ethnic cleansing, and terrorism throughout the world. How am *I* the one who is being unfair?"

"I am right, and I can prove it," he insisted.

"Proof?" I scoffed. "Your twisted tales always did amuse me. What on Earth is your verification this time?"

"Humans need direction," he answered emphatically. "You always wanted people to think for themselves, to develop their own solutions to problems. The trouble with that theory is there is no consistency. The concepts of right and wrong are too vague. Without a defined moral code, people will wander so far off track that they will not be able to provide for themselves. Homosexuality? Abortion? Wives standing equal to their husbands? No! The human race will deteriorate. Humans need someone to tell them what to do or else they will ramble around like lost sheep without a shepherd. That's all I am—a shepherd."

"Leading them straight to the slaughterhouse!" I asserted. "And what *consistency*? Your myth has caused a schism among your own family. The world now has *three* versions of your ancestral history—the Torah, the Bible, and the Quran. The only common thread is that they all worship the creation—their holy books—over the creator."

Sarcastically, I continued, "I can see how that is better than finding knowledge from a pomegranate tree."

"You were a viper," he reminded me. "You would have killed the woman I loved!"

"I only kill when I am threatened," I said, feeling my anger rising. It took all my sense of decorum not to sink my teeth into his neck to stop him from talking. I mustered enough restraint to use words instead of violence. "She needed me to protect her from *you*. *You* damaged her far more than I ever would. Even if my venom did manage to enter her physical shell, her spirit would have lived on. But you killed that spirit."

"I helped her avoid all the heartache associated with the gluttony of free will," he retorted.

"But you tell people that free will is a gift from this *God* puppeteer," I reminded him. "I heard you say it in your sermon this morning."

"Free will must be moderated just like any other indulgence," he said. "You have free will to choose certain things. Other things require guidance. If we set up policies and procedures, we can have a smooth-running society. There is plenty of room for choices within that structure."

"Such as choosing the iron maiden or the hangman's noose?" I snickered.

I do not think Adamson appreciated my humor. He glared at me and continued his explanation.

"There are times when you need to adhere to particular standards of behavior, otherwise you will lead a life of disease and shame," he said. "Especially women. They must remain soft, delicate and pure. They need a man's protection to keep them beautiful. Intelligence and strength are not feminine features. Liberation ruins a woman's charm. If a man truly loves his wife, he will shelter her from the snakes that prey upon her innocence—tempting her with the false illusion that she is somehow in need of equality. That is why I forbade Eve from communicating with you. Your friendship was as poisonous as your venom. For her own safety, we had to leave. And that is why I led President Bush into thinking the U.S. should conquer Iraq."

"Several nations have deployed military troops to Sumer," I interrupted. "They have already toppled Ishmael and are working to replace his theocracy with a nation of liberty."

"Do you honestly think their presence is about liberating a bunch of sand niggers?" he answered. "It's not even about oil— your pinko hippie friends are making damn sure that *renewable energy* replaces petroleum, and dinosaur blood stays buried in its prehistoric grave. No, dear Viper, I want control of the marsh and all other lands. I want to cover them with concrete and build temples, churches, and mosques. I want shopping centers and cheap housing over every square mile. There will be no more fruit trees growing wild—and no more animal totems giving women some false sense of independence from their men."

It was then a vision came to me:

I saw a group of men accosting Adam and Eve in the marsh, raping and beating them both. The scene was so vicious that I had to close my eyes and turn my head. Even with my eyes shut, the vision of the brutality continued in my mind.

Impregnated by her aggressor, Eve now was considered damaged goods—as if she had somehow asked for it. Adam also considered himself damaged goods—as if it were his fault another man violated his anus.

Ashamed and traumatized, Adam and Eve fled the city of Ur, searching for a life away from the memories.

At one point along the way, they met a witch who gave Eve some herbs to cure her morning sickness. The concoction worked, but her womb cramped and bled for several days. She ran a high fever and nearly died. The baby did not survive.

Adam blamed Eve more and more each day. "If she had not befriended that damn snake, we could still be living there—in our paradise."

Eve became withdrawn and sullen. Adam grew more bellicose. But he learned to channel his

anger by storytelling. He made himself the
protagonist of all his tales. The snake was always the
antagonist. Eve was the ingenue in need of rescue.
The story always ended with his heirs rising to
prominence throughout the world while skeptics and
infidels roasted over the fiery coals of hell.

For a moment, I pitied him. I wanted to hold him and apologize, but then I realized I was not the root cause of his grief. Although he blamed me for all that had gone wrong with his first incarnation, I was not the source of his sorrow.

"Stop!" I cried, opening my eyes and turning towards him. "I wanted nothing more than her friendship. You were so jealous and insecure that you fled to a place that was worse than where you came from. And now look at what you have done. You have not seen your own shortcomings or sought alternatives to your choices. Instead, you have misplaced blame and perpetuated a fable that has killed millions of people in the past six thousand years."

"I speak the truth … always," Adam insisted.

"Really?" I questioned. "You are claiming creative license on events that happened before anyone was around to check your facts. If you are so divinely inspired, who is right—the Jews, Christians, Muslims, Buddhists, Taoist, Yogis, or Pagans? Perhaps your precious God will write his answer on the office walls. Show me the deed to the Promised Land, and I will leave now, never to bother you again."

Reverend Adamson did not answer. As I stood before him, my anger grew so deep that I fantasized about ripping his eyes out of his skull.

I charged toward him. But before my hands could reach his face, I lost control of my physical manifestation. The air grew warm and overloaded with oxygen. I could move no further.

There was no mistaking the identity of the discarnate who had just entered the room.

"Dammit, Kristobal! What are you doing here?" I demanded in frustration. Father Kristobal is the only discarnate stronger than I am. Although I respect him as a philanthropist and teacher, I wish he would stop meddling in my martial affairs.

The Reverend Adamson glared at the good padré with the same condescending mien that I received.

"It figures, Viper, that you would have a Catholic for an ally," he accused. "Catholics are nothing more than pagans worshipping a bunch of dead people they have the nerve to call *saints*."

I myself had to chastise the priest as well. "Why would you want to spare the life of this bigot?" I asked. "And how can you subscribe to a religion built on the lies started by this absurdly malicious individual?"

"Zinfandel, please calm down," the priest begged. "Your fury always keeps you from exercising proper judgment. Think about what will happen if you kill the very man petitioning against the winery. Manuel is working ever so hard to portray Fermata Cellars in a positive light, but if you disincarnate Reverend Adamson, everyone will know you were the perpetrator. Xavia and Sage will not be able to live down that kind of speculation. Old Town will fail for sure, and your vines will die knowing that you were the one who led them to their demise. Is that what you want? Please, I beg you to formulate another strategy."

I hate when he is right. Although I have disincarnated many people who have threatened the success of Fermata Cellars, the stakes are higher on this project. The city council and local press are now involved. I have to avoid controversy as much as possible.

Frustrated and full of rage, I left the church office, knowing that the incident today was enough to stir up trouble. Fortunately, no incarnates witnessed my visit; therefore, there was no evidence for Reverend Adamson to use against me. But that never stopped him before. Telling lies, exaggerating what little truth did exist, alluding to wrongdoing, and creating misperceptions are all part of his *modis operandi*. I lost my first battle against him. I will not lose again. I have to think quickly in order to disprove any stories he may already be mustering.

STRENGTH

26 September in the Year of Their Lord 2003

I have not written much lately about the Order of the Green Chalcedony, so I will update you, dear reader, at this time.

Thomas and Tanya had a beautiful wedding on the twenty-ninth of June. It was held here at the winery. Xavia officiated and Brigid sang. Although the two youths were too young to drink alcohol, the Divinorums had some non-alcoholic wine available.

Erin continues to be on her own path. Hopefully she will find her footing soon, but time will tell. This morning, she disrupted my morning exercises by rushing through the cellar door and heading downstairs without even turning on the light—her chi was so powerful she glided down each step in complete grace. Her aura blistered with anxiety and anger.

"Zinfandel, are you here?" she called.

"Yes, darling, what is wrong?"

The young woman could hardly stop crying long enough to speak. Once she finally caught her breath, she told me what the trouble was.

"I have been volunteering at the local wildlife sanctuary ever since last November. I was in charge of the snakes. When I got to work this morning, they were *all dead*. Someone broke into their cages and cut off all their heads. We don't know who did it or why. The police are investigating the incident."

I held her against me and allowed the poor girl to cry on my chest. The moment her first tear soaked through my dress, a vision appeared in my mind's eye.

"Adam. It was he who killed the snakes."

I have told her and all of the members of the Order of the Green Chalcedony about my history with the false prophet.

"I figured as much," she replied. "What are we going to do?"

I had to think on this one for a bit. Adam is adept at pitting his allies against each other. He knows I am here in Rivervine and my snakes are sacred. I am sure he also knows Erin works at the zoo and is psychically connected to me; therefore, she would run to me once she discovered the crime. I am equally certain he is feasting on her fear.

"Never feed your enemy," I cautioned.

The young woman caught her breath and nodded. I have apparently trained her well because she knew exactly what I meant by that statement.

She straightened her back and inhaled deeply, looking me directly in the eye.

"Ready, Vondella?" she signaled.

"Ready, Erin."

Together, we performed a series of fluid movements, synchronizing our breath with our minds, meditating as we balanced our yin with our yang.

After a few moments, the snake enthusiast called out, "I'm having a vision, Vondella."

We continued our exercises as she spoke, her eyes still open but trancelike.

"Palm trees crash against a red sky. Sand rushes through the air—it's so fine, like talcum powder. A man's voice intones a call to prayer. Gunfire interrupts the prayer, and the ground becomes slick with blood. I am there … but I am not afraid. I am being guided by a woman in a white dress with a gold headband dotted with purple stones."

Her voice grew louder and more agitated. Her breathing hastened.

"People are calling my name. They're screaming for me. 'Specialist Tuft! Specialist Tuft!' I grab my M16 and run. The sand is so thick, I can barely see. It chokes me, fills my nose and my lungs. Even my ears. I run toward the sound of those calling my name."

She stopped her exercises and bowed to me.

I kissed her cheek, tasting a tear.

Specialist Tuft nodded and ran back up the darkened stairs.

I heard the mumbling of voices in the tasting room. And then I heard Xavia's voice cry out, "Army?"

"I have to do this!" Erin yelled back. "Please say you understand."

THE TOWER

30 September in the Year of Their Lord 2003

War is now waged. Once again, Adam has challenged me for land. And once again, his battle cry was rife with slander and unforgivable, hurtful untruths.

I knew Reverend Adamson and Councilman McCain had something devious planned, but what I heard today was nothing I could have foreseen.

A tall white-haired man came into the tasting room this afternoon, saying his name was Arnold Franklin and he was here to investigate complaints about some *nuisances* at Fermata Cellars.

I remained disembodied but followed him to the upstairs office where he sat with Xavia, Sage, and Manuel at the meeting table.

"I understand strange events occur at the winery," Mr. Franklin said. "Unexplained noises, bizarre electrical outages that don't affect any other local customers, people mysteriously getting sick after drinking Fermata Cellars wine. Is that true?"

"I am unaware of anyone getting sick after drinking the wine, unless they have consumed too much," Sage answered, avoiding the topics of the noise and electricity.

The three of them talked further about sanitation and reports from the state. They then headed down to the cellar to check for rodents and searched other parts of the building for safety hazards.

Everything seemed fine—no violations, although Mr. Franklin pointed out the city had a law stating, "Anything that is a nuisance—health, safety, noise, visual, or otherwise—may be considered grounds for abatement."

As Mr. Franklin left, he mockingly asked the Divinorums to "warn the *ghosts* that we have laws against nuisances."

He then handed them a piece of paper saying they had thirty days to get rid of the nuisance or the Divinorums would lose their business.

A short while later, Manuel pulled up some information on his writing contraption showing a list of several hundred people who have filed nuisance complaints against Fermata Cellars, all of them at the behest of Reverend Paul Adamson with the First Church of Rivervine.

"Crap!" everyone yelled in unison.

Once the employees had left for the day, I joined Xavia and Sage for a muster session in the cellar.

"How do they intend to get rid of a ghost?" Xavia asked.

"Councilman McCain knows how," I answered. "But I think I know someone who might be able to help us."

THE HIEROPHANT

2 October in the Year of Their Lord 2003

The Divinorums had a meeting with the Old Town merchants tonight to discuss the threats posed by Reverend Adamson. Instead of joining them, I paid a visit to my friend Todd Caprasen.

He now teaches at the university in Davis, but I first met Professor Caprasen when he was a college student studying the Black Land. In fact, he is the one who introduced me to the Divinorums. We have occasionally kept in touch over the years.

He had always been a night owl during the years that I knew him, so I hoped I would find him working tonight. I was not disappointed.

Todd is ever so handsome now. The gray in his beard suits him well, and he keeps it neatly trimmed. His tall stature and broad shoulders fill out his black silk suits nicely.

"Hello, my friend," I said, announcing my presence.

"Well, hello Vondella!" he greeted me with a smile. "It is good to see you."

I conjured a couple wine glasses and a bottle of Z Sharp— our driest zinfandel blend and his longtime favorite.

He accepted the glass, cheering, "You remembered! It is amazing how your wine allows me to find new perspectives on my research."

"I am glad you like it."

"You seem troubled. And I assume your visit is not a random social call."

Unable to maintain my composure, I started to bawl, telling him the whole story from start to finish—McCain, Adamson, Franklin.

"However can I help you, Vondella?" he offered. "I owe my career to you. I would be honored to repay your kindness and generosity. Besides, I worked very hard in that area to prepare it for what it is today. I would hate to see it go to waste."

"Adamson has told the people of Rivervine the Comatis are hideous monsters who do evil things in the name of Satan. If memory serves me correctly, you are a priest of the Egyptian god Set, are you not?"

"Yes. But my congregation is only thirty-three strong. I know of this Adamson person and his numbers near close to a thousand. Vondella, I assure you that your Comati friends do not want to be associated with us. The populace is far too indoctrinated to understand what my group is truly about—just like they are too programmed to understand the mystic arts. They think animism and Satanism are one in the same type of evil. Are you certain dispelling these myths is the tactic you want to use? If Adamson is utilizing traditional Inquisition-style tactics, you can be assured that he is preying on their ignorance. Perhaps you should too."

"I agree that he is preying on their ignorance, but his strategy includes frequent and forceful repetition of a fallacy. If you publicly denounce Adamson, it will be one of the few repetitions of the truth! You are so articulate and persuasive. I need you to tell the city council and the people of Rivervine that Adamson is a cheat and a liar and that his claims have no merit. You are the only one wise enough and bold enough to educate people on such an important issue."

"What do you propose I do?"

"Denounce his ideals. I need you to write to Glenda Fern—she is the editor of the *Rivervine Tribune*, and I have commissioned her to write my biography. Have her print your words in Friday's edition. The people will read them and know what a charlatan Adamson is."

"I doubt the public will believe the words of a Satanist. But they are words the public needs to hear, regardless of who says them. I will pick up a copy of the paper tomorrow morning so I can familiarize myself with this Glenda Fern woman and begin crafting my letter to the editor. I will also make sure either I or a member of my congregation attends every city council meeting until a decision is made."

"Thank you, my friend. Your assistance is greatly appreciated. Please keep the rest of the wine and share it with your lovely wife. You have an open invitation to stop by my cellar."

THREE OF PENTACLES

25 October in the Year of Their Lord 2003

On this day one hundred eighty-three years ago, Xin Hsüan and Xin Crina gave birth to their seventh child and only daughter. They named her Xin Vondella. Over time, she would come to be known as Zinfandel.

My mother told me I was a Scorpio. My father said I was a Dragon. This year, I was the guest of honor at an event the solicitor called the Zinfandel Festival.

It was the loveliest day ever. I am so touched by all the thoughtfulness bestowed upon me by the Comatis—at the behest of the fearful solicitor no less!

Visitors from many miles away gathered in Rivervine just to celebrate the end of harvest season with the Comatis.

Manuel Chavez has been planning this event all year. I am unsure if he knew today was also my birthday, but he orchestrated a fabulous street fair that involved all of the Old Town merchants, farmers, and ranchers, including the Divinorum, Rhoads, and Touchkoff families.

Everything I love about life—music, art, dance, commerce, food, and of course, wine—became the center of the townsfolk's attention. On each street corner, musicians played their guitars, tambourines, or some other instruments. Painters set up canvases along the banks of the river or in the vineyard, making magic with their brushes.

The merchants—and even some of the guests—dressed in garb from the nineteenth century and held festive activities outside their businesses. The women from the hair shop plaited girls' hair, and the animal doctors, Frank and Tony, talked to passersby about animal safety during the Halloween season.

Sage built a platform outside the tasting room where the Russians, Mexicans, and Miwok danced; at the end of the evening, young Brigid and her electrified band performed their *very* loud music. Throughout the day, Xavia and Manuel led workshops on winetasting and food pairings.

This was a memory I will savor through every incarnation.

Ironically, I still have not introduced myself to Mr. Chavez. He is such a devout Catholic that the slightest fracture of his religiosity sends him into fits of great anxiety. For example, he still struggles with the fact that he is, well … *queer*—hardly a concern for the Comatis but an abomination in his faith. More than that, though, is the uneasiness he feels toward our Pagan ways.

Yet he managed to organize a holiday celebration dedicated to the one thing he fears most: me—the devil, the serpent, the Lady of the Vineyard, the vampire ghost of Fermata Cellars.

For someone who does not even know me, Mr. Chavez sure did a brilliant job organizing my party. It was he who coordinated the festivities. Children carved pumpkins, bobbed for apples, and painted their faces while their parents purchased holiday gifts made by the hands of Rivervine's most talented craftsfolk.

Of course, Reverend Adamson tried to ruin the day. He and his associates paraded in front of the winery's entrance this morning carrying signs protesting the Comati religion. My anger raged when I noticed what they were trying to do, but decorum prevented me from causing bodily harm. Instead, I opted to shift into the illusion of a skunk and strutted in front of the protesters, spraying each one, forcing them to flee before too many guests arrived.

Once the intruders vacated, happy families, lovers, and youths coming of age had room to enjoy the goings on.

My scribe was one of the guests. I noticed her walking toward the cellar, so I figured I better meet her there.

"Hello, Zinfandel," she said, walking down the stairs. Her voice sounded cold, but her aura glowed a bright sanguine red. I could smell the semen still fresh in her womanhood.

"Welcome, Glenda," I called back with equal neutrality but trying to sound cordial. "I take it you and your soldier friend had a good night."

"Yes, but that is not your concern."

Respecting her boundaries, I nodded and allowed her to continue.

"I take it you know about the complaints against the winery?" she scolded. "The ones threatening to shut down Fermata Cellars because it's allegedly *unsafe for human occupancy*?"

"Yes, I know about them. This is the work of Reverend Paul Adamson. He is trying to swindle the city council into giving him the property to build his giant church—*a spiritual emporium*, he's calling it."

"How do you know this?"

"I heard him talking to Councilman McCain about it."

"What was McCain's reaction?"

"He said, 'Maybe.'"

"Maybe what?"

"Warner McCain tried to extort …" I could not bring myself to finish my thought.

"Yes? Extort what? Money? How much?"

"Marriage," I finally blurted out.

"Marriage? Between a human and a vampire? Now that is just crazy!"

She huffed and went back upstairs, traipsing out of the winery, unwilling to listen to more of my story. I did not see her the rest of the day.

The average observer would dismiss the episode, saying Glenda was skeptical and ready to give up on our project. But her aura told a different story.

But I refuse to be sad today. I will smile and appreciate all the goodwill the Comatis have imparted upon me.

As I shifted back up the stairs, I saw Anton and Brigid talking in a quiet corner on the left. To my right was the solicitor, pouring wine and smiling, talking with guests about how Z Sharp is the most piquant bouquet of the Fermata Cellars portfolio and how the old vine zinfandel complements dark chocolate. He also talked about the history of the winery, embellishing some of the already sensational folklore. Thomas and Tanya had baked some apple strudel to pair with the mead.

For some reason, the smell of skunk still lingered. I chose to ignore it along with the pain of the sun blasting on me as I enjoyed the outdoors. The sound of the music and sight of happy people celebrating the harvest strengthened my spirit enough to endure the torture.

JUDGEMENT

4 November in the Year of Their Lord 2003

"I don't know what I'm going to say!" Glenda yelled when I asked what she was planning to publish in the paper about tonight's abatement hearing. "Now go away! I have work to do. Just because I'm writing your biography doesn't mean you get to control the Tribune. They are two separate gigs, get it?"

"But Adamson is *LYING*!" was all I could think to retort. I do not recall ever being this upset before. I was actually in hysterics.

"It's not my job to determine who is lying and who is telling the truth. My job is to report the news—objectively and without bias."

"You could write an editorial!" I countered. "Write your objective news piece but *also* write a commentary for the Opinion section of the newspaper."

Her aura calmed down a bit as she pondered the suggestion.

"I suppose this shit show *is* worthy of an editorial," she sighed but then stiffened her back and huffed, "Let me think it all over."

She then pointed her finger at me and scorned, "But there's no guarantee I'm going to take your side on this issue."

"Reverend Paul Adamson is a compulsive, delusional, manipulative swindler who has Councilman Warner McCain on his payroll. What more do you need to say?"

"How about: What is the relationship between Mayor Carmelita Anza and the Divinorums? How come she *always* rules in favor of them? And by the way, who is this Professor Caprasen? I've *never* seen him before."

Together we reviewed the events of the evening and I explained things as necessary.

To summarize, let me just tell you, dear reader, that the meeting started with inspector Arnold Franklin giving his report, reading all fifty-some complaints aloud. "The subject parcel" as he kept calling the Divinorum property, was faulted with numerous public safety and nuisance concerns ranging from noise to fear of the devil. Apparently, Adamson got enough people to claim they were *afraid* of the unexplained phenomena such as flickering lights and optical illusions. The fact that science has not yet been able to explain how the vegetation on the Black Land suddenly regenerated also weighed heavily on people's minds. There was also a bevy of sanitation concerns and allegations that the wine was laced with some sort of illegal substance.

During Adamson's testimony, he assured the council that if they sold the property to him, he and his four hundred-plus followers would exorcise the demons and redevelop the land into a giant spiritual emporium that included a church, school, mercantile, and gymnasium. It would bring peace and prosperity to a land long plagued with evil.

The only person other than Xavia and Sage to speak in favor of *the subject parcel* was my dear friend, Professor Todd Caprasen. He explained that just because the Divinorums were Pagan did not mean they were criminals, and their land was *not* a *doorway to hell* as Adamson accused. As a professor of anthropology, Caprasen testified that it was his professional opinion that folklore and propaganda, not a group of wine-making hippies, were to blame for the nuisance plaguing the town. He even dissected the etymology of words like "devil" (Greek for "slanderer") and "Satan" (Hebrew for "adversary"), indicating that no such creatures actually stalk the streets of Rivervine.

Sadly, Councilman Warren McCain made good on his threat to me a few months ago. In a pretentious, histrionic gesture, he motioned to condemn the property and begin formal abatement procedures. Mayor Anza defended the Comatis, but she was once again outnumbered four to one. Councilmembers Pam White, Perry Josephson, and Brian Mann sided with Mr. McCain.

At the end of the evening, the council gave the Divinorums ten days to appeal the decision. If they did not file an appeal, the city then would own the property, effective on the twenty-eighth of November. The Divinorums, were, however, given squatters' rights through the twenty-first of June. At that time, they will be forced to vacate and abate the property.

When the meeting ended, everyone went their separate ways, although Professor Caprasen joined the Divinorums for a glass of wine at their house. I saw Miss Fern in the back of the room and followed her home.

"What do you think was up with McCain?" Glenda asked when we finally finished recounting the meeting.

I was forced to tell her about the blackmail attempt from last June. I also divulged my relationship with Carmelita Anza. I have no associations with the other three councilmembers.

"No one in their right mind is going to believe any of this," she insisted.

"Then they will not believe a ghost can kill four councilmembers and a pastor," I replied.

Her face went white and lost all expression. Her breathing hastened, and her heartbeat raced. She gulped, unable to let out a verbal response.

"Do not worry," I consoled. "I promise to not involve you."

Once she found her voice, she sputtered out, "I-I-I just heard you … right here … say you're going to kill five people. I'm obligated to report this!"

"Report what? That you are talking to a ghost? A vampire? They will lock you up and have you committed to an asylum for the insane. I suggest you find a rational explanation for why the good reverend wants the land and how he influenced the city council to get his way. Save the supernatural part for the novel."

"Do Sage and Xavia know your plans … for the murders? Does Mayor Anza? Anyone?"

"There is no need to concern them or anyone else. I do not need their assistance … or their permission."

"So you have no moral or ethical qualms about killing people?"

"Of course. That is why I take precautions."

"What *precautions*?" Her trepidation emitted a heavy air.

"When someone dies, they become a ghost. It does me no good to fight an incarnate only to deal with them again as a discarnate, so …"

"So … what?"

"I paralyze their spirit."

"Oh, dear God!" She started hyperventilating.

I searched the kitchen for a bag for her to breathe into. Finding such an item, I waited for the scribe to regain composure before I continued.

At last she took a deep breath, closed her eyes, and fell silent for a moment.

"I am going to put on a pot of chamomile tea," she announced. "Would you like some?"

"That would be lovely, dear. Thank you."

Her nerves never did calm down and her mind never focused, but she did manage to write her account of the abatement hearing for the newspaper. After meeting her deadline for the Wednesday news section, she started to work on an editorial for the Friday Opinion column. Once both pieces were submitted to the copy editor, she relaxed with a glass of Requiem and spent the rest of the night musing over the novel.

I returned to the cave to find my brother clapping.

"Well played, sister," he cheered. "I heard you were on your best behavior all night—did not even flicker the lights of the council chambers or make pictures fly off the walls. And then to manipulate the newspaper woman …"

"Nevermind the Comatis, brother," I answered. "How much longer do I have you?"

"Two days."

"How shall we spend it?"

He tossed me a cake of rosin, grabbed his plectrum, and said, "Something in the key of D minor."

JUSTICE REVERSED

7 November in the Year of Their Lord 2003

The Comatis all knew this would be our last ritual together. Although technically we *could* gather for Iemmol and Beltane, it made sense to end this phase of our community life at Sauin, the celebration of the final harvest.

The Comatis are in a period of transition. Without the Fermata Cellars property, the tribe no longer has its sacred space for rituals. Weighing heavy on each member's heart is the burden of knowing that they too will eventually become targets of Adamson's empire building, and they do not have the resources to fight such a well-funded, charismatic, and politically powerful opponent. What they needed from tonight's ritual was a clear message from the ancestors—everyone who ever called this place home—guiding them on a route to endurance. Would it be wise to join the new church in order to stay close to the land—perhaps even gain power from the new religious monarchy? Will the Comati legacy die, or is there hope to revive the tribe in another area? If so, where? Should they sell their property now or wait until spring when the real-estate market picks up?

Such questions, anxious thoughts, and depressive feelings poured into the Oppidum tonight after Xavia cast the circle. The crimson and black ribbons absorbed the energy, and the matching candles somehow stayed lit despite the numerous ghosts whooshing around. Incarnate and discarnate alike found solace in the incense made of rosemary, cinnamon, cloves, and sage. With so much occult chatter, none of the members played any music; it would not have been heard over the paranormal buzz. Anton and I did, however, perform our duet in the vineyard across the way from the ritual space.

Early on in our performance, the solicitor briefly made eye contact with Anton. The slight glance was enough to inspire Mr. Chavez to dwell on the mystery for the duration of the ceremony.

The most notable moment of the celebration was the group meditation. While everyone had their eyes closed and energy grounded, *my* mentor—the Sumerian goddess Inanna—delivered a message to Erin.

Inanna's beauty is recognized everywhere. Wearing her trademark white gown with a gold and lapis lazuli headdress, she radiated confidence, wisdom, and graciousness that blended wonderfully with her honey-toned skin, coffee-colored eyes, plump lips, and seductive curves.

The most important part of her visit, of course, was her message. She lifted Erin by the underarms; the young woman was barely able to balance on her toes. Inanna kissed the oracle's forehead and said, "Adamson is not a concern for the tribe. What is of most importance is the next fire to come. It will cleanse all of Rivervine in a blaze more destructive in area and ferocity than the fire of 1848. Anyone wishing to survive must leave by the summer solstice."

Inanna released the young woman. Erin then fell to the ground, sobbing.

The goddess started to fade, but I latched onto her; I had further questions to ask. We ended up walking toward the vineyard where we could speak in private. I missed the rest of the ceremony, but at least I was able to speak to the goddess directly.

"Where are they supposed to go?" I inquired.

"Wherever their hearts desire," she answered. "The light of the Comatis is internal. Sacred space is in the mind—not a vineyard, not a garden … not even an ancient city like Ur."

I heard the words. They made sense. But my heart ached nonetheless.

As her apparition disappeared, I could see Anton and Manuel talking. I was too far away to hear what they said, but the conversation ended with my brother handing his cobza to the solicitor.

My jaw dropped as I watched the soul of the most important person in my bloodline leave the occult realm. Looking over at the crowd, I saw Tanya with a newfound glow surrounding her belly.

He is gone!

I refused to cry among the vines—to curse the soil, roots, berries, and leaves with grief, panic, hatred, and despair. Instead, I shifted to the darkest, coldest place I could think of: the cellar. There I conjured my beloved violin. Letting the bow and strings bear the brunt of my sorrow, I knew full well that I was instilling the casks and bottles with melancholia. But I did not care. Let everyone who drinks our *haunted* wine taste the bitterness— putrescence on the nose and anguish in the aftertaste.

Before I could drain my well of tears, the door to the staircase opened. Standing at the top was Manuel Chavez. At that moment, it occurred to me that he and I have never met face to face before. I had to pull myself together and try my best to appear as regal as possible.

~ Page of Wands ~

This was not a good time for him to try to turn on the electric lights. He rattled the switch up and down frantically numerous times, but my depression was too strong; it absorbed all the energy in the room.

I was too weak at first to manifest an apparition, but trying to be a gracious hostess, I took a deep breath and centered my focus, conjuring an oil lamp atop an upturned wine barrel at the bottom of the stairs. I managed to climb up the stairs, swirling in an icy mist to greet him. I had to draw upon his body heat in order to have enough energy for myself. Poor darling, he shivered from the cold and quivered from the fright.

"Oh my God," he begged. "Please don't hurt me. I mean you no harm. I just want to talk about the winery. Please don't hurt me. *Please don't hurt me!*"

By the time he reached the bottom of the stairs, I had consumed enough of his energy to manifest a full-bodied apparition and was able to greet him in his native tongue: "Buenas tardes, Señor Chavez. ¿Como les puedo ayudar?"

With his normal body temperature returning, and fear consuming every body function, sweat soaked his forehead and his hands fidgeted in nervousness. Perhaps surprising him by speaking Spanish was not a wise move. I continued the rest of the conversation in English.

"Step closer, darling. I will bring you no harm." I tried to assure him, but as we locked eyes, I could read the anxiety on his irises and knew the reason he came here tonight. Sparing him the embarrassment of being forward, I went ahead and satisfied his curiosity.

"Yes, I have killed people," I blurted out. "And yes, I am the vampire about whom Miss Fern is writing."

I sensed his blood pressure dropping and noticed goosepimples bristling his arms.

"Oh, poor darling, you're shivering," I consoled, conjuring a warm cloak. "Here, put this on."

Our conversation continued—benign small talk at first as I tried to calm him down. I explained my full name and the story behind the zinfandel grape. I also told him how things went sour with Captain Sooter, and how everything ended with the fire, followed by the Divinorums rebuilding the tribe.

Bless his heart, he was a patient listener, but when I finished my monologue, he abruptly asked a question unrelated to the history of the land.

"What did you tell Glenda Fern that has her acting so strangely?"

"I need a scribe to chronicle my life. She has the gift of storytelling and an understanding of the dark mysteries. She also knows the true meaning of a vampire."

"What exactly is that truth?"

I told him the same story I told the youths and Glenda a while ago. The grimace on his face showed me how repulsed he was, especially when I told him about the menstrual cunnilingus Xavia used to feed sanguinary vampires.

In the hopes of saving his own sanity, he changed the subject—unsure if the new topic improved the direction of our conversation.

"Wh-wh-what's going on at the summer solstice?" he stuttered. "Wh-wh-why do we have to leave?"

The answer dragged our discussion down a long, cumbersome path that honestly had little to do with the upcoming inferno and more to do with my relationship with Reverend Paul Adamson. I told Mr. Chavez all about the marsh, my life as a viper, and my friend, Eve. Once he finally connected enough pieces of the puzzle, he realized that I was, indeed, the entity he feared most—the prototype of the Christian devil.

Whenever people have this epiphany about me, naturally the next assumption is that I am lying. After all, everyone knows the greatest trick the devil ever played was getting people to believe he does not exist. Unfortunately, there is no defense for such a charge. And I have, admittedly, killed people—without remorse. It is easy for a good Christian to conclude that befriending me would ruin one's immortal soul.

The solicitor's anxiety level peaked as his awareness of his aloneness with me rushed to the forefront of his mind. There we stood—in the dark, talking about murder and the original sin. The poor darling was completely vulnerable to my *Satanic* whims. I sensed the bile rushing up his gullet and heard the racing pace of his heartbeat. His limbs shook, and his mental acumen numbed. He finally fell to his knees and bawled. I knelt beside him and held him in a gentle embrace, rocking back and forth.

"My apologies, darling. I did not mean to frighten you," I said, continuing to blather in contrition. At one point, I finally allowed all my tears to gush like a broken dam. It was then the answer came to me.

"I know someone with whom you need to speak," I advised. "Go to Saint Bernadette's. Your answers will be found there."

He looked at me, confused, wondering why Satan would tell him to go to church.

I grabbed a firm hold of his shoulders, looked him in the eye, and insisted, "Go to Saint Bernadette's … or your orange tree—wherever you like."

He turned to me, perplexed, and asked, "You know about the orange tree?"

Lowering my eyes, I answered, "Yes. I am the racer snake you have befriended."

That was the final trigger to shoot him off to Father Kristobal.

THE HANGED MAN

2 December in the Year of Their Lord 2003

I knew this day would come, but foresight is not an antidote for grief. After six thousand years, I may have grown tired of fighting, but despite my fatigue, I have not yet exhausted my supply of fervency. To find that cache of strength, though, I needed a new perspective.

Once again, I have lost my land to that perpetual charlatan. Today Reverend Paul Adamson purchased the Fermata Cellars property from the city for two hundred thousand dollars. The County Assessor's Office had appraised the parcel at nearly two *million* dollars; this was the value on which the Divinorums had been paying taxes for many years. However, four of the five members of the city council agreed that since the property was haunted and therefore unsafe for human occupation, the actual fair market value was … zero. And that is how much the city compensated Xavia and Sage when it confiscated their property on the seventeenth of November.

With the Old Town anchor business gone—and plans for the property to be developed into a giant megachurch—the other Comatis realized their pagan businesses would be the next targets of Adamson's empire-building aspirations. They all met tonight and decided to sell their property as well, hopefully for a fair price this time, and relocate—hopefully where no one has heard the word "Comati" before.

Of course, with this unhappy news, I no longer have a need for a solicitor. After the meeting tonight, Manuel Chavez decided to join his lover in Chiapas, Mexico, where the two men are going to fight for freedom south of the border.

My scribe, Glenda Fern, will be out of a job as well since the *Rivervine Tribune* is closing its doors next summer. Advertising revenues have dropped, and the company can no longer afford to continue publishing. Its last date of publication is scheduled for the twenty-second of June in the Year of Their Lord 2004. The staff plans to have its swan song be the closing of Fermata Cellars and the transfer of power to the Spiritual Emporium.

Miss Fern will be gone by then, though. She has accepted an assignment with a national news organization to follow Staff Sergeant Humphries' Army troop and cover the war in Sumer.

I cannot remember a time when my heart ached more.

But I have learned that sometimes, no matter how passionately we fight for something or how badly we yearn for a certain outcome, we must pause, let go of what we cannot control, and surrender to the chaos.

Those words are obviously easier to write than abide by, but nonetheless, the fact remains that my world has been turned upside down. My plans have failed. My only choice now is to refocus.

I spent the evening in my cave—alone, of course, since Anton is now in utero. As I meditated, I tried to calm down, but I could not dismiss the rage. I realized I had to confront the one person who had the power to correct this debacle: the Nazarene mystic.

The wisdom from Father Kristobal's meditations, the divination from Xavia's spellcasting, and even the strength gained from my father's martial-arts lessons all have lacked the acumen I needed to conquer this warlock known as Reverend Paul Adamson. He has inspired in the populace of Rivervine such a monstrous combination of spiritual futility and materialistic wantonness that neither reason nor genuine righteousness can shake them out of their stupor.

I never bothered fraternizing with the weak, mediocre laypeople who stayed outside the Comatis' boundaries. Those cowards never could hold intellectual conversations or pour a decent glass of wine. I never had patience for people who did not concern themselves with higher goals such as pondering life beyond the measly existence that got them through each day.

For more than thirty years, I have invested my time and energy in the Comatis. They were my hope. I trusted them, had faith in them. They were the only ones who had both the compassion and the intelligence to manage my land. Then when I discovered the scribe and solicitor, I felt a need to give them a proper edification so they could create a conservancy for my teachings. They were all strong—strong enough to prevent the vines and all the magic in them from being squandered. Unless, of course, they came up against an enemy of Adamson's caliber.

While I busied myself developing calculated strategies, Reverend Adamson was out converting hundreds of pathetic, brainless imbeciles to his army. His strategy was simple: appeal to their desperation by telling them, "Give yourselves to me—let me do the thinking for you—and I will give you all that you need: prosperity, companionship, and security." It only took a few hours for him to convince the city council and all the citizens who filled the town hall last month that I had no property rights. The council voted four to one to accept Adamson's proposal and condemn all of Old Town Rivervine.

I lost my marsh six thousand years ago. I lost my wine cellar one hundred and fifty-five years ago. Once again, homelessness faces me and leaves me to witness the disappearance of my legacy. I wonder what lies Adamson will tell about me during these *next* six millennia. What wars will he bring to my land? What friends will he convince to betray me? What will be the *next* fruit to be banned?

The more I obsessed over the issue this evening, the more my jaw began to ache. You see, dear reader, one of the problems with being a ghost of strong mind is that there are times when one becomes so emotionally charged that she forgets she is not truly incarnate. The ghost believes so adamantly that physical sensations are actually occurring. That is why it is common to hear reports of ghosts crying, bleeding, or sustaining other injuries—the discarnate swears the sting of tears dripping onto a wound is happening just like lacerations incurred lifetimes ago.

Such was the case this evening. Not only was I experiencing physical sensations, but I became awash in confusion caused by an inability to decipher my lifetimes as various species. I could not, for the life of me, determine the most appropriate way to express the physical manifestations of the emotions I was feeling.

Memories from my life as a pit viper battled with my most recent identity as a human, causing an excruciating pain in my gums. It burned like acid on tender flesh. I felt as if hot venom ran through my sinus cavity, extending all the way up my face until it apexed right between my eyes, then trickled back down into a holding bin tucked inside my cuspids.

I was too numb to think. Fury, agony, and despair overtook any sense of reasoning I otherwise would have had. No solution or haven presented itself to help me escape the insanity that was approaching.

I submitted to the lunacy, which led me to Adamson's precious First Church of Rivervine in search of the source of all this madness—not the warlock Adamson but rather the spirit he claims is the dictator of divine providence.

When I reached the steps of the church, I found it to be completely devoid of any type of spiritual energy. I sensed no disincarnated human presence whatsoever. I could not detect a trail of a deceased deer or trampled-upon blade of grass.

Political propaganda lined the walls and the tables, but the material was nothing but meaningless pieces of paper designed to encourage the white race to breed and beat their wives into submission. Everywhere I looked, I spotted promises of salvation in exchange for monetary donations. Nowhere could I find anything that promoted a genuinely spiritual life—one that emphasized enlightenment or taking responsibility for one's land and community.

"This is so false!" I screamed. "Where is the medium of all this counterfeit righteousness? Show yourself to me … NOW!"

Never before had I encountered such a stealthy ghost. I yelled, "Appear to me, you son of a bitch!" But there was no answer. I finally realized I could not find something that did not exist—not here at least. There was nothing spiritual at the First Church of Rivervine. This rabbi of whom Reverend Adamson so fondly spoke was nothing more than a figment of some perverted imagination. The concrete floors and plastered walls offered no evidence to support Adamson's claim that this savior was now or ever had been alive.

Before my doubts could be confirmed, I felt a tug in my aura pulling me toward the home of the little Basque girl. *He is there!* my inner voice said. So I followed my instincts to the other side of town.

By the time I reached the sanctuary, I was so angry that I did not care about the statue of the woman with the snake at her feet. I did not care about the candles. I did not care about the little Basque girl. My attention was focused solely on the wall behind the podium. There he was, in the form of a wooden sculpture. His countenance looked so pathetic as he hung there ever so woefully with the nails piercing his wrists and a band of thorns encircling his head. I just stood there, staring at his emaciated body.

My rage festering, I reached for the sculpture, yanking it off the wall and hurling it to floor. With his head facing the ground, I grabbed the wooden figure and pounded it below me, repeatedly yelling, "How could you do this to me? I hate you, you son of a bitch! *You* are the cause of all my suffering!"

My chest ached from all the pounding. My tears soaked the carpet. My fear of Father Kristobal witnessing my temper tantrum *almost* made me stop. Yet I continued my assault. I was curious, though, where Kristobal was and why he was allowing me to do this. The good priest has intervened several times when my attacks have been directed at one of his sacred subjects. I wondered if I were finally becoming stronger than him or if he were preoccupied with another matter. Whatever the answer, I kept to my task.

After several rounds of pounding, I finally fell exhausted into a fit of tears, hunched on the floor beside the upside-down wooden yogi. Exhaustion, distress, and wrath frazzled my mind. The rest of the world was invisible to me at that moment.

As I lay curled on the floor sobbing, the scent of blood wafted past my nose. I inhaled the sweet, earthy fragrance, capturing the aroma deep in my lungs. When I exhaled, a sense of peace overcame me, leaving my body feeling warm and comfortable, albeit fatigued.

I sensed a man approaching me, but I was too weary to acknowledge him. The stranger knelt beside me and brushed his hand against my cheek. The scent of his blood was so strong that I grabbed his forearm and pulled it close to my face, noticing the crimson stream gushing from his wrist.

Bloodlust overpowered me, and I swept my tongue across his flesh, lapping up the juicy fluid that flowed so freely. In all my incarnations, I have never consumed such a savory meal. The palette was full of justice, strength, and self-assuredness. However, there was also a distinct note of disappointment and an aftertaste of resentment, betrayal, abandonment, and disgust.

Once I swallowed the man's blood, my body went into a state of shock and disbelief as my insanity slowed to a simmer and reason returned in a most abrupt manner. I jerked my head around to look at the man's face and confirm my suspicions about his identity. Yes, it was he—the child Kristobal never had, the teacher prophets around the world sought, the master of true wisdom. He was beautiful despite his tattered appearance. Long dark hair; sandy, glowing skin; and eyes that gazed at me with soulful tenderness and humility.

Blood striped his body where his aggressors had tortured him two millennia ago—whip marks on his back, thorn scratches on his forehead, punctures on his wrists, side, and feet. Tears soaked his cheeks. Sweat coated his ragged body. A meager cloth covered his genitalia.

My desire to assail this man transformed into a need to comfort him. I threw my arms around him and held him close to my bosom as we sat on the floor of the altar, allowing ourselves to cry together unabashedly. There the two of us sat, on the floor, holding each other and rocking back and forth, weeping.

His first words to me sounded lunatical, and yet I understood exactly what he meant.

"Seek first the kingdom of God," he uttered. "My kingdom is not of this world. I am the still, small voice."

I could not find a voice of my own to respond, so I just sat there, rocking him in my arms.

He repeated the mantra several times. Soon, I too was chanting the verse. At last, enlightenment hit me. I realized the magnitude of my mistakenness: He was not the perpetrator of the evil acts against me. It was not he who was the cause of the horror facing Fermata Cellars. He was like I had been throughout the years: another victim of storytelling who had been hijacked by faulty scribes and corrupt politicians.

I ceased my rocking and looked him square in the eyes.

"The kingdom of heaven *is* the occult realm!" I exclaimed. "And you discovered a compass for the sea of chaos."

He pulled away from my arms and sat upright with legs crossed and ears opened, listening to my monologue.

"But to chart a course, one must be still and silent, forging a bond and trusting you as captain," I continued. "We must filter out the noise distracting us and zero in on the course itself."

"You always did overthink things, *Vondella*, but yes, you are correct."

"How did you know my name?"

"I know every sailor and passenger on this ship, even those who do not know they are on the journey. Viper, darling child, Zeinferdel—whatever name you choose, I have always recognized you."

"Viper? How did you know me in the marsh? You had not yet been born."

"I was a seed in one of the pomegranates hanging in your tree."

My own voice once again escaped me.

A hush befell both of us for a few moments before he finally broached the silence.

"What happened?" he asked me. "Where did it all go wrong? I taught them so many lessons. I showed them the way to eternal peace and enlightenment. Why did they not heed my advice? How did my words become so perverted?"

My skepticism found my voice, even if I do *overthink things*.

"False prophets seek the kingdom of power and gold, and they shout with a loud, threatening voice. They do not want people to find individual paths, but rather blindly follow them. They will convert heretics and infidels at sword point if need be. Grace be damned. The term *enlightenment* was bastardized into an excuse for spiritual slavery. Your words of truth were dumbed down and given a pretty little window dressing that the masses could digest, and then ... the false agenda suddenly became glorified, turning into the political machine that we know today."

At the sound of those words, my friend hunched over in tears once again. Blood spewed from every cut, every piercing of his withered body. I sensed his despair and suffering, but I knew not what to do; there is no remedy for a bleeding ghost—the blood is a result of psychological torment, not physical torture. All I could do was hold him close to me and softly stroke his back in an attempt to console him.

At this particular moment in time, we two discarnates were filled with pity, sorrow, remorse, and a realization that we were enemies ... yet we had forgotten the original war. Was it over a marsh in Sumer or a vineyard in California? I knew of only one solution, and I saw it sitting under a red light in a cabinet behind the altar.

I reached for a bottle of Saint Bernadette's White Rose and poured it into a golden goblet I found sitting atop the altar. "This wine was made just for you," I noted as I handed him the chalice.

He accepted my offering and took a sip … followed by a horrible grimace.

"Why is it not red?" he exclaimed. "How can communal wine represent my blood if it is white?"

I explained to him that several years ago, Father Armando developed a tremor in his hand.

"Say no more," he interrupted, looking over at the altar cloths. "I understand."

He took another sip, this time with a more open mind. As he finished the contents of the goblet, he commented, "It is different. I do not care for it much, but I can see how some people would consider it refreshing."

I put the Txakoli down and conjured a bottle of Requiem, pouring some into the goblet and handing it to my host. "This one is my favorite wine," I told him. "It is my darkest red, very dry and full bodied—far more appropriate for this occasion."

He accepted the goblet with both hands and sipped it gently.

"Oh!" he smiled. "This is wonderful!"

We continued drinking and engaging in spirited discourse until both bottles of wine were empty (there comes a point in social contexts where sharing wine is more important than the flavor). We joked and laughed, carrying on like old friends. We talked at length about history, philosophy, and psychology. I was fascinated by his accounts of Eastern mysticism with magi, cabalists, yogis, and gurus. Many of his stories were quite similar to the Comatis' practices and my father's Taoist studies. We both recognized that the guiding principle in all these religions was a reverence for nature—the soil and water, trees and beasts, the winds that blow from north, south, east, and west.

"Where did humanity go astray?" I asked. "Nowadays there are so many sects that claim to know the *one true path* to heaven; if you do not subscribe to their doctrine, then you will not enter the kingdom of heaven. And yet they are all different. The Catholics, the Protestants, the Evangelicals, even the Amish— they cannot all be right, so they must all be wrong."

He responded with the same mantra from earlier this evening: "Seek first the kingdom of God. My kingdom is not of this world. I am the still, small voice."

Exasperated in frustration, my patience flew away like a flock of startled crows.

"You know what?" I chastised. "All this fighting—not just in Rivervine but the United States in general, even the world, and especially in the Middle East—would end if you used *your* power to create an illusion so real and so awesome that everyone would listen. You could set the record straight once and for all. I understand the whole *still, small voice* spiel, but humanity is so far gone. Why do you not intervene at this point?"

Once again his wounds gushed with blood and I realized I had triggered a memory—that first day of Passover two thousand years ago when he was beaten, whipped, and crucified. His face fell into a look of despair.

"They did not listen to me then and they will not listen to me now," my gory friend said, barely able to get enough breath out of his lungs. "I remember that afternoon so vividly—my disgust at the religious leaders of the time and how they integrated the temple with the political machine. I warned them that Caesar and God were not good bedfellows, for one always corrupts the other. Government should focus on justice; it cannot legislate spiritual attunement. Once dogma supersedes spirituality, a theocracy is formed, and from there the government sets an agenda that kills personal enlightenment. I am not the one who ordered divine providence. Nor did I instruct Adamson to take your land away from you. I am truly sorry, Zinfandel. Really, I am."

Ignoring his plea, I returned to my original argument. "Please tell your followers to let me keep my land. I have been a good steward of the earth. I have never allowed it to be misused."

His answer did not satisfy me. "I cannot make them do something against their will. I have cautioned them against false prophets. If they follow one despite my warning, there is nothing I can do to make them choose differently."

"But you can appear to them the way you appeared to me tonight. Tell them the truth about Reverend Adamson and the lies that have tainted your legend all these years. Please, as my friend, tell them to denounce the false prophet and let me keep my land!"

"I cannot do that, Zinfandel," he insisted. "For two millennia I have tried to persuade them to heed my advice, but I have learned that false prophets are too hard to fight—even for me. I have shown people the way. I have told them the truth. But false prophets are loud while I am the still, small voice. And now I have lost my faith in humanity."

His tone and facial expression became incredulous as he finished his response: "If their free will leads them to the false prophets, so be it. There is nothing more I can do."

"Free will is only good if people know all the facts," I countered. "They are being led by a shepherd who feeds them lies, exacerbating the perjury you were just complaining about. Why do you sit there, speaking words of abomination toward the unenlightened masses, yet you tolerate the defamation of your own good name?"

We could not agree on a solution to the problems each other faced. He insisted forgiveness and charity must be exercised at all times. I contended that inanity and cowardice were abominations.

"I reserve forgiveness and charity for those who deserve it," I told him.

He replied, "I forgive inanity and cowardice because people do not know any better."

"They do not know any better because you refuse to come forward and tell them the truth in no uncertain terms and in a language they will understand! Just like you are talking to me now."

"If I have to spoon feed them understanding, then they are not worthy of the kingdom of heaven. I have no jurisdiction in the physical realm; therefore, I cannot save them. As for you, you are open to listen to me. Remember which one of us started this conversation in the first place."

Before our debate could reach a compromise, we heard footsteps nearing the sanctuary. "Father Armando!' we hushed each other. The good priest was readying to investigate the strange sounds coming from the sanctuary.

"I suppose I should clean up here," I told him. "I do not want Father Armando to know I desecrated his sacred space."

"Why do you care so much about a Christian man?" my friend asked. It was a fair question.

"He is a good man," I said. "It is because of him that children in Rivervine have coats in winter and the hungry have soup on Tuesday afternoons. Unlike other groups that have led missions in your name, Father Armando's charity comes from the heart. He does not require a needy soul to convert to his religion before receiving such necessities as food, shelter, or medicine. Besides, Father Armando has never done anything to agitate me. I do not want to trouble him needlessly."

The yogi nodded and resumed his wooden state.

I rehung the sculpture on the wall and conjured a new bottle of altar wine to replace the one my friend and I had consumed.

By the time I returned to the cave, I had not yet finalized my opinion of this *Jesus of Nazareth* character. I was disconsolate that he refused to help me, but I understood his frustration at leading a mass of people who listened more to the false prophets than to the Messiah himself.

A part of me felt that anyone who had the power to save Fermata Cellars but refused deserved neither my forgiveness nor my pity. Another part of me realized expending energy on him was pointless. He may not help me, but he was not going to stand in my way either. I needed to find assistance from another source.

The rest of the evening found me researching heroes—discarnate and incarnate alike. I was resolved to find someone even I could look up to.

Temperance

25 December in the Year of Their Lord 2003

I am quite the opportunist, I realize. Of course, my intent had nothing to do with the outcome of last night's events, but I cannot avoid reveling in the irony of fate smiling upon a wretched sinner like me—especially on such a supposedly holy night.

I had one objective when I left the wine cellar: Give Father Kristobal a very special holiday gift that would bring a bit of old-fashioned Christmas humility to a town that had become awash in greed, discord, and spiritual disconnection.

Although it has been many years since Christmas was magical for me, I believed it would do the people good to realize what holiday cheer meant before the giant marketplaces came to town. Every year, I see people hustling to purchase the most distasteful items all for the sake of obligatory gift giving. Since this was going to be my last year in Rivervine, I wanted to leave these saprophytes with a bold statement about the insincerity surrounding contemporary customs, especially those traditions that claim to be done in the name of an impoverished Middle Eastern child. Their holiday was supposed to be about love and peace and goodwill. No one epitomized those aspects better than Father Kristobal. He was worthy of my empathy. I wanted to present him with a gift so spectacular that all these ingrates would witness it and stop cold in their tracks. Naturally, I had to execute my plan in the most elegant and dramatic fashion possible.

The real drama, though, came from a couple of accomplices who were not included in my original plan.

My scheme started with a journey to the home of the little Basque girl—the sight of the famous "crying confessional" where pilgrims and news reporters traverse afar just to hear the mysterious sounds of a man weeping on Christmas Eve.

Very few people knew the identity of that voice. Of course, I did. Who else could it be? It belonged to my benevolent teacher—sobbing over memories of his death and the heartbreak surrounding it. The twenty-fourth of December was always a melancholy night for Father Kristobal.

It was three days after the winter solstice more than two thousand years ago when the woman of his affections announced that she was with child and going to marry another man who would raise the child as his own. Any romance between her and Kristobal would not be allowed. He was so brokenhearted that he took his own life that night. According to the Gregorian Calendar, the night falls on what Christians call *Christmas Eve*.

Ever since Saint Bernadette's Catholic Church was built, my dear friend has spent Christmas Eve weeping profusely behind the confessional doors. Last night was no different, except this would be his last Midnight Mass at his home, and I knew the agony would cause his tears to flow from a deeper part of his emotional well. I had to do something to ease his pain. I could not in good conscience leave him to grieve alone.

But I had to be cautious. I could not do anything that would cause Xavia, Sage, or any other Comati to fall deeper out of favor in the community. My existence was now common knowledge, and I feared that anything I did would be misinterpreted somehow. Experience has proven that regardless of how compassionately I act, my behavior will become twisted as an act of wickedness. People fear that I am tricking them somehow—that my kindness is just bait used to lure innocent victims into a trap leading them to the fiery pit of hell.

People fear what they do not understand. They understand so little; that is why they fear so much. Those who truly know me are not afraid. No one understands me better than Father Kristobal.

Although he rarely approved of my endeavors, he always realized my motives and respected my need to do things my way. He warned me of the dangers of my actions but allowed me to experience the consequences of those actions—right or wrong. So many nights I wished I had heeded his warnings. Other times, I was glad I eschewed them. We argued incessantly over honor and ethics, yet he repeatedly told me such decisions depended on my own inner voice—that which must be heeded above any external source.

Last night, my inner voice told me to attend Midnight Mass. If the crying confessional needed a shoulder on which to shed its tears, then I would offer mine. Or better yet, an old friend.

But still, I had to be subtle. I had to remain anonymous. No one must ever know that it was I who conjured the magic. My presence would support claims of the Catholic church worshipping the devil, and poor Father Armando would be excommunicated for allowing a demon possession to occur on his watch. I may not agree with Catholic doctrine, but it has never been my intent to ensure the church's demise. The Pope is neither my ally nor my adversary. All I wanted to do last night was make Christmas Eve 2003 a spectacular evening to remember.

Without exposing my physical apparition, I waited by the pine tree at the entrance of the church parking lot. After the people gathered, the doors closed, and Father Armando welcomed everyone, I shifted into my human illusion and conjured some frankincense, a match, and a golden censer. I then sat cross-legged on the ground, placed the incense in its container, and set it alight. I also rubbed some myrrh oil on the palms of my hand, clasped them together, and rocked back and forth meditating for a while. I focused intently on my goal, begging for assistance from a magus of some sort.

Humans have used frankincense for eons as a means of purifying the air. Burning the tree resin in a gold container connects the occult and physical realms as the metal is a conductor of metaphysical energy. I included the analgesic myrrh oil in my spell to numb the pain of my friend's heartache. Father Kristobal's soul was definitely in need of such healing after more than two millennia of repressed anguish.

With my mind calm, my spirit was able to absorb the joy of the people inside the church, who were singing carols and watching children reenact the Christmas story.

Before the evening's long-anticipated grand performance, the temperature under my tree dropped nearly thirty degrees, and frozen white flakes began falling from the heavens. In the one hundred eighty-three years that I have roamed this town, I have never experienced snow. Our winters consist of rain, floods, wind, and fog; the romantic white powder never falls from the skies above Rivervine. I had to conjure a warm velvet cape to keep my physical shell from freezing.

To my right, a strong, demonstrative, male presence emerged, but no physical apparition appeared at first. Then came the aroma of Turkish brandy—oh, how I wanted a taste … and hoped this visitor brought me some.

In a swirl of laughter, the magus began to manifest his image, and I at once recognized my favorite jolly old elf. Cloaked in his signature red velvet, Bishop Nicholas struggled to find comfort sitting on the ground, especially now that it was covered in a dusting of snow. He tried to sit cross-legged, but his knees would not bend enough, so he sat with this legs stretch out in front of him, propping himself on his hands behind his back. The poor, rickety old man looked so uncomfortable that I simply had to conjure a couple chairs for us to sit on.

He took his seat but continued to chuckle while fidgeting with his garment as if checking his pockets to find something hidden.

I could feel my cheeks start to redden, afraid I was doing something embarrassing. Blushing, I asked him, "What is so funny?"

"I am just sho happy to shee you!" he answered in a heavy Turkish accent, slapping me on the thigh and continuing his laugh. "The shite of you … at church … on CHRISHMAS. I am shorry, Zhinfandel. I do not mean to mock you. But you are sho out of character here."

I continued blushing, realizing how silly I must have looked—a Heathen like me meditating on the holiest night of the Christian calendar. He laughed for a few more seconds, then paused to say, "Sheriously, I think it ish wonderful that you are here. How can I help you?"

I started to answer, but he interrupted before I could begin my explanation.

"A-ha! You want shome brandy first, I know."

Reaching into the inside breast pocket of his cloak, his shaky right hand pulled out a flask and offered it to me.

Accepting it, I lifted up the canteen and cheered, "To Father Kristobal. May he find peace at last."

As the warm liquid slid down my throat, the drop in temperature became a little more bearable.

I handed the flask back to Bishop Nicholas, who echoed my toast.

"To my good friend Kristobal!"

The organ inside sounded. The energy surrounding the building fell silent and still in an air of apprehension as everyone waited for the mysterious howl.

"Ooh!"

There it was. Just like every year.

The Turk and I arose from our seated positions, brushed the snow from our outfits, and embraced each other.

"I musht tend to my friend. He needs me," the cleric announced. Before he left, he reached inside his cloak and pulled out a small velvet sack, which he handed to me. "Merry Chrishmas," he said.

I opened the pouch and found three gold coins.

"Thank you, Bishop Nicholas, but what are these for?" I asked. "I have no use for gold."

"Look where they are from," he answered.

I gazed at the coins—they were stamped England 1687. I glanced back at his face to confirm my suspicions. He winked and nodded, confirming my assumption—I was holding in my hands the coins that purchased my greatest grandmother's ransom. Bishop Nicholas held me close and allowed my tears to stain his beautiful velvet cloak.

The bishop kissed my cheek, then disappeared. Suddenly the doors of the church flung open. The congregation oohed and aahed as they witnessed the snowstorm outside. I shed my physical apparition and stepped inside the church to follow the excitement.

The moment I entered the building, all the votive candles along the walls of the church extinguished, although the candles encased in glass jars remained lit. I did not mean to frighten anyone or divert attention away from Father Kristobal or Bishop Nicholas, but I couldn't help it. My spirit once again absorbed the energy from the unprotected flames. As could be expected, the parishioners panicked when their special prayer candles all blew out at the same time.

My embarrassment did not last long as people's attention quickly turned to the crying confessional. The moaning gave way to the sound of two men laughing and carrying on in a strange language. The congregation rushed the confessional, but the door was stuck shut. The hum of gossip and speculation competed for air space with the rich aroma of brandy. Father Armando tried to keep the peace—patting people on the shoulders, trying to herd everyone as if they were sheep. He reached for his key to open the confessional door, but it would not unlock.

Some parishioners shifted their attention outside, amazed at the snow. The children certainly loved it as they made snowballs and snow angels and tried to capture snowflakes on their tongues. Poor darlings, they were not dressed for such escapades—no heavy coats, boots, or mittens. They soiled their beautiful velvet dresses and shivered from lack of warm clothing. They did not care, though. The snow was far too much fun for the little ones to be concerned with such mundane worries as catching a chill or ruining their patent-leather shoes.

Several couples took advantage of the romantic atmosphere and kissed each other as the snow fell upon their faces, holding one another tight to keep warm.

The Turkish conversation continued in the confessional until Father Kristobal finally yelled in English, "Why not?" Then the bishop, appearing in his full physical apparition, unlocked the door to the confessional and stepped outside. All the incarnates charged the hallway to see the strange guest. He chuckled, reached inside his cloak, and pulled out little peppermint candies to distribute among the flock of children.

While the bishop was busy hoarding the attention of the parishioners, Father Kristobal found a distraction of another sort as the brandy aroma gave way to the scent of roses.

"Hello, Kristobal," a woman called. I looked over to see who owned the voice. She was a beautiful Middle Eastern lady wearing a blue woolen cloak and surrounded by a beaming silver aura. Her skin was the color of sand, and her eyes were darker than the bishop's cordial. Father Kristobal, an otherwise adept linguist, fell speechless. I knew at once she was the woman of his affection for all these years. As tempted as I was to eavesdrop on their conversation, I decided instead to leave the two of them to their private moment.

With the aid of an old friend's laughter and a lost love's kindness, Father Kristobal's broken heart was finally in the stages of mending.

My work was done here.

~ The Devil ~

I left the hubbub of Saint Bernadette's and headed back toward Fermata Cellars. As I crossed the river, a loud crashing sound rang through the air … along with the odor of Christmas goat.

A horseless carriage had apparently skidded on a piece of ice, hit a tree, and landed in the water. It was starting to sink as I approached. By the time I reached close enough to see the driver, the river was stained with blood. A teenage boy lay crouched over the wheel, his head bearing a large abrasion that was hemorrhaging.

Then I heard that unmistakable dysphonic voice calling out from behind a tree. "You brought the snow, so I made some ice."

"Krampus! What did you do? And who is that bloody face in the river? He looks way too young to be driving!"

"Constantine Adamson. I know you want the father for yourself, so I took the son."

The goat herder is famous for having a penchant for cruelty, but taking the life of an innocent youth just to exact revenge on a parent is not his usual modus operandi. I had to confirm that something more than vengeance was at play.

"Did the boy do something wrong?"

"He is just like his dad—a real asshole. Tonight he stole his mother's car. He doesn't know how to drive, but he got angry with her, so he took her keys and left."

"Smells like those sage-scented fags," I noted.

"Yeah. He was smoking marijuana. His friend said it would calm him down."

"Well, dead is pretty calm, I guess."

Our conversation halted when we sensed the boy's spirit embarking on the disincarnation journey.

The point of disincarnation is when the soul separates from the physical shell. At that time, the mind is usually extraordinarily disoriented. It attempts to manipulate the body, such as waving its arms or walking on legs, but it stays motionless because there are no limbs to maneuver. Therefore, the spirit remains paralyzed. If another force acts upon that spirit before the mind can orient itself, said force may prevent the soul from either reincarnating or reaching one's believed afterlife. The mind then spends eternity as a ghost.

Constantine's spirit behaved exactly as I had expected—unable to move without a physical shell, although he *was* able to cast a scant illusion of his recently deceased self. Once the nascent ghost started to become aware of his new state of consciousness, Krampus and I welcomed him to the next phase of his life.

The newly formed ghost hovered above his physical shell that lay in the drowned car. Naturally, he panicked, just like everyone does when they realize they are dead. The specter gawked at Krampus, then turned to me and asked, "Am I in hell?"

"Hell is a state of mind," I answered. "Just like heaven."

"Are you the devil? Or is *he* the devil?"

"My name is Xin Vondella," I said. Pointing to my cloven-hooved friend, I added, "This is Krampus. You must be the son of Reverend Paul Adamson, correct?"

"Yes, I am Constantine, and I've heard of you, you pagan whore. When my dad learns of this, he's gonna piss all over you and make goat boy here lick it all off. Now show me your tits! I bet they're *real* perky."

Not much offends me, but I was stunned to hear this vulgar language coming from such a young boy who was raised in the household of the local community's best known Christian leader.

"Did your father teach you to talk that way?"

"Sure as shit. He tells us there's nothing more beautiful in the eyes of the Lord than the blatant abuse and humiliation of women. He pisses on my mom all the time."

"Oh, really? I do not recall hearing any such beatitude before."

"Oh, yeah. He rips her clothes off, smacks her around until she's good and bloody, then whips out his dick, letting the sting of his piss purify her whorish soul. Afterwards, he makes her lick up the mess while my sister and I watch. In fact, he makes me practice on Ruthie; says she better learn to get used to it now and I better learn how to do it the right way."

Hearing this testimony was shocking even for me. This scenario was far worse than anything my father forced me to endure. I had to ask, "I take it Ruthie is your sister? How old is she?"

"Six. Now SHOW ME YOUR TITS, chink! I wanna suck those beauties! I'll bet your milk tastes like sweet and sour sauce."

With that latest pejorative, the boy lunged toward me … underestimating my response.

I was hell bent on making sure this little prick spent eternity trapped in a prison of his father's own brimstone.

His attempt at charging me landed him nowhere. The disembodied spirit simply stayed in its place.

In the meantime, I stood erect in front of the boy, looked him in the eye, pounded my right fist into my left palm, and bowed. The fight had officially begun.

Bending my right elbow at a ninety-degree angle in front of me, I kept my palm flat and fingers straight, thumb bent in, touching the base of the middle finger. Moving my wrist and forearm in a circular motion, I imagined my arm as the coil of a snake, drawing down, up, and around, hypnotizing Constantine with my fingertips until I struck—stabbing him sequentially in the eyes, cheeks … and throat.

Krampus delivered the final blow by standing on his arms with his back toward the boy, and kicking him—goat style—in the chest, knocking the specter to the ground on the bank of the river, where he came eye to eye with his own dying, bloody corpse trapped in the water.

At this point, he was extremely confused and easily controlled.

Krampus and I blazed a fiery trail.

"Smells like rotten eggs!" Constantine yelled.

"That's sulfur!" Krampus responded in his usual slurred articulation. "That's what brimstone is."

"Are you retarded? You sound retarded!" the boy sneered.

Krampus grabbed the boy's tongue, pulled it in front of his face and twisted it. He then gave the specter a new illusory image: that of a Chinese woman with four teats with red, gelatinous sauce leaking from the nipples. The woman's feet were crushed into the shape of three-inch crescent moons and bound in place, the scent of rotting flesh and dripping puss emanating from the gauze.

The two of us forced the spirit to its former home where a sobbing mother was on the phone with the police, who had just called saying they found the missing vehicle and asking her and her husband to come down to the coroner's office to identify the body. A little girl—I am guessing it was his sister, Ruthie—lay tucked in her bed, trying her best to hide a smile.

"Yes!" she whispered to her dolls. "I hope Zinfandel got him!"

DEATH

21 January, in the Year of Their Lord 2004

It is sundown on Chinese New Year—the Year of the Monkey. I am sitting under the weeping willow writing in my grimoire. I faced my fears tonight and met with my long-time adversary: the dragon-faced knot.

Ironic, is it not? I was born in the Year of the Dragon, yet I am terrified of a piece of wood that resembles the icon assigned to the year of my birth.

I was everything the Dragon asked me to be. As a child, I was vigorous, valiant, and vivacious. Nothing daunted my idealistic outlook on life. The older I grew, the more I committed to the principles embodied in my totem. I watched attentively as my mother taught me to identify each creature in the garden, learning friends from foes. I mastered every step, kick, and block during Father's gung fu lessons. I kept ritualistic guard over my brother Anton whenever he was ill.

This year, if Chinese philosophy is accurate, the agile monkey will guide me along the path of accomplishment in the face of adversity—to roll with the punches, so to speak. I am losing my home but will find someplace new to study. Adam has once again banished me, but unlike before, I will block his punch and deliver a mortal blow, striking down his perpetual slander of me.

Speaking of rolling with the punches, my solicitor, Manuel Chavez, today celebrated both his birthday and his last day of work at Fermata Cellars. He and his lover Joaquin leave Chiapas next week.

First thing this morning, he came down to the cellar to tell me goodbye. He was carrying with him an oil lamp and the dark red blanket I had given him this past Sauin.

"I guess this is it, Vondella," he said, setting the lamp on an upended wine barrel.

"I will miss you, darling."

"I will miss you too," he replied, holding up the blanket. "Hey, can I keep this?"

I smiled and answered, "Yes, of course."

"Thank you. It is a reminder of how I overcame my fear of you."

We both chuckled.

"You will have many more fears to face along your new path," I said. "You will need more than a blanket to protect you."

"Yes, I know," he sighed. "But I don't feel right staying in a country with so many privileges while so many others are suffering in my homeland. *I* could have been one of those still suffering. It is only by chance—and the generosity of the Comatis—that I even have a choice to make."

I could not hide my tears. I was so proud of him—growing from a boy with a bunch of orange seeds to a man fighting for freedom.

We held each other for a moment, then kissed one another's cheeks as we released our embrace.

"What should I do with the cobza?" he asked. "I know you wanted it kept with Lily's violin."

"Give it to Thomas and Tanya as a gift for their baby."

"Excellent idea. I will do that."

He smiled and nodded, tucking the blanket under one arm and heading back up the stairs with the lamp in his other hand.

At the end of the day, Xavia found me here by the willow. She had in her hand a thin black machine of some sort.

"Manuel turned in his laptop along with his key and company cell phone," she said, handing the contraption to me. "He was keeping a journal of some sort on it. Do you want it for this project you have going with Glenda? Should I ship it to her?"

Before I could answer, a voice that had been silent for many years called out.

"I take it!" the woman cried in a heavy Romanian accent. "I keep it safe from Dragon!"

Doina's image was barely visible. It was clear she did not have the strength to manifest into a full apparition. Yet she was so passionate about gaining custody of these memoirs.

Xavia looked at me for approval. I nodded and shrugged my shoulders since I did not have a better alternative or any reason to object.

"Fine by me," I said, turning toward my greatest grandmother. "But how are you going to keep it safe from the dragon?"

"Oh, just a little trick Romani friend show me."

Doina grabbed the machine and disappeared.

Gung hay fat choy.

TEN OF WANDS

5 May in the Year of Their Lord 2004

Tonight would normally be the Comati Beltane ritual, but since the tribe is disbanding, there was no need to hold any kind of ceremony. Most of them already have closed their businesses and emigrated to other areas. Xavia and Sage have decided to keep the winery open through the twentieth of June to sell their remaining inventory.

Glenda Fern, my scribe, is still in Sumer with her soldier friend. Brigid is going on to study music in Yerba Buena; her parents will join her after they close Fermata Cellars.

I, however, still had a contract with the fae folk. Xavia and Sage may be leaving Rivervine, but this was still *my* land and the shee were expecting their annual tribute. I had much explaining to do.

~ Idho, the Ogham of Perseverance ~

When the shee enter into a contract, the duration is for all perpetuity, even if the terms are renewed annually like they are at Beltane. Reneging on such a contract carries a penalty worse than death; the fae folk are famous for their torture techniques. They are also known for their trickery. I knew I had to keep my concentration focused tonight to avoid any of their chicanery.

As evening fell, I asked Sage to build the two traditional firepits.

"But we're not renewing our contract," he stated. "Why do we need a ritual? We're just gonna take the fae folk to San Francisco with us."

"*I* am dissolving my relationship with them," I explained. "*You* are merely changing venues. The fae deserve an explanation and an opportunity to respond."

"Good point. Maybe all of us should be here, at least Xavia and me."

"It is not necessary. We should keep it simple. I can handle it alone."

"Okay, but holler if you need us."

"I will. Thank you."

"I'll be back in a couple hours to douse the flames."

I nodded and smiled. After he left, I sat cross-legged on the ground between the fires with my hands on my knees, palms up, thumbs touching the middle fingers, eyes closed. I inhaled all the smoke and let out a long "ah … ooh … mm" when I exhaled.

When I opened my eyes, I saw an apparition mirrored in front of me. It was a woman, I guess— it was difficult to tell for sure—sitting cross-legged on the ground, the same as I was. Her image was translucent and gray, her hair a silvery white, and her eyes solid black. Her skin was the palest shade of gray, and her dress was almost equally light, although it seemed to have a tinge of pink to it. Her face was long, and her cheeks were hollow. When she greeted me, her smile bared long, sharp teeth.

"Vondella!" she greeted me.

"Hello," I responded. "I am afraid you have me at a disadvantage for I do not know your name."

"You may call me Rhiannon, unless you prefer something else."

"Rhiannon it is."

"Very well. Now that the pleasantries have been dispensed, what can I do for you? Where are the other Comatis? Why do the fires not sparkle? Have you defaulted on our arrangement?"

"It appears it is *you* who have defaulted."

"What?" she cried, obviously insulted. "How can that be?"

Keeping my cool, I explained, "I offered you a fine gold necklace with a stone center of lapis lazuli. In return, I asked you banish my enemies. But look around you."

Rhiannon turned her head left and right and even stretched to look behind her. As she came back to center, her face wore a confused countenance.

"There are no more Comatis!" I yelled. "Our tribe has gone extinct. You were supposed to protect us!"

Rhiannon's face flushed with ghastly shame. I continued my explanation.

"You allowed Adam—the same devil that stole Ireland from the Druids—to get his greedy, selfish, psychopathic hands on the Black Land. And now we have to leave—all of us, even *you*."

"No!" Rhiannon protested. "Without the Comatis, our realm has no luster. We need the glitter to make Fairy shine. This cannot be!"

"Well, then help me exact justice!"

"What do you want from us?"

"The Dragon is coming again to Rivervine, but before it burns the entire city, I want the humans responsible for this mess to suffer eternally for their part in this destruction. If, on the night before the summer solstice, you pull their brains from their bodies, they will not be able to either reincarnate or enter the afterlife of their religious beliefs. If you take their brains to Fairy, you may do whatever you want with them—make them suffer for all eternity the way only a shee could."

"Oh, my friend," she said with a great smile. "*That* is a deal that can be easily arranged. Tell me the names of the humans responsible for this outrage."

I chose not to mention Paul Adamson because I want him for myself. I did, however, offer up the four city councilmembers.

"Warner McCain, Pam White, Perry Josephson, and Brian Mann. Be sure to treat McCain with extra cruelty. He was the mastermind of this whole ordeal. The others were just sheep—incapable of thinking for themselves and more easily influenced by temporary public opinion than ethics or reason."

"Why not just let the dragon take them?"

"The dragon can take their bodies, but their souls will still be free. I want them to suffer eternally!"

"How do you know they will not go to hell?"

"Because they are convinced they are doing God's work. If that is their belief at the time of death, they will spend eternity floating on clouds and playing harp music."

She paused for a moment to consider the renegotiated terms. As she contemplated her options, I continued trying to persuade her.

"They took your flowers. They took your berries. They took everything the vineyard offered the fae. Imagine the entertainment The Good Neighbors will have exacting justice on these infidels. You could even condemn them to be a creature so grisly that it has not yet been imagined."

Rhiannon lost herself in thought for a few moments. I watched intently, wondering what her next move would be.

The last thing I saw of her was that smile—those long, sharp teeth grinning at me. Then, she disappeared into the smoke.

Epilogue

THE WORLD

June 21, 2004

To Glenda Fern
c/o Allied Journalist Network
Sacramento Bureau

Dear Ms. Fern,

You and I never met in person, but I studied under Xin Vondella, and I know she was keeping a grimoire that she wanted you to have. I do not have said book—I am currently in Arizona training at Fort Huachuca for the United States Army—but I do have clairvoyant visions that you may want to document in your novel.

This one in particular is of special significance.

I have a bloodstone ring that Vondella gave me. Of course, I cannot wear it while I'm in uniform, but I keep it locked away and take it out on specific occasions, such as new moons, solstices, or equinoxes. When I stare into that stone, I see things—images of people and scenes of what will happen to them. What I saw last night terrified me. I had to call my friends in Rivervine to confirm it was true. I am shaking as I type this, but please realize that I am not some sort of lunatic. I'm only writing to you in the hopes of solving some mysteries that may come up in the course of your project.

The media did not report what I am about to tell you. They either genuinely did not know or they are purposely hiding the truth. It sounds fantastic, but search the transcripts of the 911 calls, and you'll see it's true. If you're looking for the whole story, this needs to be part of it.

The main news that everyone's reporting is the fire and the vision of *the dragon* as they're calling it. But what I saw in the stone happened in the early hours of the morning—long before the dragon's visit that evening.

My vision had four parts, all of them involving current Rivervine City Council members.

The first incident was Mayor Warner McCain. Well, he was vice mayor when I left for basic training, but I guess he was elected mayor in 2004. Anyway, he's also the local mortician. The night of June nineteenth—going into the early morning of the twentieth—he was working on one of his corpses.

I saw, in the stone, an image of the cadaver re-animating and shifting into the vision of Vondella.

She was gorgeous—elegantly clad in a slinky black silk cocktail dress with an *extremely low* neckline. Her long dark hair flowed in waves over her shoulders, and her makeup was painted on with bright red lips and catlike eyes with long lashes.

She slid off the table so that her feet were on the floor, but she was bent over the table on her stomach. She then arched her back to make sure her buttocks protruded as she lifted her shoulders, looking to her right, tempting him to take her from behind.

He obliged, unbuckling his belt and unzipping his pants. As he bent over to penetrate her, a *monster* of some sort—I do not know what to call it, but it was like a slivery-gray old woman with long, razor-like teeth and black eyes—appeared from behind him and ran a long, sharp, wooden stake into his butthole. The pointed end of the pole came up through his chest. The monster and Vondella carried the skewer to the front of City Hall, where the old woman scaled the pole like a squirrel and then dug her fist into his head and pulled out his brain, putting it in some sort of satchel.

My vision in the stone clouded. When it cleared again, I saw the new vice mayor, Pam White, asleep in her bed next to her husband. A noise from the kitchen awakened her, and she got up to see what the commotion was. Finding her young son standing on top of the counter, she reached over to grab him. But he kept backing away, getting smaller and smaller, making it harder for her to get him. By the time she was leaned all the way over the counter, Vondella rammed another stake up the councilwoman's ass. The boy shifted into the image of the old gray woman who, along with Vondella, carried the corpse to the front of City Hall, where once again the monster scaled the pole like a squirrel and dug her fist into the victim's head and pulled out the brain, stashing it in the mysterious satchel.

Councilmembers Perry Josephson and Brian Mann met similar fates, their corpses impaled in front of City Hall with their brains ripped out.

When the stone finally cleared, I called Sergeant Griffin back in Rivervine and asked him to confirm the bodies were there. Within the hour, he called back saying they were indeed—all four of them. Family members called 911 the morning of June twentieth claiming their respective loved ones were missing, but no one heard or saw anything. The family members of the deceased were all asleep at the time of the attacks. You would think something so horrific would be noisy enough to wake everyone in the house, but it seems Vondella and this old gray woman work in complete silence. However, they did leave a mess of the victims' blood trailing from the various crime scenes to City Hall, where their impaled corpses were paraded like flags.

As for the assailants? No one can tell. According to Sergeant Griffin, the perpetrators left no blood, hair, saliva, semen, vomit, or fingerprints at any of the crime scenes. The closest thing to a calling card the perps left was a sprinkling of glitter on the victims' pillows.

Councilwoman Carmelita Anza was apparently unharmed. Sergeant Griffin told me he checked on her and she was physically fine, albeit emotionally distressed at the horror of her fellow councilmembers.

I don't understand why this isn't being reported. I thought reporters were glued to police scanners. Surely the local journalists knew what had happened—something this horrific is hard to sweep under so many rugs. Yet they all chose to keep silent. The Rivervine Police Department's public information officer did not even make a statement.

Another thing Sergeant Griffin asked me about but I did not see in the stone: The dead body of Reverend Paul Adamson was found nailed upside down to the oak that sits in the traffic island on the west side of town. There were rattlesnake bites all over the corpse, and his skin was peeling off the muscles. It's as if he was nailed first—while still alive—then attacked by a horde of vipers, making his muscles unable to cramp and forcing all the poison to run down to his brain, where the majority of the venom was found.

I have no idea what's going on in Rivervine. My parents sold the bed and breakfast inn several months ago, so I have no immediate ties to the town anymore; therefore, I was not allowed disaster leave to cope with this crisis. But I do hope you get to the bottom of it. Let me know if I can be of any assistance. I graduate from military intelligence training in August and will leave for Baghdad shortly thereafter. Perhaps Uncle Sam will let us meet up in Sumer sometime.

In frith,
Erin Tuft, Oracle
Order of the Green Chalcedony

Acknowledgements

To my mother, **Delia**, thank you for raising me to love the art of storytelling. Huge thanks to my husband, **Eddie**, for all your support and refusal to let me give up when I thought this wasn't worth the effort. Much love to my daughter, **Sabrina**—I hope I don't embarrass you too much. And to my **Uncle Harold**, thanks for redirecting my career so I don't die a starving poet.

Kristine Logan Photography did beautiful work on the cover for this book as well as the rerelease of *Fermata Cellars*. She also did my author photos and the professional photos used on my website and social media. The photos were taken at **Country Heritage Winery** in LaOtto, Indiana.

Thanks to my editor, **Colleen**, for the eagle eye and assessment of the manuscript. I didn't take all of your advice, but it helped direct the final draft.

This book has been twenty years in the making. I have poured over so many books, articles, websites, podcasts, and videos in my obsession to make this story are realistic as possible.

The following people and organizations have contributed to my research:

• The numerous winery and vineyard owners, managers, and winemakers of the **Amador Vintners Association**. Rivervine may be a fictional city, but it was heavily inspired by the Amador County region of the Sierra Foothill AVA (American Viticultural Area). Thanks so much to all my friends in the wine business for advising me as I tackled this venture.

• **Fiddletown Preservation Society.** I lived in Amador County, California for twelve years, five of which were in Fiddletown, a tiny, rural community that boasts the largest and most contiguous group of Chinese buildings from a California gold rush mining community. One of the buildings—the Chew Kee Chinese pharmacy—already has been converted into a museum. I volunteered as a docent for the museum and also led the marketing committee for the Restoration of Chinese Structures project, which was an effort to raise money to reconstruct the exterior and weatherproof the Chinese Gambling Hall and Chinese General Store. The project was completed in 2008. My experience in Fiddletown launched my interest in the Chinese-American folklore of the Gold Rush.

• **Chaw'se Indian Grinding Rock**. Also in Amador County is a state historic park that features a museum, picnic area, outcropping of marbleized limestone with 1,185 mortar holes, and a Miwok village that includes a reconstructed ceremonial roundhouse (hun'ge). The site hosts events throughout the year where they invite the public into the sacred space.

• References to vampirism were inspired by the work of the **Atlanta Vampire Alliance**, the **Temple of Set's *Order of the Vampyre***, **L.A. Judge**, authors **Michelle Belanger** and **Joseph Laycock**, and the **American Porphyria Foundation**.

• References to tarot were inspired by the *Smith-Waite Tarot Deck, Centennial Edition*; the *Evolutionary Tarot Deck* by **Richard Hartnett**; and the website for **Biddy Tarot**.

• References to the Ma'dān people were inspired by an episode of **60 Minutes** in 2009 called *Resurrecting Eden*.

• Since the subject of ancient history is so contentious, especially when comparing religious texts, I attempted to mediate by using an unbiased, peer-reviewed, secular website: **Ancient History Encyclopedia**.

• My paranormal research experience was based on time spent with **Haunted and Paranormal Investigations, Inc**. and the **Delta Paranormal Society**, both of which are in northern California.

• Anything having to do with land-use planning was inspired by my time working for the **Amador County Planning Department**.

• Archeologist **Deborah Cook** advised me on conducting research. I used this advice when writing parts for Rev. Todd Caprasen's character.

• References to Paganism were inspired by the **Sacramento Pagan Pride Project; The Sacramento Grove of the Oak** (shout out to Papa Druid, a.k.a. **Michael Gorman** and the rest of the **Order of Bards, Ovates and Druids**), and the **Sierra Madrone Grove of Ár nDraíocht Féin: A Druid Fellowship.** ADF is the modern Neodruidism group where I learned the concept of the Mighty Kindreds (ancestors, nature spirits and Shining Ones). They also introduced me to the awen symbol / | \. I would especially like to thank **Sean Harbaugh** for introducing me to the organization, **Kirk Thomas** for being so charismatic when leading ritual, and **Jon Drum** for teaching me the ogham alphabet (a course I still need to finish).

• References to parapsychological phenomena were inspired by information listed on the website for **The Society of Psychical Research**. The Society's purpose is to investigate mesmeric, psychical and spiritualist phenomena in a purely scientific spirit. A leader in this field of study is **Loyd Auerbach**, but I did not discover his work until 2019.

• The Rev. Adamson character was inspired by a troll who found me online in 1998 through a Yahoo group for fans of the TV show *Charmed*. He claimed to be an evangelical minister named **Rev. Taylor** who ran a website called **Jesus Hates Smut**. The site no longer exists, but when it was live, his "church" advocated for white supremacy as well as the "blatant abuse and humiliation of women, especially young girls," and warned against homosexuality and Paganism. It was so graphic and offensive that it inspired me to write this book, making him the villain.

• References to the fae folk were inspired by the works of **Morgan Daimler**, as well as the book *The Call* by **Peadar Ó Guilín**.

• Thanks especially to my subscribers on Patreon. Your support feeds my keyboard! Readers who would like to be part of this esteemed group of patrons of the literary arts can join at patreon.com/rivervine.

PLEASE REVIEW AND DISCUSS

The best gift anyone could give an author is to leave an honest review on Goodreads, Amazon, or other social media/blogging platform. Constructive criticism is always appreciated. Were you able to follow along with the story? Did you understand the characters and setting? What did you like or dislike?

To support my work, please subscribe to my Patreon page at patreon.com/rivervine.

Also, if you are in a book club, please consider discussing *Zinfandel's Grimoire*. Possible questions include:

• This book is about a haunted winery. Have you ever had a supernatural experience? If so, tell us about it.

• The author uses the names of tarot cards and ogham characters for chapter titles and subtitles. Do you believe in divination? If so, how do you think it works?

• *Zinfandel's Grimoire* weaves together various religious views and offers alternative mythos. Did this book make you evaluate your own spiritual beliefs? If so, how?

• Do you participate in your local government? If so, how does the Rivervine City Council differ from your own city or county?

• If this were made into a movie, who would you like to see cast in the various roles?

ABOUT THE AUTHOR

Author Gwen Alyce Clayton reads in the barrel room of Country Heritage Winery in LaOtto, Indiana. Hair and makeup by Angie Gibson. Photo by Kristine Logan Photography. Copyright 2020. Used with permission.

Gwen Alyce Clayton is an independent author, copy writer, and journalist whose work has been published in local newspapers and magazines throughout the United States. Her mission is to write quality novels and modern folklore that inspire readers to think critically while enjoying the wonder of things not yet known. She lives in Ashland, Kentucky with her husband, Eddie. Clayton holds a bachelor of science degree in public administration from Regis University. Visit her website at gwenclaytonwrites.com.